The Vampire's Witch welcomes readers back to the world of vampires, witches, and magic.

Jaret Bachmann's life spins out of control after a handsome stranger saves him from an attack along the bike path on Lakeshore Drive. His estranged high school sweetheart stalks him, the enraged ghost of his ancestor destroys his family, and his bike path savior-cum-lover abandons him after learning Jaret is a powerful witch.

A horrific family tragedy sends Jaret into deep depression. Struggling to find his way afterward, Jaret searches for comfort in the unlikely friendship of a secret vampire community.

Over time, Jaret's friendship with the vampires strengthens and he forges a new family connection with Xavier, Thomas, and Catherine. But he and Anthony are estranged, and though their souls are entwined, their hearts are another matter.

Xavier, Thomas, Anthony, and Catherine return in this, the third book in The Realm of the Vampire Council series and a sequel to *The Bachmann Family Secret*.

THE VAMPIRE'S

WITCH

A Realm of the Vampire
Council Novel

Damian Serbu

A NineStar Press Publication

www.ninestarpress.com

The Vampire's Witch

Printed in the USA

ISBN: 978-1-64890-263-5

First Edition, April, 2021

Also available in eBook, ISBN: 978-1-64890-262-8

WARNING:
This book contains sexually explicit content, which may only be suitable for mature readers. Depictions of mass murder, death of prominent characters, graphic violence, attempted rape, deceased family member, depression, and stalking.

To Don and Melody,
for sharing your family with me,
with love

Part One: Chaos

One: Dusk

19 APRIL 2010
Chicago, Illinois

Even after three years, living in a big city still creeped Jaret Bachmann out. He hated his fear of dark corners and alleys, not to mention his concern about getting beat up as a gay guy. Straight guys, no matter how peaceful they looked, worried him. In broad daylight, he felt more secure as long as he watched where he went, kept his head up, and stayed in populated areas. And he loved living in the Rogers Park neighborhood. Being in a metropolitan area was so much better for him than small town Colorado. Still, he only had a little light available before the sun went down tonight.

He giggled at himself to release some tension. His mind went to some weird place about the sun setting, like a vampire might jump out and attack him. *As if.*

Heading out to meet his best friend, Brady, Jaret relaxed once he got to the path along Lake Michigan. He passed several joggers, almost got hit by a bike, and meandered his way south. He contemplated taking the "L" but had plenty of time to walk. The spring weather warmed up Chicago, still a comfortable seventy degrees, even as the sun slowly descended in the west. The weather was perfect. Besides, he could always use the exercise.

Jaret felt safer and got his iPod out to search for music. He loved Lady Gaga; why not a little monster love? Or Train's latest CD rocked. Still, he paused at "Relax" and grinned. That song totally kicked ass. Totally. And, he hadn't listened to much of his favorite singer's first album in a long time. If he loved Lady Gaga, then words couldn't describe his adoration for Mika.

He popped in his earbuds and picked up his pace. He even danced a little, despite being in public and seeing the few passersby glancing his way as if he'd gone insane.

The path grew darker with the setting sun and the trees lining both sides of the trail. This dance mix steeled Jaret's nerves. He wiggled his butt, jumped to the side, and smiled at a little old lady and her dog as they walked by.

A few yards later, he was alone. He fretted a little but cranked the music to ignore the world around him. To comfort himself, he reached into his pocket and rubbed the ruby necklace he always brought along for protection. All the Bachmann heirloom jewels empowered his witchcraft and kept him safe, and he loved the beautiful rubies most of all. In a pinch, he could always use his magic to ward anyone off. He'd never had to use his ability to defend himself, except from ghosts, but knew he could if needed. Being a witch had its advantages.

Jaret almost missed the group of four guys sitting off to the side, watching the lake or something. He slowed when he glimpsed a bright-red shirt and thought of his boyfriend, Steve. He'd seen Steve earlier in the day, wearing this totally hot red T-shirt that clung to his chest and showed off his gorgeous biceps. He couldn't remember the shirt exactly, though he thought it had a University of Nebraska logo on the front.

Jaret lurched to a stop when he bumped into someone. "Uh, oh. Sorry. I didn't see you." He glanced up to see another guy with a pretty big belly, yet tons of muscle, not to mention a wicked scowl.

The guy yanked out Jaret's earbuds and glared down at him. "Fuckin' fairy. Watch where you're walkin'."

"Sorry," Jaret barely whispered and started shaking. He'd heard about gay bashings but had never experienced one. In fact, he had never been in a fight. He could see this dude meant him harm by the way he loomed over him.

Jaret reached into his pocket for the necklace. His shaking hands got the better of him, and his finger got stuck in the little coin pocket instead.

Growing more afraid, Jaret stepped to the side to continue until the guy moved with him and blocked his way. Jaret stared at the familiar logo of Northwestern football on the purple T-shirt. He often saw the very shirt on Steve. This guy was enormous. Not good.

His heart racing, Jaret scanned for anyone nearby watching. He spotted the group of four guys out of the corner of his eye. Any chance for help evaporated when two of them moved closer, and he saw they, too, wore Northwestern football gear.

One of them grinned and clapped. "Caught yourself a little fag, Mikey? What you gonna do with him?"

Mikey laughed and crossed his bazooka-sized forearms over his chest. Then he reached down and petted Jaret on the head like a dog. Jaret had little time to act to protect himself. There was no time to get the necklace out. He shot to the side to move around the asshole, but the guy put out his leg and tripped Jaret. He sprawled onto the path, skinning his elbow.

Jaret's heart pounded as fear almost overwhelmed him.

Instead of jumping to his feet, he fumbled into his pocket again to get the ruby necklace out. If anything, he could cause a diversion to pull their attention away from him while he ran. He raised the rubies into the air but fumbled with the necklace, tossing the jewelry a few feet away when he tripped.

The big fat guy hovered above him, snarling. Three of his buddies from across the way started toward Jaret, laughing and pointing. Though he reminded Jaret of Steve, that was where the similarity ended. This guy was muscular and angry-looking.

Jaret tried to find the necklace but Red Shirt Guy stood in his way. He sensed the gems nearby and rolled to the side to find them, but another huge leg blocked him from going farther.

His heart pounding in terror, Jaret heard nothing the four said as they laughed and sneered. He hardly saw them moving as he lay on the ground. He tried to summon the necklace back to him but could not concentrate on a spell or command. The necklace lay mocking him a few feet away. He was frozen with indecision due to fear, anger—and rage.

Where the fuck were all the people? Millions of people in fucking Chicago and no one on the main path along the lake this evening?

Jaret started to come to his senses when all four guys towered over him. "Maybe he needs a yellow shower," one hooted.

Fuck their masculine football bullshit. Jaret felt the tingling in his legs and arms as he called forth magic to protect himself. Too late, though. His delay had given his enemies too much time.

One of them stepped behind Jaret and pinned his arms to the ground as he thrashed his legs around and kicked another one in the shin. They laughed as the big guy he'd run into smacked him upside the head.

Jaret prepared himself for the beating of a lifetime. To his surprise, the huge beast instead snatched his iPod, while two others held him to the ground—one on his arms, the other on his legs.

"You can let the fairy up. I got payment for disrespecting me."

"Hold up." Another one, whom Jaret had barely noticed, looked down at him. "I think he needs to apologize. Don't you, Bill?"

Bill smiled and nodded. "Yep. Ditto, Kellen."

"What about you, Mason?" Bill shouted back. "You think he needs to apologize?"

"I did," Jaret said. He relaxed his muscles. He would never win a physical confrontation, couldn't reach the necklace, and so could only try to negotiate his way out of this mess.

Kellen knelt over and grabbed Jaret's chin in one hand, then shook his head back and forth. "Don't get mouthy. Or I'll be the one giving you a yellow shower. You need to mean it, little guy."

Red Shirt Guy moved closer to the side but still kept his distance.

"What ya think, Mason? Yellow shower? Apology?"

Mikey had moved to where the guys had sat off to the side of the path earlier. He was now playing with Jaret's iPod and ignoring the chaos he'd instigated. Another one of the men moved away, too, after kicking dirt in Jaret's face. Now Bill continued to hold Jaret, with Mason standing to the side.

"I think sorry'll do." Mason looked at both of his buddies, while never even glancing at Jaret. Was he apprehensive about their actions? "You don't want to show him your cock, cuz he'd like a stiff one."

Kellen and Bill laughed loudly, too loudly, in the fake-jock, we-are-hilarious way when no one else in the world found their joke funny. *Who among them really wanted to see Kellen's dick?*

Bill laughed so hard some of his spit landed on Jaret's face. Again, Jaret peered around to see if anyone approached on the path to help him. Nothing.

"I'm sorry. Really." *Lame. They would never go for his whining supplications.*

Kellen reached for Jaret's wallet. He opened the billfold and, one item at a time, threw the contents on the ground after pocketing the cash.

"Please let me go." Outwardly, Jaret sounded deferential. Inwardly, he seethed at all of them, at his own helplessness, and perhaps most of all at straight-man macho bullshit. Not to mention the fact he had a necklace that could have gotten him out of this mess if he'd acted more decisively. What good were witch powers if he fucked up using them?

"One more thing, pretty boy." Kellen stood up and unzipped his pants to howls of laughter from the others. Even Mason let out a chuckle though his face had turned bright red.

"I ain't afraid of his liking my meat. Giving him a little thrill as payment for the cash won't hurt. He probably wants a bit of my love juice."

Jaret squeezed his eyes shut and pressed his lips together, determined to live through the humiliation so he could injure them all with his own powers when they released him.

"I wouldn't do that if I were you." Out of nowhere, Jaret heard a male voice from behind Bill. He took a second to place the accent. British. Had a British bobby come to save him?

Jaret opened his eyes to see Kellen zip his pants and punch a fist into his other hand. The guys holding Jaret down glanced up nervously. Mason, the coward of the county, sprinted down the path with Mikey in tow.

Great, the awful and depressing Kenny Rogers song sprang into Jaret's head. He had come pretty close to becoming his own version of poor Becky, the woman who gets raped by the Gatlin Brothers, prompting her husband, previously known as a coward, to go kick some ass in the local bar. Fucking awful anyone ever thought to commit the story to a song. *Country music was so fucked up. No, fucked up was contemplating country music when three jocks and a British intruder prepared to duke out their differences with me sprawled on the ground.*

Get a grip. He closed his eyes again, unsure what else to do, and heard scuffling. Someone still held onto him, so he decided not to move.

Jaret opened his eyes when the last dude released him and he heard shouting. At first, he assumed the three guys had turned their attention to this new person. His eyes deceived him. Kellen was hanging about twenty feet in the air from a branch. His pants were gone—underwear too. Bill suffered the same fate on the other side of the path. What the fuck?

Out of the corner of his eye, Jaret noticed the nameless one struggling against a very muscular man with long blond hair.

Time to get the fuck out of there. Jaret scrambled to his feet, commanded the necklace to return to him, and dashed down the path. Thank goodness he ran every morning with his dog, Darth, so he had enough speed and stamina to get far away. He dropped onto the grass and drew in a deep breath.

"You okay?" A kind-looking woman stopped her own jog.

"Yeah, fine." Jaret hardly wanted to explain his predicament to a complete stranger.

She nodded, but seemed unconvinced. Jaret grinned and lay back on the ground to ignore her. Thankfully, she moved on, away from him and in the opposite direction from the shitheads who attacked him.

He still had his phone; somehow they missed stealing it. With shaking hands he texted Brady he was running late.

He took an inventory of himself to see if he could even go out without running home to change. He needed a washroom to scrub off his face and clean his bleeding arm. His clothes were dirty but could probably pass in the darkened bars.

Jaret brushed off his shirt and thought about just going home. But the thought of hanging out alone and rehashing this awful scene over and over held no appeal. He needed to stay out and get away from his thoughts, lose himself with other people or risk spiraling into madness and fear.

Besides, he really had no desire to head back north and end up in a tree without his pants. Except they stole his wallet and ID. Frozen with inaction again, he wondered if the guy who saved him was still there so he could get his billfold.

Shit. He had to get a grip. *No way those guys were as high up in the tree as he assumed. Not unless the guy who saved him knew magic or something.* That made a little sense, at least. If Jaret had a full complement of the family jewels, he could have sent them all into trees and commanded the gems to de-pants the guys too.

Did another witch come to his rescue?

He laughed. *Nope. Must have been a vampire, what with the sun setting and all.*

Two: Meeting Anthony

19 APRIL 2010
Chicago, Illinois

Jaret sat recovering near the pedestrian path when his senses tingled. A slight ache crept into the back of his head, and his witch instincts told him to get up and run. Too late, he looked up and saw a long-haired gentleman strolling toward him, smiling.

Jaret had better presence of mind this time to grab the ruby necklace and clutch it as the guy came over, still grinning. "May I?" he asked and pointed to a spot on the lawn next to Jaret.

Jaret hesitated, glanced around, but nodded. His senses shifted from fear to lust. This guy was hot, whatever his intentions.

"I think this is yours." The guy handed Jaret his iPod, wallet, and other belongings as he sat.

"Thanks."

"You're welcome. Sorry about the assholes. I'm glad I came along when I did."

Jaret nodded, unsure what kind of conversation to engage, wondering if the dude wanted to protect him or put a spell on him. The ruby necklace tingled in Jaret's hand, without giving off serious alarm—more like a mild warning of something a little off.

"Did you find the other two? I mean, and—" Jaret had no idea how to finish the sentence. He wanted to continue with "string them up in a tree." No, he decided against the truth. The truth might bring Jaret's sanity into question. Or worse, expose the guy as a witch and thus force him to attack Jaret too.

"And hang them in a tree?" the man spoke in a matter-of-fact tone. Like people hung from trees without their pants on all the time. "Yes."

No other explanation.

The absurdity of the scene hit Jaret full force, and he started laughing. Near hysterical, losing his breath, the laughter forced him onto his back as he clutched his side. He choked when he thought of the dude swaying in the wind, utterly humiliated as his pecker hung out there. *Asshole.* Plus his laughter was harder in reaction to the extreme fear that had peaked and now flooded out of his body. He had to laugh or risk crying.

His savior found something funny, too—maybe Jaret's laughter—and laughed along with him.

"Good. That's awesome," Jaret said.

When he calmed, Jaret checked out the man as he smirked while watching people. Jaret became completely self-conscious. The guy was stunning and totally beautiful. Tall, with gorgeous wavy blond hair falling to the middle of his back, he had steel-blue eyes. And ripped—as in muscles—a powerful guy right out of a porno flick.

Any sense of danger passed, even though Jaret's stomach turned into another knot. The ruby necklace stopped buzzing in his hand. Jaret saw the guy's Rolex and diamond earrings. He appeared older, like in his late twenties or early thirties, so he had a real job. A good real job.

"Are you okay?" the guy asked when Jaret quieted.

"Yeah."

"May I take you to the water fountain and help you clean up? It's right there." He pointed a few yards away, still close to other people.

"That's a good idea."

Jaret followed like a puppy as they went to the fountain. Once there, Jaret first swallowed a big drink of water and then cleaned his elbow. The wound stung, but he sighed in relief. Without the dirt and dried blood, the damage proved less an injury than he first thought. Jaret splashed some water on his other arm and then brushed off his clothes as best he could.

He didn't realize he had dirt on his face until he heard, "Here, let me help." Jaret stared at his biceps as the hotty cleaned and wiped his face. Jaret glanced down the hard chest in front of him, intoxicated by the brush of his firm hand across his cheek. This touch sent another wave of feeling through Jaret, more absolute desire. The guy smiled at him when he finished. "That's better. I thought a handsome young man lurked under all the grime."

Jaret blushed.

"Do you want to sit for a minute?" He pointed to a nearby bench.

Jaret nodded and led the two of them back to the grass, farther from prying ears on the bench.

"So, uh—thanks again." Jaret held up his iPod. "Really. You a cop or something? I don't know what would've happened if you hadn't come along."

"Good thing you don't need to worry about what would have happened. And no, I have no connection to law enforcement. I was merely enjoying an evening walk. Fools. Too macho for their own good."

"Did you strip them to emasculate them?"

This time the stranger laughed. "I suppose to humiliate their masculinity."

"How will they get down?" Jaret asked.

The guy shrugged. "I've no idea. Don't care. Do you?"

Jaret thought for a moment, and then he shook his head.

"Good." One of those powerful hands patted Jaret on the back. "Because they deserved what they got. They're lucky to be alive."

What did he mean? Jaret decided to leave the idea alone. He'd already dealt with enough weird shit for the evening. Well, maybe. But he also had questions. He really had to find out if another witch sat next to him.

"So, how'd you get them up there?" Jaret asked. "You know, put those guys up in the tree?"

He smiled and pointed to his arm.

Wow. So hot. Jaret almost stopped himself from saying anything, lest his words sound confrontational. But he needed to know the truth. "Um, hanging people in a tree takes more than just muscle strength."

"Not really. I suppose they looked higher up to you because you're short."

"I'm not that short. Or delusional."

"Sometimes my strength surprises me. Adrenaline takes over. I get irate when people victimize the innocent. I just snap, and before I know what hits me, someone's hanging precariously from a tree."

"Clear up in a tree with the birds." Jaret squinted at him.

He just laughed again. *Okay, so the dude didn't want to answer. Cool.* Jaret thought he better keep his distance. On the other hand, his hormones beseeched him not to walk away too fast. So he just sat there.

"Why did they attack you?"

"I ran into one of them by mistake." Jaret contemplated going into the long sordid story but skipped the details. "And maybe because I'm gay." Jaret's heart beat harder, still afraid in the initial moment after coming out to someone.

"They love to target us, don't they? Can't deal with their own masculinity. So somehow coming after gay people makes them feel better."

Us. He had said us. Oh my god, he's gay!

"By the way, my name is Anthony." He held out his hand.

"Jaret." They shook hands and held them together for a moment before Anthony released Jaret. *Whoa, was this guy hot and chivalrous.* Jaret swooned.

"Pleased to meet you," Anthony said. "Would you like to continue your walk? I could accompany you."

Jaret wanted to stay with Anthony because of the infatuation and because he still desired to know how the big bad football players had ended up in the tree. Yet Brady must be worried to death by now. As if on cue, Jaret's phone belted out Mika's "Billy Brown."

"Excuse me." Jaret grabbed his phone. Anthony stood and walked a few feet away.

"Where the fuck are you?" Brady slurred. "I'm getting snookered alone. Sad. Very sad."

"Hey. Something came up. I can't make it tonight."

"You okay?"

"Yeah. Fine. Great. I'll fill you in tomorrow. Or later tonight. Okay?"

"Sure. I'm headed downtown to meet everyone before I become the poor lonely fag drinking his sorrows away."

Jaret laughed and said goodbye. Now, what to tell Anthony?

"Do you have somewhere to be?" Anthony asked.

"No." Jaret shook his head. "I'm not going. Just some friends hanging out at a bar. I think I'll just walk for a while." He motioned down his soiled clothes. "I'm not very presentable anymore, after what happened."

"May I join you?" Anthony asked. Such a gentleman. "You look presentable to me."

Jaret's heart leapt. "Sure."

They walked in quiet for a long time, past Belmont and toward the city.

Jaret's mind raced a mile a minute. First he calmed himself about the attack. The fight frightened him, and then totally pissed him off. He cursed himself for being too slow with his jewels and for failing to watch his surroundings. Being so careless would never happen again.

As if that wasn't enough, along came his hormones. One second he wanted to jump Anthony's bones; the next he remembered he was in a committed relationship with Steve—even if things had gotten rocky lately. He had every intention of breaking up with Steve, who had taken to putting football above his boyfriend. Jaret decided to exercise caution around Anthony, who had strange powers but refused to admit them. Still, he acted the perfect gentleman the entire way.

"Come over here." Anthony wrapped his arm around Jaret and guided him off the path and toward the lake. Still plenty of people about, despite the late hour. Anthony sat on a ledge overlooking Lake Michigan. Jaret watched a barge when Anthony pointed to his right. "It's a great view of the city."

Jaret peered at the skyline reflecting back at him. "My favorite's the John Hancock Building."

"Mine too." Anthony jumped to his feet. "Come on." He held his hand out to Jaret and pulled him to his feet. "I have an idea."

Anthony hurried them toward Lakeshore Drive and took a pedestrian tunnel under to a side street where he could hail a cab. Against his wiser judgment, Jaret hopped in with him. "The Hancock," Anthony told the driver.

Before long, Jaret sat in the Signature Room on the 95th floor of the John Hancock Building, with a perfect view of the city, compliments of the hundred dollar bill Anthony slipped the maître 'd. Went with the Rolex, Jaret guessed.

Jaret's mixed feelings about Anthony became clearer. He had studied Anthony and asked the ruby in his pocket for an evaluation. The gem couldn't give him definitive answers, but the magic could give him a general feeling about anyone.

Anthony posed no immediate danger. He liked Jaret, possibly in the same way Jaret liked him. He had a protective aura about him. Despite the show of strength and evasiveness about his aptitude, Jaret trusted him with his personal safety—much like he'd felt with Steve until the last few months when Steve's actions became unpredictable. Jaret adored the sense of safeguarding offered by a powerful man, and Anthony fit the profile.

Anthony sat across from Jaret with perfect posture, his already tall frame made even more striking by his presence and long blonde hair. He acted like the superrich businessmen portrayed on television.

"What do you do for a living?" Anthony asked while they waited for their drinks.

Jaret longed for a chocolate martini. His nerves had rattled a little when he had a moment in the bathroom stall to contemplate his close call with mortality, or at least mortification. Until that point, he had mostly lost himself in Anthony's presence. *Yeah, a drink would be great.*

"Do for a living?" Jaret giggled when Anthony arched his eyebrow. "Oh, work. Nothing. I mean, college. I'm still in college."

Anthony nodded. "Studying?"

"History."

Anthony asked several other questions about Jaret's studies. Jaret answered, excited someone took an interest in his academic pursuits. Steve always acted so put out if Jaret launched into some intellectual inquiry. "I want to go to graduate school."

"A noble endeavor."

Anthony sounded so aristocratic or even seventeenth century. "What do you do?" Jaret asked.

"A number of things. I'm primarily in finance. I work at night and sleep all day."

Jaret sensed the avoidance again. "Interesting. Like stocks and stuff?"

"Pretty much." Anthony ran his finger along the rim of his glass. He even had sexy fingers. "Rather boring."

Jaret wanted to say his job must be lucrative as he glanced at the Rolex. Nah, poor taste to ogle over the watch. Instead, he took another sip of his drink.

They moved to other topics, such as hobbies and favorite music. Jaret kept his love for Mika controlled so as not to sound like a total freak. Anthony said he had no family, but a lot of friends who more than made up for it. Jaret told Anthony about his sister, Jenn, his closest friend in the world.

A couple more times Anthony shied away from a subject or line of inquiry. He never got angry or defensive, but issued vague statements or steered the conversation artfully away. His dodging piqued Jaret's curiosity.

They chatted amicably until Jaret thought of the LGBT history exhibit at the Chicago History Museum. He told Anthony about the display. "Do you ever come out through the day? Because the museum's only open during the day and you really should check it out."

Anthony called for the waitress and ordered a second round. This time, however, the sparks practically lit the room on fire as Jaret's magic picked up on Anthony's unwillingness to answer the question.

Three: Coming Out a Second Time

20 APRIL 2010
Chicago, Illinois

The awkward pause made Jaret look all over the room to avoid eye contact with Anthony. He noticed a clock on the wall, surprised the time had passed eleven o'clock. *What had gotten Anthony so worked up?* Jaret covered a slight hole in the tablecloth with his napkin—a hole that his magic had burned into the fabric through his fingertip when he realized Anthony was hiding something.

Staring out the window, he realized clouds had rolled in off the lake and now hid many of the buildings below. Only the tallest skyscrapers peeked out, blinking a warning to airplanes. And perhaps to Jaret?

Then the answer dawned on Jaret. The witchcraft. Certainly Anthony understood or had figured out he hid a secret too. If Anthony used magic to defeat the jock brigade, then he may wonder why Jaret kept his power hidden. With a really nice buzz and loving the atmosphere, Jaret risked another step.

"Not to dwell on it, but—" Anthony glanced across the table at Jaret with wide eyes. "Well, I just. It's, uh, you did some freaky stuff this evening. I'm grateful, don't get me wrong. Amazing how you saved me. I'm so cool with being saved—no matter how. But, well, I want to be honest. And I sense you're worried. Or maybe you know something but don't want to say what you think. So, let me put the issue out there." Jaret paused, worried when Anthony sat rigid, and his smile disappeared. Did Jaret sound like an idiot lush? Jaret took another gulp of his martini and then drew in a deep breath. "I'm a witch."

Jaret's hands shook, and he reached under the table for his ruby in case this went badly.

But Anthony's posture relaxed. "I've never had someone come out to me as a witch before. Tell me more."

"It's a family thing." Jaret shrugged. "Goes back centuries. See, my family has always had one male warlock per generation who protects the family. I have these jewels I inherited to give me power." Jaret set the necklace on the table to show Anthony.

"Keep going." Anthony rubbed the necklace and then handed the jewelry back to Jaret.

"You sure? Most people don't believe my story." Jaret twirled a finger beside his head. "Think I'm fucking nuts."

"Try me."

"Well, my great-great-grandfather, Henrik, sent his wife and two sons to America. He was killed before he joined them in Nebraska. He'd already scouted the area and built a house. When he returned to Prussia to get more of their belongings, his male lover freaked out and killed him instead of coming to the states. This was in the late 1800s, so being gay could get you killed. Well, being gay could today, too, right on the bike path. Anyway, Henrik's spirit returned to Fremont and haunted my family for generations. It's kinda ironic, because he became a complete homophobe and killed most of the warlocks to prevent them from using the Bachmann magic or learning about him."

Jaret paused, embarrassed the alcohol prompted him to tell this much of his fanciful background to a stranger. Yet Anthony watched him the entire time, unawed by the odd tale.

"Don't stop," Anthony said. "This is the most fascinating thing I've heard in a long time."

Jaret's face flushed. Was Anthony mocking him? Still, he pressed onward. "Okay. Well, I learned about Henrik. Figured out I was my generation's warlock when I returned to Nebraska from Colorado, where we live now, for my gramps's funeral. That's when my power came to me. I had to combat Henrik and protect myself and my family. I trapped him in a magical iron box. He's still there." Jaret laughed. "You must think I'm a drunken nut."

"Not at all." Anthony smiled. "You're charming and a lot more forthcoming since you've had a drink. I'm enjoying your story and believe every word."

Unfortunately, at this point the story reminded Jaret of Steve because they met during the Fremont fiasco. Still, telling Anthony felt good. Why, he wasn't sure. Perhaps Anthony's age comforted him, or was it the way he had saved him? Jaret felt so comfortable with him and had already explained more than he'd ever told other people.

When the waitress returned, Anthony started to order another round. Jaret panicked, remembering how much drinks cost up here. Two drinks already equaled more money than Jaret had in his pocket.

"Uh, I'm good."

Anthony scrunched his eyebrows. "Done?"

Jaret's face turned red. "I forgot to go to a cash machine," he lied.

"Nonsense. Everything is on me." The waitress grinned and scribbled something on a notepad before walking away. She returned a few minutes later with two more martinis and chocolate fondue.

"Thank you for sharing your story," Anthony said.

"Oh, yeah. Well, I thought you should know. Actually, I felt like you were worried about something. I told you so you'd be comfortable."

As if reading Jaret's mind, Anthony responded. "So I'd be comfortable telling you I know magic too?"

Jaret smiled and popped a chocolate-covered piece of banana into his mouth. "Yeah. Yep." He nodded. "What's your story?"

"I learned magic from friends. A group of us. We all know sorcery. We use the power to protect people. We vowed to conceal our ability from everyone else and only use it for the good of humanity."

"Which is why you saved me, right? You're kind of like the police. Or maybe more like superheroes. Were you afraid to tell me about magic?"

Anthony hesitated. "Yes. Not everyone reacts well to such news."

Jaret knew Anthony lied again from the pause before he spoke. He recognized the subterfuge even before he glanced down and saw the ruby glow a warning.

"Yeah, it's not usually a great conversation starter." Jaret grinned and ignored the ruby. "Hi, I'm a witch. I know magic. People usually freak." They both laughed. "So, you got those guys in the trees with magic, right?"

Anthony twirled the same piece of pound cake in the chocolate he started with. "Precisely. Can you forgive me for not telling you?"

"Yeah. I get it. It's cool. And thanks again for saving me. And for the drinks. I can't really afford this place."

Jaret stopped himself from any more drunken chatter, afraid he'd sound like some twinky call boy to Anthony and the patrons around him.

"You're more than welcome for everything. Actually, I have one more confession, if I may?" Anthony played with the stem of his martini glass. "May I take you on a proper date next weekend? When you haven't first been attacked? Not that you don't make a beautiful damsel in distress."

Jaret blushed. A date? With this total Greek god sitting across from him? Wow.

Shit. Steve.

"Well, um."

Anthony seemed to slump. "It's not a command or expectation."

"No. But I'm in a relationship."

"I see. I didn't mean to be forward."

Before he totally lost the moment, Jaret let the drunken chattiness come roaring back. "No, let me explain. I'm breaking up with him. I have to. I've actually been thinking about splitting up for a long time. He's turned into an ass. Or he's afraid or something. My magic indicates something is wrong, but I can't tell what. Anyway, I need to end our situation. I delayed for a lot of reasons. Probably a bunch of psychological bullshit in my own mind, you know?"

Jaret paused, took a big drink from his glass, and shrugged his shoulders and smiled. "Here's the thing. You know the guys on the path? Well, they all play football with my boyfriend. They're his friends."

Jaret allowed the bombshell to sink in before he said anything else. He could almost see the wheels churning in Anthony's mind.

"Was he part of the attack?" Anthony asked, a slight smile at the corner of his mouth.

"No." Jaret shook his head. "He wasn't there. But if we go out and he sees them, he has me stay behind and pretends not to know me. I doubt he'll do anything about what happened."

"You sound like you have another story to tell me."

"More like part of the one I already told you." *Shit. How did this guy get him so chatty when he usually shied away from conversation?*

"I'm all ears." Anthony grinned and leaned toward Jaret, his eyes sparkling up this close. He reached over and brushed a strand of Jaret's long hair behind his ear.

Jaret paused, wondering how to begin this sordid account. "Well, first you have to know we were way too young to get as serious as we did. I mean, we started dating just a few years ago. We hadn't even finished high school when we met and got serious. It's embarrassing."

"I was young once too. Relax. We all grow up, look back, and think about the mistakes we made. Youthful indiscretions are what shape us into the adults we become. We can't regret them forever."

Funny, how again Anthony sounded so mature yet appeared only a few years older than Jaret.

"Right, well, mistakes. That's a good word for it. During all the shit with Henrik, I met Steve in Fremont. He's a football player. I fell for him, because of his body and this mesmerizing masculine charm. Believe it or not, he protected and nurtured me through the mess at my gramps's.

"We fell in love. Or, we felt like we were in love at the time. Now I wonder if our emotion was more lust. Teenage dreams, not reality. But we fell hard. I mean, really, really hard."

Anthony laughed at the double entendre, which caused Jaret to join him.

"Yeah. Lots of hardness." When he controlled himself again, Jaret continued the story. "Anyway, we both graduated a few weeks later and arranged to go to Northwestern. We planned to live together. But before we got here, Steve decided to move into the dorm where all the football players lived. His coach said he needed to be a good teammate, all in and shit. I was so disappointed. But now, thank God we didn't ever start rooming together. Sharing a room would be awful, since it's all falling apart.

"See, we moved here as boyfriends, planning to live out and proud. Which I do. Steve, not so much. Instead of using Chicago as a safe zone, he closeted himself more and more because of the football team. Yet I stayed with him because of who he used to be. And because I feel like some entity took control of him. Like a spirit infiltrated him." Jaret sighed. "I'm pretty sure, though, I made up the possession part to explain how Steve came to love football more than me. And his teammates are super important to him."

"The charming group I met earlier?" Anthony asked.

"Yeah. Them. Well, Steve and I grew farther apart as he got closer and closer to the football team. I think he got more afraid of coming out here than when he was in fucking Nebraska. Because being on the team meant so much. And I met my best friend, Brady, who's also out like me. And Steve likes him okay, but he hangs out more with the team, and I like being with Brady. In fact, since I have Brady, Steve decided he could stay in hiding to protect his standing on the team. To the point we can only see each other in private or at some distant location. Steve even put a halt to our trips to Boystown. He went to a gay bar one time after we turned twenty-one. Now he refuses to go back. Whenever we discuss being out, my magic tingles with alarm, so I drop the subject."

Jaret almost told Anthony about his big fight with Steve the other night. Too embarrassing. Steve came over to Jaret's for a night together. They'd barely started eating when things turned bad.

*

"We could go downtown this weekend." Jaret took a bite of pizza and measured Steve's response, who ate in silence. No reaction. "There's a new gay bar close to Michigan Avenue. A couple guys went last weekend and said it rocks. Brady's going." Brady actually disliked Steve. For Jaret's sake and because of their friendship, Brady never dwelled on his feelings about Steve. But hiding his thoughts was not one of Brady's strong points either.

"I gotta go to clubs with the guys, you know. To keep up appearances. You could go with Brady. We'll meet after."

"Romantic."

Steve dropped his pizza onto the box lid and stood up. He grabbed at his football jacket and toppled the chair over.

Jaret's dog, Darth, reared up and put her forty-pound self between Jaret and Steve. Despite her medium size, she cast a fierce presence when upset. She had the colorings of a Doberman, a short stub of a tail, and pointy ears. The hair on her back stood straight up as she glared at Steve, so Jaret patted her butt to calm her down.

"What?" Jaret asked. Dumb. He knew "what." He pulled Darth to him, not worried about Steve's latest little outburst. His temper flared all the time. He never got violent because the protective football jock inside of him kept him from lashing out at his gal. A pounding headache roared into Jaret's mind, like the one he used to get when the angry ghost Henrik haunted him.

"You can't accept who I am, can you?" Steve shook his head and righted the chair. He sat and ran his hands through his short brown hair. "I'm not some prissy guy who wants to go dancing and have trolls stare at me. I love football. I live for it. You knew what football meant when we started dating."

"Prissy, like some fag with long hair and no muscle tone?" Jaret tilted his head so his own long hair fell to the side.

"Don't turn this on me. You know what I meant. I love the way you look. I'm just different. I can't be like you and play football."

"So football means more to you than me?"

Steve slammed his jacket to the ground. "No. You mean the most. I just gotta be me, too."

As they argued, his headache continued to tell Jaret some force affected them, but again and again no concrete explanation came to him.

They bickered for a few more minutes before Jaret cried from the frustration of wanting something Steve never intended to offer. His tears prompted Steve to soften and nurture him.

"Babe, I'll come with you Friday for a little while. Don't cry." Steve rubbed Jaret's back and they made up, even though each knew he lied through his teeth.

*

Nope, even with his drunken chattiness and lust for Anthony, Jaret did not want to share that charming memory. His own passivity embarrassed him.

As if sensing his thought, Anthony moved their conversation forward. "So why are you still with him?"

"Good question. Our history? I still kinda swoon when we're alone." He hoped his admission would not lose Anthony, but continued as if someone had injected truth serum into his veins. Or a lot of alcohol. "Steve acts like the big jock protecting and loving his girl. Maybe I need a therapist, because I love when he treats me that way." He laughed at himself, and thankfully so did Anthony.

"What else?" Anthony asked.

"Bottom line?"

"Cut to the chase." Anthony nodded.

"I guess I keep hoping the loving, protective guy who helped me through the problem with Henrik will return and become the man of my dreams. At least, I kept up the illusion until the last couple weeks when it hurt too much to ignore the truth." Jaret sighed. How could he segue back to Anthony? Maybe he needed this opportunity to give him the courage to move forward. "Anyway, if you don't mind, I'd love to go on a date. I promise I'll be single by next weekend. If you can deal with my situation, I'd love to accept. I know my handling of the circumstances sounds slimy and all."

"Not in the least." Anthony smiled and lifted his drink in the air. "A toast. To new beginnings." They clinked their glasses together. "I'll pick you up at seven, one week from today." Then he frowned at Jaret. "Provided you're single."

Jaret knew he had a big sloppy grin on his face. He couldn't help the feeling. They got up to go, Jaret wondering how to get home. He figured Anthony didn't live in Rogers Park. More like Lincoln Park. Or the Gold Coast.

"Would you like a ride home?" Anthony asked.

"Sure."

"Follow me."

Anthony led them to a back elevator and then on some behind the scenes journey through the John Hancock Building, including parts Jaret had never seen. They stood in front of a convertible Porsche in a matter of moments.

"This is yours?" Jaret asked.

"Yep." Anthony opened the passenger door for Jaret.

On the exit ramp toward Michigan Avenue, Jaret glanced at Anthony. "How did you get your car to the John Hancock Building if we came in a cab?"

"I live here."

Jaret gulped and looked straight ahead. A rich witch. That didn't suck.

Four: Friendship

20 APRIL 2010
Chicago, Illinois

Jaret burst into his apartment and greeted Darth. "Hey, girl. What you up to? Was your night as exciting as mine?"

She wiggled her little tail at him before spinning around in a circle. Jaret almost belly flopped onto the couch, while Darth hurried to the side and started licking his face. He reached down to pet her.

After taking Darth outside to do her business, he thought about going to bed. Nope, way too much energy coursed through his veins. Instead, he jumped up and ran over to his iPod, putting it into the stereo so he could listen to Mika. His mind raced with thoughts of Anthony and their date next weekend.

Jaret turned the sound up to drown out the other music blaring throughout the building. He usually hated these nights when everyone at once defied decorum and blared their shitty music, forcing everyone else to suffer listening to it too. Like they all lived in a dorm instead of an apartment building. Some of these people worked. As in adults with real jobs. Yet tonight he joined the revelry.

Too giddy to sit tight, Jaret leapt to his feet, gave Darth a big kiss on the head, and turned off the music. He headed for his computer, wanting to watch a video instead of just listening to the music. He loved Mika. A perfect way to celebrate this totally rocking night.

Who would have guessed, as Jaret lay in the middle of the bike path, waiting to get pissed on by an asshole, the evening would turn around to one of wonder?

As the computer booted up, he glanced at the picture of Brady and him at last year's Pride Parade, smiling and barely holding back a major laugh-fest because of something one of them had said. If Jaret's family provided an anchor of love and support, Brady offered a life line to reality and good times.

They'd met their first year, in an English class, when they were thrust together by the professor to analyze some awful poem. They did the usual dance of exchanging names and pleasantries and then tried to dive into the literature.

"Um, I can't tell if the butterflies are insects or little penises floating around." Jaret snorted.

Brady laughed very loud, covering his mouth when the professor glanced over. "Then the author isn't a size queen."

Soon enough, they had each other laughing and a burgeoning friendship developed, first because of their shared sense of humor, and later over beers when they exchanged coming-out stories. They enjoyed academic discussions, music, hanging out in gay bars, and simply making life fun. Jaret had never had such a close friend outside of his relatives.

Brady was cute as a button with black hair, deep brown eyes, and a slight build. Not Jaret's type, which actually helped because Brady felt the same way about Jaret, so they never had to deal with any sexual tension.

They could almost always make each other laugh. Over the last couple years with Steve going more and more haywire, Brady yanked Jaret into reality by taking him out to clubs, laughing, and reminding him he had a lot more going for himself in life than misery with a closeted jock.

And Brady introduced him to Mika.

Jaret sighed when Mika stared back at him from the computer screen. So cute, with those big brown eyes and curly hair. Jaret fell in love with his music from the internet. When Brady showed him Mika's picture they both swooned and turned into total fanatics. His music was powerful and original. The sound transported Jaret to a happier place and helped him escape reality. Then total insane lust took over for them when Mika admitted he was gay.

A couple of Mika's sad songs spoke to Jaret too. He hated and loved the one Mika sang about a lover slipping away while he slept. Hated the lyrics because they reminded him again and again how many times Steve performed the role to perfection. Loved the song because he felt connected to someone else who'd experienced the same devastation.

Wow, Mika dancing around in his underwear to start this song. To die for.

Jaret spun around and belted out the lyrics to "We Are Golden" along with Mika. He jumped and then grabbed up a batch of gems. Jaret still grinned when he thought about the fact he possessed family heirloom jewels that held magical powers only he could control. He tossed them in the air and watched them sparkle to life, creating a disco right in his own bedroom. Then he commanded them to create the image of Mika.

A ghostly Mika and Jaret danced all over the room. Jaret laughed and picked up Darth, her body going rigid as usual when she lost control of herself. Against her will, she danced in Jaret's arms until she licked his face and lurched away. Darth shook off and straightened her collar before turning in circles and lying down with a canine harrumph.

When the song ended, Jaret ordered the gems to return to their box and then flopped onto the floor next to Darth. She licked his hand.

"You love Mika, too, don't you? Is he your favorite singer?"

He hugged Darth, and she gave him a big lick across the cheek. Moments like these reminded him how much he depended on her and had his entire life. Growing up, when Jaret felt so different because of the ghost visions and his sexuality, she remained the rock in his life. Loving him. Seeming to get inside his head and know what to do to make him feel better.

Not wanting to dampen his mood, he ignored the gray hair on her snout, concentrating on the fact she still jogged with him at her age, albeit a little more slowly.

He scratched behind her ears and then pulled her close when his phone rang. Another Mika song as his ringtone, this time "Billy Brown."

"Hey, Brady. Why are you calling so late? No late-night hookup tonight? What's up?"

"Dude!" Brady screamed into Jaret's ear. "A lost night of finding love has turned to gold. You won't fucking believe what I just found out!"

Jaret held the phone away from his head. "Uh, what? You've gone deaf and have to shout everything?"

"Uproariously funny. Change your tune, or I'm keeping the news to myself. Trust me—you'll be pissed you didn't give me some love."

Jaret laughed. Brady always made him laugh. Thank God for good friends or Steve would surely have driven him right to the loony bin. "Okay, I give. What has you screaming excited?"

"Mika! Fucking Mika, dude!"

"You're fucking Mika? I *am* jealous."

This time Brady laughed. "No. I wouldn't have called you in the middle of hot sex. Only afterward to rub it in. Mika's coming to Chicago this summer."

Jaret took his turn to squeal. He hopped up off the floor and jumped up and down. "No fucking way!"

"Yes, fucking way. Right to Chicago, so we don't have to plan a trip anywhere."

"Awesome!" Jaret danced around the room. "When can we get tickets?"

"Soon. I'll keep you posted. Should I get 'em?"

"Sure. Sounds good."

"How many?" Brady asked.

"Just me."

"Cool."

Jaret thought about explaining his peculiar evening, but Brady shouted into his ear again.

"Can you send the apparition of Mika you conjured the other day to me? Have him walk down the street to my place."

Jaret thought about how he had used his magic for Brady, so they could dance with a 3-D Mika. They both found the hologram absolutely hilarious. "You know the rules. No magic in public. Plus, you sound too drunk to get it up."

"Never, my friend. Never. Always willing and able. Okay, fine. No Mika. I'll settle for some alone time with him next time I'm there."

Jaret laughed so hard he coughed. "You can't have sex with an apparition. Or even know what he likes sexually."

"Oh, just give me a few minutes alone; he'll become whatever I want him to be. Mika is so gorgeous."

"Do we even know if he's bi or gay? Top or bottom?"

"Again, doesn't matter once I get a chance. We know he's into men, which is all I need."

"Maybe I could just use the gems to force his compliance for one night."

Brady laughed. "Um, that's called date rape. Not cool. Besides, you always claim to follow some magic code of ethics with your shit. Enchanting someone against their will doesn't jive."

"Right. Except I can fantasize about anything I want. No restrictions there."

"Hey, I just thought of something. Can those gems give you sexual pleasure? You know, like the sensation of getting a blow job?"

Jaret barked a laugh. His mind drifted to thoughts of his friendship with Brady, especially after Brady learned about his sorcery.

They had hung out several times and grew close enough so one evening, after a night on the town and still too wired to go to bed, Jaret's inebriation loosened his tongue.

*

"I gotta tell you something. You won't believe me. But I'm a witch."

"And a bitch." Brady giggled at himself.

"No, seriously. I'm a witch. The thing I've always hinted I wanted to tell you but couldn't, remember? Because most people don't believe me or make fun of me."

Brady stopped laughing but tilted his head at Jaret. "Is this the alcohol talking? Gone to your head or something?"

"Wait here." Jaret jumped to his feet and headed for his bedroom to retrieve his gems. He returned to the living room and sat next to Brady. "Don't freak." He lifted the lid of the tiny chest and had the gems dance before their eyes.

"Fuck. You're seriously a fucking witch?" Brady spoke with awe but no sense of fear.

"Yeah."

Brady nodded. "Cool."

"So you're not scared of me or anything? Not running for the hills?"

"Well, I never met a witch before. At least you're not green and old and scary and shit." Brady smiled. "Seriously, it's cool. What can you do? What power do the jewels give you?"

"It's hard to explain. Sometimes even I don't know. First, my ability comes through or from these gems somehow. They've been in my family for centuries. Get this!" Jaret clapped his hands in excitement. "Every generation of Bachmanns has a gay male who controls the gems and the magic. Always gay! Always a witch. How awesome is a gay family witch tradition?"

"How far back?"

"Long as we can tell. There's a book in the family, a history, to explain the legacy."

"And all were pole smokers?"

Jaret laughed at Brady's slur. "Yep. All fudge packers."

"So tell me, what can you do? Or is your power some ancient secret and you'd have to kill me if you let the cat out of the bag?"

"You need to promise not to tell anyone. Most people freak out. And I don't want to become a scientific experiment or anything bad. I probably shouldn't have told you this much."

Brady grew serious and crawled over to Jaret. He gave him a quick hug and then sat beside him. "Dude, your secret's safe. I won't tell anyone. I'm honored you wanted to share with me."

Jaret had a hard time telling Brady how much his words meant. He thanked him, then decided to try to explain his power. "With the gems, I can move stuff around. Mostly they defend me from ghosts and bad stuff. They can close doors, open windows. Trap spirits against their will. Once, they even controlled a storm. But I never know for sure what will happen until I need the magic. Then I think something, maybe something specific or just, 'I need help!' and they do the rest."

"Radically cool. You're like the *Bewitched* woman from the old TV show."

Jaret decided they had gotten too serious. "Sometimes I just play around with them. Here, let me show you. Name someone you'd like to see dance naked."

Brady arched his eyebrow and then held his chin in his hand while he contemplated. "How about the hotty from the basketball team who sits in front of us in speech class?"

"The one with the low pants so we see his crack?"

"Yeah. Him."

Jaret closed his eyes and envisioned the guy, then asked the gems for help. When he opened his eyes, three of the smaller jewels had floated between Brady and him. Soon enough, a small apparition of the basketball player moved right out of Jaret's mind and onto the floor in front of them. He did a strip dance to Brady's whoops and hollers.

Jaret had no idea what the guy really looked like naked, so whatever appeared once the clothes came off stemmed from his imagination, not reality. But he did know the tight bubble ass wiggling in front of him came pretty close to authenticity because he had stared at the firm ass so much in class.

*

If Brady had become his best friend before Jaret revealed his magic, then nothing could ever separate them once he had handled Jaret's most intimate secret with grace and understanding.

"Hey!" Brady's shout on the other end of the phone brought Jaret back to reality. "Did the phone drop the call, or did you figure out how to make the jewels give you a blow job and you've lost yourself in sexual pleasure and forgot about your pal Brady?"

"It would seem wrong to manipulate the jewels for sex. Degenerate or something."

"But it's okay to make them show you dancing naked guys? You've got some mysterious rules with magic. Hard to follow them."

They chatted for a few more minutes before agreeing on a time to rendezvous tomorrow for lunch and hung up. Jaret grabbed his coat and Darth's leash, ready to take her out and then finally get to sleep.

Part Two:

Boyfriends

Five: Jenn

26 APRIL 2010
Chicago, Illinois

Jaret yawned and stretched as the sun peeked through his window. He reached down and patted Darth on the head. After a brief moment of early morning amnesia, Jaret grinned. A giddy anticipation swept over him.

Reaching for his jogging clothes, Jaret contemplated his date with Anthony. They had exchanged a couple of texts through the week to confirm their plans. Jaret worried Anthony would dismiss him or make excuses to avoid their first scheduled date. Nope. His last message had indicated he would pick Jaret up around seven.

A pang of guilt riddled him, however, as he jogged beside Lake Michigan. Unafraid because of the early hour, the sunshine, and Darth trotting along beside him, he regretted he didn't break up with Steve as Anthony had insisted. The one time Anthony referred to his relationship in a message, Jaret answered other questions and rambled without addressing the inquiry.

Not that Jaret had any second thoughts. No way. The feeling of a group of jocks threatening him, all friends of Steve, was burned into his memory. All the people Steve hid Jaret from knowing. He constantly implored Jaret to not expose their friendship, let alone their relationship to his football pals. Three years of subterfuge and closeted dating came to a head on the bike path a week ago. Jaret was done.

Instead of confronting Steve, though, Jaret spent the last week avoiding him. The first email from Steve probed to see if Jaret was pissed about not going dancing together. Jaret never replied.

Three voice messages went unanswered too. Jaret had class, studying, and in his free time either wanted to hang with Darth, talk to his family on the phone, or hang out with his friends. He had finished with Steve so had no reason to see him.

In an ultimate act of cowardice, he called Steve one time—when he knew Steve had football practice. He left a message about how the football gang had attacked him on the bike path, saying Steve needed to choose between macho abusers or Jaret. Steve never replied.

Nor did Steve ever show up at the apartment. Jaret waited for him to appear so he could break up. If Jaret didn't have the energy or desire to instigate the meeting, Jaret at least planned to eliminate their life together when forced to interact. Either Steve's regret, embarrassment, or fear kept him away. Maybe he was afraid because of Jaret's message.

Jaret got to the halfway point on his run and turned around, pulling Darth away from the squirrel threatening her on the path. She barked in triumph as the poor rodent raced the other way.

Truth be told, the attack last week simply compelled Jaret to confront what he'd known for some time: he had emotionally finished with the relationship. He stayed with Steve because he hated admitting defeat and because of the totally hot sex with a jock. The memories of charming Steve from Fremont reminded him of the good person lurking under the terrified internalized homophobe. He wanted to avoid dealing with their failed love. More than anything, Jaret had persisted with the relationship because he so dreaded the breakup scene. He had no stomach for the drama. Made him queasy.

But an end had to happen eventually. Jaret had to escape this unhealthy situation. He only hoped Anthony could forgive him the slight indiscretion today.

Jaret showered after he got back, fed Darth, and spent a couple of hours reading and working on a research paper. By midafternoon, he lost focus as he watched the clock tick in slow motion toward the bewitching hour.

When his phone sang out, he grabbed it right away.

"Hey, Jenn," Jaret greeted his sister warmly. "What's up?"

"Not much. Hanging."

Jaret plugged his earphone in and sat back to chat for a while. "What's new in your world?"

"I broke up with Edward. He only sat around playing video games, which bored the shit out of me. I needed to move on. Plus, I'm trying to save up to go to Europe sometime. He insists we have to finish community college first."

"He may have a point." Jaret stopped himself from saying more, not wanting to risk her getting angry with him too.

"Community college is stupid. It'd still be here when we get back. Oh! And Lincoln came and spent the weekend with me. That was so awesome. Our brother is so sweet. We had a great time. So, what's up with you?"

"A lot."

"Spill the beans."

"My classes are going well. I love my course on the history of witchcraft persecutions. It's so unique and interesting. But, here's the big news. I'm breaking up with Steve. An incident pushed me to the edge."

"An incident?"

"Um, yeah." Jaret then launched into the story about what happened on the bike path.

"He's such a total fucking asshole," Jenn shouted through the phone. "I knew it."

"He wasn't there though."

"Doesn't matter," she yelled. "All his butch bullshit. I told him once I'd rip his balls off if he ever hurt you. I was serious. I know people, you know." Jaret had no doubt. People said such things all the time in jest. Not Jenn—she meant every word. She earned some extra spending money by waitressing and had a lot of loyal customers. She rocked at her job. She could call in all sorts of favors, from free legal advice from top attorneys to putting out a hit. She was too kind to call out for a murder, but the possibility was still in her arsenal.

Jaret laughed. "No thanks. I'll send him on his way."

"So what's taking you so long?"

"I'm avoiding him." He paused, predicting his sister's reaction to his next comment. "And the fear he's not himself haunts me."

Jenn sighed. "I hate to sound like Mom and Dad when they told you seeing ghosts wasn't real, but I think the magical warning is more a way for your mind to explain the situation and protect Steve than anything real. Otherwise, you could detect something concrete. Do something about the problem."

"I think you're right. I do. Still, I'm not great at this breakup thing. I've been dodging the issue all week."

"Sounds great. Impressive." Jenn giggled. "Maybe you can get an ulcer over the whole thing. Maybe shingles, like Dad got when he was stressed after Gramps's funeral."

"Right. I know. But it's going to be so melodramatic. He'll never accept that we're over. Any rational person would know. He's lost in this make-believe world, all of his own creation. It's not going to be easy. But you're right. I need to be done with the relationship."

"Fuck him. Just tell him to fuck off. Want me to call him for you? I will."

Again, Jaret laughed at her protectiveness. "No, I'll do it."

"Break up tonight and then go out and dance your ass off."

Jaret hesitated. He could share anything with Jenn. "You have to swear to secrecy because I don't want people knowing I did this before I broke up. But, I have a date tonight."

Jenn squealed with delight. "Tell me!"

"I met him last week. You know the guy I said who saved me on the bike path? It's with him."

"You mean the other witch who put them in the trees?" Jenn laughed.

"Yeah, him."

"Two witches dating. Awesome! How totally hilarious, right? I wonder if you can use some kinky magic in bed."

"Stop!" Jaret chatted with Jenn for a few more minutes and then hung up, emboldened anew to end everything with Steve.

Six: First Date

26 APRIL 2010
Chicago, Illinois

Jaret had no idea if he had a shot with Anthony despite feeling encouraged after his conversation with Jenn. She reminded him to follow his heart, no matter the hurt from before or where his next move might take him. She had a good way of pointing him in the right direction too. "Trust your instincts," she said when he confessed his concern about Anthony concealing something from him.

Jaret promised Jenn, and himself, to take the dating slowly because barreling quickly into his relationship with Steve had proven a complete disaster.

After another quick walk with Darth and plenty of primping later, Jaret waited for Anthony to call. When he did, Jaret raced to the elevator and down to the lobby where Anthony stood, wearing tight black jeans, a loose white cotton shirt, and looking oh so gorgeous. Whoa. As in, Jaret went into instant heat.

"Hey." Jaret stood awkwardly.

Anthony smiled. "I'll never get used to modern greetings."

Jaret scrunched his brow and giggled. "Modern greetings?"

Anthony leaned over to kiss Jaret on the cheek. "Never mind. Come along."

As they drove down Lakeshore Drive to a surprise location, Jaret tried to relax in Anthony's presence. No use. His nervous energy took over. They rounded a bend and turned onto Belmont, heading west. A short while later, Anthony paid a valet and ushered Jaret to a quiet table at the back of a nice restaurant on Halsted.

"I've passed this place a million times," Jaret said after Anthony ordered a bottle of wine. Jaret said nothing about never having had anything but boxed wine or his parents' cheap Riesling.

"Have you ever eaten here?"

"Nah."

Anthony placed his napkin on his lap. "You don't need to be ashamed. I understand you're in college. I don't expect you to have a lot of money."

"My grandpa left all his grandkids enough to go to college for free. And a little spending money left over. Enough I have my own apartment instead of living in a shitty dorm. Which is especially cool because I got to bring my dog. I couldn't be somewhere without her. But the place eats up most of my money. So it's not like I'm poor. Just, you know."

"I know." Anthony reached over and patted Jaret on the forearm. "Relax."

Anthony swirled the beautifully deep burgundy wine in his glass and then took a sip. He closed his eyes and nodded appreciatively at the waiter, who poured more for both of them. Jaret had never tasted anything so smooth and delicious.

They talked a while longer before Anthony stared into his glass and then looked at Jaret.

"So why didn't you break up with Steve?"

Jaret's had stupidly hoped to avoid the conversation. "Is this what it's like to date a witch? They know all your secrets?"

Anthony grinned and shook his head. "No magic. I won't use my spells on you. Call it intuition. You avoided the subject in our correspondence. Tonight, you never mentioned Steve or breaking up with him. I thought you might. I could only think of one reason for you to avoid the topic." Anthony appeared a little remote, sad even.

"Yeah, well. It's complicated. See, I want to. I'm going to." Jaret paused, searching for the right words to keep Anthony from bolting. His hands shook as he reached for his glass and took a drink. "This isn't bullshit. Seriously. I'm done. That's the problem. I need to break up because he's an ass and I've already moved on. No emotion there except memories. However, I want to protect him. He'll be so dramatic. I think he can't control himself with so much of the shit he does. But I'm going to break up."

Anthony reached over and stopped Jaret by placing his hand on his arm. "Slow down. I believe you."

"Thanks. Because I *am* going to break up." Shit, he didn't want to fuck this up. Even if nothing more than a fleeting rebound, he so desperately wanted to date Anthony. "I swear. I left a voice mail for him. I avoided seeing him, yeah. Not good, I know. Lame."

Jaret finally quieted with nothing else to say. Anthony swirled his wine again, sniffed the aroma, and then reached under the table and patted Jaret on the leg.

"Take your time. Here's what I need from you. Until you put an end to your relationship with Steve, we're friends. Tonight"—Anthony motioned at the table in front of them—"is a dinner between friends. Not to worry, it's on me. But no date."

"Yeah, I mean, I totally understand. You have to know I'm a monogamous kind of guy. I can't handle thoughts of anything else. Are you?" Jaret blurted out the question before thinking. Sometimes his mind and mouth raced forward before thinking through the implications or appropriateness of the moment.

Again Anthony stared into his wine before speaking. "I am when I'm in a relationship. Between relationships? Honestly, I can be a complete slut. I'm not proud of my behavior." Anthony paused again, a sad expression spreading across his face. "I like the companionship. And sex. Love to orgasm. But what I like, what I long for, is a relationship. A monogamous one. I suppose playing the field is a way to avoid my own emotion. Kind of like you with Steve."

"So you've had a long-term relationship before?"

"Once." Anthony smiled. "A very committed and loving relationship, but a very long time ago. Things ended badly." Anthony's mind seemed to drift away to a different place for several minutes. Jaret fidgeted as he waited, unsure what to say. "Then there was one quick relationship. We proved incompatible as lovers, wonderful as friends. I've been afraid to enter one because I fear the pain if it fails."

Jaret wanted to probe further. But a sense of finality overcame him again. Without a word, Anthony signaled the end of this conversation. Jaret had one last question, though. If Anthony expected Jaret to break up, Jaret deserved to know Anthony's intentions.

"So, I mean...well...you know... I was wondering. I mean..." He stumbled on his words, unsure how to articulate his feelings. "If...I mean...*when* I break up. Am I one of those companions? Or what?"

The words hung in the air, and Jaret had to force himself to breathe. Why did Anthony take so long to respond?

Anthony's eyes met Jaret's and stared deeply into them. "I feel a connection with you I haven't felt in—" He stopped. "Let's just say years. I would like to date you. And until I know where we might go, I have no need for other companions."

A little bit of a riddle. Not direct. Jaret wanted something specific, but he would accept mysterious. After all, he still technically belonged to Steve. Jaret smiled and drank more wine. "Cool."

Anthony roared with laughter. "Cool." He lifted his wine glass to toast and clinked the crystal to Jaret's. "To cool and wherever it may lead."

Seven: Breaking Up

28 APRIL 2010
Evanston, Ilinois

Last night's call rumbled through Jaret's head:

"Steve, we need to meet. Tomorrow in the library, in our usual study room."

"That's great, sweetie. It's been way too long. I could just come to your place. Better to meet there, so we could do everything we need to do?"

Jaret sighed. "We need to talk, and I think it'd be better in the library."

"Well, I suppose. Because I need to apologize. I'm so sorry for what happened with those guys. I really am. We'll work out our differences."

"Can we just agree to meet tomorrow?"

"Yeah, we will. We'll get back on track. Tomorrow, in the library. I can't wait."

A pit sat in Jaret's stomach from the second they hung up until he sat on a bench in the middle of campus, willing himself to get up and go to the library but dreading the moment after last night's conversation. Steve had no clue.

Jaret finally got off the bench and made his way to the lower level and headed to the back. Steve sat inside, a bright smile spreading across his face when he saw him.

Shit. He's so fucking clueless. Jaret closed the door. Steve came over and tried to kiss him. "Stop it." Jaret pushed him away and pointed out the window in the door, toward the stacks of books. "Someone may walk by. It'll look weird enough we're in here together, never mind you standing so close to me. The next person might be one of your football buds."

"I told them you tutored me for money," Steve said.

"Did you mention you fuck your tutor?"

Steve frowned. "Don't be an ass. The lie keeps them from snooping."

Of course, Steve had some prestidigitation worked out had anyone ever caught them. Jaret had learned "prestidigitation" the other day in his literature class and loved the word and how it described their relationship to perfection. Probably too big a word to pop on Steve, however. Jaret wondered if Steve would even get the concept of a ploy to divert people from the truth. But Jaret was using the word to avoid the reality standing in front of him.

"Well, they may think I'm for hire. But you wouldn't want them to see us swapping spit and think you hired me to suck your cock, would you? Worse than if they saw me on the path alone and decided to beat the shit out of me. Because then you'd have to ignore how your good friends beat up your boyfriend. And how you said nothing about the attack afterward. Makes more sense to ignore if it's just a tutor you fuck on the side."

Steve backed away and moved toward the table. He sat and motioned for Jaret to join him.

"Any of your little buddies end up in a tree of late?"

Steve frowned. "I suppose we've got a lot to talk about."

"Not really. I just have one thing."

Steve held up his hand. "Wait. Let me get this out first."

Jaret rolled his eyes even as he acquiesced.

"I'm not totally pissed at you." Steve smiled as if he made a huge concession. Jaret bit his tongue and resisted marching out of the room. "I was when you told me about the incident. And then I talked to the guys, and it totally pissed me off at first. Wait, how did you know about the trees?" Steve looked puzzled but ignored the way Jaret arched an eyebrow.

"Did you say you were pissed at *me*?" Jaret did not believe his ears.

"Not anymore." Steve shook his head. "But yeah, at first. Sure. We agreed to keep things on the down-low. I got a real shot for serious playing time next year because I'm a junior. We didn't want to fuck that up, remember?"

"*You* didn't want to fuck up the football playing, as I recall." Jaret started bouncing his knee up and down in nervous rage.

"Whatever. So there I am, waiting to hang with the guys who can help get me there, and they don't show for hours. They finally come into the dorm, explaining a crazy story about getting put into trees naked, and the whole episode starts with a description of you. One of them, unfortunately, recognized you because he saw us together once. Which, by the way, is why I came up with the tutor story. To protect us."

"*You*," Jaret stressed. "To protect you."

Steve dismissed his comment with a wave. "They got into an argument because one of them wanted me to take you to them so they could finish the job. Get revenge. The others wanted to leave the situation alone, given how they ended with some huge guy kicking the shit out of them. But they described you, and you being there put me in a bad spot. Because they also said you were dancing around all faggy. Thank God, you didn't pull out some gem and start the magic shit and all. That would really be bad. So yeah, I was pissed because I got in the middle of your problem—created by you insisting on being all gay." Jaret almost screamed but Steve held up a hand to stop him. "I've had some time to think. I forgive you. And the good news: they let it go, as long as I promised to warn you next time you tutored me. And I know you did the best you could, given the circumstances, because you were probably scared."

Steve had no idea how much the library protected him at the moment. In Jaret's apartment, the gems would have gone into action and strung this fucking asshole up on the ceiling. Put him naked in a tree. Steve forgive him? How had Jaret missed the fact, in addition to becoming more and more of a closeted shithead, Steve had also morphed into a complete and utter loon?

Then Jaret paused. Perched in the back of his mind, the magic buzzed. Jaret stared into Steve's eyes, as if a spirit lurked in his head, controlling his action. As fast as the notion entered Jaret's thoughts, the idea disappeared. Jaret knew what he had to do for himself, regardless of what compelled Steve to become a dick.

Steve stopped his monologue and waited for Jaret to respond. He smiled, as if he had done Jaret a huge favor. Where did the charming and loving football jock from Fremont go?

Jaret clenched his teeth and whispered in order to measure his tone. "You were pissed at me?" He tapped his fingers on the table. "We don't even need to get into all this." The rage coursing through Jaret left him at a loss for words. "You should have been up in the fucking trees with them."

"How did you know about what happened?" Now Steve's voice had an edge.

Jaret stifled a grin, the image of those butch jocks de-pantsed in the tree too much. "I was there at the beginning, remember? How did they get down?"

"Firemen. They wanted to know how the hell the guys got up there. The guys didn't want to tell them some other guy beat them up. Too embarrassing. I'm not sure how they dodged an explanation."

This time Jaret laughed out loud. Those turds with no pants being saved by Chicago firemen. Hilarious!

"What's so fucking funny?" Steve asked, his face bright red. "Those are my friends. You could have saved them, you know? Used those fucking jewels for something good for a change instead some pussy ghost thing of a fag singer. Made up with them by helping them."

Jaret had enough. "Okay. Let's stop. I wanted to meet you because we're done. Done." The softer letdown Jaret had practiced before getting there evaporated with Steve's dense ire. "I can't accept what they did to me on the path. And you siding with them, I won't accept either. Forgive? Maybe in time. I get you're in a strange place. But I'm not dating a guy who's willing to allow other people to kick the shit out of his boyfriend so he can play football. We agreed to something different before we came here."

"They weren't going to hurt you. Just a little roughhousing."

"And pissing on me?"

"Piss wouldn't hurt you." The last two words trailed off, almost inaudible, as if even Steve realized the absurdity of his stance.

Jaret slammed his fist on the table. The pain hurt. He reminded himself never to punch wood again. "A little piss, what's the harm? You're so utterly, hopelessly, fucking clueless. That's why we're done."

Complete silence filled the room. Steve slumped over in his chair. Jaret remained as pissed as ever.

"What do you mean, *done*?" Steve asked in a whisper.

He needed a definition for done, and Jaret almost popped prestidigitation on him. Jaret took a deep breath to level his voice. "I'm breaking up with you."

Steve shook his head. "You can't. We're going to be together forever. Remember?"

"No, we're not. We planned forever before you decided to keep me in a bottle and just rub the sides for your genie when you needed me. We came to Chicago to come out, not to go farther into the closet."

Steve grew quiet for a long moment. "It's temporary."

"Until when? You still haven't told your parents. You don't have any gay friends except through me. You're more in the closet here than you were in Fremont. There, at least you'd hold my hand in the middle of the night or let me suck you off in the park. Here? I only see you in the dead of night in private locations. Like you're a vampire who comes to me for sex. Nothing more."

"I can change. We can fix this. You can't give up so easily. We've been together for over three years."

"Try four." Jaret found his empathy and looked at Steve with remorse. "This has been coming for a while. It's not just last weekend. Last weekend pushed me to do what I've known was coming. Steve, it's not working." Jaret's eyes teared when he saw Steve's eyes glass over. They had so loved each other at one time. Young, innocent lust and rapture had given way to turmoil and broken hearts.

Steve nodded and wiped at a tear trickling down his cheek. He looked up and placed his hand on Jaret's cheek. "You were my sweetie, you know?"

Jaret reached over to grab Steve's hand and held it for a minute, then placed his hand back on the table.

"I know. You'll be okay."

Jaret stood, moved to the door, and paused. He turned around to see Steve had laid his head on the table and shook with convulsive sobs. Jaret gulped back his own desperation and willed himself out of the room before he did something stupid like give Steve another chance. He almost returned when he heard a maniacal laugh echoing through the room but forced himself to leave.

He raced back to his apartment and engulfed Darth in a desperate hug. Only then did he allow the full extent of his tears to pour out. Did he want Steve back? Of course not. He knew the drill, because they had come to the brink a few times before. Steve would act the perfect boyfriend for a while until he slipped back to being the jock who so hated himself. The homophobia ran too deep. Steve could not imagine himself without the football identity which overpowered their love.

The pain hit hard tonight. He cared about Steve and at one point could never have imagined their breakup. Jaret prayed Steve would find a way to come to terms with himself one day.

After a good cry and plenty of comfort from Darth, Jaret got up to make himself macaroni and cheese, his favorite comfort food. He felt a million conflicting emotions. He put some Mika on and decided to spend a quiet night alone, contemplating.

The depth of his remorse surprised him. Not regret because he broke up. Ending their relationship was inevitable. Still, Steve and he had such beautiful dreams together. He was saddened their ambitions ended with such a loud thud. More than anything, he mourned his lost innocence. No more dreams of falling in love one time and staying with Steve forever. He understood how much work was required to love someone. Both had to have the same level of commitment, the same vision for the future.

Jaret turned the corner when "Blame It On the Girls" blasted through his apartment. Had Mika met Steve and wrote the song specifically about him? He could see

Jaret's life when he sang the lyrics. Steve wanted to blame Fremont, football, his parents, and society for the reasons he stayed in the closet. And he had a point with each and every one of those examples. But plenty of reasons to avoid coming out sat in Jaret's life too. At some point, however, Jaret and a lot of gay people came to grips with their past and all those current threats, let them go, and understood they alone possessed the power to move themselves forward.

Jaret found peace as he munched on his mac and cheese and watched *The Wizard of Oz* for the one millionth time, Darth nestled close to his side.

Eight: Transitions

29 APRIL 2020
Chicago, Illinois

Jaret hurried home from his evening class, eager to send Anthony a text. He had spent the day studying for his finals the next week and telling Brady all about his breakup with Steve over dinner.

After sympathy and gauging Jaret's mood, Brady let loose with a torrent of expletives.

"He is such a fucking loser, manipulative, asshole, douche!" Brady yelled so loudly a number of people in the cafeteria glanced over and frowned.

"Shh." Jaret blushed.

Brady rolled his eyes. "Seriously. I have to get this off my chest. You're a wonderful, sweet, and caring man. You're going to make some power top one of the happiest men on earth!"

"Will you stop it!" Jaret looked around to see who was listening.

Brady forged ahead without acknowledging Jaret's discomfort. "I've held my tongue for too long. Fucking shithead. Shit for brains. Dumber than a llama. Fuckwad, bitchy shithead. That's the nicest thing I ever thought about Steve and how he treated you."

"He wasn't bad. He was confused and in turmoil."

"See! That's my point!" Brady raised his hands in the air with exasperation. "You're too nice, bro. Way too nice."

Brady calmed down after his diatribe. Jaret appreciated the fact Brady had kept all the venom to himself, for the most part, as long as he dated Steve. But he felt wonderful hearing the truth because Brady's opinion supported Jaret and his decision.

Once home, Jaret sent the first text to Anthony as he walked Darth for the last time before bed.

I did it.

Are you okay? I'm proud of you.

Fine. Glad. Relieved.

Why?

Ready for a real date.

His fingers shook as he typed those words.

Jaret walked Darth for a while longer, picked up a super smelly poop, and headed back toward his place. Fifteen minutes had elapsed since his last text to Anthony, and his heart began to sink when he got no response.

He rounded the corner and fumbled for his keys when he heard Darth growl. His head shot up in alarm until he saw Anthony standing nearby, leaning against his Porsche.

Jaret grinned and waved. He walked over, but kept a slight distance because Darth kept growling.

"Is this Darth?" Anthony asked.

"Yeah. She's usually well behaved."

"Maybe she doesn't like other witches." Anthony knelt and put his hand out for Darth to sniff. She did, and after a minute calmed enough for Anthony to pet her on the head. She kept close to Jaret.

"I'm surprised you're here." Jaret played with Darth's leash and stared at the sidewalk.

"You said you were ready for a real date."

"Now?"

"Why not?"

Jaret thought about class the next day. The last week of the semester was crucial. He was tired and needed to get up early to jog in the morning. Instead, he smiled and decided he had too much discipline in his life. "Yeah, why not? Where are we going?"

"Your choice."

"Let me put Darth in my apartment. I'll be right back."

Jaret rushed through the lobby and up to his place. He let Darth in and then ran to the bathroom to pee and brush his teeth. He glanced in the mirror and straightened a few stray curls of hair before hurrying out the door.

Anthony opened the car door for Jaret and helped him in. Again Jaret swooned in the presence of such a gentleman. Once in the driver's seat, Anthony looked at him. "Where to?"

Jaret thought for a second before answering. "Want to go to the lake? It's awesome at night."

"Perfect," Anthony answered as the motor roared to life and they headed out.

Anthony parked in a lot close to the lake and ushered Jaret out of the car toward a spot in the grass under a tree and overlooking the water. They sat quietly for a while as the waves lapped against the shore, enjoying the cool spring breeze and the utter tranquility.

"Would you like to go for a walk?" Anthony asked.

Jaret thought for a moment. It sounded romantic. Yet fear crept into his mind about being alone on the path. In his hurry to get going, he had forgotten to bring any of his jewels.

"I'll protect you." Anthony ran his hand along Jaret's back and got up. He pulled Jaret to his feet and kept one hand clasped in Jaret's as they sauntered along. "Nothing will harm you when we're together. You have my guarantee."

Jaret believed Anthony, and yet his very trust brought back Jaret's sense about Anthony concealing more secrets. How was he so assured he could protect Jaret? Was his magic so infallible?

They chatted about various topics, as people do when they first meet and need to learn details about the other person's life.

"I grew up in Fremont, Nebraska, until my dad got a new job and we moved to Colorado. What about you?"

"I'm originally from England. I've lived a variety of places since."

"Like where?"

Anthony paused. "All over the place. Very nomadic. Where do you want to live after you graduate?"

Once again, Anthony avoided talking about his past.

"No idea." Jaret shrugged, deciding not to push the issue. "I'll figure out where to go when the time comes. Probably wherever I get into graduate school."

By the time they turned around and headed back toward the car, Jaret had already determined he wanted an official relationship with Anthony. Brady cautioned he should take time before diving into something right after Steve, but Anthony was too much to pass on or risk a delay. Hot and well established. With a sexy accent. But more important, Jaret felt safe with him, protected, in much the same way he first experienced with Steve. Whatever Anthony hid would come out in time.

"So," Jaret's voice quivered, "you know a lot about my sorcery. Tell me more about yours."

"Well, as I told you earlier, a group of friends and I, with the same powers, came together to use our ability for good. It's not profound, really. Much like your power, what we do depends on the situation and the individual warlock or witch involved, and the threat we face."

Anthony opened the passenger side door for Jaret, and soon they headed back toward Jaret's apartment. "You seem worried." Anthony reached over and grabbed Jaret's hand. "I'll introduce you to my friends next time they're in town. To help you feel better."

Anthony had never gone so far as to make such a promise, which Jaret took as a positive sign.

They parked outside Jaret's building and talked a while longer, as Jaret grew tired. He finally willed himself to go upstairs, knowing he would pay a price tomorrow if he failed to get enough sleep.

"When do you want to hook up again?" Jaret asked.

"Do you have plans on Friday?"

Jaret shook his head.

"Good. It's a date. Our second official date."

Jaret reached for the door handle and got out, thinking he would lean back in and say good night. Instead, Anthony got out of the car, too, and escorted him into his building. As Jaret got his key out of his pocket, Anthony reached over and pulled Jaret close to him. Jaret looked up into those beautiful blue eyes and felt the strong hands wrapped around his arms. He closed his eyes when Anthony reached down and kissed him gently on the lips.

Intoxicated with infatuation, Jaret glided up to his apartment. He danced around and petted Darth before crawling into bed. He drifted to sleep despite his witchy senses warning something watched him. He glanced around, feeling almost as if Anthony's presence were nearby, but dismissed the sensation as the lingering effects of the kiss and closed his eyes.

The two days until their next date went by fast because Jaret had so much to do during the last week of the semester. He finished his most important papers, organized his studies for next week's finals, and barely had time for anything else but an occasional chat with Brady or texting Anthony. He ignored the texts and calls from Steve.

Life moved along pleasantly until his last class finished late Thursday afternoon. He looked forward to a break as Brady and he planned to go out in Andersonville to celebrate surviving another semester.

Jaret bounded out of the building and headed home. A block away from campus, along a residential street, his senses tingled, so he wrapped his backpack around both shoulders to secure it and grabbed gems in each hand. They vibrated with alarm.

Jaret spun around to find Steve walking several paces behind him. He stopped.

Steve smiled and jogged up to Jaret. "Hey."

"What do you want?" Jaret said with an edge.

"Aren't we still friends? Can't friends hook up and chat? I could walk you home."

"That's rather awkward, don't you think? You can blame me. I'm too immature for a friendship after what we tried to have together." Jaret turned around and resumed his journey.

Unfortunately, Steve kept pace beside him. "I think you gave up on us too soon."

"I know you do. So we disagree. We can't have a relationship if both parties don't agree to it." Jaret hurried to get away.

"Listen." Steve grabbed Jaret's arm and stopped him. "I guess I'm asking for a second chance."

Jaret rolled his eyes. "No."

"Please. Baby, I love you so much." Despite the bad vibes, Jaret was sad for Steve. But Jaret continued walking again as Steve implored him with soft words, promises, and his undying love. More lies. In Jaret's lobby, Steve asked if he could come up for a visit.

"That's not a great idea. Steve, it's over. I know you hate this reality. I know you want something different. I just can't. You hurt me. I have to move on."

"I know, sweetie. Listen babe, I can change. We can work this out. You mean so much to me. I feel like—totally empty inside and lost. I was wrong. It won't happen again."

Jaret wondered which "wrong" Steve referred to but had no desire to persist with the conversation. He unlocked his door and started inside. "I'm sorry," he said and went upstairs.

Had the apology ended the argument, Jaret could have understood Steve's actions as part of the grief. Jaret came to terms with the loss a few months ago, Steve had only grasped the breakup for the first time the other day. He would take time. But the next morning, Jaret hooked Darth to her leash and found Steve waiting for the two of them outside his building, wearing running shoes and sweats. Steve beamed a hello.

"Why are you here?" Jaret asked.

"I thought we could work out together."

"No." Jaret shook his head. He took a deep breath to find as much patience as possible. "Like I said yesterday, I can't transition to the friend thing. It's not my style. We need to stop seeing each other so we can both come to terms with all of this."

Darth tugged at her leash and grabbed it in her teeth, trying to pull Jaret along. He headed toward the lake. About halfway down the path from his turn around point, Steve ran up to his side. "I decided to go ahead and run anyway."

"I can see." Jaret slowed, knowing Steve jogged faster than him. Instead, Steve kept pace.

Darth ran along, oblivious to everything but the creatures around them, so at least she enjoyed a pleasant morning run.

Jaret lurched to a stop, and so did Steve. Darth lunged forward until her collar choked her. She looked back at Jaret with her ears folded back in irritation.

"Uh, you're stalking me." Jaret drew in a deep breath as his heart and body cooled from having run.

"No, babe. Nothing so sinister." Steve whispered the words, with a crestfallen look on his face. And Jaret knew the truth of the statement.

"Then you need to leave me alone. We're through. I don't want to see you. We can't be friends. It hurts too much."

Steve hung his head and asked, "So you won't even give us a little shot?"

"I gave us many shots. So, no. I don't want to. Actually, I might be seeing someone."

"Already? Nice. Fucking tramp." Steve turned and ran the other way.

Jaret wondered at the ease with which he got rid of Steve, then wished he had not revealed anything related to Anthony. It *did* look bad. He'd told Steve about the relationship out of anger, not from any calculated reasoning.

Great, an angry stalker. Jaret determined to keep his gems close at hand and start using more protective spells at night before he went to bed. A wave of panic swept over him. How had he forgotten to get his key back from Steve?

Nine: Desperation

2 MAY 2010
Chicago, Illinois

"So he's stalking you now?" Jenn spat through the phone.

"*Kind of.* It's probably not bad. Just awkward. I mean, I'm trying to understand because he still really loves me." Jaret tried to convince himself as much as Jenn.

"I get what you're saying. But this isn't okay, right? I mean, this is so not cool. You've got to be careful. Maybe you need a restraining order or something."

"No, nothing so extreme. I'm being careful. Trust me. I think it'll be better once I get my key back."

"He has a key to your apartment?" Jenn shouted.

'I'm not deaf." Jaret held his cell phone away from his head for a second. "Chill. But yeah. I never got the key back. He doesn't come up here. I'll be careful. Anyway, I didn't call about him. You asked about Anthony."

"Don't think you'll get off the hook so easily next time. Use your magic to keep him the fuck away. Can't you tell those gems just to go get your key?"

"I could if I was close enough. But he'd know if I did use a spell on him. That's not the best way to handle things."

"Whatever. Let's move on before you go back to blaming his being an ass on hocus pocus. Tell me about this Anthony." Jenn's voice went from annoyance to excitement.

Jaret filled her in on his date the other night with Anthony and their walk along the lake. "I felt so protected with him nearby." He explained more about Anthony. Something stopped him from revealing to Jenn how he suspected Anthony kept some major secret from him. She had already ripped on Steve enough. He wanted to protect Anthony so early in the game.

After thirty minutes, they hung up. Time to get ready for his date. He and Anthony had decided to go to a movie and then out for pizza.

Jaret enjoyed seeing an action-packed superhero film, especially since this one starred one of his Hollywood crushes, Robert Downey, Jr. Anthony, on the other hand, guffawed through much of the movie.

In the lobby, Anthony laughed. "That was one of the most completely absurd movies I've ever seen."

They stepped outside, with Jaret smiling at Anthony. "Where's your sense of imagination?"

"Not in anything to do with the movie."

"It was a wonderful superhero flick! Just like you on the bike path the other day."

"I can only hope I'm not as silly and naïve."

Jaret laughed again as they held hands and walked down the street toward a little ice cream shop.

Jaret had a twist cone. Anthony moved the M&Ms around with his spoon but Jaret never saw him eating any ice cream.

"What were you listening to when I got there?" Anthony had first asked Jaret the question when he arrived and heard Mika in the background. Something sidetracked them and Jaret had never answered.

"Mika. He's totally my favorite. His songs kick ass. Some are, like, I-have-to-dance-to-them numbers, and then all of a sudden there's some moving, sad song. He writes his own stuff. Who writes their own songs anymore? It's so incredible. His composing gives him a real connection to his music. His sound is so original. I can't listen to him enough."

Anthony asked a few questions, showing interest in Jaret's favorite pastime. "Doesn't Katy Perry write her own stuff?"

Jaret nodded and took a lick of his ice cream. "Sure. Her stuff is hot too. I love it. I just like Mika better. Plus, he came out. Cool, right? He's coming to Chicago this summer. Major hotness! I've never seen him live. His concerts seem so incredible. I have one on DVD. We can't wait to see him."

"We? You mean someone else is obsessed with Mika? You aren't going with Steve, are you?"

Jaret was hurt. "I told you we broke up. No way. I'm going with Brady. And yes, he loves Mika just as much."

Jaret tried to move on, but his mind kept coming back to Anthony's question about Steve. "Did you really think I'd go with him?"

"No. I'm worried about how he keeps showing up."

Jaret grinned. "Are you jealous?"

"No. You're right. I shouldn't have asked. I trust you. It's more a need to be protective than jealousy. I'm sorry."

"Apology accepted."

"Remember his friends attempted to beat the shit out of you on the bike path."

"I know. You're right. You and Jenn both. I gotta be careful. Think of it this way, without the attack on the path, we might not have met." Jaret took another lick of his cone.

"That's very sensual."

Jaret blushed. They had done nothing more than hold hands and briefly kiss, Anthony ever the gentleman in their courtship. But he obviously had other thoughts. Jaret searched for a witty reply, but just stood there, his ice cream starting to drip to the ground.

Anthony grabbed his wrist and held the cone upright. He ran his finger down the side and stopped the flow of ice cream, then held up his finger to Jaret, who licked off the ice cream.

Jaret felt nothing else but his rock-hard dick. How embarrassing. Anthony, on the other hand, winked and laughed.

"You're precious." They moved to his car, heading to take Jaret home.

Jaret shifted in his seat, attempting to cover up his boner. "How long do we date?"

"What do you mean?" Anthony smirked, despite knowing full well what Jaret meant.

"Don't make me say it."

"I'm very slow and deliberate in such things. I don't want to make a mistake." Anthony rubbed Jaret's leg and inched toward his penis and stopped. "It's just as hard for me, no pun intended."

Jaret laughed. "Yeah, well. I get it. And I appreciate your decorum. I want to take dating slow too. But it's not like 1800 anymore, either. We don't need any parental permission."

Anthony laughed, grew quiet, and then laughed again. "Be patient with me. I told you I decided to give this relationship a shot. I can't hurry into one. I have to shelter you."

What did Anthony mean? Probably better not to ask. They rode quietly the rest of the way to Jaret's apartment. This time, Anthony took him all the way to his apartment door and stepped inside.

They greeted an excited Darth, who still eyed Anthony with a wary eye.

"You keep a nice place." Anthony surveyed the small apartment.

Jaret rolled his eyes. "It's not quite the Hancock."

Anthony wrapped his arms around Jaret's waist, lifted him off the floor a couple of inches, and held him there as they kissed, his tongue deeply probing Jaret's mouth. Jaret hardly had time to wonder at the strength Anthony took to do this as the passion swept over him. Darth even stopped jumping on them to say hello and sat nearby, her head tilted in bewilderment.

Anthony set Jaret down. "Don't mistake what I desire from you." He reached over and pulled Jaret back to him. This time his hands ran down Jaret's back and then grabbed his butt, squeezing almost in desperation.

Anthony stepped back and smiled. "I'd better go." He brushed his hair out of his face and turned to leave. Jaret followed him the few steps to the door, where Anthony turned around for another goodnight kiss. "You can go take care of yourself. Just promise you'll be thinking of me."

Jaret almost came in his pants. He locked the door behind Anthony and then went to his bedroom to do just as Anthony instructed.

Jaret was almost asleep when his phone rang. He answered it.

"I saw the dude holding your hand when you went into the apartment. Did he fuck you?"

Jaret cursed himself for not looking at the name before he answered. "You shouldn't call me. How did you see?"

"I'm not fucking blind. I happened to walk by your place. Did you fuck him?"

Jaret walked to his window and looked into the parking lot where Steve sat in his car.

"You always walk by in your car?" Jaret asked.

"So I wanted to see you? Kill me. We were boyfriends for years, and two minutes later you're banging another guy."

"We're not banging." Jaret rubbed his forehead. "And it's none of your business."

To emphasize his point, Jaret asked several of his jewels to swirl into the air. He cracked open the window and sent them spinning downward. He made sure Steve noticed them, and then zapped him. A quick, harmless shock to make his point.

Steve hung up and started his car. As he drove out of the parking lot, he flipped Jaret off through his open window.

Part Three:

Revelation

Part Three:
Revision

Ten: Ruined Concert

JULY 2010
Chicago, Illinois

The most exciting night of Jaret's life arrived. He sprinted home from the library in the hot July sun, so pumped about the Mika concert he could hardly keep himself focused on anything but singing Mika songs all day. He had enough time to walk Darth, change, and head out to meet Brady and a couple of other friends before the concert.

He opened his apartment door to Darth's typical exuberance and almost immediately spotted the first sign of trouble. His heart pounded as he pushed Darth aside and hurried into the office. The bottom drawer of his filing cabinet stood open, which he always kept closed. Jaret never left the apartment with a drawer open.

He closed the drawer and walked through the rest of the place, where he found a note in Steve's handwriting on the kitchen table.

Call me about tonight. It'll be awesome. Love, Steve

Jaret summoned the gems and set them in motion, recreating before his eyes what happened earlier in his apartment. He saw Darth run to the door and greet Steve, though she seemed hesitant, as if something warned against his presence. Still, she knew him enough not to bark or behave as if an intruder entered.

Steve went right to the office and rooted through Jaret's drawers one at a time, until he found the file where Jaret kept tickets and special items in the bottom drawer of the filing cabinet. He took out Jaret's ticket to the concert and put it in his pocket. As the gems recreated the scene, they buzzed with an alarm, Jaret had not experienced since his fight with Henrik in Fremont.

Jaret's heart sank. They'd tried to get a ticket for Anthony earlier in the week, after Jaret spent eons convincing him to go to the concert. Unfortunately, the concert had sold out. Anthony told Jaret to dance his ass off without him. "Just promise not to run away with Mika," he finished. His only entrance tonight was with the stolen ticket in Steve's possession.

Jaret snatched his cell phone and called Steve.

"You haven't dialed my number since you tried to break up with me," a too happy Steve answered.

"I *did* break up with you. I called because you stole my property."

"Merely exchanged the ticket. It's an early birthday present. I got us the best seats. You'll be right up front. It'll be good for us to go do something. I'm even willing to risk being seen. See how much I'm trying, babe?"

"But maybe you need to bring a female date along for cover. It wouldn't be the first time."

"Don't start like this. Come on. Let me treat you."

Jaret sighed. "I'm going with Brady and my friends. He got our tickets so we all sit together."

"Don't be like this," Steve whined.

"Steve, we're not a couple anymore. I can't be friends. Bring my fucking ticket to me."

Steve sighed. "Nice. Real nice. I'm doing something special for you. Just meet me; let me try to convince you."

Jaret contemplated how to respond and decided he had to meet him or he'd never get his ticket. "All right. Ten minutes. Outside my apartment." Jaret hung up on him.

Before heading down, Jaret grabbed some gems, intending to use them to steal his ticket back.

Jaret glanced out his window and spotted Steve standing in front of the apartment, so he sent the gems after his ticket. They came back swirling in the air with nothing. Jaret then commanded with his mind for a blue sapphire to locate his ticket, and his magic showed him. In some cesspool of shit and piss, ripped into a thousand tiny pieces. Destroyed. Beyond even Jaret's magical ability to repair.

Jaret's eyes teared with desperation and rage as he ran out of his apartment, sprinted down the stairs, and stormed toward Steve.

Steve held up his hands in a defensive posture. "Babe, relax. I know you get worked up. Trust me. I've got better plans."

"Relax? You fucking destroyed my ticket. You don't care about me; you're trying to ruin me."

Jaret wanted to call Anthony but knew he was still asleep. Brady had left early for the restaurant. Besides, no one else had a ticket for him. Trapped and blinded by disappointment, he clenched his hands into fists and fought against crying or punching Steve.

"Sweetie," Steve reached over and rubbed Jaret's shoulder. Jaret jerked his body away. "Come to dinner with me, and we'll discuss a special way I can get you to the concert."

"Okay." Jaret ground his teeth together but caved to Steve and accompanied him to dinner. Neither said a word as they drove to the restaurant. He figured he could endure a boring meal, get Steve to take them into the concert, and then call Brady for their seat locations from inside and join them, since no one could use Jaret's ticket anyway.

Jaret texted Brady that something came up, and he would meet them at the concert. Then, he tried to control his racing heart even as they sat and ordered a drink. Steve obviously planned to use his dad's credit card since he took them to a pretty nice place in Boystown. He always played it this way when he wanted to woo Jaret back. When the waiter arrived, Steve ordered an expensive bottle of wine.

"You hate wine. Buying me shit won't work."

Steve wiggled his eyebrows and ignored what Jaret said. Jaret was annoyed and yet wondered again if something possessed Steve. "I think we should use this time to consider getting together again." Steve grinned.

"No."

Steve waited for what felt like hours before saying something else. "Nothing else?"

"Nope. We've talked about this. We're not going over the same ground again."

"Sweetie, you have to let me show you how much I've changed."

Jaret rolled his eyes, which prompted Steve to slam a hand on the table. "Why do you have to be this way? I had to tell my dad I was taking my girlfriend on a special date just to arrange for this dinner. All for you."

"You still don't get it. You made my point. All the lies and deception. We're through, done, finished. I get how some people struggle to come out. Many never do. I'm not trying to judge your decision, but I do need to assess your actions compared to my goals and desires. We don't work together."

"Can't we talk about us?"

"No."

They ate an appetizer and then finished dinner in complete silence. Eating his last piece of steak, Jaret glanced at his watch. "If we don't head for the concert, we'll be late."

Steve paid quickly, and they soon hurried down the sidewalk toward the concert hall. A block away, Steve grabbed Jaret's arm and brought them to a halt.

"Babe, don't hate me. I knew you'd forgive me if you understood the situation. If we had our night together and everything got back to normal."

"What the fuck are you talking about?"

Steve bowed his head and kicked at a stone on the ground. "I don't have tickets. I couldn't get them. Even my dad's connection fell through."

Jaret felt dizzy. He wanted to throw up. Or enlist the gems to kill Steve. No, even at his most desperate moment Jaret looked at Steve as nothing more sinister than a deeply scarred and afraid person. So instead, Jaret wanted to entomb Steve in the iron box with Henrik.

"Great way to win me back. By convincing me not only are we through, but you're a complete and utter asshole."

"Don't be a shithead. And lower your voice." Steve reached over to touch Jaret.

"Don't fucking touch me. Don't get fucking near me. You're the biggest ass I've ever known. Don't ever talk to me again."

Jaret stalked off, praying Steve would stay behind.

He did, shouting an enormous "Fuck You" as tears poured down Jaret's face. He raced to the arena and arrived after the concert started. Desperate, he asked at the box office but they had no tickets. He searched around desperately for a scalper. Shit. The two he found wanted more cash than he possessed. Sitting in the middle of the parking lot, Jaret slumped over and balled his eyes out.

He thought of calling Brady. Why ruin his friend's perfect night? Jenn would only scold him. And Anthony, how he wanted to reach out to Anthony, but he was so utterly humiliated at his own stupidity he didn't have the courage. He had never gotten his key back from Steve. Still didn't have it. Didn't even ask for the key in the shouting match. He had gone to dinner with Steve instead of calling Brady or Anthony for help. He could point out a thousand ways his naiveté and fear of hurting Steve played perfectly into the situation. He mourned by himself, struggling against the competing forces of being irate with his own stupidity and lost in his own self-pity.

Jaret eventually headed home and greeted Darth with a big hug, comforted by her kisses. She set her snout on his leg after he slumped onto the couch, as if knowing he needed her.

The next night, Jaret met Anthony at a favorite coffee shop and told him what happened.

"Why didn't you call me? I can't believe you didn't call me."

"I was embarrassed," Jaret whispered.

A vein in Anthony's forehead looked like it might burst. "In the future, I expect, no—I demand—you reach out to me when anything like this happens. No more hiding."

Anthony's stern voice, combined with the love behind the words, brought Jaret to tears.

Anthony softened his tone. "I'm sorry. I must have sounded like the dominating ass you dumped a few days ago. But I could have gotten you into the concert. We'll get you to a concert someday. I promise. I'll find out when and where he's performing in Europe."

Jaret jumped when his phone rang. "I gotta take this." He waved the phone at Anthony and then answered it. "Hey, Brady."

"I got your message about the fucking asshole and why you missed the concert last night. Jesus, Jaret."

"I'm so sorry I missed our big night. The concert meant so much to me, to us. I feel like the worst friend in the world. Shit. Do you hate me?"

"Dude, I don't think I could ever hate you. Listen, I was disappointed too. Only because I wanted to share the night with you. I'm not mad. At least not at you. I feel bad for you. I still got to see Mika. But you need to wake up about Steve. Stop bending over and taking it up the ass. This is not a good boner up the ass, this is an unlubed baseball bat over and over and over."

Jaret's eyes teared at the thought of what he'd missed at the same time he laughed at the baseball bat analogy. Anthony reached across the table and held his hand.

Brady seemed to sense the same emotion when he spoke again. "We'll make up for it. Lots of good times ahead for us. Talk soon, okay?"

Jaret hung up and clutched Antony's hand.

The following day, Jaret changed the locks on his apartment. Anthony paid Jaret's landlord for a high-end deadbolt.

Eleven: Stalker

16 OCTOBER 2010
Chicago, Illinois

Jaret glanced out the window again to see if Steve still sat in his car outside the apartment. Yep. For over four hours, Steve had stared through the window at the front door or up at Jaret's window, probably trying to force another interaction. He had done this at least once a week since Jaret broke up with him.

"Go to the police," Jenn had said for the fourth time during their conversation yesterday.

"I will."

"Promise?"

"Yes."

But Jaret broke the promise and instead waited until Anthony scolded him later the same night.

"This is getting dangerous." Anthony frowned at Jaret. "I want you to go to the police and file a report."

"Steve isn't violent. He never has been."

"So you're going to wait until he is?"

Jaret paused, embarrassed at the thought of going to the police. "What report can you file about a love-sick guy? You can protect me. Put him in a tree too."

"Not all the time. I want you to go to the police."

"I'm having a difficult time with what to do."

Anthony breathed deeply. "Then allow me to confront him. I don't have any problem telling him to back off. A conversation between men. As a big, tough football player, he should understand the machismo."

Jaret shook his head. "No, you two fighting over me makes me feel too much like a damsel in distress, with knights jousting over my virtue. Please don't. Steve and I have a history, good or bad, and I need to handle this myself."

"I'll stay out, as long as you handle his behavior, soon. As in, I'll give you two days."

"I'm taking you seriously, I promise." Jaret lost his emotional battle, tears of frustration dripping down his cheeks.

Anthony pulled him into his arms. "I know July was a few months ago. But you have to see Steve's behavior hasn't been stable. He had a break from reality. He will again. He went into your apartment against your will."

"I wasn't there. He never hurt me."

"No, you weren't. He just went in and ruined your whole summer. I didn't think you'd ever stop crying about the ticket. But now his act doesn't matter? I'm trying to protect you."

Seeing Steve sitting down there in his car, Jaret pondered how fucked-up Steve had become, even worse since the July Mika concert fiasco. Despite Steve's quest to get Jaret back, he had found a new girlfriend as "part of his cover" with the football team. At least his getting playing time during games, and thus the necessity of practice, film sessions, and travel, kept him from spying on Jaret too often. Except this morning.

Still, Jaret never feared Steve. Even Steve's psychotic behavior before the Mika concert never caused Jaret to worry about his personal safety. Steve's stalking annoyed him more than anything. Jaret wished Steve would give up and go away, convinced the closet caused all of the bad behavior in Steve more than anything. He had no gay outlet or hope for the future. Plus his family expected him to act the perfect part of a straight son, and though Steve wanted to break free of Fremont and their authority, he could never bring himself to force the issue.

Jaret went so far as to perform a ritual to see if Steve was possessed but discovered nothing conclusive. Once and for all, Jaret dismissed demon possession as an invention in Jaret's own mind to explain Steve's behavior rather than a true explanation.

So this morning Jaret cleaned the apartment, did a bunch of homework, and then played on the computer while he waited for Steve to disappear. He kept expecting him to leave for practice or something.

Jaret finally decided to force the issue. He dreaded the confrontation the whole way down, especially knowing the bickering would become an instant replay of every interaction they'd had since July.

He tapped on the car window. "Go away."

Steve rolled the window down. "But I love you so much. My love for you will never die."

"Nice melodrama." Jaret grinned at the absurd comment.

"Don't laugh at me. You're breaking my heart. I'll never stop my devotion to you."

"What about Judith? You splitting your devotion these days, between your future wife and me?"

Steve ground his teeth together. "She's a beard. You know I need one until the season ends."

Jaret rolled his eyes. Steve's utter insanity kept Jaret from going to the police and making Steve's life worse, though his reasoning was exactly why Jenn and Anthony recommended the opposite.

Jaret spun around and walked back toward his building. He motioned toward the driveway and pointed as he walked away. "Go."

Jaret got upstairs and went to his computer, needing a distraction. He checked his email and groaned.

> *Babe, when you just walked away, it ripped my heart out. You stomped my love into the ground again. Give me a second chance and you'll never regret your choice. You told me the rich fucker you're dating promised to take you to a concert anywhere in the world. Just like the douche you're dating, I can fly you anywhere for a Mika concert.*

Jaret hit delete and searched the internet for new Mika videos to distract himself. His phone rang with Steve's number popping up. He silenced the ringer.

With Steve's incessant behavior, Jaret wondered again why he continued to protect his ex-boyfriend. Something in his magical being tingled an alarm, not to protect himself from Steve, but to protect Steve from something. The vagueness of the sensation frustrated Jaret, especially after he asked the gems for assistance and they came back with nothing. As he'd explained to Anthony and Jenn, there was no perfect solution. A restraining order would get the police involved, but to what end? The authorities wouldn't incarcerate Steve or prevent him from showing up. The order would give Jaret recourse after the fact, but Steve wasn't violent, despite his desperate love. But clinging to love wasn't a crime. He needed help, and Jaret wondered if he could get Steve counseling instead of involving any authorities. He understood Steve more than anyone else, which led him to shelter the guy, even after all Steve had put him through.

As usual, again tonight, Steve disappeared after Jaret waited him out. Jaret took Darth out and went about his routine. Truth be told, by this point he worried going to the police would escalate Steve to violence or worse, suicide.

Besides, the minute Steve drove away Jaret turned his attention to a bigger concern. Over the last couple weeks, Anthony had grown more distant and elusive, especially when Jaret probed for the secret Anthony still kept from him. He had even canceled a couple of their dates and still refused to escalate their intimacy. Jaret called Anthony out last time they were together as they bickered about Steve. Anthony pledged to protect Jaret. At the same time, he insisted Jaret take the appropriate steps to protect himself too.

"Because you can only guard me at night," Jaret shot back. Jaret came closer and closer to the inevitable confrontation with Anthony. He needed final confirmation of his suspicions, and he had worked all weekend to develop the spell to figure out his secret.

Twelve: Revelation

19 OCTOBER 2010
Lake Michigan

Jaret almost chanted the ritual a thousand times over the last three days. He had researched the spell completely, gone to his trunk of sorcerer's materials a hundred times, and confirmed its utility through the jewels, which seldom failed him.

Jaret sat on the floor with his legs crossed, the gems surrounding him in the exact pattern they themselves had revealed.

So why had he delayed the spell? Why, just last night, had he gotten this far and chickened out?

Because he cared a lot about Anthony. After his too-fast falling for Steve, he resisted the idea he had fallen in love with Anthony, and neither had ever spoken those words. Yet he couldn't deny he was completely smitten. Not the lust alone, though the sexual allure was a powerful force in his attraction. He also adored Anthony's ability to be protective without smothering him. Anthony had a mature presence about him to comfort Jaret and calm him. All of this added up to a definite magnetism Jaret wanted to pursue.

Which brought him to the problem. While Anthony continued to express fondness for Jaret, professing his complete infatuation, he had pulled away in the last few weeks. Fewer calls. Fewer dates. Always with some explanation about getting too close too quickly and the complications of their relationship, though he would never explain the details. Jaret had pleaded with Anthony for more information but found pushing too hard resulted in Anthony distancing himself even further.

If Jaret took the step to ask the gems for answers, he had to risk losing Anthony forever.

Despite his reluctance, annoyance poked at the back of Jaret's mind. Anthony insulted Jaret's intelligence to think he could keep his secret from him. Jaret may be a young college kid, but he had matured a lot since learning about his destiny as a witch. He had defeated the enraged ghost of an ancestor and protected his entire family. He had learned to control and use his magic, without other people finding out. He knew a lot and controlled a vast amount of magic.

As far as intellect, he had come to Northwestern determined to go to graduate school after obtaining his bachelor's degree. He possessed a rare worldly outlook for someone his age—a combination of common sense, academic learning, and knowledge about hidden realms.

When he first guessed at what Anthony hid, his theory sounded fanciful. Anthony only showed up in the dark. He claimed his job kept him up through the night and he slept during the day, a routine which he never varied. Something right out of a cheesy vampire novel, right? Or one of those low budget gay horror movies.

Still, if witches existed and jewels could perform magic at Jaret's behest, why not vampires? Vampire power would explain how those bulky football players ended up in trees despite being outnumbered five to one. Anthony being a nosferatu made the nocturnal habits make sense. And being undead was a secret Anthony's would be reluctant to share.

Jaret had no choice. He winked at Darth, laying under the kitchen table, always leery of Jaret's spells. She panted while keeping her distance.

Jaret closed his eyes and cleared his mind of anything but the gems' energy. He had every single one of them arranged in a circular pattern with their highest power pointed at him. When he opened his eyes, he saw nothing but blackness around him—Darth, the apartment, and even the jewels having disappeared.

Except for the five-pointed diamond, which hovered right above his vision. The largest of his diamonds always signaled security and safety. If Jaret planned to go somewhere, the diamond told him he could feel safe. If, on the other hand, the gem flickered out and was replaced by a red ruby, Jaret knew to stay away.

An undefined spiritual force materialized before Jaret, with no recognizable shape. Colors danced before his eyes. Jaret turned his head to the left and right, then glanced beneath himself. He found nothing but blackness except for the swirling rainbow of squiggles and bubbles before him and the white diamond above him.

He stared into those colors and found answers as the bubbles showed glimpses of Anthony. Jaret knew by instinct they showed the true past, not fanciful images or make-believe. In every scene, despite the horror of what occurred, the white diamond floated above Anthony's head to indicate Jaret's safety.

Jaret saw Anthony in a darkened alley, protecting some woman from a rapist, who he then leaned over and killed.

Anthony glaring at a woman yielding a knife, fangs descending from his jaw.

Anthony with a long-black-haired gentleman, laughing as they hunted in some unknown locale. This tan-skinned person also had a diamond over his head.

Anthony, sitting on a tree in the middle of the night, peering into Jaret's room and leaping to the ground to chase Steve away.

Anthony ripping off the head of a man.

And just as terror almost ripped through Jaret at the sight of these awful images of his lover, Anthony sat with another vampire, a kind-looking soul with short hair, hazel eyes, and wearing a cross around his neck—he too with the diamond to signal he posed no threat to Jaret. Jaret heard them discuss a vampire ethic of killing only hardened criminals, rapists, murderers, and foul beings of the earth. They spoke of the honor they had of defending humanity with their vampiric power. Then the long-black-haired one entered and laughed at them, though he never disagreed. He teased about their righteous goodness as he kissed the short-haired one on the cheek.

Vampires, all of them. And the white diamond insisted over and over Jaret had nothing to fear.

The colors churned before Jaret, with Anthony and the diamond coming out of the middle of them in 3-D, waking from a coffin, dressing rapidly, racing at inhuman speeds through the streets of Chicago to Jaret's apartment, through his window, and standing before Jaret on the floor in the midst of his jewels.

Jaret opened his eyes and saw Anthony standing before him. Not angry. Not unkind. But not happy either. The five-pointed diamond still sat directly in front of Jaret in the circle of jewels as the magic dissipated and reality came back into focus.

Darth had growled from under the table until she saw the look of alarm when Jaret opened his eyes. She raced to Jaret and put herself between Jaret and Anthony. Jaret reached out and petted her while looking at Anthony with concern.

"We need to talk," Anthony said. "Don't worry. I would never harm you."

"I know." And Jaret did. Despite what he had learned, he understood on some primal level, because of the diamond but also from his own instinct, his complete safety even after learning Anthony's deadly secret.

"Come." Anthony lifted Jaret into his arms and carried him effortlessly to the couch, no longer concealing a vampiric strength. Darth had taken her cue from Jaret and allowed the moment without so much as a growl. As Anthony and Jaret settled next to each other, Darth curled up on her dog bed next to them.

"I woke with a magical alarm warning me someone had learned of my nature against my will."

"Do all vampires know magic too?" Jaret almost laughed despite the seriousness of their conversation. Of all his questions and all they had to discuss, why blurt out about the magic?

"No. Only members of the Vampire Council."

"Vampire Council?"

"Later." Anthony sighed. He removed his arm from around Jaret and cupped Jaret's face in his hands. "I'll tell you everything eventually."

"Why not now?" Sometimes Jaret lost patience with Anthony's elusiveness and wanted to demand answers, even though he knew his insistence would only make Anthony more stubborn. But why keep anything back once Jaret discovered the ultimate secret?

"I don't even know where to begin." Anthony looked up and then pulled his fingers through Jaret's hair. "I always control outing myself. And I haven't been so drawn to someone in centuries. I'm confused. Unsure of myself. At a loss."

"Centuries?" Jaret felt stupid with his short utterances. The news had him befuddled.

"Did you think I was born yesterday?" Anthony smiled, still gentle and loving. "Yes, centuries. I don't know how to take this slowly or ease you into the truth. I suppose I relinquished my opportunity by avoiding this very conversation for so long. You're a historian. Think about this. I was born in England under the Roman Empire."

Jaret tried to wrap his mind around that news, his academic training moving backward, through the American Revolution, the Glorious Revolution, the Reformation, Medieval Europe, and beyond. He comprehended the timeline, but couldn't rationalize the being next to him. "What does this mean?" Another idiotic question.

Anthony laughed and hugged Jaret. "Aren't you afraid of me? Aren't you worried about sitting next to a vampire? You amaze me."

"I trust you. I may be a few centuries younger, but I know when my jewels warn me about danger. Or tell me I'm safe. Besides, even though she growls because she knew you were a vampire before I did, Darth would never act so chill if you posed any threat." Jaret leaned into Anthony.

"Of course."

"I have the rest of the night. We have a lot to talk about."

Anthony giggled and wrapped his arm around Jaret to pull him close. "Indeed."

And so they spent the night, Jaret never tiring as his adrenaline and curiosity kept him awake.

Anthony told the briefest of self-histories, especially given his actual age. "I grew up during the Roman Empire. Have you studied the period? It's far more interesting than even the most brilliant of history books can tell. I was converted to vampirism early in life and soon after accepted into membership on the Vampire Council."

"Vampire Council? Now can you explain this council?"

Anthony nodded. "A body that enforces a strict vampire ethic to govern all vampires and commands we only kill those worthy of death. This is what I referred to when I used to mention the witches who came together to protect the innocent. I was referring to the Council, and the job of all vampires. The Council first began to protect vampires from exposure to humans. But now the Council has expanded its duties to include the fact we must defend innocent humans by dictating vampires only kill the deserving and never reveal ourselves. We feed our need for human blood to survive without murdering indiscriminately."

"This is fascinating." Jaret lost all ability to express his wonder about the news. Even as he felt safe and relaxed, the reality of vampires shocked his system. Especially when he added the fact that he had a very hot vampire as a boyfriend. "What else?"

Anthony smiled. "Are you listening as a historian or boyfriend?"

"Both." Jaret grinned.

Anthony paused, his expression growing sad. "I promise to explain to you someday. But I can't tell the whole story today. Please don't push on this. There was a vampire war, and all Council members except myself were annihilated. I alone had to enforce our laws, defend humanity, and conceal vampires. I lost my lover in the war, which is why I don't want to dwell on the past tonight. The loss is still very painful after all these centuries."

Jaret honored Anthony's request and changed their discussion despite his intense curiosity. "How long were you the only Council member?"

"Centuries. Until someone very dear to me, Xavier, defied the vampire laws, so I had to hunt him down. But his lover, and my best friend—Thomas—attacked me. In the end, he forced me to expose I was the entire Vampire Council, because I had led everyone to believe a group of vampires still held court together. We reconstituted the Council with them on it, as well as two others—Harriet and Xavier's sister, Catherine. Thankfully, I'm no longer alone in the task."

As Anthony spoke, Jaret recognized the long-haired vampire from his visions as Thomas, Anthony's best friend. The story sounded the stuff of fantasy. Until Jaret reminded himself that he was a witch. If gems could control the world at Jaret's behest and help him fight ghosts, then vampires could certainly exist. But how did Jaret's mind accept all he learned without alarm for his own safety? Did he trust the gems so much, or were other forces in play? Perhaps Anthony's steady presence comforted him. Or Jaret's experiences allowed him to process the unacceptable without threat.

Anthony cried a blood tear when he finished. "I'm remembering Julius. He was my lover." Jaret fought back a slight alarm at the revelation vampires cried blood and concentrated on Anthony's story to forget about the tear.

"I attach deeply to those around me, friends, companions, everyone. I feel connections deep within me." Anthony paused and wiped at his tears as he stared at Jaret. "I've loved two people with profound depth. My first lover, taken violently from me. And then Thomas, before he admitted his subterfuge and the fact we were, and are, incompatible as lovers."

The thought of Anthony's sexual experience overwhelmed Jaret with jealously and pangs of fear. What did all the experience mean? Jaret pushed the panic back into the recesses of his mind, afraid of what it meant and how to cope with his insecurity. Still, the feeling gnawed at him that Anthony revealed a previous relationship with

Thomas. "Wait. What do you mean by subterfuge? You and Thomas are lovers?"

Anthony shook his head. "Not are. Were." He sighed. "I converted Thomas in the 1700s. He was enchanting, outgoing, and absolutely beautiful with his half-English, half American Indian blood. He figured out I was a vampire and pretended to play a passive role, knowing I would never go for a dominant type. He did love me. I think, though, he even more desperately wanted to become a vampire."

Jaret frowned in confusion. "Passive? Dominant?"

"Ah, modern parlance would be better. How about bottom and top?"

Jaret blushed and nodded his understanding. "So what happened next?"

"I changed Thomas, thinking I had a new lover. Later he revealed his dominance. We tried to make our relationship work. Stupid, really. We ended up fighting most of the time. Incessant bickering. Thankfully, we got over the tension and became the dearest of friends. Much like you and Brady."

"But I feel like something still bothers you."

Anthony grew quiet. "I took a long time to even want to try to love again. I don't expect you to understand what it was like to watch Julius die. I don't want to talk about losing him. Then, when I was finally ready to attempt love again, Thomas betrayed me. He had no way of knowing the personal struggle I took to convert him and ask him to be my lover. He knew I cavorted with all sorts of men and acted the perfect slut before we got together. How could he have known the wounded soul within? Still, he hurt me. But I said I don't want to dwell on these miseries. What else do you want to know?"

"Do vampires get married?"

"Interesting question. I don't know if marriage is the right word. Many couple for life. Especially the male vampires. I've never attempted to analyze why."

The idea gave Jaret hope, though his mind could not go to a place where he became a vampire and left his human life behind. He could not stretch credibility too far for one night.

"I loved Thomas as a friend despite what he'd done to me," Anthony continued without prompting. "I sound insane." He laughed. "You'll have to meet him to understand. He infuriates me. I could have killed him. But as I said, I'm loyal, and my bond with people runs deep. Once you're in, you're in.

"And Thomas has saved me from myself over and over again. He gets violently angry with me. Well, not just me, though Xavier has gotten Thomas's temper under control. He wanted to kill me when I put Xavier in the iron box over the fire."

"Whoa! What iron box over what fire?"

"A vampire prison. After I found Xavier disobeying the laws—he was freeing slaves—I incarcerated him in the Council's magical prison, where he lay in a coffin over a pit of fire. The Vampire laws demanded the sentence because Xavier had exposed himself as a vampire while hunting for a free Black who'd been captured and forced into sexual slavery. That was his real mission. He liberated slaves in the process as a fringe benefit."

Anthony started to move on with his story about Thomas until Jaret stopped him. "Wait." Jaret held up his hand. "Tell me more about what Xavier did." Jaret's mind whirled at the idea of knowing someone who witnessed the past so intimately, and at a vampire so concerned with humanity.

"He went to liberate a free Black person who had been captured into slavery. He was saving him for a friend. Xavier couldn't handle being around Southern slavery, so he started freeing slaves all over the place. This was in 1822. So I caught and imprisoned Xavier for his crimes. Thomas discovered a spell to protect himself from my magic, the Council's magic, thus forcing me to admit the truth I alone served as the Vampire Council. With Thomas immune to my power, I had to free Xavier before Thomas exposed the truth to all vampires and humans alike, thereby threatening our very existence. Afterward, to maintain vampire laws and protect humanity, Catherine, Harriet, Thomas, Xavier, and I reconstituted the Vampire Council. The alliance freed me from the solitary onus of governing."

"Wow."

Anthony smiled at Jaret's response. "May I get back to my own story now?"

Jaret nodded and smiled back.

"Anyway, during the prison episode, Thomas got mad at me, threatened this exposure, and we compromised. He stopped his insane plot, I freed Xavier, and then Thomas forgave me. He moves on quickly after our fights, as if it's perfectly natural to hate your friends from time to time. The creation of a new Council, which in so many ways Thomas instigated, saved me from myself."

Anthony stopped and ran his hand down Jaret's arm. "Are you okay?"

This time Jaret laughed. "I think so." He grabbed Anthony's hand. "It's a lot, you know? Like—holy shit, I just landed in the middle of an Anne Rice novel. I've gone bonkers and think it's all real. I accept vampires and vampire laws and vampire fights, as if I'm strolling down the street watching people eat ice cream." Jaret stopped. He really did comprehend everything he had learned, as fanciful as Anthony's story sounded. Unfortunately, the sun crept onto the horizon before Jaret could articulate the one fear lurking in his mind. He had no idea what all of the vampire stuff meant for them—Jaret and Anthony.

Thirteen: Double Date

20 OCTOBER 2010
Chicago, Illinois

Jaret slept until noon and still felt tired. When Darth poked her nose into his face, desperate to go potty. Jaret willed himself to jog. He nurtured himself, however, by deciding to skip a day of classes and just try to process last night.

As Darth trotted along next to him, Jaret came to terms as much as possible with the fact he currently dated a vampire. A very old vampire. And a member of some Vampire Council. So, a very old and powerful vampire.

Still, he had no idea what the vampire thing meant for him and needed those answers. Soon.

Once home and showered, he distracted himself with a book and then TV. When his phone rang with a call from Jenn, for the first time Jaret could ever remember, he let it go to voice mail. No way he could explain all of this insanity to her, and she would absolutely know something was up.

Thankfully, the afternoon went by rather quickly and before long, he sat on the red line on his way to meet Anthony at his place.

Anthony greeted him with a hug and ushered him into the living room, with a stunning view of the downtown skyline, though Jaret preferred the view of Lake Michigan from the bedroom for a number of reasons. He sat on the couch, waiting for Anthony to return with some wine and felt as fidgety as he had on their first few dates.

Too nervous for chit chat and explaining he had to sleep that night, Jaret cut to the chase. "So, I get the situation. At least, I think I do. I mean, you're a vampire. Check. I dig it. I accept why you hid the truth. Not an easy one to pop on someone, even a witch. Cool. You know, like, you kill people to survive. I took the longest time to wrap my mind around the concept, even with some ethic making you only kill the bad guys. But okay. I'll just repress death and deal with your killing over time. At least being a vampire explains why you avoid eating, even though you can if you want." Jaret sipped his wine, desperate for a buzz. "Centuries—dealing with the time factor takes a little more to wrap my mind around. Vampire friends? Well, duh, of course. A vampire with magic. Shocking at first, you know? But if I'm a wizard and all, why not a vampire wizard, right?"

Anthony smiled. "The Harry Potter of vampires."

"Only sexier. So you die with fire? Or the sun?"

"Yes. And only through those means. None of the other myths are accurate."

"What if someone whacked your head off?"

"Depends." Anthony shrugged.

Jaret roared a laugh. "Depends? Your head rolls down a hill and into a stream but can crawl back out?"

"This is gross. Don't think about the image for too long. But if the head stayed close to the body, they'd pull together, reconnect, and heal. But if someone kept them apart, they'd live and try to seek each other out. Unless they were burned or thrown into the sun. So the head could float all the way to the ocean but if the body and head discovered one another, the vampire would be right back to living. Or undying. Whatever you want to use as a label."

Jaret chuckled again. "You're right. Gross. And weird."

"Indeed. You should see the reconnection happen."

Anthony had sat in a chair opposite Jaret but stood to move next to him. He wrapped one arm around Jaret and held his shoulder in those strong fingers. With his other hand, he took both of Jaret's and held them tightly. "You're jittery. I've never seen you like this."

"Yeah, well. This discussion makes me jittery."

"I thought you were okay with my being a vampire."

Jaret paused. "I am, with what I said. But there's still us. Right? You've avoided our relationship as much as I have."

Anthony nodded and seemed distant again, sad. "True. There's us. I'll be honest. I won't hide anymore from you." Anthony rested his head against Jaret's. "I don't know what to say, because I don't know about us. I can't make you a vampire. I've checked. You're too powerful a witch, which makes your transformation dangerous and forbidden by the code. The combination of the magic you already control with the strength and heightened senses of a vampire would be too volatile. I can't risk the conversion, for your sake as much as anything. Plus, changing you would require you to leave your family. I know you. You'd never agree."

Jaret's heart sank with each of Anthony's words. He wanted to protest the part about being too powerful a witch, which seemed completely unfair. But what the hell did he know about vampire rules? He almost said something when Anthony spoke again.

"Did you hear what I said about your family? You'd have to fake your death and leave them behind. It's too dangerous to stay in contact with those we knew in our human life. The Council is strict about forbidding human interaction with those we knew in life."

"I thought you said once Xavier stayed in contact with his sister? Isn't she even a vampire now?"

"True. They were an exception to the rule, and a dangerous one. Catherine discovered the truth because Xavier couldn't let her go, and Thomas hid the situation and before I knew what was going on, Catherine knew about Xavier and Thomas while she was a human. She concealed vampires despite being human because she wanted to protect Xavier. Then, Catherine's transformation came about during Xavier's quest against slavery. Agreeing to allow her to live as a vampire was part of the truce Thomas and I reached. You couldn't just walk away from your family, either. We can't have you creating a *Twilight* clan."

Jaret laughed despite his feeling of sadness. Right. Anthony did know him. No way he could convert to the undead and ditch his mom, dad, Lincoln, and Jenn, not to mention Darth.

"So where does all the truth leave us?" Jaret's voice quivered. "That's the end, I guess?" His eyes teared.

"Frankly, I wish it were." Anthony nestled even closer to Jaret. "Life would be easier if I could turn you into just another trick. I tried. And I almost got up and left Chicago without a trace. I knew even with your powers I could hide from you."

"Why didn't you?"

Anthony scrunched his brow. "I should have ended this the minute I learned the facts. But instead, like a complete and utter fool yet again in my long and miserable life, I fell in love."

The soft kiss sent Jaret to places he had never before gone. He fell limp in Anthony's arms as he carried him to the bedroom and slowly undressed him. Jaret's every sense tingled as Anthony licked up and down his body. He nearly came at the vision of Anthony naked before him, more beautiful than he had ever fantasized.

With Steve, sex always felt so animalistic and frantic. Passionate and good, yes, but not tender caresses as with Anthony. Not the building tension and excitement of tasting Anthony, of licking at the precome and then stopping. The desire deep within him as Anthony licked his ass and then stuck his tongue in, followed by a longing for Anthony that almost sent the room spinning around him. The instant of pain and then the raw excitement of Anthony's cock sliding in and out, in and out. When Anthony grabbed Jaret's dick and stroked, Jaret screamed in ecstasy and shot come onto his face, which Anthony licked as he clenched and began spurting inside of Jaret.

Jaret wrapped his legs around Anthony and pulled him closer, smashing Anthony even deeper inside of him.

When they finished, Jaret fell asleep in seconds as he held tight to Anthony lying next to him.

Jaret woke with a start, disoriented and naked in a strange bed. Still dark. The clock by the bed read five o'clock. When Darth jumped up next to him, he really got confused.

"I got her for you." Anthony came in, wearing jeans and a T-shirt. He sat on the bed next to Jaret. "I knew you'd panic if you woke up here with her at your place. I have to go to sleep before the sun rises." Anthony petted Jaret's head. "Do you have plans tonight?"

Jaret searched his brain to even figure out the day. Saturday. Nope, nothing planned. "No."

"Good. You're coming with me. I'll take you to dinner and then I want you to meet my friends."

"Vampires?"

Anthony tilted his head and nodded.

"Cool."

Anthony laughed. He leaned over and kissed Jaret. "Yes, cool. I even got Thomas to promise to behave. I think Xavier threatened him or something."

Anthony started to walk away but something turned him around. Perhaps he sensed the same tension between them as Jaret felt at the moment? Or had he used his witchcraft to read Jaret's mind, because he answered a question without ever hearing one. "I don't know either. There isn't going to be an easy answer. Maybe we don't need one. Can we agree to go with our situation for now without answers?"

Jaret thought he agreed. "Still, that could hurt. A lot."

"I know." Anthony smiled. "Believe me, I know. I'm willing to risk the pain for you."

"Okay."

Anthony grinned even wider, came back and kissed Jaret on the cheek. "I'll see you this evening, my love. Eat and drink anything you want. The kitchen is fully stocked."

"I thought vampires didn't have to eat or drink? I mean, other than—you know."

"True. We only need blood for sustenance. But I love wine. Thus my full wine cellar." Jaret recalled an enormous wine fridge in the kitchen. "I got most of the food because I knew you'd eventually be here."

Jaret's heart almost melted as they kissed goodbye.

Jaret flopped back onto the bed when Anthony had gone, reaching over to pet Darth and feel her next to him. He spent the day in Anthony's apartment, exploring every inch of space.

He also stopped to consider Anthony's wealth. His place took up at least half a floor of the building. Millions. More than Jaret could comprehend.

Jaret tried watching a movie and did some reading. No matter what he did, he kept wondering about his life and the most recent development. Would he want to be a vampire? As much as he accepted Anthony's status as such, he had a hard time thinking that a conversion could apply to him. Jaret came to terms with all of the truth when he boiled the situation down to what really concerned him: he wanted a relationship with Anthony but had no idea what he meant, how long their relationship would last, or about Anthony's intentions. It would rock to have superhuman power, to be able to run across the entire country in a night, or lift two or three people and carry them around without thinking about the weight.

Much as the nonchalance went against his typical behavior, Jaret decided he had no choice but to go with Anthony and the ambiguity, to see where the relationship took them without any grand promise for the future.

Despite an initial hesitance to meet Anthony's friends and spend a night with three vampires, Jaret had a wonderful time meeting Thomas and Xavier. Thank God the five-pointed diamond had signaled Jaret's safety with all three of them, clear back when he first discovered Anthony's nature. Thomas and Xavier, too, awed Jaret with their utter beauty. He laughed a lot at Thomas, who teased Anthony and prodded for details about their love life. Yet Thomas treated Jaret nicely, and in a private moment said something to almost give Jaret hope.

They had all decided to take a walk through Chicago. As Anthony and Xavier sprinted away, Thomas smiled. "Damsel in distress ahead. They heard her scream. I'd help, especially if I were alone. But it's just one asshole. They can take care of him. They like being the police better than I do. Heroics and saving humanity and all suits them better."

Thomas and Jaret walked along a downtown street. "You don't agree with the ethic?"

"On the contrary, I do. Well, most of the time." Thomas flipped his hair back and stopped. Jaret halted too. "It's just they have more faith in humanity. They care about people more than I do. I have a lot of hate. I don't trust people as much. Nor do I think the vampire ethic and all the rules can control or predict every situation."

"Fair enough."

"What about you?" Thomas asked.

Jaret had never considered the question. "Probably somewhere between. I mean, after studying history, I think society, and by extension people, are just a bunch of selfish assholes. There's a lot of hate in the world. But I believe in individuals, especially those around me. It's hard to give up on the people I'm close to." Jaret thought of Steve and how long he had taken to end their relationship.

"Interesting. You'll get along well with Anthony. He'll talk your arm off about this, so don't get him started unless you want to hear about his philosophy for hours." Thomas laughed. Jaret did, too, knowing the truth of what Thomas said.

They started walking again and then Thomas pulled Jaret to a bench and sat him down. "Forgive my forward behavior. But hear me out. He's going to be impossible. Absolutely impossible." Thomas rolled his eyes. "He's already told me about the rules and his fear. He'll fight this tooth and nail. He fights off everything, and the more personal, the more he fights. I've known him for centuries, and he never changes. He has angst about picking a car to drive, let alone anything more intimate. Here's the bottom line—he's afraid. Give him a chance. Don't give up. I'll help when I can, but I have to be careful not to piss him off. There are times in life when you have to fight for what you want."

Before Jaret could ask any questions, Anthony appeared beside him. "What does he want you to fight? One of his ridiculous battles against the religious right?"

Thomas laughed, jumped up, and punched Anthony in the arm. "You have as much fun as I do teasing the religious wackos."

Fourteen: The Dance

31 OCTOBER 2010
New York City

Thomas and Xavier stayed in Chicago for the rest of the month until Thomas announced one night while Jaret visited them with Anthony that he had to go to the Halloween parade in New York City. He and Xavier went ahead the next day. Anthony stayed with Jaret until the weekend because Jaret had classes.

Over the days since he had met Thomas and Xavier, Jaret was drawn more and more to Xavier. Xavier had a nurturing way about him that made Jaret feel sheltered and protected, cherished as a soul but without the complication of a relationship like when Anthony did the same things.

One evening, sitting alone in Anthony's living room with Xavier after Thomas and Anthony ran off to buy a Wii so they could all play bowling, Xavier sat next to Jaret. "Thomas told me he warned you about needing to fight for Anthony."

"Yeah." Jaret wondered where the chat might take them.

"He's right, of course." Xavier smiled. "Thomas knows Anthony better than anyone. But you also have to protect yourself."

They fell silent, Jaret wondering how to take the comment. Before he came up with anything to say, Xavier spoke again. "I don't mean to dissuade you. But I also want you to protect yourself. If you ever need to talk about your relationship, come to me. Promise?"

"Sure." Jaret nodded, though he sensed Xavier had kept something from him. His heart sank, because he had fallen hard by this time for Anthony, adoring every bit of his protectiveness, sexiness, and maturity. He had captured Jaret's heart despite the warning signs to pull back. "You don't think our relationship's going to work, do you?"

Xavier shook his head. "I didn't mean to imply anything. But I don't think anything is guaranteed either."

The raw honesty drew Jaret even more into trusting Xavier.

"I guess I just don't know what to do. I could leave." He paused. "I don't want to. But I don't want to sit around to be crushed like a bug either. I'm confused."

"I understand. Love is always complicated. The movies in this contemporary age make love seem too easy, like the stuff of fantasy. The make-believe land lasts for a very short time before reality sets in. And with the vampire and magical complications for you two, I just want you to protect yourself too." Xavier wiped at a blood tear.

"Did I say something wrong? Why are you crying?"

Xavier had a nice, easy laugh. "I'm easily moved to tears. Thomas often complains I'm too emotional, even though he loves my moods at the same time. I'm feeling a lot about your fears and insecurities. I wish I could make them go away for you."

"You care about me already? We just met."

"Like I said, I'm an emotional person, and Anthony has great taste in men. I find you very endearing. Just promise you'll take care of yourself."

"I am. Promise. Can I ask you a rude question?"

Xavier laughed again. "Sure."

"Does crying blood creep you out?"

"I take it you're creeped out?"

"A little. The blood is rather unusual."

"I completely agree. I have no idea why we turn to blood tears after converting, any more than I understand how vampires are made and survive for centuries." He shrugged. "I just deal with the reality."

They heard the front door open as Anthony and Thomas returned.

That weekend, Anthony flew Jaret to New York City so they could join Thomas and Xavier for the Halloween parade. Jaret had a marvelous time with them, feeling protected and free to join the revelry without concern for his safety. He was amused that all four of them dressed as Goth vampires.

Lost in the revelry, Jaret ignored his phone's buzz after he saw Steve calling him yet again. He dismissed the call. He did talk to Brady a minute later, having to shout into the phone above the roar of humanity until he moved to a quieter corner.

"Dude! You have to come to this next year. It's insane."

"Sounds cool. We have to get to Mardi Gras too! Okay, have fun without me."

Jaret laughed. "I will. Later, dude."

The night seemed perfect when Anthony led them to their rooms in yet another flat he owned, this one with Thomas and Xavier. Anthony pulled Jaret into his arms and danced with him to Mika's "Lollipop." When his playlist shuffled to "Toy Boy," the mood changed and the haunting words of Mika with a poor dismissed boy being a puppet for love to those around him sent them both into melancholy.

"It's hard for me sometimes," Jaret said and pulled away. He sat on the edge of the bed, where Anthony joined him but kept several feet between them. "The not knowing. You know? Like, I get the truth. I don't want to push you. I know I can't. I hate the fucking vampire rules."

Jaret hesitated before he glanced at Anthony. Anthony sat stoically as usual during the conversation but grinned, which put Jaret at ease. "I don't always love them myself, even if I have to enforce them."

"Yeah, but you're like some vampire cop who also loves the rules. Can't get away from them."

Anthony laughed. "You sound like Thomas. He always reprimands me for taking the rules to the extreme."

"He has a point."

Anthony nodded. "I understand. But I've experienced enough to know that it's not simple. Yes, I protect myself by following the rules. I also protect others. You, for instance."

Jaret gulped back the tears welling inside. "Yeah. It's just, you know, eventually we have some decisions to make here. Hanging out in limbo land has been fun and all. Mostly because I got to stay with you." Jaret looked at Anthony, wanting to close the distance between them. His fear kept him from moving even an inch. "Except continuing made me, you know..." Jaret stopped. No way he wanted to finish his thought.

Anthony arched one eyebrow. He leaned back, his long blond hair falling gently onto the bed. "You keep saying you want to know; you want to make plans. But you can't even bring yourself to say the words."

A tear trickled down Jaret's cheek. "You don't have the patent on being hurt." Jaret could remember every time he had told Steve how much he loved him, each one a crushing blow since Steve had turned from a lover into a nightmare. Sure, Jaret had admitted to himself a thousand times he had fallen for Anthony over these last few months. Completely in love. But if he said *love* out loud, the noise made his feelings truer. No taking the revelation back. No running into a shadow when Anthony finally declared they had to stop seeing each other because some vampire ethic mandated their separation.

Anthony leaned over and pulled Jaret into his arms. "You don't have to." Jaret rested his head on Anthony's rock-hard chest, thankful for the reprieve.

Anthony rested his chin on top of Jaret's head. "If I had better answers, I'd tell you. I'm running from the rules too. I know it's not fair I kept a distance. But every day with you makes me want you all the more. Then I hear you talk to your parents or brother and sister and know you can't just walk away from them and be with me. Even if you could, you're a powerful witch. More powerful than you even know. What your energy would do when mingled with the blood of a vampire—" Anthony rubbed Jaret's arm. "I can't imagine. The ethic is right. You might be too much, and I don't want to risk the results."

They sat quietly for several minutes. Jaret's mind raced. He came back to the same place he had time and again. He desperately wanted to force the issue and make Anthony proclaim their future. Then he retreated, leery of the answer and content for the moment to let the problem hang in the air because at least unsaid, he could pretend they had a future.

Jaret felt better the next night. He spent the day exploring New York by himself and decided not to drink as much as he had the previous evening. He wanted to loosen up and take his cue from Thomas, who seemed to find a way to enjoy every moment. Sometimes Jaret accomplished as much, sometimes he knew he just kidded himself.

As they took a private plane back to Chicago in the middle of the night, Jaret and Anthony chatted comfortably.

"You should own your own plane. This rocks."

"I don't need a plane, remember? I could have run with you in my arms back to Chicago even faster."

Jaret smiled. "Yeah. Creeps me out for some reason. I'm not ready to go there yet."

Anthony laughed. "You accepted I kill to survive. You accepted vampires. But my carrying you across state lines goes too far?"

Jaret laughed. "I didn't say my feelings made sense." He thought about getting back to see Darth, excited even though he knew when Brady stayed in his apartment to babysit, Darth was spoiled rotten. "Don't you ever want to say, 'Fuck the Council? Fuck the rules?'"

Anthony gave him a puzzled look.

"You know, always with the rules and fucking up your life. I mean, I can't imagine centuries of being captive to the ethic. Thomas lets go sometimes. I think even Xavier does. But not you."

"I've explained to you why." Anthony grabbed Jaret's hand. "I know the consequences if the laws disappear. Too dangerous. Besides, believe me or not, I'm more relaxed about enforcement than people believe. More than ever before because of the newly formed Council. They help make exceptions to the rules or change them if need be."

"So have them change the rule about my magic."

For the first time in weeks, Jaret glanced at Anthony and realized he was hiding something. "It's not so easy," Anthony said after a long pause.

Jaret drifted to sleep in the following silence. He woke up in his apartment with Darth snuggled next to him unaware of how he got there but guessing Anthony carried him.

He got up, found a note saying welcome back from Brady, and took Darth on their morning jog. Classes went well, and thankfully he and Anthony had agreed not to see each other until the following weekend. Jaret needed time away to clear his mind.

Jaret lost himself in the routine of his life. He caught up with his Mom and Dad, and left Lincoln a quick message to say hello. He and Jenn talked for over an hour, mostly about her trying to decide what to do with her life, and about a new hot guy she'd met.

He loved his history classes and spent more time than needed on a couple of research papers. He almost felt normal again when he got home and found Steve sitting on his sofa, petting Darth.

"How'd you get in?" Jaret asked and clutched an emerald in his hand. At least he had not let his guard down enough to forget to carry a jewel with him at all times.

"The super let me in. Remembered me from before." Steve got up and walked over to Jaret. "Relax, babe. Put the jewelry away."

Steve took the emerald from Jaret with a soft grab. Jaret allowed the theft, knowing he could summon the gem back to him if needed. He could call forth all the jewels since he was in the apartment.

"Babe. We never got to have the talk I wanted." Steve stood close and reached out. Jaret stood rigid. Steve sounded like the hot jock who had swept Jaret off his feet their senior year of high school. Self-assured. Built tough. Protective, yet soothing.

Anthony had more maturity, sure. But as much baggage. Maybe life was easier with a closeted jock than a rule-bound vampire.

Jaret came to his senses when Steve leaned over, ready to kiss him.

Jaret ducked under his arm and stepped away. "Why can't you get it into your head this is over, Steve? Shit."

Jaret sat on the couch. "Sit down." He motioned for Steve to sit opposite him in a chair. Instead, Steve came to the couch, too, but at least sat at the other end.

"I haven't handled this well, I know." Jaret grabbed a pillow to hug to himself. "But we both know our relationship didn't work out. I'll always hold a place in my heart for you because what we had meant so much. But we have such different views of the world and what we want. Our dreams don't mesh. We'll keep hurting each other, over and over and over. It's not worth the pain for either one of us."

Steve seemed to contemplate. "What about all the promises to each other?"

Jaret nodded, accepting Steve's confusion. The change from their infatuation to the present moment confounded him sometimes too. "We were young. Lame excuse, I know." Jaret fidgeted with the pillow. "Too naïve. We didn't really know each other as well as we thought."

"I want a second chance. Please." Steve reached over and placed his hand on Jaret's knee.

Jaret shook his head. "I'm sorry I hurt you. I'm sorry for handling this breakup poorly, and being so shitty. But we have to move on."

They both cried before Steve got up without saying a word. He walked to the door, and Jaret followed. Steve spun around and grabbed Jaret in his arms, clutching him in a tight hold. Jaret felt Steve's hard dick pushing against his stomach, and against his will, Jaret got excited too.

"I get what you said." Steve crushed his face into Jaret's hair. "I'll go. But I won't give up. Ever."

Steve kissed the top of Jaret's head and then turned around and left the apartment. Unaware he was holding his breath, Jaret remembered to exhale when Steve disappeared.

Good. Maybe the conversation put an end to the nonsense about staying together. At least, Jaret wanted to convince himself as much despite Steve's last words. He needed to believe he had put an end to all the crap with Steve. Jaret could only have one mess of a relationship to deal with at a time. If he could put the stalking Steve behind him, then he could concentrate on the insanity of dating a vampire with a code to forbid witch-cum-vampires from existing. Jaret made a mental note to ask Anthony about the hypocrisy of the notion all the Vampire Council members knew magic, but Jaret's power would be too much to handle.

Jaret went to his computer, put on some Mika, and sat with Darth in his lap while the sun set. He found a few minutes of sanity from time to time in these moments alone with his dog and Mika.

Fifteen: Love Dance

23 DECEMBER 2010
Chicago, Illinois

Jaret's heart ached at the thought of leaving Anthony behind for the next two weeks while he traveled back to Colorado for the holidays. He *was* excited to see his family. Still, the strain with his relationship had increased of late and he hated to leave on a negative note, feeling a pit of despair in his stomach almost all the time.

"Let's just at least set a date to talk." Jaret heard the whine in his voice as he held onto Anthony. They sat in Anthony's living room overlooking the city, but neither noticed the view.

"There's nothing to talk about. I can't convert you. No matter what you promise about your family or keeping your powers in check, transforming you is forbidden."

Maybe too much wine sharpened Jaret's emotion. He pushed away from Anthony and walked to the window to watch outside. "Fine, then maybe we're finished." Jaret folded his arms across his chest and twirled around to see Anthony's reaction.

Anthony lowered his head and folded his hands in front of him. He refused to look up or say anything.

"I guess your answer is silence."

Anthony looked up, the blood tears spilling down his face. Still, he remained silent.

Jaret stumbled on his way to the door to get his shoes and walk out. Anthony followed him.

"What are you doing?"

"Getting out of your hair." Jaret tumbled over as his foot missed the shoe.

Anthony reached out and steadied him. "Stop. We don't need to do this right before you leave."

Jaret slammed his fists against his side. "I just tried to say the same thing! Let's figure out a time to talk about us."

This time, Anthony shouted back. "We can't. Because a conversation will lead to more arguments and confronting our very bad reality. This will not last forever."

Now Jaret burst into tears. "Then we're finished. Done. So don't fucking touch me. Get out of my way. I'm going to get my dog and go home."

Jaret slammed the door behind him before realizing he only wore one shoe, and Darth was still inside. He slumped against the wall and bawled.

Anthony eventually opened his door and bent over to pick up Jaret and carry him into his living room. They sat silently for over an hour, holding one another. Sometimes Jaret squeezed Anthony so hard his muscles hurt.

"We'll talk later. Not tonight. Not now. Okay?" Anthony ran his fingers through Jaret's hair and kissed him on the forehead. "I love you. Just leave us at loving each other."

"I love you too." To the point I can't live without you. But Jaret kept the thought to himself, not wanting to intensify the moment.

Part Four: The First Time

Sixteen: Pace

17 MARCH 2011
Chicago, Illinois

Still in his early twenties, Jaret thought he'd begun to understand life more deeply than most of his peers. Not just because he'd faced death his senior year in high school or because of the magic that gave him unique powers and abilities.

In the last year he had come to comprehend the patience required to get through the ups and downs of life. He had experienced the slow pace of change and the monotony of painful emotions. He dwelled within the longings one kept hidden for fear of being hurt. Life presented one piece of suffering after another.

In his youth, he had always wanted quick answers and solutions, for life to move along as fast as a basketball game; up and down the court, shoot a basket, and move to the other end. Instead, he discovered how slowly things shifted and changed. How when you wanted something concrete—needed tangible results, even—life's direction could take a painstakingly long time to make the next turn.

It was not as if some unknown force propelled him forward. He had plenty of free will. Except the choices and answers at his disposal repelled him.

Almost a year ago, he broke up with Steve and started to date Anthony. Good.

Then the complications. Steve took to stalking him. As much as he had wanted to believe Steve would get over their relationship, he had to admit he had a bigger problem on his hands than a little love sickness. Yet he had limited options to cope. When Jaret finally relented and allowed Anthony's involvement in the Steve problem with a promise of no physical threats or violence, Anthony's intimidation had no effect on Steve. So Jaret had a possessive football player/ex-boyfriend who showed up off and on, desperately trying to coerce him back into the awful relationship. Almost a year of dealing with Steve shit? Fuck.

Jaret could handle one complication, even one as big as the problem with Steve. But add to the mix his strained relationship with Anthony and he confronted an enormous mess. Since outing Anthony as a vampire and taking their relationship to the next level, not much had changed. They loved each other. Yet in fits and starts Anthony would pull away, come back, and then Jaret would distance himself only to show up crying at Anthony's door and begging forgiveness. They had no more solutions to their dilemma today than they had in the fall. Jaret and Anthony both wanted the commitment. Neither dated anyone else nor desired an outside tryst. Yet Anthony had, if anything, become more stubborn about the fact Jaret's witchcraft prohibited him from ever becoming a vampire. And frankly, with the requirement he leave his family behind Jaret doubted he could take the next step.

Still, eternal life? With Anthony? It had an appeal. Thomas and Xavier seemed so happy and content after over two centuries together. Why not Jaret and Anthony? Because of some gems and a spell or two? Bullshit. And Jaret told Anthony his feelings about the vampire ethic, but the conversation didn't go well. Any discussion about their future always ended in an argument and frustration over their differing views on the situation.

So, Jaret sat today, trying to accept he had no answers to these problems. He doubted one would suddenly appear on the horizon like a knight in shining armor coming to his rescue and making everything great again.

Darth had a much easier time with life. Jog, eat, sleep, play. Worry about Jaret until he appeared, and repeat the pattern all over again. Jaret often thought he'd rather be a dog. Shorter life, true, and you had to have a hankering for poop or at least enjoy a good butt smell. Other than excrement, a dog's existence seemed like a pretty decent option.

Jaret realized life provoked such insanity in people. If only he could take life slowly and allow the rhythm of his existence to play out, however methodically. Anthony obviously had all the time in the world, and with a vampire protecting him Jaret could wait for a few years too. As for Steve, something would give eventually, right?

Jaret turned to the one source of never-changing stability in his life. He decided a month ago to tell Jenn everything. Everything. He kept it from Anthony, who would freak about the news. Funny, though, Xavier had first suggested telling Jenn because he recognized in Jaret and Jenn the same relationship he had with his sister, Catherine. Xavier recommended talking to Jenn could help Jaret through the turmoil.

"Hey," Jenn answered on the second ring. "Are you a vampire yet?"

"It's morning, Sherlock Holmes. You figure it out."

Jenn laughed. "Testy. What's up?"

"Nothing much." Jaret sighed. "I know what you're going to say. There's nothing to update. Just some mornings are better than others, you know?"

"I know. I love you." Jenn's singing that in his ear always made him feel better. She grounded him. "That's the shitty part, right? Not my love." She laughed at herself. "How you don't have any options, really, except to wait out whatever happens. Anthony has decisions to make. He holds all the cards. Unless, you know, you decide you can't deal anymore and—boom—shitcan the whole thing."

Jenn let her idea hang in the air. She told Jaret a month ago what she thought of dating a vampire. "Bad idea." Jaret had countered he loved and trusted Anthony. "Okay, so I'm not there and all. But dating the aloof undead doesn't sound like a great idea. I mean, he can delay this forever. Literally. You're only going to have one shot at this life." Jenn eventually backed off but implored Jaret to protect himself.

"I wish I could be like you. Just move on when a relationship ended." Jaret asked about Jenn, and they chatted for a while longer. More than anything, he needed to hear Jenn's reassurance. "Love you, little cowpoke," Jaret said, using a funny nickname they'd annoyed each other with growing up.

Jaret spent a quiet Sunday playing with Darth and reading. Nothing heavy. He felt down today, like the weight of everything pressed on his shoulders and threatened to smash him into the ground. At least Jenn cheered him up.

When he checked his email later in the afternoon, he found a new message from Xavier. He, too, made Jaret feel better even in the midst of his misery.

> *Dearest Jaret,*
>
> *I told you months ago I understood your anguish more than you could realize. Thomas and I took years before we figured out our relationship. I realize we met in a different time and place, when things moved more slowly. Still, when next we get to see each other, I'll share some ideas about how to cope as the two of you try to figure this out.*
>
> *Two, you must understand Anthony's nature. He moves methodically and anguishes over anything with even the slightest possibility of bending a rule or guideline. Thomas and I can help with his personality too. Be patient. I know it's much easier for me to write such a thing than for you to live the reality.*
>
> *The most difficult thing will be leaving your heart open and vulnerable. I had the hardest time opening up to Thomas. Whatever happens with Anthony, your life will be fuller and more complete if you learn to risk it all to gain much. Even the pain of failure will enrich your life. Trite, I know. But true.*
>
> *Love, Xavier*

Xavier had a way of comforting even while speaking the truth, telling Jaret things he'd rather not hear. Jaret watched his favorite vampire movie, Francis Ford Coppola's *Dracula* and went to bed cuddled next to Darth. He had survived another day. Sometimes he hoped for nothing more.

Seventeen: Steve

18 MARCH 2011
Evanston, Illinois

The next morning after his melancholy day and watching a movie with Darth, Jaret got halfway through his jog when he stopped to tie his shoe. Nothing much to the pause, except this sudden halt allowed him to see Steve running alongside a parallel path closer to the lake.

"Shit." Determined to finish, he jogged until he got close to his apartment and stretched while Darth lay panting next to him. When Steve came up, Jaret refused to acknowledge him.

Of late, Steve had started to play some new game, in which he stood in front of Jaret or nearby without saying anything. Eventually, he'd erupt and accuse Jaret of being rude.

When Jaret walked toward his building, Steve hurried alongside. "Aren't you at least going to say good morning?"

"No."

"I just happened to be out for a jog, you know? Thought we could say 'hi' at least."

Lame. His behavior got more and more lame. "Funny you always happen to take a walk, go to the library, jog, or half the other normal things you do, at the same time and in the same place as me."

Steve's voice grew softer. "You used to like when we ran into each other."

"We were dating." Jaret lurched to a stop and stared at Steve. "I wanted to see you. But you normally didn't want to acknowledge me. Now suddenly you want to follow me around like a puppy. Go see your girlfriend. Take her to breakfast. Or, better yet, go get help. Figure out how to come out so you can have a happy life as yourself. We're not an item anymore."

Steve's lower lip quivered. "If I got help, would you come back?"

"No." Jaret shook his head. "We're over."

Steve reached over and grabbed both of Jaret's shoulders. The movement came quickly and with force, startling enough Darth jumped at Steve and nipped him in the arm before Jaret could call her off. Jaret struggled out of Steve's grasp. His face bright red, Jaret yelled louder than intended. "You're fucking creeping me out. You've got to stop this stalking shit. Fuck, Steve. Get a fucking grip."

Even through his anger, though, a sensation gnawed at Jaret. Something magical tingled when Steve touched him. Not in the sense of passion or emotion, but of magic. Of a force surrounding Steve, perhaps against his will. These warnings often caused Jaret to back off his anger.

"I can't live without you." Steve stared at his feet. "Is that what you want? For me to disappear?"

"Steve, don't. Don't go there."

"Why? You don't care anyway."

Steve walked away dejected. Jaret wanted to follow to make sure he didn't go and do something stupid. But he also knew the routine was nothing more than business as usual and the insinuation another idle threat to get his attention. Still, the circumstances sucked.

Eighteen: Dinner

22 MARCH 2011
Chicago, Illinois

Another week and no more answers came Jaret's way. Steve showed up two more times, alive and well, and Anthony went along as if in a normal relationship without a care in the world.

Jaret earned an A on one of the most difficult research projects ever. Pumped, he called his parents and then Anthony right after sunset.

"Remember the beast of a research paper trying to kill me? For the asshole professor? You won't believe this. I got an A!"

"Wonderful!" Anthony shouted. "To celebrate, I want you to wear the outfit I bought you for Christmas. I'm taking you to a surprise location."

After dressing and primping, Jaret waited in his apartment for Anthony. Anthony had his own key, so he usually came upstairs to escort Jaret instead of just having him come down or appearing out of nowhere with his vampire ability. Jaret found such old-world chivalry quite charming.

Riding toward downtown, they chatted about Jaret's paper, updated how their previous couple of days had gone, and at one point Anthony reached over and held Jaret's hand.

They pulled up outside Table 52, an extremely nice restaurant near downtown Chicago. Jaret had heard about the place on TV and from a friend but never had the means to eat there. Anthony tipped the valet and then went to their table, back in a corner.

After Anthony ordered a high-end bottle of wine and the waiter checked both their IDs, Jaret laughed.

"What?" Anthony asked.

"How old does your driver's license say you are?"

Anthony got the joke. "I'm twenty-eight."

"Good. I don't think they'd buy three thousand, or whatever."

"Indeed." Anthony lifted his wine glass in the air. "A toast, to your academic achievement." They clinked their glasses together.

The wine went down smoothly, more so than even the wines Anthony had back in his apartment. Jaret could definitely get used to this lifestyle. Still, he was troubled that he had no idea just how long the moment would last, and what Anthony really wanted from him. He enjoyed the clothes, the high-rise apartment, and the cars. Who wouldn't? But ultimately, he loved Anthony, not the material things. He loved how he transformed sex from making out as an animal lust to lovemaking; how he shielded Jaret from harm but gave him room to live his life; how he refused to treat Jaret like an infant. Thinking too much about their future, he grew more and more quiet, almost silent by the time the famous banana dessert arrived at their table.

"Penny for your thoughts," Anthony said.

Jaret smiled. "One minute, you talk like any twentysomething guy in the world, and the next you say something to remind me of your real age."

"How so?"

"No one says 'Penny for your thoughts.' Maybe 'What the fuck are you thinking?' Or 'Spill it.' Or just 'What?' But the whole penny thing sounds more like my grandpa, may he rest in peace."

Anthony laughed, thankfully, because halfway into his monologue Jaret started to worry he'd offended him. "I could try Latin instead—my native tongue? And I hope I don't remind you of your grandfather very often. There are so many disturbing images and implications to the thought—" Anthony cut himself off. "I don't even know how to continue."

"Nor should you." Jaret shook his head. "You don't have anything else in common with Gramps." Jaret leaned over the table and whispered, "I never wanted him to bang me like I want you. Now."

Anthony waved to the waiter and got their check. In a matter of minutes, they tripped over each other getting into Anthony's condo and fumbled to strip off their clothes. Anthony pushed Jaret onto his bed and removed his final sock, then licked from Jaret's toe up his leg, sucked on his belly button, and tongued his ear. Jaret pushed up to rub his cock against Anthony's stomach.

With one arm bracing himself up, Anthony took his free hand and flipped Jaret over. Jaret moaned with pleasure when he felt Anthony's tongue rim the outside of his ass, then dart in and out. Jaret lifted his butt and pushed his ass toward Anthony, until Anthony's finger, and then two, slowly entered him. Anthony held Jaret up as he fucked him, reaching around and stroking Jaret to the rhythm of Anthony's pleasure. Vampire strength added a whole new level to the sexual experience.

Before he knew what hit him, Jaret blasted all over the bed. He enjoyed the feel of Anthony inside him for several more minutes before he noticed Anthony's leg muscles flex and his body spasm.

Anthony gently put Jaret down on the bed, then collapsed next to him. He pulled Jaret into his arms and kissed his cheek. "Your ass is the most remarkable ass I've ever had the pleasure of defiling."

Jaret grinned. "I doubt it. You've seen a lot of butts."

"Precisely. Which is what makes me an expert on your particular ass." Anthony moved his hand down Jaret's body and squeezed his butt. "I could do the same thing all over again, but I think you have something else you want to talk about."

"What?" Jaret looked into Anthony's eyes.

"The penny. You diverted attention from the matter by commenting on the language I used. Then you seduced me. A clever ruse from a wicked little witch. I'm not so easily dissuaded. You've been melancholy of late. Again at dinner. Why are you hiding from me? It's like we just started our relationship last week. I thought we'd moved beyond these mind games."

Jaret fell silent. Did he dare get into the truth? The topic risked much, perhaps everything. Besides, why reveal his inner turmoil when no one but Anthony could change the circumstances, which he refused to do? Anthony accused him of playing a mind game. Funny, because who held the puppet strings in this relationship? Anthony. He kept things close to the vest and avoided any reference to their long term future. Jaret struggled with his instinct to bury his emotion again versus their promise to each other to open and honest communication.

"It's nothing we haven't talked about. There's nothing we can do. You know? Still, some days I deal with us better than others."

Anthony ran his hand through Jaret's hair. "Is there anything I can do?"

"Nope." Jaret stopped himself from pleading to become a vampire or attempting to get some oath of eternal affection. He remembered their awful Christmas Eve scene and wanted to avoid the drama. Still, Jaret's eyes welled with tears of frustration.

Anthony pulled him closer. "The truth isn't any easier for me. I wish I had clearer answers too. I take for granted how the days, weeks, and even months go by without our addressing the problem. I keep hoping for a miracle solution. We have to be patient. We've been together a short time, to a vampire."

"It's a long time to me." Jaret wiped at the tears. "Listen, I promised to wait. Or whatever. I can't leave you. I don't want to. So, I'm willing to deal with the bullshit, I guess. But you have to understand it's rough for me sometimes. I mean, I won't always be peachy with the whole thing. Okay?"

"Peachy?"

Jaret laughed despite his mood. "Don't start the language thing again."

"We have difficult decisions to make. Very painful ones. I don't know what any decisions will mean." Anthony cupped Jaret's face in his hands. "I keep studying the ancient documents and the ethic, looking for anything to give us a better option. No easy solution exists. If you can give me some time, I'll accept how hard waiting is for you."

"Okay." Jaret laid his head on Anthony's chest. Sometimes he needed to forget the reality of dating a vampire like he tried to repress his own sorcery. How he longed to be normal. "I told Jenn it's not easy falling in love with a vampire."

"You told Jenn?"

"Yeah." Jaret spoke with hesitation, worried about the edge in Anthony's voice.

"What did you tell her? Everything?"

"What does everything mean?"

"Don't be coy." Anthony pushed Jaret away so he could look into his eyes. "Does she know about vampires?"

"It's not a big deal." Jaret rolled away. He always hated when Anthony got stern. "She knows about magic. Almost got killed by the irate ghost of an ancestor. She's dealt with a lot. And keeps the magic all a secret. I tell Jenn everything. So if this becomes some major crisis, well, not much I can do about the past. Because I love you. Jenn's like, I don't know. Part of my soul."

Anthony stared at Jaret for a moment and then took a deep breath. "I suppose you need someone to talk to."

"Good point. I mean, you talk to Thomas and Xavier about everything. But I'm supposed to keep a tight lid on my knowledge. Bullshit. A total crock. Not much different than Steve making me keep a lot of secrets so I had to suffer by myself." Jaret saw that his words cut deep by Anthony's downcast eyes and slumping shoulders. "Sorry. Too harsh."

"No harsher than my attitude. I trust you." Anthony pulled Jaret back to him. "I'm glad you have someone to talk to. It's good for both of us. Forgive me. I was reacting out of a very old defense mechanism. Even with you, I struggle against my instincts sometimes."

Jaret nodded. He kissed Anthony's chest and hugged him. "Most of the time I just pretend it's all okay. Because, see, there isn't a world I can imagine without you in it."

"At least we agree on something." Anthony kissed the top of Jaret's head.

Nineteen: Life Sucks

24 MARCH 2011
Saugatuck, Michigan

Jaret walked along the Lake Michigan shoreline as the sun started to set. Not enough yet for the vampires to awake, but close enough Jaret looked forward to seeing them again. Darth had returned with her ball, so Jaret tossed it into the water and laughed when a wave smashed into her. She barked a reprimand at the lake, grabbed her ball, and swam back.

Anthony had planned a short holiday in Michigan for Jaret's sake, after the latest incident with Steve. Despite himself, Jaret replayed the scene in his mind where he stood in front of his apartment, waiting for Anthony to pick him up.

In the movies, TV shows, and news reports, the victim always screams for help. Not Jaret. For whatever reason, when he felt the hand clasp around his mouth and the other arm wrap around his stomach and lift him up, he struggled but remained quiet.

Whoever kidnapped him knew about the gems, because once he dragged Jaret into the bushes, he grabbed Jaret's pocket before Jaret could call them forth for assistance and held them tight in one hand while tying Jaret's hands behind his back. The assailant slid the gems into a silver pouch with some power to render them ineffective. Jaret swore the bag was his own magical sack. He hardly believed what happened when the dark figure cut off Jaret's pants with a knife and tossed them aside. Then he carried Jaret and dropped him into a car trunk. All the while, Jaret accepted fate with a passive attitude, struggling a little but not enough to matter. Weird, how a magical vibe filled the air with some sort of alert but not one of imminent danger to Jaret.

But the trunk freaked him out. Jaret tried to get out, to no avail, and the gems in the sack several feet away did nothing but signal Jaret of magic in the air. The trunk lid slammed shut. Still Jaret failed to respond by banging on the car and making noise. He lay there as the car wove through Chicago and stopped at some unknown location.

"You fucker!" Jaret screamed when the trunk lid opened and Steve looked down at him. Steve cut him loose from the rope. "You fucking maniac." Jaret jumped out of the trunk, feeling awkward to stand in some forest in his underwear despite being in the situation against his will.

"At least you're not naked like those poor guys up in the tree." Steve smiled. Still acting like all was well, nothing amiss in the world.

Jaret reminded himself to keep his wits about him and not antagonize Steve too much for fear Steve would get violent or leave him in the middle of nowhere. In some ways, he wished Steve would go apeshit and give him the excuse to fight back. Instead, Steve always seemed pathetic, like Jaret was kicking a little puppy if he spoke against Steve.

"Do you have any pants I could have?" He motioned down his body.

Jaret ignored the fact Steve clutched his ass when he reached into the trunk, or how he moved his hand around to the front of his crotch. Steve handed him a pair of his football practice shorts. Too big for Jaret, he cinched them tight with the drawstring.

"Why are we out here?" Jaret asked, his confidence returning with the pants. "Kidnapping is a felony. I should report you. What the fuck is wrong with you?"

"Babe, we needed to talk. I didn't know how else to get you to listen. You're so distant. So hard to reach. You were never like this before."

Jaret almost began his standard litany about the end of their relationship, blah, blah, blah, when he remembered his current predicament. He had pants. But still no jewels or transportation.

"Here," Steve reached into the trunk. "I got you a present. I bet he never got you this. See? I know you better than anyone." Steve held up a poster signed by Mika, from his first album. "Do you like it?"

"Steve." Jaret took a deep breath. "I can't accept gifts from you anymore." Damn. He had nothing else to say. The problem being Steve's mental illness blocked out reality. Jaret found he could reason better with Darth. Despite adding kidnapping to the list of charges against his former boyfriend, Jaret sensed that a power beyond Steve's control intensified his actions.

"Here's the thing." Steve moved closer, placing his hand on Jaret's shoulder. "We were meant to be together. You even promised as much. I'm not giving up. No way. I know you better than anyone. See? That's why I knew to get you the Mika poster, right? I'll make up for the missed concert, sweetie. I promise."

"That's not the problem." Jaret pulled away.

Steve stayed close behind. "Jaret, don't make me do something more drastic."

"What?" Jaret whipped around and looked at Steve. "Don't do the suicide routine again. It doesn't work."

Steve shook his head. "Henrik. The ghosts. I know about them. They'll help me because they were there at the beginning with us. They'll understand."

Jaret glared at Steve. "Are you fucking nuts?"

"You know I'm right."

"Uh, no. You're wrong. Let's see, Henrik tossed you around the attic like a rag doll and almost threw you out the window to your death. So, your brilliant plan is to call on him. He's real keen on gay people too. Loves how we suck cock. Jesus. You've gone nuts." An idea hit Jaret in the chest like a ton of bricks. Henrik. What if Henrik, despite being locked in Jaret's magical box, had seized control of Steve? Did Henrik explain the aura Jaret sensed around Steve?

Steve started to speak, but suddenly fell to the ground in pain. Anthony stood above him, clenching Steve's shoulder with one hand with enough power to send him to his knees. Steve passed out.

"Is he okay?" Jaret asked.

"You're welcome for the rescue," Anthony said and pulled Jaret into his arms.

Jaret laughed. "Oh, yeah. Thanks. But you didn't kill him, did you? Is he okay?"

"Physically, he'll survive. Mentally, he's far gone. You have to go the police."

"I think it's more complicated. Anyway, I don't want to deal with him. Can you just take us wherever we were going on our date like none of this happened?"

Jaret grabbed the sack with his gems, and sure enough, Steve had stolen the magic bag they were in, complete with the embroidered Bachmann crest.

Anthony stared at Jaret with disbelief. "You're incredible. He kidnapped you. Stole your fucking pants. He stalks you every day, but you want to leave him here and go about life as usual? I should kill him before he escalates the situation further."

Jaret reached out and touched Anthony's arm. "I'm not afraid of him. And I know his behavior is bad. But the danger comes from magic, not him. I think Henrik got hold of him. He needs protection too."

"How long have you suspected?"

Jaret pondered a moment before answering. "I had a sense of something off for a while, but until tonight I never pinpointed what. Leave him here. He'll wake up and go home. Give me time to figure out how to handle the problem. I can."

"You promise you will?"

"Yes!" Jaret nodded. "I don't enjoy pantsless kidnappings. Well, unless maybe you snatched me."

After more convincing, Anthony took Jaret home first to retrieve a new pair of pants and then they went on their movie date.

At home before bed, Anthony reiterated his feelings about Steve. "This situation is more serious than ever before. Especially if Henrik figured out a way to manipulate him. You need to do something, and fast. No more bullshit or dodging the danger."

"I know. But he still didn't hurt me. He could have taken me to some dark location and cut me into pieces."

Anthony shot back, "The next time he might."

"Well, Henrik would like to. But I beat him before, and I'll beat him again."

*

Which brought Jaret back to the shore of Lake Michigan and this weekend, when Anthony got Jaret out of Evanston, away from Steve, and to a weekend away with his vampire friends.

As dusk finally set, Jaret walked back to the rental unit. Darth headed for the little backyard of the cottage so Jaret followed her. He sat on a bench to let her play for a while. Leaning against the back wall of the house, he looked into the trees and breathed in their peaceful presence.

"Where's Xavier?" Jaret heard Anthony ask through the window above him.

"Still asleep." Thomas answered. "After all these years, he still can't take any hint of sunlight. I thought he might outgrow his sensitivity someday. All of those angels and gods who talk to him in his sleep must wear him out. They keep him there to the bitter end."

"I wish they'd come to me with an answer about what to do with Jaret."

Jaret felt guilty about overhearing the conversation. On the other hand, he wanted to hear what Anthony had to say and had no intention of leaving the spot.

"Where is he?" Thomas asked.

"He left a note to say he's on the beach."

"Good. You and I need to talk." Jaret heard a chair scrape across the floor after Thomas spoke. "You're wrong. You're misinterpreting this whole matter. As usual, you're taking the ethic to some asinine extreme."

"What do you mean?"

Thomas sighed. "I'll keep the concept simple and in twenty-first century terms for you. You're utterly, totally, and completely fucked in the head."

"Nice. Am I supposed to interpret your meaning?"

"My idea doesn't require interpretation. Remember, you're not the only one on the Council anymore. We've helped you for almost two centuries now. Imagine. You're not solely responsible for interpreting the texts and the magic. You're making yourself into a martyr again for no reason. None whatsoever. Xavier and I checked the documents too. Xavier sent them to Catherine and Harriet for their advice. None of us believe the rigid reading you gave to the passage prohibiting the turning of Jaret. Is my meaning clear to you?"

"He's dangerous. You can't deny that the ethic warns about the danger."

"The law says to monitor a witch before making them into a vampire. I believe you've monitored him a lot, complete with an anal probe. And the ethic says to put tight controls on their power and that such people make ideal candidates for the Council, because of their very power."

"The one who almost destroyed us had such ability too. I can't risk everyone else for my own foolish gain."

"You're impossible."

Jaret heard someone smash a table and likely obliterate the furniture.

"That should help," Anthony said. "Destroy the place. Your temper always solved so many problems in the past. It usually leads to brilliant insights."

"You're pissing me off!" Thomas screamed. "Why can't you allow yourself to find this happiness? I know how much you love him, so don't try some nonsensical denial. He adores you. He's a good person. He's a risk worth taking."

"And what if we're wrong? What if the combination of his vampiric power and the magic he gets from those gems overwhelms his very being? He's still learning the extent of his ability! I suspect he has magic within him without the aid of the jewels, but he doesn't realize it yet. We could put him at risk. Or give him too much power to handle. Do you know what would happen to me if he died because of my changing him? I realize I'm not alone on the Council anymore. But we all need to follow the guidelines. Those laws were created for a reason and based on centuries of experience."

"That's where you're wrong and always have been. The Council should use the guidelines in making their decisions. Note, you called them guidelines. Not laws. Or rules. Or regulations. What worked before Christ was born may very well be different here in the twenty-first century. Give the entire Council control over this matter. Don't make this decision on your own."

The two men went silent for several minutes before Anthony spoke again. "Even if we could overcome this problem, there's still the matter of his family. He'd never leave them behind to become a vampire. He'd end up wanting to turn them all. Even you have to agree we could never do that."

"Let him make the decision. Or at least for him to make one with you. He's not a child."

"He's barely twenty-one!"

"And lived a thousand lives already. He holds more responsibility for his family than anyone should at his age. Trust him. Trust your instinct. You know, the one guiding you to love him with so much passion."

"Um, guys?" Jaret heard Xavier suddenly speak right above him. He glanced up to see Xavier smiling down and leaning out the window. "For two vampires with super senses and extra caution about your safety, you can be dithering idiots. I do believe the subject of your conversation overheard at least part of what you said."

Next, Anthony peeked out the window, followed by Thomas, who roared with laughter.

Twenty: Come to Jesus, or to a Council

24 MARCH 2011
Saugatuck, Michigan

"Will you get up here?" Anthony called to Jaret. Thomas continued to lean out the window and laugh beside him. Xavier winked at Jaret, who sat red-faced, embarrassed at having been caught listening to their conversation. Jaret called to Darth and went inside, soon joining them in the small living room.

"We'd better leave you two alone. I think you have something to talk about." Xavier stood near the door as he spoke, motioning for Thomas to follow.

Thomas arched his brow. "But if we leave, Anthony will spin this in some deranged way again. Shouldn't we be here to help? It's a Council matter, after all."

Xavier's eyes grew wide as he stared at Thomas. "Their relationship is none of your business."

"Well, it most certainly is. As a member of the Council and this lunatic's best friend," he pointed at Anthony, "I have an oblig—"

Before Thomas could finish, Xavier swooped across the room and clamped his hand over his mouth. "Enough. Come with me. We'll hunt. You'll enjoy feeding. If you're really good, you'll get lucky in the woods somewhere."

Xavier led Thomas out of the cottage and said goodbye, leaving Anthony and Jaret in an awkward silence.

Jaret anticipated Anthony moving closer. Whenever faced with some tension between them, Anthony tended to close the distance and provide reassurance that whatever the problem, they still had their deep connection. Instead, Anthony sat opposite in a lounge chair and motioned for Jaret to take a seat across the room. Jaret's stomach did a summersault.

"Well, can we talk?" Jaret asked when the silence became too much.

Anthony fidgeted in his seat before launching out of it and pacing. He stopped and looked down at Jaret. "Nothing's changed. There's no point."

"Thomas disagreed. He said there's a chance—"

"Thomas speaks before he thinks. I'm sorry you had to hear him because he gave you false hope. He's wrong."

"He said the others agreed with him." Jaret heard the whining in his voice and hated the sound, yet desperation began to well within him. The gems tingled a warning in his pocket.

"They're all young." Anthony returned to his seat. "They don't understand the vampiric forces and documents the same way I do. I've taught them much. But they didn't live through the war. They still need to work to understand how to protect ourselves."

Jaret's palms sweated. "You don't trust me. Do you?"

Anthony shook his head. "Not true. Listen to me. You're a powerful witch. You admitted you still learn new capabilities with those jewels every week. You're going to become stronger and stronger. You possess a gift—a special gift." Anthony gazed out the window, refusing to make eye contact. "Vampire magic is at least as strong. If we placed you on the Council, your power would double. You'd be a dangerous weapon. I'm not saying you'd turn on us. But power corrupts. I can't know what the strength might do to your body. No one with such strength has ever been created. I'm afraid the transformation might kill you. I won't stand by and watch you die."

At least Anthony had issued an official refusal to convert Jaret. No more ambiguity or leading him on. Jaret sat crestfallen. He'd always suspected Anthony would never turn him. Still, he had hoped. Foolishly, perhaps, but what else could you do when young and in love with a vampire?

"Besides, you wouldn't leave your family."

"I know." No matter how much they argued about their future, magic, or converting Jaret, Anthony always won when he reminded Jaret about his family. Try as he might to envision an eternity with Anthony, he could never bring himself to the moment of disappearing from his mom, dad, brother, or sister. Perhaps Jenn more than any of them. Every time Xavier mentioned his relationship with Catherine, Jaret became jealous they had forever together.

Jaret patted the couch and called to Darth, who jumped up beside him. He pulled her close. "I guess we had to deal with this, huh? I mean, it's not like we could run from this conversation forever. I suppose it's good."

Anthony glanced at Jaret with an incredulous look. "What good could come from this conversation?" His harsh words silenced Jaret. "That the talk forced us to admit the truth?" Anthony rolled his eyes. "I liked hiding from reality far better. You still don't get what this means, do you?"

"Get what?" Jaret placed his chin on the top of Darth's head.

"Reality."

"I can't be a vampire. You've been telling me for months. I got it."

Anthony shook his head and got up to pace again. "I take the blame. For letting us go this far. I'm an idiot. I accept responsibility. I knew all along the right course of action. It was just..." He paused, for the first time looking at Jaret. "You so utterly seduced me. I'm sorry."

"Sorry for what? What's going on?" Jaret reached for Anthony.

Before he touched him, Anthony walked away and stared out the front window at Lake Michigan while Jaret sat holding Darth on his lap. The room swirled around Jaret, and then the gems pulsated a relaxing charm. Somehow, they knew to try to calm him.

"We'll be boyfriends. One human, one vampire" Jaret spoke in a whisper. "Okay? Cool. At least we have our situation defined. I mean, I won't get old and fat and gross for a while, right?"

Jaret stopped when Anthony turned to him with pity written on every inch of his face. "We love each other.

Right? I mean, our love is what makes anything worthwhile."

"I forget sometimes just how young you are." Anthony stopped in front of him. He still refused any physical contact. "The solution seems so easy to you, yes? Just continue the subterfuge. Pretend all is well and good with the world. Do you understand what would happen?"

Prestidigitation, now the word slammed into Jaret's life once again. Anthony sounded so cold and calculated, nothing like Jaret had seen before. "What's happening?"

"If we continued this charade, we'd fall deeper and deeper in love."

"Isn't that the point?"

"No, it's not the point. We'd get closer and closer, until I watched you die. Do you think I could live through losing you? What's the point? You need to live your life as a witch and fulfill the Bachmann legacy. I need to continue my service on the Vampire Council. We have two separate roles on this earth. As deeply as we intertwined our lives, so we must separate them. At once. For the betterment of both of us."

Jaret cried. He grabbed Darth for comfort, who looked up and licked his cheek. When Anthony approached, Darth growled. He held up his hands and backed away.

Anthony remained quiet while Jaret composed himself and stood to leave the room.

"Where are you going?"

"Why do you care?"

"Don't leave this way."

Jaret stared at the ground, bewildered. "You don't get to have a lot of say in how I leave. Because you left first, not me. We're through. I'm not daft. I get it. You're the big councilman in charge. I have a hard time tossing what we had aside like some shitty old used piece of toilet paper. No problem for you. You use a vampire patience thing. For you, in vampire time and all, it's probably like we knew each other for five or ten minutes. Had a good fuck and thanks for the come. Fine. I had a different experience. So don't try to dictate any terms of separation now. Don't worry. I'm not a stalker, either. Cheerio." Jaret mocked a British accent as he turned and walked out of the room.

He held himself together until he got to the room he shared with Anthony, then slammed the door shut after Darth came in behind him. He cried with her in his arms for a long time, before slowly starting to pack his belongings. No way he wanted to stay in this vampire-infested shithole another minute. Time to get back to reality. To history lessons, to classes, to drinking on the weekends with Brady. A good dose of reality would do him good.

He had packed his bag and started to wonder how he might get back to Chicago when he heard a soft knock at the door.

Twenty-One: Xavier

24 MARCH 2011
Saugatuck, Michigan

Jaret ignored the first knock and continued packing his things to leave Michigan and the vampires behind forever. Then someone pounded on the door.

"Go away," Jaret said to whomever was bothering him. He never wanted to see Anthony again.

The beating got louder so Jaret locked the door. "Does 'go away' mean something different in vampire than English?"

He heard someone chuckle softly on the other side. Then the lock opened on its own, and Xavier stepped in. Xavier, with his protective and comforting nature. Always encouraging. Always understanding Jaret on a level he had no way of explaining.

"In vampire"—Xavier said as he stepped into the room—"it means barge in anyway." He stepped over Jaret's bag and sat on the end of the bed. "Going somewhere?"

"Home. Oh, can you get my keys from Anthony? The last time I left them with a boyfriend it didn't turn out so good."

Xavier tilted his head and looked at Jaret. "You're a smart-ass. I like that in a man. But I'm afraid getting your keys back won't do any good. He could get in anyway. You might as well save yourself the trouble."

Jaret sat next to Xavier. "You know, I'm partially being funny right now as a defense mechanism?"

"Partially?"

"Maybe a little more. The point being, I'm not really okay with chatting. I'm holding myself together not to embarrass myself."

Xavier leaned back on his elbows. "Ah. So I see."

"You know he broke up with me?"

"I heard as much."

"So why are you here?"

Xavier sat up and patted Jaret on the knee. "One, to take you home. You're my friend. Two, to offer as much comfort as possible. You know he loves you, as do I. I realize neither is worth very much right now."

Jaret gulped back another wave of tears. "I don't want to do the vampire running fast thing. It upsets Darth."

"Then I'll drive."

Without more conversation, Xavier helped Jaret finish packing and then drove him back to Chicago and toward his apartment. As they drove along Lakeshore Drive, Xavier spoke. "I don't believe in false hope or saying things to make people feel better. Such attempts always seem to end badly for everyone concerned."

"Good. Because I don't want to hear any nonsense."

"Let me say one thing, please?"

Jaret glanced at Xavier and nodded.

"You're a special person. Whatever your fate or future, I wish you well. I'm going to give you a way to contact me if you ever need anything. You're my friend. I won't abandon you."

"Anthony said he was my lover and look where his promise got me."

They pulled up outside Jaret's apartment. Xavier turned off the car and sat back.

"I don't expect you to understand or accept this. But maybe you'll hear me out. He hurts. Despite his gruff exterior and in-charge persona, he has deep emotional wounds. He has a hard time admitting them. It's been centuries since he lost his lover, and still the loss burns inside him. He operates out of fear much of the time. Fear of himself. Fear of being hurt and losing everything again."

Jaret tried to sound sympathetic, but he only had bitter left. "Well, nice self-fulfilling prophesy."

Xavier grinned. "True enough. I'm asking you not to give up."

"You know, Thomas and you both have told me the same kind of thing in different ways a number of times. I tried, see? I tried to wait out Anthony's issues. But *he* dumped me, remember?"

"Don't burn any bridges."

Jaret got out of the car and put Darth on her leash. He grabbed his bag and leaned back in the car window. "Seems like he already torched every available bridge."

"I'm here if you need me."

Jaret nodded and turned back to his apartment. Sometimes life seemed a lot more doable with nothing but his dog, his books, and his own little world.

In his living room, he went right to the stereo, popped in his iPod, and turned to the Mika song he'd played over and over in his mind during the entire ride home. In "By the Time," Mika sang about a lover who sneaks off as he sleeps. Mika laments his despair to wake up to find his lover gone without a word. He wonders what on earth he's going to do.

How had Mika so gotten into Jaret's head? How had Mika seen the exact desolation consuming Jaret, years after he wrote the song? Jaret listened to the song over and over and over. The misery of the lyrics gave him comfort.

Part Five:
Devastation

Twenty-Two: Jenn

9 May 2011

Chicago, Illinois

After Anthony unceremoniously dumped him, Jaret moved forward as best he could. He concentrated on doing well in every class, on every paper, and in each and everything he did at school. He spent hours alone at his apartment with Darth, reading recommended books by his professors, choosing his own additional studies to undertake, and avoiding the real world as he lost himself in academic pursuits.

To be sure, his close group of friends never allowed him to fall too far into an abyss. Brady in particular dragged him to the bars, though Jaret had no appetite for hitting on guys or for them hitting on him.

"You don't have to stick their tongue down your throat or let them blow you in the bathroom to enjoy the moment." Brady held Jaret by the wrist as he pulled him onto the dance floor late one Friday night.

At first, Jaret barely wiggled his butt and tried to pretend he had to go get another drink. Brady grabbed

Jaret's hips and pulled him close, smiling and grinding into him. Jaret had enough of a buzz to laugh, wrap his arms around Brady's neck, and grind back for a minute before the two twirled apart and raised their arms in the air.

Both whooped when a dance remix of Mika's song blasted onto the dance floor.

When they stopped to refresh their drinks, Jaret smiled.

"Thanks for making me come out tonight. Letting loose on the dance floor released some tension."

"Lots of sweaty, happy, and half-naked gay men will chill a guy."

"Whatever." Jaret rolled his eyes. "I needed the release."

"Right." Brady held up his glass for a toast. "Sometimes friends are for getting you away. To remind us in the midst of misery good times will be just around the corner." Brady pinched Jaret on the butt. "Now, more dancing!"

In addition to Brady, other friends met with him for various events or lunch, always cheering Jaret up with their support and presence.

And having kept his mom and dad out of the loop from the beginning about Anthony, they nonetheless gave him a loving reprieve when they called to catch up or to congratulate him for doing well on another assignment.

Jaret could barely contain his excitement as he waited for his mom to answer the phone. "Mom, guess what?"

"What? You sound excited."

"I am! Dr. Engelder said I'd have no problem getting into a good graduate school!"

"A surprise to you but not to us. We already knew you'd accomplish your goals! Oh, wait a second." Jaret heard his dad ask something in the background. "It's Jaret. His professor said he'll get into graduate school when he applies."

This time Jaret could hear what his dad said. "Of course! We know he will."

"Well, good job, honey. We're proud of you. Oh, Lincoln wants to say hello."

"Hey brat." Jaret smiled at his brother's crass greeting. "I promise I'm coming to Chicago soon to see you."

"Yeah, yeah, yeah. That's what you always say."

"Seriously, I am. I gotta go. Here's Mom."

But Jenn remained his lifeline to sanity and love more than anyone else. She came for a visit and insisted they would worry most about having fun and exploring the city of Chicago. Tonight, they sat in a coffee shop, people watching and joking about anything and everything.

Jaret stifled a laugh when yet another guy approached Jenn.

"Hey, you're so beautiful." The guy stood beside Jenn and smiled.

Jenn nodded toward Jaret. "I'm having a private moment with my brother, so thank you for the compliment, and you can move along."

He frowned and walked away without another word.

Jenn wrinkled her nose after being hit on for the third time. Not since before Anthony dumped him had Jaret enjoyed a weekend so much, nor had he laughed so hard. He felt as if eons had passed since he'd let himself embrace life's pleasures. All because of Jenn.

Jenn, of course, knew the entire tale about Anthony and comforted him whenever he needed her steady presence and undying love. "Don't get sad on me. Unless you want to talk about *him* again."

Jaret shook his head. "No, I'm good. Really. Today has been a lot of fun. Maybe I'm jealous about all the hotties drooling all over you tonight."

Jenn punched him in the arm. "Oh my God, look at the guy over there! Who does he remind you of?"

Jaret glanced across the street and spotted a guy wearing a cowboy hat, which stuck out as rather odd in Chicago. "No idea."

"J.R."

"Wow, he does look like J.R. I can't believe Mom and Dad allowed us to watch *Dallas* while we were growing up. Pretty heavy content."

Jenn snorted, almost choking on her coffee. "But Mom loved the reruns. We had all the DVDs and watched some of the episodes over and over."

"Look over there. It's Han Solo." This time Jaret pointed to someone across the street who looked like one of their favorite *Star Wars* characters.

"Wonder if his dog's name is Chewbacca?"

They grew quiet for a moment, so Jaret blew into his coffee to cool it. Despite what Jaret had said, Anthony lingered in his mind. Though almost two months had passed since their breakup, Jaret had failed to move forward and push him from his memory. He had no inclination of becoming a Steve clone and stalking Anthony. He held no demented fantasies about entrapping Anthony in their love life forevermore against his will.

But no reality had forced him to forget their love either. Too strong and passionate for the months they'd spent together, Anthony lurked in his mind and pulled him into melancholy all too often. He loved Anthony with his entire heart, and Anthony loved him as much, or so he claimed. Those wounds would take a while to heal.

"Should we head to a bar?" Jenn asked.

Jaret grinned. "You're not of age."

"Wasn't yesterday either. But the combination of my charming smile and fake ID works every time."

While Jaret had never tried such a thing before he turned twenty-one, Jenn did all the time. No use trying to stop her. At least Jaret could protect her if they went together. "Which one?"

"Don't care. As long as it's a gay bar. Less chance of getting hit on there."

"Didn't work last night."

"Shit! What the hell was a straight guy doing in there, anyway? He wouldn't leave me alone."

Walking toward the L and back to the safer climes of the gay bars, Jenn and Jaret laughed at her misfortune.

"Oh! There's another bar! Let's go there!" Jenn tried to pull Jaret across the street.

"Instead of going out, why don't we head back to my place and watch the Mika concert I wanted you to see?" Jaret glanced at Jenn to see her reaction.

Jenn smiled and put her arm through his. "Sounds great. If we can get a bottle of Jack to take home."

"Already in the cabinet."

A quick ride to Rogers Park, and Jaret and Jenn took Darth outside before popping some popcorn, making drinks, and settling in for the concert. Jaret sang along, feeling uplifted by the music and dreaming of someday attending a live Mika concert. Jaret and Jenn danced together to a couple of tunes and then sat up talking for several hours before fatigue got the better of both of them.

The next morning, the gems glowed oddly next to Jaret's bed when he woke up. He rubbed his eyes and touched one to get a sense of why they had become so active. Holding a diamond ring in his palm and closing his eyes, he saw premonitions of a dark force in his future.

Unfortunately, Jaret had yet to master the art of seeing the future very clearly with the Bachmann jewels. Sometimes they gave him exact warnings, other times vague portents about avoiding a location or person, and then there were these moments of a fuzzy feeling of danger ahead. He remembered they had given him this ambiguous foreboding the week before Anthony broke up with him, but the image today was darker and more sinister. But danger to whom? Where? And how?

Jaret ignored the gems as best he could as he drove Jenn to the airport.

"So, you ready for the family reunion?" Jaret asked. Instead of flying back to Colorado, Jenn had a ticket to Omaha where their mother and father would pick her up and drive her to Fremont. The annual Bachmann family reunion was taking place over the weekend with everyone in attendance except Jaret.

"I'm excited to see everyone," Jenn answered. "But I still call bullshit that you're not going. Everyone wants you there. You shouldn't be allowed to get out of the reunion. I mean, what's the point of a Bachmann reunion without the family witch?"

Jaret smiled. "I know. I really hate missing everyone being together. It's the first time I won't be there. I have too much to do before graduation, and the timing is awful."

Jenn stared at him. "You know, hiding from everyone won't make you feel any better about Anthony."

"That's not the problem," Jaret lied.

"Whatever. You're already on thin ice with everyone for prohibiting them from coming to your graduation, just because you're going to grad school and have more graduations in the future. They wanted to be there. You don't want to deal with your feelings. So you're not ready to face a bunch of drunk, happy family members. Fine. I'm not trying to make you go. I can't. But don't try all the crap on me because I see right through your nonsense."

Jaret drove silently for a while, wondering how to respond. Jenn pinpointed the problem. He hardly felt like putting on a good face for the family and pretending all was well with the world when he still had so much healing to do.

Outside the airport, Jaret got out and helped Jenn lift her suitcase out of the trunk. The gems in his pocket whirled to life, once again with forewarning of danger. Jaret hugged Jenn tightly. "Thanks so much for this weekend. You helped more than you can imagine."

"You'll get through this. I promise. I love you."

Jaret clung to Jenn a moment longer than their usual goodbye, worried somehow the jewels indicated something about Jenn. He had no idea, though, what to say or do about their alert. At the doorway, Jenn turned around and flashed her big smile at Jaret as she waved goodbye.

Jaret cried on the way home, wishing he and Jenn had more time and regretting more than ever his decision not to attend the family reunion. Still, he hardly felt up to the trip. Jenn had tried to persuade him getting away might do him good, to be around the people who loved him.

Jaret played some Mika in the background as he grabbed his phone and fell onto the couch. He dialed his parent's cell phone as Darth wandered over to the side of the couch and put her snout on his stomach.

"Hey, Mom. It's me. I just dropped Jenn off at the airport." He listened to his mom's usual questions about how their weekend had gone and if they had behaved. "We tried to behave. And we had a great time, anyway. Where you at?"

"Somewhere in the middle of Nebraska."

"Looking forward to the reunion?"

"Of course. You know the Bachmanns, plenty of drinking and catching up. Plus the annual putt-putt golf tournament. Lincoln's still upset you won't be there to be his partner."

Jaret heard his brother in the background. "Yeah, you dork. I have to be with Dad instead. I'm doomed."

As he chatted with his mom a while longer, Jaret again noticed the gems tingling in his pocket. He looked over to see if the other jewels had done anything and shot up straight in his chair at what he saw. The jewels from the jewelry box had floated out and hovered in the air around the iron box in which he had jailed Henrik.

Jaret chatted a few more minutes with his mom and then his father, all the while feeling something horrendous awaited his future. He hung up and got the jewels out of his pocket, noticing a higher energy level in them than usual. He released them, and they too drifted through the air and joined their fellow gems in a circle over Henrik's box.

Jaret went into the office and made sure the golden key, the one way to unlock the magical box in which he had trapped his angry ancestor, sat safely in the locked drawer. He touched the key but felt nothing.

Next he returned to the living room, trying to see into the jewels for a better answer. Something about Henrik alarmed them, but the warning made no sense to Jaret. Only the golden key could unlock the box, and Jaret had no intention of releasing Henrik during his lifetime. He cast a couple of spells. Nothing told him anything more than what he already knew.

Jaret shouted in frustration. "Get the fuck back in the box, then. Stupid fucking things. What good are vague warnings about nothing?"

The gems floated through the air and replaced themselves neatly in the jewelry case.

Jaret's phone rang, distracting him from the problem.

"Hey," Jenn said on the other end. "Just got to Omaha. Have a good weekend. I promise we'll be thinking about you."

"Thinking about you too. Have fun. I love you."

"Love you too."

After he hung up, Jaret glanced back at his jewels, which glowed brightly. *Shit*.

Twenty-Three: One More Attempt

10 MAY 2011
Chicago, Illinois

Jaret tossed and turned throughout the night in a restless sleep of worry. In one dream, he saw his family in distress, in another something came after Darth, and then a dark force stalked after him. In other nightmares, he relived his breakup with Anthony over and over, the last time waking up as he screamed. Darth licked his face in worry.

Jaret glanced at the alarm clock and moaned. Five a.m. He'd never get back to sleep before he had to get up. He wished he had another hour of sleep. He rubbed his eyes and reached down to pat Darth on the head.

After fumbling around his apartment and getting a drink of water, he peed and dressed for an extremely early morning jog. At least few people littered the path, so he did not fear any hooligan football jocks because they preferred the night.

Jaret decided to spend some time trying to figure out what the gems meant to tell him. He'd hoped his dreams would offer a clue, but nope, not unless his entire world was about to implode, or the earth was coming to an end. His nightmares had signaled danger at every turn.

Which left him without any answers.

After showering and eating breakfast, Jaret fed Darth and sat at his desk with the box of jewels in front of him. He got their basic message because he had experienced their power a number of times. Something disturbed them. Not immediately, as in their sensing a present danger, but more as if an aura hung in the atmosphere predicting future trouble.

When he touched them, whether by picking one up or sticking his hands into their midst, they tingled and hummed.

He attempted to see into them as he had when he had determined to find out the truth about Anthony and had discovered his vampirism. The gems offered nothing but blackness behind his closed eyes.

Before he got angry again and tossed all of the jewels in the garbage, Jaret went into the living room. He jumped from the buzz of his intercom. Setting his book aside, he answered.

"Hi. FedEx with a package you need to sign for. Can you come down?"

"Sure."

Jaret grabbed his keys and headed toward the elevator, at a loss for what anyone would send him by such official means.

Hoping at least for a hot delivery guy, he instead thanked the portly middle-aged gentleman and took the thin envelope up to his apartment. As was her custom,

Darth insisted she sniff the new goods the minute Jaret came through the door.

"TSA on the job. Thanks, girl. I'm safer than an airplane." Jaret scratched Darth behind the ears and went back to his office.

He set two gems on top of the envelope to see what they detected. Nothing, though their slight prickling continued as from before.

Nothing supernatural alarmed Jaret, yet he sat staring at the envelope for a moment without opening it. Had Steve sent something creepy? Maybe Steve invented a new and scarier way to stalk him. Jaret reached for the envelope and tore at the red strip.

His heart rate sped up when he saw the signature. A horrendous gift from Steve would have been much easier to take than a letter from Anthony.

Not that Jaret had come any closer to getting over their relationship. At least the limited communication had numbed him. He envisioned and dreamt of a time when Anthony invoked nothing but a dull memory. He could still see Anthony vividly when he closed his eyes and almost feel his arms wrapped around his waist. But he'd forgotten the masculine smell of Anthony's cologne until he detected the faint scent on this piece of paper.

Jaret closed his eyes, wondering whether or not to read the missive. He wished he had Jenn's cold detachment whenever her relationships ended. She dismissed the guy from her mind and moved on, never wanting to hear from him or deal with him again. If he called, she dismissed the attempt. If he left a message, she deleted it without listening. The same with any texts or emails. She could vanquish someone from her life.

She'd rip this up. Or throw the letter in the garbage. But no, Jaret read the note.

My Dearest Jaret,

I won't torture you by spilling out my heart in this letter. I know you must hurt as much as I do. Since nothing can change our status, I see no reason to dwell upon the misery.

Still, I think of you often and wish you nothing but the best. You deserve the most in life. Money hardly solves anyone's problems. It never has. But cash can make things easier. I have more than anyone deserves. As a way of apologizing and trying to communicate how much you meant, and still mean to me, please accept this token of my love.

There is one condition. I have sources who informed me Mika intends a European tour in Summer 2013. Place this check in the bank and use the money for whatever you need. You will never want for money again in your life. But you are required to attend a concert and spend as much time as possible in Europe. Take Brady or Jenn, or perhaps both, with you.

I wish things could be different. Life doesn't always work the way we wish.

Love, Anthony

Jaret slapped in anger at the tear trickling down his cheek. Why did he still feel so much passion for this asshole? Jenn had called Anthony every name in the book, yet Jaret defended him because he loved him. The letter, though, hit below the belt.

Jaret's trust fund provided more than enough to keep him comfortable all the way through graduate school. If he did well, life as a professor promised a comfortable enough living. But imagine what he could do with two million dollars. He wondered if he had to pay taxes on vampire hush money? This check came with no instructions. Typical Anthony, thinking everything is so clear and easy. Just spread around some money and all will be well.

Jaret's hands shook as he clutched the check in front of him. How could he explain the wealth to his parents? And he thought coming out to them sucked. Seriously, how did anyone deal with this much money?

He pondered all his questions for a long time before sitting down to respond. He had no idea how to get a letter directly to Anthony, but Xavier had given him his contact information. Jaret could get a letter to Anthony through Xavier.

Dear Anthony,

My instincts tell me to begin this letter by telling you what an absolute and utter asshole you are. To blast you for arrogance, and to warn you to get the hell out of my life.

My heart, unfortunately, tells me otherwise.

I don't know what to do with so much money. Vampire blood must teach you a lot you never learn in human life. I almost fed the check to Darth. She likes to rip shit up, remember?

Okay, that was bitter. Sorry. You probably already figured out the snotty tone is because I love you.

I'll take the money. Just not with any conditions. I'm not doing some tour of Europe to see Mika. You and Steve have so fucked up all my dreams about seeing him live, I think I better kill the fantasy. I'll listen to him and enjoy his sounds instead.

You wouldn't want to give me another chance, would you? I could slice off an arm or leg to weaken myself, to keep my power under control. I still don't get why Thomas and Xavier have a different idea about our dating and what the ethic dictates. Your explanation always sounded like bullshit.

I wish you'd told me I was too immature for you. Or humans smelled too bad. Or you liked big buff guys, not nelly little twinks.

Do me a favor and just lie to the next guy, okay? Don't fuck with him like you did me.

Seriously, can I have another chance? Please?

Maybe you'll come back now you can see you pushed me into schizophrenia. Give this letter to any psychologist, and they'll admit me to the nut farm in a nanosecond. Nuts as Steve, you're probably thinking. Oh well.

I love you too. Come back to me.

Jaret put the letter in an envelope, sealed it, and added a quick note to Xavier. A hundred times on the way to the mailbox he almost ripped it up and threw it in the gutter. Should have, really. He laughed at his stupid pining. Like a lost teenager after a first breakup in a super bad romance movie. Like Bella being a dumb fuck for Edward. If anything, such neediness probably chased Anthony further away. Way to act like a twelve-year-old.

But spelling out his feelings in writing was therapeutic. He managed to pack a lot of twists and bipolar emotions into a few paragraphs. He held no delusions Anthony would return to him because of the letter. Only a fool like Steve would think such a thing. At the same time, Jaret let out how he felt and directed the intense emotion at the appropriate target.

To further defy Anthony, Jaret listened to Lady Gaga when he got home and not Mika.

He spent the rest of the day feeling better. He had released the emotion trapped inside. He also decided to keep the money. Placing the check in a safe location in his office, he talked to Darth. "If my heart's gonna hurt forever because of him, at least I'll have lots of money. Right? Being rich can't suck. Think of all the Snausages."

Twenty-Four: Steve Sucks

11 MAY 2011
Evanston, Illinois

Jaret thought of Anthony's check in his office first thing in the morning. He'd tossed and turned all night, wondering what to do with so much money. He doubted he could prance into the local bank and deposit the sum without all sorts of alarm bells going off.

Sleeping on the problem seemed to help for he woke with a probable resolution. He would call Xavier for advice. Knowing the sun would keep him from answering, Jaret went ahead and left a message for his friend.

"Xavier, it's Jaret. I have two things. First, I sent a letter to you for Anthony. I don't have any other way to contact him. Could you please deliver it? I attached a note to you too. Also, he gave me a check for a lot of money. I wanted to rip it up. But I could use the cash. I mean, it's a lot. Anyway, I'm really calling for advice about the check. I don't think you can just waltz in and get this check cashed or whatever. I thought maybe vampires knew how to deal with two million dollars at a time. So can—"

Jaret had rambled for too long and Xavier's voice mail cut him off. He hung up and decided to head to class a little early.

He walked because the shining sun uplifted his spirits. The brightness gave him a peace of mind he could weather all the storms and somehow come out stronger. His optimism lasted until he spotted Steve ahead with a group of friends from the football team.

Jaret tried to walk by without acknowledging Steve. At least in broad daylight with students all over the place, he doubted a replay of their lake path attack. He kept his head down and hurried by.

"Jaret!" He heard Steve calling him after half a block. Shit.

He kept walking, pretending not to hear.

"Hey, stop." Steve tugged on his backpack and pulled Jaret to a stop.

Jaret halted. He refused to turn around, so Steve walked around to face him.

Jaret stared at the ground. "People will see you talking to a fag."

"Don't call yourself bad words." Steve put a hand on Jaret's shoulder.

"Okay, so they'll think you're a fag for talking to a gay guy."

Steve's face turned bright red. "Why do you have to be this way?"

"Because you're stalking me. I'm funny about being depantsed and kidnapped."

"Could we have a civilized conversation?"

Jaret remembered to breath. "Doesn't work."

"I love you, babe." Jaret strained to hear Steve's whisper.

Jaret found himself at a loss for words, once again befuddled by Steve's behavior. He walked slowly toward his class building, searching for a way to get rid of Steve but also attempting to figure out the contradictions of Steve's actions and professions of love. A magical force buzzed in the air. "Please don't make us do this again. I have to get to class."

"Will you just meet with me one more time. Today sometime. Please? We can meet in public, so you don't freak out or anything."

Jaret tried to think of a gracious way to get out of a meeting, but his damn sensitivity got the best of him. "The coffee shop in two hours." Jaret pointed to a local place across the street. "I'll have about thirty minutes before I have to go."

Steve smiled too broadly. "See you then."

Jaret jogged off as if late, despite the fact he had almost an hour before class. He found a quiet corner and sat on the floor to read until he wandered off to class and enjoyed one of his favorite professor's lectures. His next class went too quickly despite a couple of dry presentations by other students, and too soon Jaret found himself meandering toward the coffee shop in no hurry to get there.

After kicking at a stone, Jaret sighed, haunted by Steve's latest interaction. He almost thought he would allow Anthony to deal with him if they were still together. He'd finally moved toward thinking he had to do something to cut Steve out for good, like Anthony and Jenn always insisted. He had no stomach for taking this to the police, though. Partially because he did not trust the masculine and racist bastion of civil protection. They might taunt him as had the group of football players. Who needed their bullshit? Besides, he had no evidence of any wrongdoing, other than Steve showing up at the worst possible times or following him around campus. True, Steve had stolen Jaret's Mika ticket, albeit ages ago. Probably beyond some statute of limitations. The thought of some entity controlling Steve crept into his mind, but again no evidence pointed to anything concrete.

Jaret kicked the stone down the sidewalk again. He still felt terrible about the end of their relationship. His foot missed the stone but he kept walking to the crosswalk.

Jaret admitted in some sick and twisted way he did nothing about Steve as a way to assert independence from Anthony. Childish and utterly stupid, true enough. But he couldn't help wanting to defy Anthony's orders. As a boyfriend, Anthony had protected Jaret and made him feel safe. Now his decrees felt paternalistic. Anthony had no say over his life. He voluntarily gave up his voice. So why should Jaret listen to him?

He got his phone out and read the recent text Anthony had sent.

I assume you went to the authorities about Steve?

Nothing else, just an order. *Fuck him.* Jaret shoved his phone back in his pocket.

Never mind the soundness of the advice, or the general concern Jaret himself continued to harbor. He was making a point by handling Steve with caution and also because if magic were involved then no authorities could help anyway.

When Jaret stepped into the shop, Steve got out of his chair and waved Jaret over to a private corner, almost out of view from anyone else. Typically, they had to meet in secret. The clandestine location reminded Jaret of one of the reasons he'd fled their relationship in the first place.

Jaret plopped his backpack to the ground and sat opposite Steve without a word. Steve stared at him awkwardly for what felt like hours, before Jaret fidgeted in his chair. "Um, I'm getting something."

When Jaret moved to get up, Steve shot out of his chair and to Jaret's side. "I've got it. What do you want?"

"You're buying?"

"Of course." Steve spoke like he always bought, which was another sore point. Despite Steve coming from a wealthy family, once they had gotten to college, he insisted they split everything on every date. Meaning sometimes Steve did things without Jaret because Jaret had created a careful budget with his trust fund money. Steve claimed he could never buy because his father would ask who else went along, expecting a date. With a girl. Now Steve wanted to buy?

"Extra-large café mocha." Jaret did not need the caffeine or the caloric intake, but chose the most expensive beverage to be an ass.

Too fast Steve handed Jaret his drink and sat opposite him. More awkward silence. Jaret blew on his coffee, wiggled his leg up and down, and squirmed around. "So, why are we here?"

Steve cocked his head and smiled. Weird. "We're friends. Friends hang together."

Jaret squinted at Steve. "No, we're not. We're ex-lovers. And this is creeping me out. I thought you had something specific to talk about."

"Not really." Steve reached across the table and tried to take Jaret's hand, but Jaret pulled away. "I had a new idea, though. Maybe we could work on being friends. Like, hang and do a few things together. Then, if that goes well, we could try the relationship again. Something like a trial period. So the end isn't so sudden. What do you think?"

A million smart-ass retorts flew through Jaret's mind, all inappropriate and unhelpful but amusing to him. God, why had he decided to take a stand against Anthony on the issue of Steve? He took a sip of his drink to stall for time. "Okay. I've tried to understand. Seriously. I tried to soften this as best I could. I know you don't believe me. But I have. And none of our efforts ever worked. So here." Jaret drew in a deep breath and exhaled. "I don't want to be friends. And there's no way we'll ever date again. Ever. We can argue all we want about the reasons and blame each other, but it's not going to change anything. We're through." Jaret pointed to Steve and then to himself. "Done. Forever. I don't know how to be your friend. And I don't want to be your boyfriend. Being together hurts too much. You've got to move on and stop being all crazy psycho."

Steve had lowered his head and stared at his shoes through Jaret's entire monologue. His face turned bright red even as his eyes seemed to tear. He said nothing and failed to move. After a couple of minutes without a response, Jaret got up, grabbed his coffee and backpack, and left the restaurant without another word. He turned around at the door to see Steve had not moved an inch.

Twenty-Five: Attack

11 MAY 2011
Chicago, Illinois

After the coffee shop drama with Steve, Jaret went home and called Brady.

"Oh, my God. Steve is so nuts. He was pleading again to get back together. Can you come over? I'll buy pizza. I need to relax or something."

Within thirty minutes, Brady buzzed him and walked into the apartment to an enthusiastic greeting from Darth. Brady danced in a circle and squealed to get Darth even more excited. "Crank the Mika and order the pizza, for God's sake! I'll get the Jack out."

Jaret ordered a pepperoni pizza and Brady handed him a drink. He sipped the Jack Daniels and Coke and closed his eyes to feel the burn down his throat. His eyes opened wide. "Holy shit! Did you put any Coke in there?"

Brady bent over laughing. "Not much. It'll help loosen you up faster."

They chatted about classes until the pizza arrived, then turned their attention to baser topics.

"Who's the hottest athlete in America?" Brady asked. "And don't say Steve."

Jaret flipped him off. "The quarterback for San Francisco has my attention. He's not super handsome but there's something so sexual about him. Like, bend me over the sink and fuck my brains out."

Brady almost slammed his head into the table from laughing so hard. "Dude, the alcohol so lets out the Jaret fantasies! Awesome. I'm still in love with Tom Brady. I can't get him out of my system."

Jaret took Brady down to the lobby when he had to go meet a friend to study for a chemistry test. As Brady reached for the door, Jaret whispered, "James Franco is a hotty, in terms of actors."

Brady swung around. "Not! Totally George Clooney."

"You just like older men."

"To each his own." Brady came back and gave Jaret a big hug. "You'll be fine. Promise. Call me if the creep shows up again. Better yet, call the police."

Jaret nodded and smiled, grateful for his friend. He watched Brady dart away then went back up to his apartment. He cleaned a little until he remembered his phone had rung while they ate. He saw Lincoln's number so sat down and listened to his voice mail.

"Hey. It's me. You know, your brother. I gotta talk to you. I've been thinking. Jenn told me more about Steve. Listen, I'm not much for big brother advice and all. But I think she's right, and everyone else does too. Add my name to the list of people who think you need to go to someone about Steve. If not the police, what about the dean of students or something? Be careful."

Jaret smiled. His brother's concern meant a lot. Lincoln's message also forced him to reconsider everything, especially in light of the conversation Steve and he had at the coffee shop. If the situation worried Lincoln, who had such a happy-go-lucky attitude about life, Jaret had to take note. His brother never told him what to do or hovered over him in some protective way.

Plus, Lincoln had given him the best advice yet. Maybe someone at the university could point him in the right direction. If they told him to go to the police, then he had more credibility with the authorities. He determined to make an appointment with the dean of students in the morning.

Jaret lay back on the couch to return Lincoln's call when his buzzer sounded. Wondering if Brady had forgotten something, he went over and answered. "Yo."

He heard the sounds of traffic and a door opening in the background. No other sounds came to him. Not unusual. Either someone *hilarious* had gone by and buzzed people in random or another fool had locked themselves out and just buzzed people until someone let them in.

Jaret decided to have another drink. He went to the kitchen and grabbed a Newcastle before starting back into the living room.

Darth suddenly charged at the door and barked. Two seconds later, someone knocked.

Figuring someone had let Brady in, Jaret answered. As Jaret pulled the door open, he giggled and said, "James Franco" when he almost dropped his glass. Steve stood in the doorway, frowning and drunk.

"Steve," Jaret sputtered.

"Let me in." Steve pushed by and slammed the door shut.

Darth positioned herself next to Jaret, the hair on her back sticking straight up.

Steve pointed at Darth. "Control your fucking dog."

"You're scaring her."

"We need to talk."

Jaret stifled his typical response. He needed the jewels and a safer distance before he said anything else. "Okay." Jaret slid along the wall toward the jewelry box. He cursed himself for having put away all of the gems and closing the box during Brady's visit. They had continued to tingle some warning and got on Jaret's nerves, so he locked the case to take a break from them. The problem being if he locked the box, he had to open the lid again before they could get to him.

Steve slammed his hand against the wall and blocked Jaret's path with his arm. Darth reared up and nipped at him.

"I said to get her under control."

Jaret reached down and grabbed Darth's collar to keep her close for his own safety.

"Let's go in another room or she'll never calm down." Steve turned around and started for Jaret's bedroom. Jaret followed, unsure what else to do. If he lunged for his phone, Steve could get to him before he even touched it. He tried to veer toward the jewelry box, but Steve turned around and clutched Jaret's arm. "No," Steve said and pulled Jaret along.

Despite the gems being locked away, the air was tinged with magical alarms, worrying Jaret even more because Steve was not in control of himself.

Once in Jaret's room, Steve pulled on Jaret and flung him onto the bed. Then he kicked Darth in the head. She fell out of the room, and Steve slammed the door on her as she charged at him baring her fangs. As Darth clawed in desperation at the door and barked, Steve stalked over to Jaret and hovered above him.

He pointed at Jaret. "You're still my boyfriend, and I don't like the way you've been treating me."

Jaret lay frozen. No way he could overpower Steve. Yet he wouldn't sit idly through a rape scene. He'd rather die fighting.

"You gonna fucking talk to me?" Steve reached over and yanked at Jaret's hair, before pulling Jaret's face over and smashed his nose into his crotch. "Don't you miss some of this?"

Jaret was disgusted Steve had gone entirely hard. A headache pounded in Jaret's head at touching Steve, a headache to warn him of a supernatural presence. He could finally confirm a spirit possessed Steve. "You never treated me like this before. This isn't you," Jaret whispered with no hint of the rage coursing through his veins. Steve released him and half fell onto the bed next to him. Jaret did his best to stay calm and ignore Darth as she continued to attack the other side of the door.

"I know. Forgive me." Steve's face still burned crimson, but he lowered his voice. His breath smelled like shitty beer. "I miss you. I don't feel like myself."

Jaret took his opportunity. He dove for the door and had it open before Steve could register what happened.

Darth roared into the room and wrapped her jaw around Steve's leg before Jaret could command her to stop. Jaret pushed himself toward the jewelry chest and fell into the wood. He glanced back to see Steve at the bedroom door, screaming in anger and pain as Darth came along beside him, her teeth implanted in his calf.

Jaret fumbled with the lock and released the gems. Without needing to concentrate or issue specific commands, they whirled into action and surrounded Steve, paralyzing him and revealing some other form around him.

Darth released her grip and scampered to Jaret.

The gems shoved Steve toward the front door. Jaret took the chance of exposure and had the gems imprison Steve until they forced him out of the building and a safe distance down the block.

Within a few seconds, every one of them flew through his bedroom window and back into the chest. Jaret enchanted a spell around his entire apartment to alert him if anyone approached. He locked all his doors and windows, then cast more spells to make sure no one could enter without his reversing the magic.

Only then did he take a deep breath and sit back on the couch. He cried tears of relief and clutched Darth close. He felt around to see if Steve had injured her, but she seemed unharmed.

Steve had had blood tricking down his calf. *So what.* Jaret hardly cared. If he tried to go after Darth or told anyone, then Jaret would file charges against him. He could defend Darth on the grounds of his own self-protection.

Besides, what was with the ghost? A bad aura around Steve? Some other being? The presence of something supernatural lived up to the alarms and fears Jaret thought prompted Steve's behavior all along.

But Jaret intended to file charges anyway. *Fuck going to the dean.* In the morning, Jaret had every intention of heading right for the police station and escalating the tension with Steve to force an end to the stalking and to force the other entity out of hiding. He had to get a restraining order. If Steve ever came back to him, Jaret would threaten to out him all over campus, and he possessed plenty of visual evidence.

Jaret chugged the remainder of his drink and made another one. Darth refused to leave his side, to the point she walked with him the ten feet from the couch to the kitchen. He turned on the television to no avail because nothing distracted his attention.

Instead, he pondered how much life could suck. He never dreamt someone would try to attack him, least of all someone he knew so well. Steve, of all people, whom he had intended to spend the rest of his life with at one time.

At least Steve had failed. And the violence forced Jaret to do what everyone had been pleading for. Enough was enough.

Twenty-Six: Henrik's Revenge

12 MAY 2011
Chicago, Illinois

Jaret's hands trembled when he got to the campus police station the next morning. He knew he had to go to the Chicago Police since the attack had taken place in his apartment but suspected the campus police would be more sympathetic to his story and offer more help.

He was correct. The officer listened and took a lot of notes. She explained what they could do as campus police, and then gave him the number of a friend and colleague who worked with rape victims in Chicago. "She'll be good, I promise."

"Even though I wasn't raped?"

"We're going to make sure he doesn't."

Jaret called the Chicago officer and set up an appointment for the next morning. He promised her over and over not to communicate with Steve, to stay with groups of people, lock his doors, and she felt a lot better when Jaret told her about Darth.

"My dog won't be in trouble for biting him, will she?"

"No. He intruded into your apartment, and she defended you."

Jaret managed to enjoy his one class of the day, feeling he had things moving in the right direction enough to lose himself in the lecture about witch crazes of the 1500s. He called Jenn and filled her in, then left a message for Lincoln.

He last called an enraged Brady who followed him around the rest of the day like a bodyguard. He met Jaret at his building after lunch so they could walk together to campus, then escorted him to each class and greeted him afterward.

"I don't know how the president doesn't punch the Secret Service guards in the face sometimes," Jaret said to Brady as they got a snack in the cafeteria.

"Huh?" Brady took a big bite of an ice cream sandwich.

"You're like having a bodyguard everywhere I go. It gets annoying."

Brady laughed and pointed at Jaret. "It's for your own good. You should feel lucky to have such a charming and cute security detail."

Jaret smiled. "What would you do, anyway, if he showed up? He could beat the crap out of both of us at the same time."

"Sure." Brady nodded. "But I can scream really loud. Want to hear?" Brady cleared his throat as if readying to practice.

Jaret reached across the table and clamped his hand over Brady's mouth. "Stop."

"I will, if you let me guard you," Brady mumbled through Jaret's fingers. Then he stuck his tongue between two of them.

Jaret yanked his hand away, laughing.

Later, it took a lot of doing to get Brady to allow him to walk the final block home alone. "You live here," he said and pointed at Brady's apartment complex. "It's only one block in broad daylight. I'm fine." He held up the whistle the campus officer had given him. "I have my rape whistle. Even louder than your screaming. I'll call the minute I get to the apartment."

Brady still forced him to delay until a gaggle of students from the university, at least twenty of them, headed in the same direction. Jaret followed a short distance behind until he saw his complex looming a couple of buildings ahead.

He jumped when a dog rushed at him, his heart pounding when he looked down.

"Darth? What are you doing here, girl?"

Darth greeted him with even more enthusiasm than usual. She jumped and licked his face, spinning around in an anxious whirl of energy.

Stunned to see her outside, Jaret reached down and checked her tags even though he had no doubt she had somehow gotten out of the apartment.

Holding onto her collar and moving as fast as he could in a hunched position, he got to his building and scrambled for his keys. The elevator took forever to get to him. He hurried into it and pushed the buttons, not wanting to wait for the older woman who had stuck her key into the outer door.

His anxiety grew worse when he got to his hallway and saw his door standing wide open. He reached into his pocket and pulled out the gems, which hovered in front of him. They tingled an alarm but seemed passive, given the situation, sending him an alert from the past but none from the present.

Jaret inched toward the door and peered inside. He saw nothing. He stepped into the apartment and watched as Darth ran around to every room. She stopped sat his office door and refused to enter, uttering a guttural growl.

Jaret left the front door open and got his phone out, ready to call the police.

He almost threw up. Standing in his living room he spotted the iron box in which he had imprisoned Henrik, sitting inside the half-closed door to his office. But instead of being locked tight, the lid was wide open and the golden key placed inside the lock. Henrik had escaped.

Jaret rushed forward and then leaned over and vomited all over the carpet when he peered into the room. Steve lay across the floor, his neck at a crooked and inhuman angle.

Jaret started to reach for him, but knew without touching him. Dead. Henrik had killed Steve.

Jaret searched the atmosphere for signs of his dead ancestor and found nothing. Seeking a more definitive answer, he asked the gems for help. They floated to his kitchen table and hovered above. There, scratched into the wood, Henrik had scrawled a message:

Roses are Red, and They'll Screw You.

I Killed Your Lover, and Next Comes—Who?

Lovely to be free, Jaret. Thank you for falling in love with an imbecile. He's been calling for supernatural help to win you back for a while. He had no clue I found him despite my being in the box. Seems he connected ghosts in his subconscious to me and revived a bit of energy I'd left with him so long ago in Fremont. How marvelous. He released me and pleaded for my help in reuniting you with him. I executed him swiftly for his transgressions. You may thank me later. Off to the Bachmann mansion in Fremont. I hear tell they have a family reunion this weekend?

In a frenzy, Jaret raced for his phone and dialed his mom and dad's cell number. Nothing but their voice mail. "Hey, it's Jaret. It's urgent. Call me as soon as you get this."

Next he called Jenn, Lincoln, his aunt and uncle who lived in the ancestral home, and even his two cousins. No one picked up. Jaret kept leaving the same message over and over. Time and again he swallowed the rising bile when he saw Steve's body out of the corner of his eye. He had no time to mourn or dwell on this horror because his family needed him.

He thought of calling the police. How could he explain a dead body in his apartment? Even if they didn't suspect him, which seemed doubtful—hey, 911? A ghost killed my ex-boyfriend—the authorities would trap him in Chicago when his family needed him in Nebraska two minutes ago.

As he ran all over his apartment like a chicken with its head chopped off, packing and preparing to race to Fremont to defend his family once again from Henrik,

Jaret left more messages, this time for the vampires in his life.

He struggled to find the right words to leave for Anthony. "I need your help. I know we're over. And you said you can't help me anymore. But it's so urgent. Not about me. About my family. I think they all may be in trouble. Well, me too. Please. Call me."

Next he left messages for Xavier and Thomas. He found clearer words for them without the desperation and sense of defeat. He even managed to let Xavier know a corpse lay in his office and wondered if vampires had a way of managing such scenes. Yet they wouldn't get these messages for several hours. Jaret could almost be to Fremont before the moon rose to wake them.

He fumbled around for Darth's leash after he packed his car. Before he ran out of the apartment, he stopped and got a sheet to place over Steve. Only then did he notice the tears streaming down his face.

Panicked, he wasted no more time on Steve, locked his apartment, and raced down the stairs with Darth in tow. He kept telling himself to be calm as he drove, to be patient to avoid an accident. Getting pulled over for speeding would only delay getting to Nebraska. Worse, crashing because he barreled down the interstate would mean he may never arrive to protect his family.

Pushing it as much as he dared, Jaret drove about ten miles over the speed limit and cautioned himself whenever the speedometer started to inch upward. In Iowa, he passed three different state patrol cars with people pulled over.

Outside Fremont, he almost lost control of himself with fear when supernatural warnings engulfed his entire being. A headache even worse than the ones warning him of Henrik's presence back in high school pounded into his brain. The gems glowed with fierce colors in the passenger side foot well. Darth sensed the danger too and alternated between whining and growling when they passed the Fremont cemetery and drove all the way to the streets near his grandfather's house. The ache in his head almost made him vomit.

Twenty-Seven: Fainting

12 MAY 2011
Fremont, Nebraska

Jaret gripped the steering wheel, his palms sweating. His ancestral home sat before him. Dark—foreboding. His head hurt like hell.

He realized he'd stashed his cell phone in the center console and forgot to check for calls. He pulled it out and saw several messages from Xavier and Thomas but decided to listen later after he made sure about his family's safety.

Darth barked like a rabies-infected beast, and he pulled her close to calm her. "Darth, no barking." She quieted even as she panted hard, her eyes never leaving the house. "I know girl. I'm spooked too." Jaret blew out a breath and reached into his pocket to feel the Bachmann gemstones he'd brought along. His nerves quieted a little to know these stones gave him power over the supernatural. Even Henrik.

Still, he trembled and delayed the inevitable trek up the large porch that wrapped around the old Victorian house. His mind whirled with the events of the last year leading him to this moment and inspired fear deep within his soul. Something had gone terribly wrong. Henrik had returned to exact vengeance against the family. Against Jaret.

He wiped the sweat from his brow and looked at Darth. "Ready?" She panted an unknown answer and growled, almost under her breath.

Jaret stared at the ground as he stepped toward the porch, then watched each foot climb one step at a time. Slow. He reached down to make sure Darth had stayed by his side. Only then did he feel the hair on her back standing straight up, the rumble of warning still in her belly.

He pulled the house key from his pocket, making sure to grab as many of the jewels as possible in his other hand. He touched the front door. The pounding headache always warning him of hauntings threatened to drop him to his knees, so he asked the gems for strength to continue, which they granted. Still, his head hurt more than he could ever remember. Even more than the time, at this very house, Henrik attempted to kill him and Steve.

Then he felt the presence in his very bones. Henrik had indeed returned to Fremont. Angrier. Irrational. Set on destroying the family and everyone in his path. Jaret knew the truth without needing confirmation. Henrik waited inside for him. He had no choice but to enter.

The door creaked as Jaret slowly opened it. Darth whined a protest and lurched back before charging forward in front of Jaret after he proceeded inside. She had never abandoned him. Jaret relied on her inner dog voice to push her forward, knowing she would defend him with her life if necessary.

Jaret choked back the bile when he set foot in the entryway. He smelled rot. Human waste and death clung in the air like thick smoke. Henrik had transformed the mansion into a haunted house, complete with streams of blood flowing down the stairwell and dank mold covering the walls. The grand house of his childhood, when his loving grandfather had safeguarded the family, had turned into a house of horrors.

His head swirled and he fought with all his inner strength against the desire to faint away and make reality disappear. He glanced up to see if Henrik waited at the top of the stairs, as he had so often in the past, but saw nothing but Henrik's addition of uncharacteristic cobwebs covering the grand chandelier.

An evil wrapped itself around this house, something tangible and horrific. His heart sank, something deep within telling him a tragedy had occurred, the likes of which he had never witnessed. Next, he peered into the living room. He saw ripped furniture, toppled tables, glass shards everywhere. Henrik had made mould grow on the walls here too, and blood covered every surface. Deep, crimson blood everywhere. On the carpet. In the chairs. Smeared across the ceiling.

Again the room began to swirl and his knees buckled. Jaret clutched at the jewels, begging them for more strength than he had ever needed. They responded and again he stood upright, though losing his last, tiny semblance of confidence. On the long drive from Chicago, he'd reminded himself he had defeated Henrik in the past and jailed him inside the iron box. The gems fought for him, too, along with an increased knowledge about his own powers.

Such reassurance worked until his mind forced him to confront the memory of death when he had walked into his apartment and saw the iron box opened, the golden key in its lock, and Steve dead. To avoid panic, Jaret reminded himself Henrik could have designed all these theatrics to scare him. Maybe he spared them. The Bachmann family legacy meant everything to Henrik, so he had to keep them alive, right?

Jaret smelled the death and decay in the air. This time, he leaned over and threw up. As he worked to right himself and ignore the macabre scene, Darth lurched forward and howled a warning bark before snarling and growling. She positioned herself between Jaret and the staircase, barking as if a pack of wolves headed toward them.

Jaret scanned up the stairs, following the flow of blood, until he saw feet standing upon the landing. He glanced up the blue wool pant legs covered in blood, saw the bloodied hands contentedly folded in front of the man's groin, and continued up the stained and dripping shirt until he stared into the bright-red eyes of a smiling Henrik. A ghost, no doubt, but never before had Jaret seen him so solid and in command.

Henrik smiled, blood covering his teeth. "Hello, Jaret."

The stairs spun away, and Jaret's last sight was the enormous spider spinning away in the chandelier when the world went completely black.

Part Six: Adoption

Twenty-Eight: Saving Jaret

12 MAY 2011
Fremont, Nebraska

Jaret's distraught message sent Xavier into a frenzy. Jaret had sobbed into his phone about the ghost of his ancestor getting out of his metal box turned prison and murdering Steve, then leaving a note threatening Jaret's family in Fremont. That much Xavier had understood. Jaret had rambled about a few other things, but Xavier couldn't decipher the words, even after listening several times.

Thomas received a similar message. Thomas glanced at Xavier and they read each other's minds—they had to intervene and help their young friend. Forget the difficulties with Anthony or the hope they both harbored someday Anthony would come around and accept Jaret into their family. They had to act fast. In the short time they had known him, Thomas and Xavier had expressed to each other how much they admired the young man and enjoyed his company. Without a formal declaration or ceremony, he'd become part of their family, whether he wanted the acceptance or not.

"Thomas, you need to go to Jaret's apartment and see what happened. If there's a body, treat the scene like a vampire kill and conceal the evidence to protect Jaret."

Thomas kissed Xavier without saying a word and raced out of their flat.

Meanwhile, Xavier searched the internet for Bachmanns in Fremont, Nebraska and found three listings. He wrote them all down, praying Jaret's family had listed their number, and he had the right address among them. He had no idea what he'd do if he arrived in Fremont without the correct information. Figuring out what magic to use might take a while, and he sensed he had little time to spare, so any further search was too risky. Not trusting his vampire sense of direction and needing to make the best use of his time, Xavier pulled up maps of Fremont and memorized all the streets, especially the location of the three Bachmann residences.

He finished as Thomas swooped through an open window of their condo. "Steve's dead, as Jaret described. Something twisted his head almost completely around. I'll need to take care of the body but wanted to see you first."

"I have to go to Fremont."

"Then we have to go." Thomas walked across the room and took Xavier in his arms and squeezed him. The feel of Thomas's lips on the top of Xavier's head made him fall limp in his lover's arms. Thomas's powerful presence and love flooded through Xavier to give him courage.

Xavier looked up into Thomas's eyes. "Thank you. We'll go. But I think I'd better go first. Can you take care of Steve? I don't want Jaret to have to deal with the mess, and no one in the public should learn what happened."

"I'll move the body and stage the death somewhere else, as you suggested."

"Good. Make sure nothing ties Steve back to Jaret." Xavier pulled Thomas to the computer. "This is Fremont. I'm going to one of these houses. Find me there."

They both hurried to the window to jump to the ground and start running when Thomas stopped Xavier and held him. "Be careful. You can't help Jaret if this thing harms you. I'll never forgive you if you get hurt on one of these errands from God."

"God didn't send me this time."

Thomas tilted his head and smiled. "Are you sure? You still think God sent you to free the slaves, which led to Anthony imprisoning you, and to my almost killing Anthony."

Xavier laughed despite the seriousness. "Anthony says he almost killed you. Yes, God sent me on the slave errand, I'm sure. And to help the poor during the French Revolution before you converted me."

Xavier contemplated. Of course, he never knew the answer to such a theological question. Perhaps God did have another plan for him again this time. "I thought you were an atheist?"

Thomas laughed. "More agnostic, as you know. Besides, I didn't ask because of me. I asked because I know you."

Xavier nodded and smiled. He kissed Thomas on the lips. "I'll be careful. Hurry."

They leaped to the ground five stories down and ran as fast as their vampire legs would carry them. Xavier arrived in desolate Fremont in no time.

Having grown up in Paris and spent his entire human life there, followed by over two centuries as a vampire living in large urban areas, Xavier always felt vulnerable and adrift in smaller towns. Fremont was not some village in medieval Europe, but it was small enough. He took a matter of seconds to check the first residence, a small house on the outskirts of town. Wrong Bachmann.

Xavier next stood outside a foreboding Victorian house that must have stunned its neighbors when first built. The mansion still held a grand presence, with a big wraparound porch, ornate trimming, and the house and yard taking up an entire city block. Xavier's vampiric eyes detected a faint glow of red inside. Darkness surrounded the place. Not literal darkness—the forces of darkness. They hovered above and swirled around, alerting him to their presence within.

Xavier gathered as much information as possible by using magic from the Vampire Council and his own observations. He had to know what he faced, what danger the menace posed to him, and then determine a way to combat the ghost. His hands shook more when he spotted Jaret's car in the driveway. He stepped onto the porch, then looked into the living room window and saw Darth barking her head off and jerking backward, as if imploring Xavier to come help her. Only one thing could send her into such a total frenzy. She was protecting Jaret.

Xavier closed his eyes and called forth the magic Anthony had taught him when he became a member of the Vampire Council. He'd felt better when he'd learned a ghost really had little power over a vampire. This one could throw things around and physically attack, but nothing of such a nature could harm a vampire.

Cool air surrounded Xavier while comforting arms gripped him. Anne. His dear friend of long ago, who had so often watched over him, came to offer comfort. Even after all these years, he knew her presence at once. They had spent so much time together during his life in Paris that Xavier recognized Anne's energy without seeing her. She had saved his life when he fell into total despair and helped him go to his life with Thomas, while he had saved her grandson after slave catchers captured him. They had an unshakable bond, despite her being long dead and Xavier a vampire.

Anne's spirit spoke inside his head. "I'll contain him in the house. Go. Now."

With Anne's assurance, Xavier strode into the house. Darth greeted him at the door and jumped at him with urgent alarm. She scampered a few feet away and spun around, again barking at Xavier.

A lump caught in Xavier's throat when he saw Jaret's limp form lying in the middle of the grand entryway at the foot of an enormous stairway. Xavier grabbed him into his arms.

He looked up at a ghost, covered in blood and holding a knife dripping with thick crimson goo, as the spirit moved down the stairs with an eerie calm. He recognized Henrik from Jaret's descriptions. The rage on his face almost froze Xavier until he heard Darth barking, so he whipped around and hurried to leave.

Henrik tried to slam the front door closed before he got there, but Xavier sent a magic thought to counteract his attempt. With the force of his mind, the door stayed open, and Xavier hurried outside with Jaret. Holding Jaret in one arm, Xavier reached down and scooped Darth into his other and raced away. He had no idea where to go, and so stopped a few blocks away in a deserted park to collect his thoughts.

Xavier needed a safe place for them for the rest of the night and the next day until he could determine a more permanent solution. Resorting to his primitive vampiric nature, Xavier went to the Fremont cemetery. He leapt onto the roof of a chapel and mausoleum at the entrance that stood about three stories high. He broke into a crypt and laid Jaret gently on the floor, where Darth curled up next to Jaret and lay her head on his stomach.

Xavier knelt over and placed his hand on Jaret's forehead and enchanted a spell of protection and then one of rest. He ordered the elements to keep the witch asleep until he instructed otherwise, then repeated the incantation on Darth.

Ensuring no one else could enter and find Jaret or Darth, Xavier left and returned to the Bachmann house.

He discovered Thomas there, walking calmly around the block in contemplation.

"I assumed you'd return when I figured out someone from the Council had taken Jaret out of here." Thomas walked over and held Xavier's hand. "Are you okay?"

"No." Xavier took a deep breath. "Did you go inside?"

Thomas shook his head.

"I think they're all dead."

Thomas frowned. "Who?"

"His entire family. I sensed the carnage from outside and then saw a couple bodies."

"Everyone?"

"I think so." Xavier searched his mind again for what he had learned. "Mom, Dad, brother, sister. I think even his aunt and uncle and cousins."

Thomas cast his head down. "My God." He leaned into Xavier. "Are we safe?"

Xavier nodded. "The spirit can't harm us. From what I can tell, he's enraged all the more because of being powerless against vampires. Anne trapped him in the house to help us protect Jaret."

"Anne?"

"You're full of questions tonight." Xavier smiled. "I felt her presence. She assured me she could marshal allies to contain him."

They both stared at the house for several minutes until Thomas broke the silence with a soft whisper. "You don't have much time before the sun will force you to bed."

"I need to go back in. To make sure I'm right about what I saw and felt." Xavier looked at Thomas. "We're going to need a home here. Can you—"

Thomas cut Xavier off before he finished. "I'll have our people procure a house by tomorrow night. Don't worry. Do what you need to do."

Thomas squeezed Xavier's hand and pulled out his cell phone as he walked a short distance away. Before Xavier even returned his attention to the ghost, he heard Thomas talking quietly to someone.

Xavier walked toward the house.

Twenty-Nine: Henrik
Gone Mad

13 MAY 2011, 1:00 A.M.
Fremont, Nebraska

With his hand on the doorknob, Xavier took a deep breath. Xavier recalled the presence sauntering down the stairs toward Jaret, a knife in its ghostly hand.

Xavier opened the door and stepped into the foyer. If possible, the forces of darkness had taken even firmer hold.

"Sodomite!" The words thundered and shook the very foundations of the house.

In a controlled voice, Xavier spoke to the ghost. "You've no power over me. Your histrionics don't impress me in the least. I know magic more powerful than any of your ghost antics."

The chandelier swayed back and forth before crashing down at Xavier's feet. Xavier looked around to find the ghost, but Henrik had hidden from him. Still, he possessed each and every one of these rooms and maintained strong power despite imprisonment in the house.

The demon curled itself around Xavier's back and licked with a phantom tongue at his ear. "I'm going to fuck you with a stake and then throw your diseased body out the window."

Xavier walked forward. "You're not the proper ghost of decorum Jaret described. You used to have manners. You sound more like a bad demon from a poorly made horror movie. Crass. Uttering nonsense for shock value."

The spirit lurched away and spun around near the ceiling.

Xavier determined to do his job quickly and leave, not wanting to engage Henrik any more than necessary.

"I'll follow you." Henrik hovered above as Xavier stepped into the living room. From pictures at Jaret's apartment, he recognized the corpses of Jaret's mother and father. In the sitting room nearby, he saw Lincoln, who had died while hammering at the window.

"You can't follow me outside of this house, can you?"

The demon growled.

"Confirms what I thought. You're in prison again. Just a bigger one. My friend Anne has more power than you, doesn't she? She's trapped you here. And guess what? I added more spells. You're a rather feeble ghost for one trying so hard to be demonic."

Upstairs Xavier located Jaret's aunt and uncle, taken by surprise in the study while sitting with their grandchildren, also dead. Next, he found the bodies of the cousins. Last, he came upon Jenn's body. Unlike the others, the spirit had placed her in the middle of the hall in peaceful repose, a dark message to Jaret despite her quiet presence. No doubt designed for Jaret to discover and send his world into chaos. Xavier would never tell anyone of this scene, not even Thomas.

Xavier gently closed Jenn's eyes and patted her head where she lay on the carpeted floor. The spirit wailed in anger and took a stake and tried to jab it into Jenn's cheek. Xavier enacted a spell to protect her body. Henrik tried to stab him then, to no avail.

With the sun fast approaching, Xavier had to leave. He walked down the stairs.

At the front door, Henrik spoke. "You'll be my bitch."

"Good night," Xavier said.

Xavier walked out the front door and found Thomas waiting. He took Thomas's hand and led him through Fremont to the cemetery. Inside the crypt, after Xavier released her from the spell, Darth wagged her tail but refused to budge from her spot near Jaret.

With everything secure, Xavier sat on the ground near Thomas and collapsed into his arms. Only then did he release the emotion inside him, pent-up and building since receiving Jaret's message. He had controlled his feelings and all the angst he felt for Jaret through the entire night, being strong for the poor soul who had suddenly become lost and alone in the world at the hands of forces the likes of which Xavier had never seen.

Xavier wondered at the intensity of his emotion. All the destroyed hopes? All the misplaced trust? The crush of tragedy? How utterly and completely humans ruined one another, even in death? Did Jaret embody the goodness and innocence Xavier so wanted to find in humans, only to discover once again hope would get destroyed amid their madness?

Perhaps.

Or perhaps his emotion was as simple as the bond the two had developed in their short times together. One could never explain how friendships and intimacy sprung up over time or all of a sudden, yet planted themselves deep and stayed for good.

He wept on Thomas's chest. The blood tears poured out every emotion. He had almost lost control when he saw Jenn displayed on the floor, the pure evil of Henrik worse than any horror story Xavier had ever heard. Jaret had confided so often to Xavier about how close he felt to his sister. They'd shared stories, Jaret about Jenn, Xavier about Catherine.

Xavier could imagine the horror Jenn's death would bring to Jaret. His family lost. Such a thing would completely devastate anyone. But Jenn's death took the misery to another level. Unlike Xavier, who at least had Thomas in such an eventuality, Jaret's lover had abandoned him.

Thomas clutched Xavier in his arms the entire time, offering Xavier his loving and commanding presence without interfering in the devastation Xavier felt for Jaret.

As Xavier drifted to sleep, still clinging to Thomas, he cursed Anthony and his damned wounded soul. Centuries of existence and Anthony still held onto the guilt he felt at losing his first love. Still, he hid behind obligation and law and order to protect himself from becoming vulnerable.

A merciful, complete and utter sleep took hold of Xavier before the emotion threatened to descend him into mournful chaos. He and Thomas had to remain strong for Jaret.

Thirty: Last Rites

13 MAY 2011
Fremont, Nebraska

Xavier woke the next evening with a quiet determination and strange calm. His breakdown in Thomas's arms as he fell asleep purged much of his turmoil. He had a duty to Jaret.

"Are you okay?" Thomas asked when Xavier opened his eyes. Thomas had been awake for at least an hour but he stayed in the crypt tonight instead of venturing out.

"I wouldn't say okay." Xavier closed the distance and wrapped his arms around Thomas's waist. "I'm under control. I can do this, which I believe is what you're asking."

"You won't shut me out, will you? Or sneak away again?" Thomas reminded Xavier often of the time he had slipped away from France to America in the 1800s on a mission to liberate a captured freedman from slavery. Xavier had pledged over and over such subterfuge would never happen again, but still Thomas worried.

Xavier pulled Thomas close. "I promised never again. I'm going to need you every step of the way."

"Even if some fucking archangel commands you?"

Xavier recalled the dream visits from St. Michel. "He was terrifying, you know. Real. But even if he returns, I'll tell you because I know you'll go with me."

Thomas backed away and leaned over to pet Darth. "What are we going to do with them?"

"I put Jaret under a sleeping spell. Darth insists on staying near him, to the point of fighting sleep, I think because she needs to protect him. Jaret'll be fine for a few nights, if needed. I don't want to wake him until I can focus all of my energy into him, and him alone."

Xavier glanced at Thomas, who stood up with a scrunched brow. "Have you considered a mercy killing?"

As if sensing what Thomas said, Darth growled.

Xavier paused and took a deep breath. "Of course. Who wouldn't? And I dismissed the notion with complete horror for having ever pondered such an action."

"Don't be angry with me."

"I'm not. I don't know if you'll understand this. Now's not the time to go into detail. But I'm going to adopt him whether he wants me to or not."

"He's an adult, not a ward of the state or some orphan from a Dickens novel." Thomas came over and rubbed Xavier's shoulders.

Despite himself, Xavier giggled. "I know. He'll be a very wounded adult though. And a young one. Over the course of getting to know him while he dated Anthony, I came to care about him on a very deep level. Maybe because you and I can't have children. Or perhaps it's just a bond with two people who happen to come together. I'm going to protect him. I'm adopting him, and he's going to live. Now I have work to do. I'll take Darth out and bring her back. I doubt she's going to want to leave Jaret. And she doesn't seem to like you right now because she heard what you said. Quit smirking, I know the dog doesn't know English but I'm also not in my right mind."

As expected, Xavier had to capture Darth in his arms and carry her from the crypt. She bit at him and struggled, but he forced her outside. She did her business and then raced to the base of the building. Xavier got her back to Jaret as soon as possible. By the time they returned, Thomas had come back with dog food and two bowls, one for water and one for the food. Until he set them right next to Jaret, she refused to even look at them. With her body plastered to Jaret's side, she reached her head over and ate and drank.

Outside, Xavier breathed in the night air and looked at the stars. So peaceful and serene. No sign of the chaos churning in Jaret's life as he slumbered in a forced dream world.

"What did you do with Steve?" Xavier asked.

Thomas laughed.

"Only you could find something funny right now."

"Sorry." Thomas still smiled. "I staged his death as usual and well away from Jaret's place."

Xavier rolled his eyes. "Is everything a game to you?"

"It's not like I really care how Steve died. He had no redeeming qualities. Look what his insanity wrought." Thomas swept his arm in front of them, as if Henrik and the dead Bachmanns stood before them. "Maybe Steve was a tragic story, the product of a demented society. I know Jaret thought the ghost possessed him somehow. Still, he did this to Jaret. So, he died. From your perspective, I'd call his demise divine justice."

Xavier reached over and pushed Thomas's long black hair behind one of his ears. "There you go again with the theological references. I'll make a believer of you yet."

Thomas stifled another laugh. "I use language you'll understand."

"Whatever."

"So, what now?"

"Do we have a house yet?"

"I'm meeting someone there soon. They even managed to furnish the place, according to the text from my woman in Chicago."

"Where?"

"Across town." Thomas pointed in a direction. "He called it the May House, apparently the last name of the guy who built it. Pretty big. Redbrick, two stories plus an attic. And a big fenced-in yard for Darth. We can put Jaret in a bedroom and hide ourselves in the basement."

"Charming."

"I didn't have time to worry about our quarters, and I improved over the opulent crypt in which you stowed us."

Xavier became quiet, contemplating what he had to do while Thomas went and secured their temporary home. "Good. You meet your person, while I go to the Bachmann House. Oh, what about Jaret's car? It's outside the house too."

"I already moved the car to the new house's garage."

"You had a key?"

"No, I hotwired it."

"I knew I was married to nothing more than a common thief."

Thomas cupped Xavier's face in both hands. "You haven't fed for a while. Are you strong enough? Don't you need me to go with you?"

"I'm fine. I'll feed soon, I promise. Fremont must have some degenerates lurking around. But not tonight." Xavier loved the warmth of Thomas's strong hands as they held his head and forced their eyes to bore into one another's very being. "I want to do this alone."

Thomas nodded. "I'm not surprised."

"Because of religion. Faith."

"Not surprising either." Thomas grinned. "Do what you need to do."

"I'll need you to help make the appropriate arrangements. So, there's no doubt about Jaret's innocence."

"Not difficult. You go and meet me at our new Fremont home later. Who would've thought we'd own property in such a place. Do you think it's gay friendly?"

Xavier laughed. "Why can you make me laugh at the saddest moments? Will you go away? I'll be there soon."

Xavier steeled himself for his next task. He walked more slowly to the Bachmann House and paused outside. He took his time putting on his priestly robes. He had no idea why, when Thomas remained in Chicago to deal with Steve's death, Xavier had called Thomas and asked him to bring his clerical garb to Fremont. But Xavier's reason became clear when he figured out his duty at the mansion.

Without acknowledging Henrik as he ranted and raved and threw things around the house, Xavier gathered each body and placed them side by side in the living room.

With blood tears streaming down his face, he delivered the funeral service from memory—the same one he had done all too many times as a priest during the horrific French Revolution. He remembered Jaret mentioning the Bachmanns were Lutheran, but Xavier only knew the Catholic Mass. He gave them their rites and placed the sign of the cross over each face as he closed their eyes.

Pleading for God's forgiveness, he then loaded them into the large Chevy Traverse parked in the driveway, thankful for the large vehicle where he could put the entire family, albeit cramped. He hoped the authorities would buy so many people packed into the car. He buckled each body in as if on a family trip. The house behind him rumbled the entire time. He placed Jaret's father on the floor between everyone and then drove the car out of town.

Xavier pulled to the side of a road on the way to Omaha and placed Jaret's dad in the driver's seat. Sitting on top of the dead man, Xavier drove down the road like a maniac. Going around a curve and toward a ravine, he steered the car off the road. Airborne, Xavier saw the tree as the car flew toward the woods. Before the vehicle smashed into a grand old oak, Xavier launched himself out the window and rolled far away.

The car exploded.

Xavier got up and knelt before the inferno. Again he prayed for the souls of each person inside. He pleaded with God to take them to heaven, and to forgive him for defiling their bodies even more than Henrik had already done.

He stayed there by himself, crying and wondering how Jaret would ever survive until he leaned sideways into the being who materialized beside him, allowing the presence of his brother in his military uniform of long ago to comfort him. The medal on his chest pressed against Xavier's cheek as they embraced.

Then Xavier felt another presence for but a second. She stared at him and screamed into his head, "Protect Jaret. Help him survive—" Jaret's mother started to say something else but disappeared.

Michel stayed with him for a long time without a sound, until Xavier felt strong enough to leave the scene of this "accident" and go to Thomas.

"I love you," Xavier said to Michel as his brother drifted away. Michel smiled at Xavier before he disappeared.

As Xavier returned to the cemetery, he met Thomas at its gates.

"I called the police from a pay phone," Thomas said. "I claimed to have seen a terrible accident and gave them the location."

"Good. We need to call our lawyers next." Thankfully, paying ten times the usual salary kept these faithful employees happy despite the strange hours at which Thomas and Xavier called them.

"I'll call." Thomas got his cell phone out. "Scott? It's Thomas. I told you about the young man we're helping tonight. I need you to find the Bachmann lawyers, hire them through your firm, and get everything in order for Jaret. Pay whatever's necessary. As always, this must be discrete."

Thomas walked away to finish the conversation, while Xavier again got Darth and let her out. Darth seemed to trust Xavier more this time and resisted little when he took her outside. Still, he returned her quickly to Jaret's side where she clung to her master.

It took over an hour for Thomas to explain all the intricacies and details to the lawyers and return to Xavier. "Did they understand?"

"They got the message and are going to work out the details right now. They stopped asking too many questions a long time ago."

"Come on. We should get going." Thomas carried Jaret while Xavier picked Darth and her bowls up and they moved across town to their new home at vampiric speed. Darth squirmed a little but stared at Jaret in front of her with Thomas and so allowed the movement.

Xavier had Thomas place Jaret in the master bedroom and closed the door after Darth jumped into bed beside him.

"A couple of our servants from Chicago arrive this morning." Thomas played with Xavier's fingers as they walked down the stairs. "They know to leave him alone. I don't want them going in there without us. I'm not sure how Darth would react. But I'm sure they'll love Fremont after the nightlife of Chicago."

Xavier laughed. "We pay enough. They'll get over themselves."

"When will you wake Jaret?"

Xavier thought for a moment. "Soon. We need to do more at the house, first. And let the authorities think they contacted Jaret about his family. We'll have to pretend to be him when they call. Then I'll bring him out of the trance."

Thomas and Xavier retired to the basement, where they at least had a chest-cum-coffin big enough to sleep together.

Xavier clung to Thomas as he fell asleep. He felt the sun climbing above the horizon even from the depths of a basement. Sorrow engulfed him too. He found a mission in saving Jaret, but how could he ever deliver the boy to anything but complete misery? He even wondered about euthanasia again but could never bring himself to do such a thing, even if part of him wondered if Jaret might prefer death to living without his family. He would have to convince Jaret to allow the adoption into a new family, with two odd but loving and passionate fathers.

Somehow, someway, he would do more than save Jaret's physical being. As impossible as the task seemed, Xavier would find a way to redeem this wonderful man's very soul and bring him out of the depths of hellfire he would experience upon hearing the news.

Thirty-One: Imprisoned Ghosts

14 MAY 2011
Fremont, Nebraska

"What do you mean, we can't get rid of him?" Thomas asked Xavier.

They sat in the living room of their new home in furniture brought to Fremont from the finest stores in Omaha earlier in the day and arranged by their staff. Two servants from Chicago had organized the house and even begun remodeling a couple of rooms. The large formal living room, however, had needed nothing other than furniture.

Jaret slumbered in peace in the master bedroom above them, with Darth glued to his side. Xavier kept him under the enchantment because he and Thomas still had work to do. When he brought Jaret out of the trance, he had to focus his attention exclusively on the poor boy.

"I tried the few things I knew how to do. Nothing worked. I even talked to Anne when she appeared. She had no answers. In fact, the spell she used to keep him in the house began to fail. I had to use our magic to trap him there."

Thomas stretched out on the couch, his tight jeans exciting Xavier despite the situation. They hadn't had sex in a few days because of the turmoil, and Xavier's loins tingled at the mere thought.

"Am I just a sex object to you?" Thomas asked and smiled, as he read Xavier's mind.

Xavier blushed.

Thomas jumped off the couch and came over to Xavier. He lifted Xavier, sat down, and then held him on his lap. He rubbed at Xavier's crotch and licked his ear, sending shivers down Xavier's spine.

Before Xavier knew what hit him, they lay naked on the living room floor after a passionate but quick bout of lovemaking. When Xavier reached for his underwear, Thomas grabbed his arm.

"I like you naked."

"But I don't like one of the boys coming in and seeing us naked. Come on. We have stuff to do."

"I could bugger you instead."

Xavier smiled. "You're incorrigible." He kissed Thomas's nose as he pulled on his jeans. His snug T-shirt wrapped around his defined torso.

Then Xavier flicked the tip of Thomas's penis, which had grown hard. "Stop."

"What?" Thomas rolled over, laughing. "Like I can help the problem. Get your ass away from me to make me limp."

Xavier tossed Thomas's clothes to him. "Get up. We have to focus."

"So Anne's magic failed even though you managed to keep him in the building. Will your new spell hold?" Thomas dressed as Xavier watched him.

"I think so. If anything happens, I should be alerted to the change."

"Is this ghost still pissed off?"

"Of course. Cussing and ranting like a drunken sailor. I didn't know ghosts, like people, could have psychotic breaks. From everything Jaret told me, Henrik had a bad temper. Still, he also carried himself with a great deal of decorum. He was very proper. The entity in the house now has nothing but malice in his soul."

Xavier started to say more when Thomas's phone rang.

While Thomas attended to some business, Xavier reflected on Henrik's attitude. He used base threats and ugliness to try to scare Xavier. When Xavier went about the business of covering up the deaths and cleaning the house, Henrik shadowed him, ranting the entire way.

Strange, however, he had less power than before. Xavier sensed him trying to throw items around the room, smash through the windows, and attempt to upend the furniture. None of his attempts worked. Xavier's spell had controlled Henrik better than Anne and her compatriots from the other side.

Xavier had left the mansion with the assurance Henrik could cause no more harm unless someone entered the house. Even then, Xavier wondered if Henrik had lost some of his power. Other than a ranting and inappropriate ghost, the house looked in order.

"Who called?" Xavier asked when Thomas returned.

"Jaret's phone rang. The Nebraska State Police."

Xavier's heart sank. He'd anticipated as much, even set up the call. Still, the moment reminded him what he had staged the night before.

"What did you say?"

"I pretended I was Jaret. They broke the news to me about my family. It wasn't a long conversation. I called our lawyers and informed them that the bodies have officially been found and pronounced dead. They've set the legal work in motion for Jaret to inherit everything. Of course, at some point he'll need to be involved. But it's all set for now."

This time, Thomas's phone rang. Lady Gaga sang out a ring tone. "It's the shithead."

"That's not helpful," Xavier scolded.

"Anthony," Thomas said into his phone. "How good of you to get around to calling. No doubt busy on some vampire police work... I'm not being an ass. Well, maybe a little. I assume you got all our messages, explaining the situation. We've got things under control. But you know how much your help would mean right now... I'm biting my tongue so hard I think it's going to bleed. Maybe I'll snap it off so I don't say anything nasty. If I do, I'll send my severed tongue to you." Thomas laughed at Anthony's response. "Agreed. I'll be there tonight. But Anthony, you're still an asshole. He's going to need you."

Thomas hung up and looked at Xavier. "I know this will shock you, but he still says he can't see Jaret. He claims being together would reopen painful wounds for both of them and do nothing to help Jaret out of this crisis. He's still worried about Jaret's magic." When Xavier started to protest, Thomas put his hand in the air to stop him. "I agree with you. But he's not listening. He never does. We've talked about their relationship a million times. We both know he's afraid of the relationship and all the shit about Jaret's magic and being careful is bullshit."

Xavier sighed. "I know. He's too afraid and hurt. I think he's insane."

"He's more than insane about this. He's completely demented and has been for centuries. Underneath his gruff and formal exterior, he harbors tremendous feeling and even greater pain." Thomas rolled his eyes, ever the sympathetic one. "I did make progress with him. He's agreed to hear me out if I'll come back to Chicago to help with some vampire problem. That's all he'd tell me."

"Is the matter serious?"

Thomas rolled his eyes again. "With Anthony, everything to do with the Council is. But no, we need to spank someone and be done with a small nuisance."

Xavier saw Thomas to the door and kissed him goodbye. Xavier often had to calm Thomas down and keep his temper under control. Yet whenever something called Xavier on a mission, Thomas managed his emotions and did everything possible to assist him. Xavier needed his steady assurance in the current circumstances.

"Don't be too hard on him." Xavier patted Thomas on the back. "I know how much he can annoy you. Bitching at him won't do any good. We can't help him if he's always pissed with you."

Thomas grinned and winked. "Would I do anything to antagonize him?"

"You're making my point."

When Thomas had gone, Xavier called Anthony and left a message. "Anthony, he's on his way. He just talked to you. Where did you go? Anyway, I'm calling to remind you not to let him get under your skin. I don't agree with you anymore than he does. I *do* understand where you're coming from, though. Just don't get in an argument with him. Even if you don't think it's a good idea for you to see Jaret, he needs all of us focused on him right now. Please? Okay, love you."

Xavier spent the remainder of the night making sure all arrangements had been made regarding Jaret and his family. He visited the house to assure himself the magic had a tight hold over Henrik. To appease Thomas, he found a worthy victim and fed, and his stamina returned.

In the last couple hours before the sun sent him to bed, Xavier drank an exquisite bottle of French wine and plotted a strategy for waking and informing Jaret. Xavier already knew tomorrow night would be one of the worst of his life in a very, very long time. Perhaps worse than anything since he witnessed the murder of his brother during the French Revolution.

Thirty-Two: Grim Reaper

15 MAY 2011
Fremont, Nebraska

Xavier wished the sun had never set on the previous day.

He woke within his coffin and longed for Thomas. They talked on the phone, Thomas explaining all was well between him and Anthony in Chicago and promising to return soon.

Xavier prepared himself for the awful task ahead. He dressed in something casual and black, fidgeted around the house, and then got Darth and let her into the backyard. As always, she hurried to accomplish her business and raced back to the door and demanded to go back to Jaret. She almost fell a number of times on the hardwood floors as she scurried through the house and up the stairs.

Xavier sat on the edge of the bed and watched Jaret sleep with Darth now curled next to him. He brushed a strand of Jaret's long hair out of his face, then ran his fingers along Jaret's cheek. Such a beautiful boy, with long lashes, slightly curly hair that fell down to past his shoulder, and soft skin.

A perfect match for Anthony. He had all the physical attributes Anthony adored, with his slight runner's build, bubbly solid ass, and hazel eyes. His personality, too, fit well with Anthony. Jaret liked having Anthony in charge but at the same time never backed away from challenging him. He added a lightness and playful demeanor to Anthony's seriousness.

None of which mattered at the moment. Xavier was about to destroy Jaret's world and the weight of the responsibility pressed down on his shoulders, as if he'd done the killing himself and now had to confess to murder.

He kissed Jaret's forehead and then said a silent prayer for both of them. Then he spoke the words to reverse the enchantment and awakened Jaret.

Jaret sat up with slow movement and glanced about the room. Darth twirled around and started licking his face with fury, her little stub of a tail wagging back and forth. Jaret smiled and allowed her passion before he pushed her back down and held her in his arms.

At first, he seemed frightened, then confused. He frowned and looked at Xavier. A slight smile spread across his face but disappeared just as fast.

"Where am I?" Jaret asked with a froggy voice.

Xavier drew in a deep breath and sighed. "Our home. Thomas and I purchased a house in Fremont for all of us."

Jaret frowned. His face lit with recognition, as if he remembered how he got to Fremont and what he had discovered there. He shook his head. "I don't understand. I was at the house. How did you find me? What happened?"

"We need to talk. But first I want you to shower and eat something. If you'll do that for me, I'll explain everything."

"What happened? Tell me? How long was I asleep?"

Xavier reached over and patted Jaret's shoulder as his voice grew more panicked. "Quite a long time. Now, please, listen to me. I put you under a magic spell so you'd survive without eating. You'll get hungry soon, so shower first, and then when you're ready, let's get you fed. We'll talk afterward. Do this for me. Okay?"

"I've been out a long time?"

Xavier nodded.

"I don't feel like I missed more than a couple minutes. I'm not hungry. Or weak or anything."

"I know. My spell on you affected your body. Now, go."

Jaret resisted at first but acquiesced when Xavier refused to budge. He showered in a matter of minutes, ran downstairs in sweatpants and a T-shirt, and gulped down two bowls of cereal.

Too soon, they were seated together on the couch. Jaret's leg bobbed up and down, he twiddled his thumbs, and his arms visibly shook. He lifted Darth onto his lap and kissed the top of her head. Then the fidgeting began again.

"Henrik did something, didn't he? He killed Steve and came to get my family. I saw him. And lots of blood."

Words flooded out of Xavier as if from an alternate reality. Perhaps his mind played such a trick on him to help him cope with the news he had to impart. He had to remain strong for Jaret, all the while dying a little inside with each part of the story.

"I came to Fremont right after I got your messages. I walked into the house soon after you fainted, or at least I suspect as much, because Henrik was coming down the stairs with a knife. I carried you out of the house and concealed you in the Fremont crypt until we could get this house." Xavier motioned to the home around them. "I put you under the spell once in the crypt.

"And you're right. Henrik did awful things. There's no way of explaining this to make the truth okay or soften the blow. Jaret, he killed your entire family." Xavier waited a second for Jaret to react. Instead, he stared at Xavier.

"Everyone?" he whispered.

"Yes, everyone."

For the first time since Xavier met Jaret, Xavier witnessed the full power of Jaret's sorcery. As Jaret became more distressed, the jewels drifted up of their own accord from the jewelry box Xavier had set on the floor beside Jaret in the bedroom. They swirled above his head with greater speed. Electrical currents shot into the air from Jaret's being.

"I staged your family's death in an automobile accident to protect you. We're having our lawyers arrange with yours for you to inherit everything. I know this is awful, but I chose an accident because no one would believe a ghost killed everyone. A subterfuge was the only way to ensure you weren't accused of the murders."

Finished, Xavier trailed off and stared at Jaret.

The jewels plopped to the floor around them. The magical currents ceased altogether. Jaret stared straight ahead, the only sign of any feeling or reaction came from how he pulled Darth to himself and seemed to try to squeeze the life out of her.

Otherwise, he swayed back and forth as if catatonic. As if he returned to the state of sleep Xavier had placed him in for the last few days.

After several minutes of this nothingness, Jaret erupted. As if a dam burst, he slumped over and cried without control as he buried his head in Darth's back. Ever the dutiful companion, she sensed the moment and remained frozen in his arms, her only job to offer what little comfort Jaret had left in the world.

Xavier got up and went around behind Jaret. Without taking him away from his dog, Xavier reached around and held Jaret tight, hoping the contact might offer some solace for a situation beyond Xavier's comprehension.

As Jaret mourned, Xavier reflected on the tragedies of his own life. First, the unexpected death of his father that sent the family into a dull ache. Xavier had found his dearest friend, Maria, raped and dying, then helped quicken her passage to heaven. The murder of his brother at the hands of a demented witch doctor stung more. Xavier had witnessed the killing and still cursed himself for being so drunk he could do nothing to stop the carnage. Catherine's husband, Jérémie, died too. Xavier watched Anne die, and other friends along the way.

But even the worst of Xavier's tragedies came one at a time. They spaced themselves out to allow the pain to become a memory, a deadened ache at the back of his mind.

What if he could wrap all the tragedy and misery into one single moment? What would he feel? How would he have ever recovered from such complete devastation? Because in his arms sat a soul going through such a torture.

Xavier had no idea what to expect. Literally hours passed without any of them moving. Darth lay in Jaret's lap, Jaret clung to her, and Xavier clutched Jaret.

Without a word, Jaret got up and took Darth to the back door. He watched her run around the yard a couple of times until she ran back to him.

Xavier anticipated Jaret wanted to feed her, so he showed Jaret her bowls and the dog food, again without any verbal communication.

An hour before Xavier would have to return to his crypt, he guided Jaret back to the bedroom and sat him on the bed.

"I'm going to place you back under the spell. I'm not going to hurt you. But I don't want anything to happen today." Xavier almost added he feared what Jaret might do to himself or Jaret would rush off to the Bachmann mansion.

Jaret complied without complaint. As Xavier enchanted Jaret, the jewels floated back into the room and into their jewelry box. Darth slumped over in her spot next to Jaret. Her kind eyes seemed to stare at Xavier, pleading with him to help her distraught master.

Xavier closed the door and went to the basement. Before getting into his own bed, he cried blood tears for several minutes. Certainly not the pure agony Jaret must feel. But bad enough. Painful enough. Blessed sleep once again took over.

Thirty-Three: Dysfunction

16 MAY 2011
Fremont, Nebraska

Xavier sensed someone lifting the lid to the trunk in which he slept. Nothing alarmed him or provoked his vampiric defenses. He felt strong arms raise him out and carry him to a chair, where the person sat with Xavier in his arms. As Xavier came out of his sleep, cool hands caressed his cheek and played with his ear.

Thomas's long black hair tickled his cheek when Xavier opened his eyes and looked into those piercing brown eyes. He fell in love all over again with the way Thomas's mere presence could protect him even during the worst trials of his life.

"I got your texts. You did it." Thomas leaned down and kissed Xavier. "Are you okay?"

Xavier sighed. How could he answer such a question? "I'll survive." Xavier leaned into Thomas. "Telling him was awful. I prepared myself for the absolute worst." Xavier paused, remembering how numb and silent Jaret was after hearing the news about his family. "He was catatonic. As if all feeling left him."

"Where is he?" Thomas asked.

"I put him back under the trance. I was afraid of what he'd do to himself through the day. Or worse, I imagined him running off to confront Henrik. There was no one to be with him."

Xavier relayed more of the story to Thomas. "How did the Council mission go with Anthony?"

"We had some fool vampire getting drunk and then telling people he was a vampire. He meant telling them to sound like a joke. He was in the Goth clubs, where everyone claims to be a vampire. He went along with the charade of the entire bar, except he was really biting them and drinking their blood. Not killing them, mind you. But another vampire saw this happening and alerted the Council. Anthony got the magical notice. We talked to him and convinced him to stop because it's too dangerous." Thomas shrugged. "You'd think he was an idiot newbie. But we haven't allowed a new vampire in almost a century. No, this one was older than me. Just bored. Anthony had met him before and told me he had the intelligence of a moronic ape."

Xavier laughed, happy nothing more serious had demanded the Vampire Council's attention. At least Thomas had given him a momentary diversion from his misery.

Too soon, Xavier caught Thomas up on the whole miserable tale and decided they needed to wake Jaret. Part of Xavier wanted to let Jaret sleep for eternity, blissfully unaware of reality.

Before they got upstairs, however, Xavier asked about Anthony. Thomas pressed his lips together and a vein in his forehead throbbed. "Relax." Xavier placed his hand on Thomas's forearm.

"He won't come. He says it'll only make things worse."

The news disappointed Xavier, as much as he had expected the answer. "I still think he'll come around. We have to help him. He's so hurt."

Thomas rolled his eyes and sputtered a harsh laugh. "It's been centuries. Literally. Centuries."

"Not everyone heals the same way. He's afraid. We both know how much he loves Jaret."

"That's what pisses me off!" Thomas shouted. "You should've seen him when he talked about Jaret. It was the strangest mix of euphoria and sadness I'd ever seen in one person at the same time. I want him to snap out of his mental block."

They started up the stairs again as Thomas talked. "He's coming to Fremont. He promised to check out the house with us, to know for sure we locked Henrik inside. But he won't see Jaret. At least he's involved. I guess."

"Anything helps." Xavier nodded. Actually, the news encouraged him. He knew Thomas would only get annoyed all over again with Anthony if he said anything. But the fact Anthony even came to Fremont meant his soul was leading him where his mind refused to go.

Thomas assisted Xavier through the night with Jaret. They woke him, helped him take care of Darth, and forced him to eat but allowed his complete silence.

At the end of the night, Jaret willingly went back to the bedroom and curled up with Darth to go under the vampire spell. He never once spoke as Thomas filled him in on the legal details and asked for his signature on a couple of documents. Darth never left his side.

Thirty-Four: Catatonic

31 MAY 2011
Fremont, Nebraska

Xavier and Thomas remained with Jaret in Fremont for the rest of the month.

Jaret never spoke a word to them. He never left the house. He refused a funeral or memorial service, instead having his family cremated and interned in the Fremont cemetery with no remembrance.

Darth remained at his side every minute of every day.

A week after Xavier first awakened him, Jaret began playing Mika every night on his iPod.

Part Seven:
Healing

Thirty-Five: Rag Doll

8 JUNE 2011
Fremont, Nebraska

A few weeks after Xavier's revelation to Jaret about the tragedy of his family, Xavier witnessed faint signs of Jaret healing despite the fact he still refused to talk, even when his phone rang, or Thomas and Xavier spoke to him.

Jaret remained lost in his own world and suffered. He cried often.

Yet, a week ago he started jogging each night after Thomas and Xavier woke him. Then they trusted him enough to convert him back to a human schedule, so he switched to running in the morning. Darth danced with utter euphoria at this development and continued to cling to him every minute of every day.

Next, Xavier caught Jaret texting. Jaret tried to hide the communication but realized the vampires figured out he was reaching out to someone. Xavier also received a text message from Jaret's friend, Brady. Xavier had reached out to Brady, asking him to contact Jaret, and Brady indicated he had already been doing so. Xavier noticed Jaret never answered his phone calls, though he always listened to the messages. Brady wrote to Xavier to explain that after sending numerous unanswered messages, Jaret returned a text out of the blue and they had started a somewhat regular correspondence. Brady wrote, "I can feel his pain, even in texts."

Jaret listened to Mika's albums almost every day. Strange to hear the often happy and upbeat songs Jaret played at full blast throughout the house despite his morose attitude. He even wiggled a little to the music and laughed a few times at Darth's antics when she pranced around to the music with him.

Little steps, not anything to get Xavier excited or to pretend Jaret had recovered in any significant way. But Jaret had moved from the rag doll of the first few weeks to something more animated and attuned to the world around him.

Darth warmed to Xavier and Thomas and began to trust them, too, enough so Xavier stopped placing any spell on her. Xavier wondered what might have happened if not for Darth. As much as Thomas and Xavier sat with Jaret, talked to him, and tried to lead him out of his cocoon, only Darth evoked any kind of real emotion. Her mere presence soothed Jaret. The flood of emotions coursing through his body at every second of the day only came out when she sat by his side and he held her in his arms. Xavier melted at her loyalty and total devotion. Without Darth, they most likely would have lost Jaret.

Still, Xavier wondered at how long Jaret could survive as a rag doll. He ate to survive. He barely communicated, and Brady said he texted he loved Brady and thanked him for thinking of him but nothing else. Any other questions from Brady went unanswered. Xavier longed to place a spell on Jaret and snap him out of the funk. Except such machinations would create a temporary solution and embitter Jaret when he figured out Xavier's subterfuge.

Xavier and Thomas sat with each other, drinking wine and enjoying the fireplace. The chef they had imported from Omaha had taken Jaret into the kitchen to serve him his favorite homemade macaroni and cheese. When Jaret got out of his chair without a word to go with the chef, Darth followed at his heels.

"I appreciate all you've done since we came to Fremont." Xavier sipped the Bordeaux. "I know this isn't ideal." Xavier wanted to gauge Thomas's mood regarding their current situation but also feared the answer.

Thomas smiled. He ran his fingers through his long hair before he laughed again, got up, and walked over to kiss Xavier on the cheek. Then he sat on the floor in front of Xavier.

"What's so funny?" Xavier asked.

"You." Thomas hugged Xavier's leg. "After all these years, your subtlety amazes me. You forget I can read your mind. You don't have to walk on eggshells with me."

Xavier smiled and ran his hand through Thomas's hair. "So answer the question I avoided asking."

"I'm fine. I understand what we're doing, and why. I agree with you. In fact, unlike some of the other missions you've been on, this one actually makes sense to me. It's the right thing to do. We're adopting him, whether he wants us in his life or not. Perhaps it's our way of finally having a child. Now, do I love Fremont? Decidedly not."

"Come on," Xavier said. "The town has a certain comfort and charm."

"If you're painfully straight and provincial."

"That's not fair."

"Neither is life." Thomas laughed. "Small town America isn't my cup of tea. Eventually we'll get him out of here. He's still gay, even if he's sad. He can't last long here, either."

Xavier paused. "Do you think he'll recover?"

Thomas got up and scooted Xavier over, so they sat in the chair together. "Yes, I do. For one reason. He has you."

Xavier looked at the ground. "I've hardly done well by him."

"You saved his life." Thomas lifted Xavier's chin and stared into his eyes. "He lost almost everyone. There isn't a human alive, except perhaps a serial killer, who could survive such a thing without a great deal of pain and turmoil. He'll never heal to his former self. But can he live a full life and find some peace and happiness? Yes. The human spirit is resilient. And the only reason he's come this far is because he has someone who nurtured him."

Xavier wiped at a blood tear. "Thank you. I won't abandon him. I've determined to see this through to the end."

Thomas smiled and tapped Xavier on the nose as he got up to return to his own chair. "I'd expect nothing less."

They sat quietly and watched the fire crackle and provide warmth. A few minutes later Darth trotted into the room, glanced at the fire, then jumped onto a couch.

Seconds later, Jaret meandered in and headed to join her. He often sat in the room in total silence with Xavier and Thomas. Xavier appreciated his presence, thinking being together was positive since Jaret stayed with them instead of sequestering himself in some private part of the house.

In the comfortable silence, Xavier contemplated what to do. He had wondered for over a week at whether or not to remain in Fremont. They had purchased the house and decided to keep the home regardless, because Jaret might want someplace to stay in his ancestral town, now that the Bachmann home was out of the question. But why did they stay here? No one lived here who could help. Jaret could jog with Darth and ignore reality from any location in the world.

Xavier understood one thing alone rooted them here. He had not determined what to do about Henrik. Over the last few days, he convinced himself beyond a doubt Henrik had no means of escaping the house. The combination of Anne's spell and the vampire magic held him within its confines. He even stopped destroying the place and had no power but to rant and rave whenever Xavier or Thomas appeared. Yet Xavier doubted they could just leave him as a prisoner in the mansion in the middle of an active town for years upon years.

The impasse stumped Xavier every time. They had no long-term plan for Henrik, and no idea how to even go about designing one.

Thomas and Xavier decided to speak as if all was normal around Jaret about everything, whether or not he reacted. They wanted as much a sense of normalcy as possible.

"Have you thought any more about Henrik?" Xavier asked Thomas.

"As little as possible."

Xavier glanced at Jaret, worried Thomas's smart-ass humor might offend him. He was pleased to see Jaret's mouth curl into a slight smile.

"I don't think we can just leave him there. But I don't know what else to do."

"Nor do I." Thomas shrugged. "I don't mean to be flippant. We've thought about him. We either need to leave him alone or eliminate him. Killing him off requires a very powerful and dangerous magic. If we decide on murdering a ghost, we need a lot more studying and planning."

Xavier poured more wine for Thomas and himself. Then he got another glass and poured Jaret some too. When he held the glass out, Jaret took it and smelled the wine. Then he took a drink and closed his eyes, as if savoring the taste. Xavier returned to his own chair.

"That's what we need to do. Get rid of him permanently. We can summon Harriet and Catherine." Left unsaid was the need for Anthony. Anthony had even agreed to assist with the matter if they determined to move in this direction. "He's too dangerous just to leave there."

Thomas and Xavier chatted a while longer about developing their strategy for going after Henrik, when Jaret's voice startled them.

Thirty-Six: Resurrection

JUNE AND JULY 2011
Fremont, Nebraska

Thomas and Xavier had almost plotted out the timeline for going after Henrik when Jaret spoke. "I don't want anyone going into the house. It's mine, and I forbid entry." The room grew silent. Thomas and Xavier glanced at one another as if a ghost had entered. "I'm depressed. Probably still in shock. I didn't become deaf and dumb."

After another pause, Thomas roared with laughter, prompting Xavier to laugh, and even Jaret to smile.

"So you aren't comatose after all." Thomas got up and went over to sit next to Jaret, followed by Xavier. "Do you think you can join the living again?"

"Ironic coming from you." Jaret took another drink of wine. "I never left humanity, really. Just disengaged. But your plan is too dangerous. I won't allow interaction with him. Vampires or not. Leave him alone. Leave him be." Jaret's lower lip quivered, and his eyes welled with tears. "I won't let him take anyone else away."

Then he sobbed. When Thomas and Xavier both reached over and engulfed Jaret and Darth in an immense hug, Jaret responded and put his arms around them. Xavier made no attempt to control his own tears and let them burst forth.

In the moment, regardless of how he phrased his interaction or what his intention, Jaret had returned to the living.

When they recovered enough to sit back and resume the conversation, Xavier addressed Jaret. "I promise we won't do anything against Henrik until you allow us. You'll know everything before an attack happens."

With their business concluded, Jaret returned to his silence but allowed himself a more animated participation in their evening. He would smile and laugh, or often simply nod or shake his head. He stayed with them for a while longer before saying good night and going off to bed.

When he disappeared and left Thomas and Xavier alone, Xavier again burst into tears, this time of joy because Jaret had made his next step toward recovery. Xavier never pretended Jaret had miraculously healed. He knew what a long process they had entered but tonight signaled a gigantic step forward.

The next night they got more of the same from Jaret. Two nights later, he asked if they minded if he played Mika while they sat and talked in the living room. He even left the house for more than just his morning run, and according to the servants, had gone grocery shopping and talked with the chef about his favorite foods.

Gradually their routine shifted to a more engaged Jaret. He still cried and refused to talk about what had happened. He could enter a conversation for several minutes and then retreat into his silence just as fast. But he seemed to heal, or at least fought to move forward.

On a few occasions, Xavier overheard him talking to Brady.

Then one weekend in July, Brady appeared at their doorstep. Xavier greeted him with a hug. "What are you doing here?"

"Jaret invited me. Didn't he tell you?"

Xavier shook his head as he ushered Brady into the living room.

"Is it okay?"

"Of course! I'm glad to see you. He's still not well."

Brady nodded. "I can tell. I mean, who would be? I thought maybe I could help or something. I'm usually pretty good at getting him to chill for a while. He means too much to me just to leave him alone, even though he insists he wants solitude."

Jaret embraced Brady in a tight hug lasting several minutes after Xavier fetched him. Brady and Jaret spent the weekend together, talking, listening to Mika, and taking walks around Fremont. To give the friends plenty of room, Thomas and Xavier removed themselves from Fremont.

They also needed to protect Brady from learning about their vampirism. He knew they had befriended Jaret through Anthony but nothing else. When Thomas and Xavier returned, and just before Brady left, Brady confided to Xavier how Jaret finally opened up about his misery and sorrow.

"He cried a lot and said he'd never recover from losing his family." Brady choked back a sob as he spoke. "Of course, who would? Or could? I don't know how to explain him, though. His transformation was amazing, the way he finally let out the pain. Don't get me wrong. I don't think I've ever been more depressed in my life. I wanted to hold him in my arms and squeeze all the misery out. But at the same time, I felt like his purging was what needed to happen. I don't think I was the sole catalyst. He changed because of timing, the alcohol, and then me. But he came through a big moment."

Xavier needed every ounce of self-control not to weep blood tears in front of Brady. Xavier reached over and squeezed Brady's arm. "You caused the change. You mean a lot to him." Jaret releasing some emotion to Brady meant a sea change in his healing, giving Xavier more hope for the future than he had in a long time, if ever.

A few nights later, after Jaret let Darth out for the night and the two of them headed to bed, Jaret turned around and poked his head into the living room. He had not spoken throughout the evening. "Guys?"

Xavier looked up from his novel. "Yes?"

"I think it's time to leave Fremont. I mean, you can stay if you want. I'm just, well, it's just time to leave. Okay?"

"Sure." Xavier shrugged nonchalantly, not wanting to betray his inner hope and excitement at the latest development.

Thirty-Seven: School

AUGUST 2011
Chicago, Illinois

After Jaret surprised them in July with the announcement he wanted to leave Fremont, Thomas almost tripped over himself to make the move happen. In fact, after Jaret went to bed, Thomas rattled off almost every major city in the world as a possible destination.

"How about if we let him decide?" Xavier asked.

Thomas opened another bottle of wine. "Our imminent departure from this backwoods pasture, I mean Fremont, demands a celebration!"

"Right you are."

Thomas pointed at Xavier and smiled. "He can decide. As long as he doesn't say Omaha. Or anywhere else rural and isolated. Like the Colorado boondocks."

"Thomas."

Thomas held his hands in the air. "I'm just saying."

The next night Jaret explained to them his desire to return to school. "I talked to Brady a lot about going back. He agrees it's a good idea to maybe get back to a routine and see some of my friends. I planned to get my MA, anyway. I was already accepted. Oh, and I asked Brady about the whole Steve thing."

"Steve?" Xavier asked in surprise.

"Yeah. I mean, so you told me what you did with his body. But I didn't know if the campus said anything about his disappearance, or if I'd have to deal with his death. Brady said his death was a topic for about a week and then people moved on. They didn't do some memorial or anything."

"Ah." Xavier nodded. "Of course."

Thomas orchestrated their return to Chicago for early August. "I'll sacrifice my time and make the advance arrangements. Unfortunately, my work requires my returning ahead of you two."

Xavier and Jaret laughed at Thomas.

"You're such a martyr," Xavier said.

Thomas did a perfect job of preparing the way for them and explained the plan to Xavier one evening. "I got rid of Jaret's old apartment by paying off the lease to the landlord and moving Jaret's stuff to a new house near DePaul University. I bought a three-flat and had to pay millions of dollars to hire crews to renovate it into a one family home, complete with a decked-out basement and secret chamber for our coffin."

Xavier shook his head in amazement. "I still marvel, even after all this time, at how fast you can get people to do things that take others well over a year or more."

Thomas grinned and rubbed his thumb around two fingers. "Capitalism, dear boy. All about the money."

"Which explains the problem with this world."

"Indeed." Thomas nodded. "But gay vampires deserve what they can get for themselves."

"You're incorrigible. I don't agree."

Soon enough, the trio and Darth had moved into their new abode and re-accustomed themselves to living in Chicago. Thomas liquidated the previous property Xavier and he owned there. With the three of them instead of two, Thomas wanted Jaret to have his own space away from them. The new house felt more like a permanent residence as opposed to a vacation home, which Thomas chose because Jaret would live in Chicago as opposed to Thomas and Xavier dive-bombing the city from time to time. Thomas went all out.

Xavier attempted, on a couple of occasions, to engage Jaret in a conversation about Henrik. Despite Jaret's obstinacy, Xavier knew they had to do something about the imprisoned ghost. The charade about how Jaret kept the house because of his mourning could only last so long before Fremont neighbors and authorities started to wonder. But whenever Xavier broached the topic, Jaret shut down. Otherwise, he more and more returned to discussing things like a normal human. A very depressed and sad one, to be sure, but at least a connected one.

So, Henrik remained in Fremont, trapped in the home he had built and surrounded by memories of the family he destroyed.

Xavier thought Jaret had another breakthrough when Brady came over one night for dinner. As they dined, with Thomas liberally pouring wine, after a spending binge on hundred dollar bottles of Xavier's favorite *Vouvray* from the Loire River Valley, Brady casually mentioned the counselor Jaret had seen.

"How'd it go this morning? Feel better?" Brady asked.

Jaret rolled his eyes. "You have the biggest mouth of anyone I know. Bigger than a hippo's."

"Not bigger than Mick Jagger." Brady's rebuttal made everyone laugh. "Besides, they needed to know, and you'd never tell them." Brady jerked his head toward Xavier and Thomas as he spoke.

Jaret smiled sheepishly. "Don't make a big deal about counseling. I get too emotional to talk."

"Yeah." Brady looked over at Xavier and Thomas. "He barely mentioned his move back to Chicago to me. I had to pry out of him where he was going. Even had to threaten to strip naked and run down the street screaming his name before he let out the truth. Let alone getting him to talk about seeing a shrink."

"Stop. No big deal. I see her three times a week, right around the corner at Flourish Studios. Plus, Jodie— she's my counselor—doesn't think I need medication. Thank God."

And thus, Xavier and Thomas learned Jaret had started seeing a psychologist. Jaret sounded so pleased they thought he could survive without the medication that Xavier cried.

Once again, Xavier felt so grateful for Brady's presence in Jaret's life.

Recently, Xavier had taken to following Jaret from time to time, not because he feared he might hurt himself or relapse, but because he worried about his safety. He would never forgive himself if something happened to Jaret.

One night in particular confirmed the need for the extra security. As Brady and Jaret strolled home, a thug followed them. When he sped up and whipped open a switch blade, Xavier raced over and grabbed him from behind. Before the thief could even scream in terror, Xavier jumped high into an oak tree and clapped his hand over the guy's mouth.

Xavier savored the blood, having forgotten again to feed in a number of nights. The depraved life passed before Xavier's closed eyelids. Robbery, rape, beatings. Nothing redeeming in the miserable soul. Xavier carried him downtown and posed him on lower Wacker Drive, another degenerate who drank himself into oblivion, according to the police when they found him.

However, thanks to Brady, Xavier and Thomas could take nights out for themselves from time to time. One night, on a walk along Lake Michigan, Xavier confided a worry to Thomas. "What if it's all a mirage, and he's healing too quickly?"

"What do you mean?"

"I don't want his recovery to be false and forced."

Thomas contemplated a minute and then grabbed Xavier's hand as they passed Navy Pier. "I'm not worried. He's still quiet. He lets himself cry. His previous happy demeanor and laugh has not returned and nothing sounds fake."

Thomas's assurance comforted Xavier. Not as much, however, as the conversation Xavier had with Jaret a few nights later, before classes started. Jaret had purchased a new car with Anthony's money after selling his previous one because it reminded him of his last drive to Fremont. Xavier lectured him about being careful and not becoming a target in his convertible.

Jaret laughed and said, "Okay, Mom."

The words stunned them both once they fell out of his mouth. The color drained from Jaret's face, and he slumped onto the couch. "I miss her so much," he sputtered through tears.

Xavier again held Jaret in his arms for a long time.

When Jaret stopped crying, Xavier pulled away but stayed close with only Darth sitting between them.

"Will Darth be okay when I'm not here?" Jaret asked.

Strange, Xavier thought. Until he pondered the question. Nothing made Jaret embrace his emotion more than his dog. When most vulnerable, he reached to her for protection. He felt exposed and alone and reached out to her, his anchor, with this question about her safety.

"Nothing will ever happen to her. You have my word. The entire staff knows she comes first."

"Thank you. You know, I'm not good at the emotion kind of thing. Jodie tells me so a lot. Even before everything, I wasn't good at letting myself be vulnerable. So, I'm not good expressing emotion." His eyes teared. "Now, especially. See, if I open up or say thank you to you and Thomas, then I'm admitting to myself you mean something to me. But no one is ever going to mean anything to me again because then I won't hurt so much when something happens. See? My mind is working those thoughts over and over."

Jaret lifted Darth onto his lap and held her as he wiped at another tear.

"It's okay to never heal." Xavier surprised himself with the words.

Jaret reflected in silence. "I don't understand."

"Yes, you do." Xavier reached over and held Jaret's hand. "This world expects you to move on. And to some extent you will. You have to. You'll find happiness again. You'll work. Have friends. Despite everything you think, you'll be vulnerable again. But the pain never goes away, so don't expect it to."

Jaret leaned over and kissed Darth on the head. "I don't know how to live this way."

"You just have to learn. I've been alive since the 1700s. Think about the length of time. And every day I think about my father, and especially my brother. I think about my friend Anne, even though I see her ghost sometimes. And Maria. Friends gone for decades still haunt me. All of them. They live inside me. I came to feel more of a sense of peace because they'd become such a part of my being. Their memory gave me some sense at least a part of them still lived. But I miss them. Every day I miss them." Xavier handed Jaret a tissue. "I hope I'm not bungling this. You should probably be hearing the ideas from Jodie, not me."

"Please, don't stop."

Xavier sighed. "I'm just trying to say you'll miss them forever. They're a part of who you are. That will never change. Don't go looking for some grand moment of revelation and healing. Healing will happen in a painfully slow manner over a long period of time. And part of you will always be sad. Always. And the emotion is a good thing, because the hurt turns you into the person you'll become. And the ache keeps their spirit alive in you."

"For you too?"

"Every day."

Xavier led Jaret up to a special room he maintained for himself. He showed Jaret his keepsakes, such as his father's quill pen, some of Michel's medals, and an empty bottle of wine Anne had kept as a reminder of the last time Xavier drank himself into oblivion during the French Revolution as he came to terms with his true self and his love for Thomas.

When Xavier escorted Jaret to his bedroom, Jaret let Darth inside and paused at the door. "I love you." Then he scratched his ear and ran his hands through his long hair. "I don't mean like *love* love. I mean, you know. Like, you know."

Xavier smiled. "I didn't take your words wrong. You're part of my family. I love you too."

"Yeah," Jaret cried again. "My family. I love you both."

He closed the door, and Xavier stood outside for several minutes and listened to Jaret crying. He placed his hand on the door and said a prayer for his dear friend who had become like a son to him.

Thirty-Eight: Estes Park

DECEMBER 2011
Colorado

Jaret kept Xavier apprised of the fact he and Jodie worked through most of November in preparation for Jaret to return to his family home in Estes Park. He surprised Xavier with the idea of going to Colorado for Thanksgiving. Xavier convinced him to wait a while longer and work through the emotional implications first, so he delayed the trip until Christmas.

Xavier had arranged, soon after Henrik killed Jaret's family, for people to go to the house in Estes Park to clean and care for it until Jaret returned. Xavier always knew he would go back at some point, but until Jaret mentioned Thanksgiving and now worked toward Christmas, Xavier had not known how close Jaret was to wanting to go back.

Jaret had walked into the living room one night as Xavier read. He set the book down and looked at Jaret. "What's up?"

"Not much. Thinking about going back to Estes later this month."

"Returning won't be easy," Xavier said.

"I know. I have so many good memories from home. But for some reason, going back will make their deaths real. Like, I know they died. But then it's really real. I talk about going home at every session with Jodie. To understand whatever I feel is okay. And to expect being there to be hard. Which reminds me I wanted to talk to you about something."

"Of course. Anything."

"Where's Thomas?"

"Out. Doing God knows what damage to the world." Xavier still avoided mention of Anthony. Thomas and Anthony had a night on the town, just the two of them.

"Good. Not because I don't love him. I do. But sometimes I find talking to you easier."

Xavier smiled. "No offense taken. I understand." Xavier patted the couch next to him as an invitation to Jaret. They both laughed when Darth jumped up instead. Jaret sat on her other side.

Jaret chatted about nonsense for a few minutes before he got to the point. "I need to ask a favor. I hate to, after everything you've done for me. But it's important."

"What?"

"I want to go back to Estes mid-December, after finals but before Christmas. Otherwise, I'll always associate the holiday with going back. You know? Anyway, what concerns you is I need someone to go along. Brady needs to go to his dad's. I was wondering if you and Thomas would come with me. I mean, I need the support."

"You can count on us."

The rest of early December went by rapidly. Xavier observed Jaret but none of his behavior was out of the ordinary. Jaret spent most of his time studying for finals, going to class, and in counseling with Jodie. He went out a couple of times with Brady. One night he returned, more down than usual.

"What's going on?" Xavier asked.

"Going to clubs leaves a bad taste in my mouth. I don't know. The partying. The guys hooking up, some already in relationships. Reminds me of—" Jaret stopped. "Reminds me of stuff."

Xavier assumed he nearly mentioned Anthony before he retreated.

"The scene is too happy for me right now. I'm not ready for real happy."

But during finals week, Jaret became more and more morose. He slipped back into talking less and took to his room alone with Darth on most nights. Xavier's heart broke to see him again at the depths of desolation, yet he understood. He expected despair when Jaret arrived at key moments of transition.

The night they packed the car for the drive to Colorado, Thomas again tried to convince Jaret to go with vampiric speed.

"I might need my car." Jaret put Darth in the back seat as Xavier climbed in after her.

Thomas stood outside the car with the passenger door open. "At least let me drive."

Xavier pointed to Thomas then pointed to the passenger seat, commanding him to get into the car. "It's not about you." Thomas obeyed.

They drove to the house in Fremont that Thomas had purchased for them, spent the day there with all of them sleeping, then sped through Nebraska and northern Colorado until they arrived an hour before dawn the next morning in the mountains.

Jaret gave away no emotion as he drove up the beautiful canyon from Loveland to Estes Park, nor any indication of his state of mind as they drove around Lake Estes and toward Sanborn Drive. He slowed the car to a crawl as they wound around Fish Creek Road and pulled to the curb at a large bend.

"It's right around the corner," Jaret said.

Thomas reached over and placed his hand on Jaret's arm. "Do you want me to drive?"

Jaret nodded and unbuckled his seat belt. They both got out of the car and switched places; then Thomas pulled back onto the road. Xavier reached up and grabbed Jaret's shoulders in each hand.

Jaret motioned for them to pull into a driveway. They sat in front of a medium-sized brown home with magnificent pine trees surrounding a deck that wrapped around three sides of the house.

Jaret opened the door, and Darth leapt out. She started to trot away but he screamed at her to return. She lurched to a halt and came back to him. "Coyotes and even mountain lions," Jaret explained. "They eat little animals. She's not real little. Still."

Then Jaret fell silent. He reached into his pocket for a set of keys and walked up a flight of stairs and onto the deck. He paused at the front door before putting the keys in the lock and opening the door.

Inside, Darth sprinted from room to room in a familiar manner and wagged her tail whenever she passed Jaret. Thomas and Xavier stayed behind Jaret as he mimicked his dog and went from room to room. In what was obviously his own room—they could tell from the Mika poster and history books—he sat on the bed next to Darth.

"Wow, this is hard." Tears burst forth, breaking Xavier's heart.

The sun came up too soon, forcing Xavier to a basement bedroom first.

"I'll stay with him until the last possible minute," Thomas promised. "I can stay up longer than you. Go to bed."

The next few days passed in a flash. One night, Jaret asked Thomas and Xavier to join him in the living room.

"There's a lot of memories here. I think I'd like to share some of them."

"We'd love to listen." Xavier sat back to listen while Thomas poured them all a drink.

"The brass deer thing"—Jaret pointed to a foot high deer near the fireplace on the floor—"if you put it here next to my chair, a ghost knocks it over."

"A ghost?" Thomas asked.

"Yeah. Pretty sure the lady who built and lived in the house until she died is still here. I've seen her. This was her spot. She hits the deer when she goes to sit in the chair. My mom could sense her presence, which says a lot since most of the time I got scolded for saying I saw ghosts. I could never say anything because they always freaked if I talked about ghosts."

"What else?" Xavier took a sip of his drink. As usual, Thomas made it too strong.

"See the ridge up there? Right next to the driveway? If you watch, you'll see a bobcat walk right along on the prowl."

Thomas got up and walked to the window. "Isn't that dangerous?"

Jaret nodded. "Yeah. You can't leave dogs outside and shit. But I grew up with wildlife. So you have to be careful. Oh! Look at this picture." Jaret got up and took a needlepoint Christmas picture off the wall. "My mom did this. One every year. I have to keep them." Jaret wiped at a tear.

He quieted for a bit but then chatted a while longer before he retired to bed.

One morning, Jaret declared they needed to decorate the house. "I have one picture up, which is nothing. My mom had a lot of other stuff." He set a box on the kitchen counter. "Look, my mom's Christmas dishes. I have to be careful not to break any." Then he showed Xavier one by one the other holiday scenes she had sewn.

Jaret hurried down a hall and opened a closet. "Help me with this." He pointed to a large shape covered with a black plastic bag. Xavier carried the object to the living room for him.

"A Christmas tree." Xavier smiled as he removed the bag and noticed an ornament with a picture of a very young Jaret. "How cute."

Jaret rolled his eyes.

They spent the afternoon decorating.

"Did they always leave the tree decorated and with the lights around it, shoved in the closet?" Xavier asked.

Jaret laughed and cried at the same time about the tree. "They hated decorating the tree so kept it in there with a bag over it. I always hated how we didn't decorate the tree anymore. But the fact always made me laugh. Still does." He held an ornament for several minutes, staring into the sparkle for a memory he kept to himself.

On Christmas Eve day, Jaret went to the store and purchased a mountain of food. Xavier awoke to Thomas and Jaret in the kitchen preparing a feast.

"Are we having an army to dinner?"

Jaret actually laughed. "Tradition. This meal. You and Thomas have to eat with me. I know you don't like to poop—"

Thomas placed his hand over Jaret's mouth. "No one wants the image. Stop there."

They had a divine Christmas Eve dinner in which Jaret opened up about holiday memories. At one point before dessert, he grew very quiet and then lifted his wine glass in the air. He barely choked out his toast. "To the Bachmanns."

Thirty-Nine: Harriet's Visit

JANUARY 2012
Estes Park, Colorado

The day after New Year's Day and a week before they needed to return to Chicago for Jaret's next semester, Xavier knocked on Jaret's bedroom door. Jaret had a bad couple of days after he started cleaning the house and reorganizing closets and rooms. He explained he owned the house, had to take care of it, and planned on keeping possessions but wanted to clear out some clutter. Each closet, each shelf, held some memory Jaret had to process.

"May I?" Xavier motioned to sit on the bed near Jaret.

Jaret nodded. He set aside a box of pictures and picked a few up he had spread around the floor. Darth slept on the end of the bed.

"You'll be honest with me if this is a bad idea?" Xavier had gone over his plan a million times, thinking about the positives and negatives and all of the probable implications. Still he fretted, afraid to cause Jaret any unnecessary pain.

Jaret tilted his head and creased his brow. "I don't lie to you."

Xavier nodded. "I have someone I want you to talk to." Xavier paused, searching for the right words. "Remember the conversation we had about never healing?"

"Yeah. Your advice helped a lot. Still does."

"I'm glad. But that's not why I asked. I think you could be helped if you heard the same thing from more people or were exposed to more ways of coping with loss than from me alone."

Jaret reached over and petted Darth.

Xavier slapped his knee. "I'll stop. Here. There's someone in my life who did suffer as much as you—if not brutally more. I want you to talk to her. Again, not to force some false healing. But so you see you're not alone, to get what I meant about the sorrow being a part of you and remaining sad even as you struggle for a way to move on and allow yourself some happiness."

Jaret frowned. He played with Darth's collar and appeared to fight some emotion. "No one experienced what I did."

"Give her a chance. For me?"

Jaret got up and motioned for Xavier to lead the way without saying anything.

Harriet sat in a chair in the living room, as beautiful as ever. She radiated warmth and understanding as she stood and brushed her hand along the designer jeans she wore. Her red sweater glowed warmly against her skin.

"Jaret," she said and held out her hand. When Jaret reached out and shook it, she held his hand firmly and led him to a loveseat, forcing him to sit right next to her. She had a commanding presence few challenged.

Even Darth accepted the situation and walked over to sit at Xavier's feet.

Xavier had racked his brain for a way to help Jaret beyond what he had already done. He knew Catherine could help but thought introducing her to Jaret was a bad idea. The parallel to Jenn might overwhelm Jaret, even though Xavier knew Catherine would love Jaret to death.

Xavier had no idea why he'd taken so long to think of Harriet in connection with Jaret.

"I hope you don't mind Xavier told me about you. I'm a member of the Vampire Council, so he had to."

Xavier wanted to blend into the background, so he didn't correct her. His telling Harriet about Jaret had nothing to do with vampire business whatsoever. She probably framed her introduction as such to protect a confidence between Jaret and Xavier.

"When I suffered the same thing as you, only people who'd experienced profound grief could really reach me. I had people around me who cared. One in particular sat with me for hours to help." Xavier knew she meant Anthony and avoided his name at Xavier's request. "Much as he helped, only those who'd lived a similar tragedy could reach me at the deepest level."

Jaret began to cry as Harriet continued.

"I suppose you're used to vampires by now? I ask because I've got to give you some rather old history. You're a historian, right? You'll know how old."

Jaret nodded. He glanced around the room and then kept his eyes on Darth. She lifted her head and perked her ears.

Harriet held Jaret tight with both of his hands in hers. "I was a slave in the Old South. I won't tell you my whole story, but someday you may want to know. I escaped because another vampire needed me to carry on his work of protecting slaves from the most vicious masters. I accepted the duty out of a sense of obligation. I took no comfort in eternal life. My immortality gave me no hope at the time. I did my duty as a calling to do more for the slaves than I could as a human. Anyway, after I escaped with the assistance of the vampire, my master tortured and killed my family before I knew his intentions. I thought them safe because they were healthy and worth a lot of money.

"I'd been told I had to leave them behind to become a vampire and accepted the reality. Again, as an obligation with no choice. But I had planned to watch over them from afar. To protect them. To watch them grow old and maybe even try to help them escape if I could without violating the ethic."

A combination of her story and Jaret's crying pushed Xavier over the edge to near weeping himself. Harriet, too, wiped at the blood tears in her eyes.

"In one night, they were all gone. You're not alone. You'll never be alone. A family member of Xavier's is part of my family too."

"No one survived but you? And you decided to go on?"

Harriet grinned with sympathy. "I did for them. If I had my choice, I would've joined them. Selfishly. And not a day goes by I don't think of them and pray they watch me from heaven, proud of what I accomplished. I am who

I am because of them. I'll never forget them. You won't forget your family either."

"Does the memory...um...ever...you know...like... stop hurting?" Jaret stumbled over his words.

"The pain changes. Oh, the hurt still stabs me in the heart sometimes. Like I lost them yesterday. Other times, I feel a more comfortable presence. I'm not going to lie to you. It never stops hurting altogether."

Harriet closed what little distance remained between the two of them and pulled Jaret into a tight hug.

When Jaret asked Harriet another question, Xavier took the opportunity to remove himself from the room. They needed time alone to cope with their shared misery. Xavier felt warmed by doing the right thing in bringing Harriet to Estes Park as he'd watched Jaret open up to her.

Knowing Jaret was in good hands, Xavier snuck out to the Stanley Hotel. There, in the finest of rooms with wine uncorked and her arms wide open, Catherine rushed across the room and hugged him.

"Don't break my ribs," he said and kissed her on each cheek.

"You'd heal. How did it go?" she asked.

"Pretty good. Harriet was magnificent. She was very open with him. More open than she's ever been, even with me."

Xavier spent a nice night with Catherine, catching up on her trip to China and how much she despised the Communist rulers. She told of her exploits in Japan, followed by a holiday in India with Harriet.

Xavier updated her on the situation with Jaret, though he had kept her abreast of most of the story via email as he went along.

Harriet and Catherine left a couple days later. They had agreed with Xavier to keep Catherine's presence a secret. Xavier saw them off as they hurried toward Alaska, excited to experience the longer nights there for the first time in their lives. Xavier noticed their traveling together occurred more and more frequently though they denied they were a couple.

"Watch out for Sarah Palin," he said.

Catherine waved her hand in the air. "If we see her, we'll get her into bed and take pictures."

Xavier returned to Thomas and Jaret, who had put the finishing touches on the house as they prepared to leave.

"You okay?" Xavier asked.

Jaret nodded. "Thanks for introducing me to Harriet. I like her a lot."

"I knew you would."

"And I want to meet Catherine next time. If she's part of your family, it's important to me."

Xavier looked at Thomas, assuming he'd spilled the beans. Thomas shot his hands in the air and his eyes opened wide.

Jaret smiled. "It's like last summer. I'm sad. Depressed. Not stupid or deaf. I can pick up on what's going on."

Jaret decided to drive back alone with Darth so Xavier and Thomas could go fast without riding in the car.

It had taken a lot of convincing on Thomas's part for Xavier not to shadow Jaret the entire way.

"You're a nervous mother hen. You're going to smother him to death. Stop. You can't always protect him from every danger he might face."

Xavier and Thomas spent a nice night in Chicago on their own, topped off by more wine. They hunted together, playing one of the games Thomas so loved.

Xavier giggled as they settled behind a dumpster in an alley.

"Shh." Thomas slapped his knee. "You'll ruin everything."

"Because you blend so well." Xavier motioned for Thomas to consider how his ass stuck out.

"The bait."

"It *is* a good ass."

"Will you be quiet? Here they come."

Three guys approached with guns drawn. Thomas and Xavier had spotted them earlier because they were doing target practice in their backyard, clearly up to no good.

Before they reached their destination, Thomas jumped out in front of them. He grabbed two of them, throwing one against the wall and killing him. The other he began to drink from.

Meanwhile, Xavier chased down the third thug and slammed him to the ground, drinking from his neck. He almost gagged when the stench from the man's pants hit his nostrils. He had shit himself in fear.

One night later, Jaret drove into their garage right on schedule, and again their routine returned as Jaret started his final semester, and Xavier and Thomas watched over him. Indeed, things had progressed enough for Xavier to determine to take the next step in this healing process.

Forty: Clandestine Meeting

APRIL 2012
Austin, Texas

"You left him alone with Thomas? Is that wise?"

Xavier laughed at Anthony's question as they settled down on a couple of bar stools at a high table along the wall in a large dance club. Gay boys danced around them, people laughing and having fun on a Friday night.

"Thomas gets him to let loose more than anyone else, except maybe his friend Brady. You know how incorrigible Thomas can be. Sometimes his quirks work to our advantage. Jaret even agreed to try a night out dancing with Thomas. We'll see."

Anthony nodded but had withdrawn at the mention of Jaret going out. Good. Xavier wanted to expose him as much as possible.

"I'm so used to meeting you in these situations with a gaggle of boys," Xavier said, another intentional jab. "You never used to miss an opportunity for fresh meat, what with all these hung Texans around."

Anthony stared across the table without smiling. He had pulled his long blond hair into a ponytail but instead of any revealing clothing, he wore a crisp button-down shirt and pleated shorts. "I haven't played the field in a long time."

"Since you met a certain someone."

"What's the point? Did you meet me to dig at a wound? To taunt me?"

"Have you been with anyone since then?"

Anthony grabbed his glass and chugged. Then he went to the bar and had another shot of liquor before he returned with yet another drink.

"No. I haven't." He sipped at his drink this time. Xavier remained stoic, waiting for the next moment to pounce. He had learned from Thomas, despite his own inclination to nurture and take things slow, Anthony also needed a kick in the ass sometimes.

Anthony glanced around the room before meeting Xavier's eyes. "So my relationship with Jaret exposed me. We all know I used to be a slut to cover the pain. Anonymous sex doesn't work anymore. Not that my sex drive disappeared. But I need time to get back to my old self. Are you happy now?"

Xavier took a drink of his raspberry rum and Coke. "I didn't push you to the brink to make myself happy."

"Then why?"

Xavier paused before answering. He took a drink and sighed. "This isn't my style. Let me start over?"

Anthony nodded but still frowned across the table.

"Thomas told me I had to get your attention, or you'd never listen to me. I don't know if he's accurate, but

I've seen your reluctance to engage in something unless Thomas tweaks you first. I can't approach you with the same harshness. I hope you'll hear me out anyway."

Anthony's shoulders slumped and lost their rigid posture. Still he said nothing, so Xavier waited. Eventually, Anthony spoke in such a soft tone Xavier needed his vampiric senses to hear him. "I know why you're here, and nothing's changed."

"I disagree. Two very significant things have changed. Hear me out."

"Okay."

"First, one of your main contentions regarding Jaret had to do with his leaving his family. They're gone. You don't have them as an excuse anymore."

Anthony stared into the distance. "True. But he's still too powerful a witch."

"So there's only one obstacle, not two."

"What was your other point?"

Xavier gathered himself so as not to make a scene in front of others. "A matter of life and death. Or it could be. He needs you, Anthony. I can't begin to fathom what he's experienced. But I see the effect on him every day. He's lost his carefree demeanor and will to live. He's decided to survive. He still needs something to help him make the next step. Hope. He needs hope."

"And you know I can't offer hope because of the Vampire Council. The ethic is very clear about the danger he poses."

Xavier scooted his stool closer to the table and leaned toward Anthony, his face now inches from

Anthony's. He stared into his blue eyes as if peering into his soul. He had one opportunity to capture Anthony before he might lose him forever to the demons suppressing his emotion and scaring him away from long-term intimacy.

"That's the biggest piece of bullshit I've ever heard from you. Almost two hundred years ago, you lost the ability to hide behind the Council. I have it on good authority you'd lose the vote about Jaret by four to one. Harriet, Catherine, and Thomas all agree with me. Besides, reaching out to him doesn't have to mean he becomes a vampire, let alone a member of the Council. Hide behind these invented black-and-white laws of yours if you wish only to protect yourself. Eternity doesn't have to be constant mourning for the past unless you let your sorrow rule. Moving on won't dishonor your old lover. But continuing as if you're in a coma might."

Anthony glared at Xavier with an icy coldness. Xavier half expected Anthony to throw his drink in his face. Xavier pulled away and sat upright on his stool.

"I don't talk about my feelings because I'm frightened." Anthony bit his bottom lip, then rubbed his eyes. The chilled atmosphere evaporated. "I honored him by living and enjoying life. And I do. You know, as does Thomas. I could never bring myself to embrace another relationship because I'm scared. Scared to death of losing him again. I watched him die. Then, after centuries, I tried again—only to have Thomas fool me into making him a vampire and then abandoning me. In the modern parlance, a relationship doesn't work for two 'power tops' to stay together. I'm from a different era. Things moved slowly, even slower than when you lived as a human. I figure as a vampire I can take five hundred years to heal each time. I've given myself the luxury. I can't start something with Jaret and then lose him, too, whether to human death or because of the ethic. Another loss would most certainly kill me."

"Reach out to him. Even a simple message would help."

The hint of a blood tear appeared at the corner of Anthony's eye. "Don't you see? I can't."

Xavier allowed the silence to linger. Never had Anthony been so open and honest about what inhibited him. He had exposed a raw emotion buried deep within himself. Nothing he said surprised Xavier. Had someone asked beforehand, Xavier could have predicted every word. Anthony had hidden for centuries as the sole member of the Vampire Council, in part to protect vampires out of a sense of duty, and in part to protect his own emotions. So long as he had his obligation, he could hardly drag someone else into his business by courting them.

But two centuries ago, after Xavier had gone rogue and went about freeing slaves in America, he thought Anthony had been liberated from this burden when they reconstituted the Council with the four new members joining Anthony.

Yet still today Anthony maintained a rigid interpretation of the rules and what the ethic stipulated. Anthony forced the others to negotiate with him to see reason on many occasions when everyone else thought the changed realities in the world mandated a tweaking of the ethic.

It became so much clearer tonight. True, Anthony had a personality attracted to order. He often did see the world in black-and-white terms. But more than his personality trait, he still hid in the ethic to protect himself. So long as he could always find a legal excuse, he never had to cope with his lack of a relationship. In his constructed world, the forces around him commanded his single life, not his own emotion.

Xavier reached over and grabbed Anthony's hand. "You can change. Even a stubborn old vampire like yourself can change."

Anthony got up and motioned for Xavier to follow. They wandered the darkened streets of Austin. Without witnesses, Anthony allowed himself to cry. Though he kept them moving and avoided any verbal engagement with Xavier, he did allow Xavier to put his arm around him.

"The sun's almost up." Anthony stopped outside his flat and unlocked the door.

Inside, Xavier stood in the living room before retiring to bed. "Are you okay?"

Anthony smiled. "You're a good priest. Not only do you stare into people's souls and see the truth, but you get them to confess. Perhaps more to themselves than to anyone else."

Xavier hugged Anthony and kissed him on the cheek. "Don't close up."

"I can't promise you anything."

Xavier started to walk away but stopped and turned around. "I'm not expecting you to. I'm simply asking you to live within the gray areas of life. He needs you. Frankly, you need him too."

Anthony nodded and again smiled as Xavier went on his way to the guest coffin in Anthony's flat.

Forty-One: Mika in London

JULY 2012
Chicago, Illinois

For the first time since saving Jaret from Henrik, Xavier understood the rage of a parent. He loved Jaret to death. He respected his depression and the emotional turmoil he still struggled against. But Jaret's obstinate behavior of the last month boiled to the point Xavier fought to keep his emotions in check.

Thankfully, Thomas had stormed out of the room a few minutes before when his exasperation had become too much.

Jaret sat like a statue with Darth in his lap. His furrowed brow gave away his fury, as did the tightly closed lips.

As a college graduation gift in May, Thomas and Xavier had purchased airline tickets for Jaret and Brady to fly to London to stay in a five-star hotel, along with front-row tickets to the Mika concert in July. Thankfully, no one told Brady because Jaret refused to go.

They'd argued about the trip several times. Each time, Jaret shut down and stopped talking. Only once did he explain his reasoning.

"I'll only go with Anthony," he said. "He and I planned the vacation, and then he dumped me. When Mika came to Chicago, Steve fucked it up, and I let him. It's obvious that some supernatural force is dooming me. I'm not meant to see him live. I'm done talking about going to London."

He never let up on pretending something mystical doomed his desire to see Mika in concert. "Each failed attempt could be an omen. Not good to ignore any omen ever again."

Tonight, Jaret repeated this refrain. "Too risky. Can't ignore the gods' warning. How clear does the alarm have to be, other than every time I try to go something tragic happens?"

Jaret finished this monologue for the umpteenth time, and Xavier had enough.

Xavier stood across the room and let out an exasperated breath. Before he spoke, he reminded himself Jaret was still depressed. Lashing out at him would do no good, and may possibly cause harm, if Jaret thought he was losing Xavier as his new family.

Still, he needed to hear the truth. They couldn't walk on eggshells around him forever and always protect him from the troubling things he still had to confront.

Xavier knelt in front of Jaret and placed his hands on Jaret's knees.

"I love you. I'll always love you. And I understand what you're going through. But all of your reasons for not going are bullshit. At least have the decency to tell me the truth. You can punish yourself if you need to. But promise me you'll talk to Jodie about the concert because your reasoning isn't rational or fair. You deserve to have fun. You earned this trip. You've wanted to see Mika in concert your entire life. The guilt controls you."

"I won't go without Anthony," Jaret said as tears streamed down his face.

Xavier stood and pulled Jaret against his stomach. He clutched the young man's head and leaned over to kiss his hair.

Then he held Jaret's head gently in his hands, as if a priceless artifact.

"I love you." He patted Jaret's hair and walked out of the room.

Part Eight: Henrik and the Rogue Vampires

Forty-Two: Vampire Council

25 AUGUST 2012
Washington, DC

"Explain again why we're up here?" Thomas glanced around the roof of the National Cathedral as he asked the question.

Xavier punched Thomas in the arm. "Aesthetics. The beauty. The grand view. The gargoyles enchanting us. And as long as we avoid the security, no one knows we're up here."

"Well, who starts this meeting? For a group enforcing rules, we don't have many to dictate how we operate."

Anthony laughed. "The biggest rogue in the history of vampirism seeks more rules? I can't believe it."

"No," Thomas said tersely. "But we make such a big deal about calling all of us into session, meet at the oddest of places, and then gawk around without anyone seeming to know how to get the party started."

Catherine linked her arm through Thomas's and led him to one view of the city. "How can you not take a moment and appreciate this? No one else can get up here at this hour. We have an exclusive tour, and you want to get on with some meeting?"

"We're intruders. Common criminals."

Everyone laughed at Thomas and gathered near him.

Anthony motioned toward Thomas. "Well, then, why don't you begin?"

"I don't want to. It's not my thing this time."

"It's everyone's problem." Harriet stepped forward. "The magic seldom alerts all of us to an emergency of its own volition. Having a ghost trapped in a house, unmonitored, was enough of a problem. Our jurisdiction doesn't include spirits. But our friend Henrik pulled in some vampires."

"Henrik did?" Thomas asked.

"Didn't you read the report? The magical missive came to all of us." Xavier said, exasperated.

Thomas shrugged. "I knew you were reading, and I was busy watching *Dallas*."

They all laughed at him again before Xavier kept them on task. "Henrik has apparently called forth some vampires to work with him. Or they discovered him and are manipulating the situation. We're not sure what they're up to. But something is going on in the Bachmann mansion demanding the Council's attention."

"Yes," Anthony said. "Something has to be done about Henrik, whether or not Jaret agrees. A trapped and angry entity flirting with vampires endangers us all."

"What's the solution?" Catherine asked.

Xavier answered her. "I think Anthony, Thomas, and I need to go to Fremont. Soon. I spoke briefly with Jaret, and we agreed Henrik needs to be trapped back in the iron box. I won't allow Jaret to go, but I think we can handle Henrik."

The five agreed to have those three take care of Henrik.

As they sauntered through the quiet Washington evening, Thomas grabbed Xavier's hand. "Seriously, we could have done the meeting on a conference call, let alone in some exotic location. Ridiculous."

"Anthony and I think it's important to get everyone together sometimes for Council business, face-to-face."

"Let's get together for parties instead."

They walked quietly until they reached their block. "I hope Jaret will be okay while we're gone." Xavier still hated to leave his adopted son for long periods of time.

Forty-Three: Catherine

2 SEPTEMBER 2012
Washington, DC

"One more time, for me." Xavier pulled Jaret into the breakfast nook and sat next to him. "I haven't been away from you for this long, and I need to know you'll be okay."

Jaret smiled but rolled his eyes. "I can talk about your being like my mom without crying, at least. Mostly because you're a lot worse than her. Like, I don't think she was this protective when I was three."

"You've been through a lot. Humor me."

Jaret smiled. "I'm fine. *I am.*" Then he glanced out the window and tilted his head.

"What?" Xavier asked, alarmed.

"Nothing bad." Jaret smiled. "I wonder sometimes why you took me in. You know? We've talked a little about what you did. But this is intense, don't you think?"

Xavier grinned. "Indeed. I don't know what you want me to say. You mean a lot to me. Like the son I never had, maybe? I wish I had something profound to tell you or some moment of revelation to explain everything.

Instead, I grew to care about you as a friend over time without some grand scheme. Then, when Henrik murdered your family, and you called us for help, I knew what I had to do for a friend. At that moment, you became part of my family and I loved you. I operated on instinct, obligation, and love all at the same time."

"Just like that?"

"Just like that." Xavier nodded. "I suppose we could contemplate the deeper longings we meet for each other. Parent and child? Lost families? Older brother and little brother? But I'm not sure an exact definition is necessary or even possible. I know our bond developed and took a profound hold over me."

Jaret sat in thought for several seconds before he smiled and nodded. "Same for me. But I'd say it's closest to you being my surrogate parent. Because I need one and love our relationship. Okay?"

A blood tear materialized at the corner of Xavier's eye. "Beautiful. And, for the record, I feel the same way." Xavier wiped at the tear. "Now tell me. You'll be okay while I'm gone?" Xavier repeated what had started the conversation, bringing them back to the moment at hand.

"I need to stay here and do a lot more exploring, to have some fun. I know what you're doing with Thomas and Anthony, and I don't want any part of the attempt. I can't be so close to Anthony. I never want to see the house again. So, you go do what has to be done." Jaret played with a napkin on the table. "Sure, I'll worry a little. But I trust you guys to be careful and win. I'm going to stay here and try to figure out my future. I can't think of a better place." Jaret waved his hand out the window, indicating Washington, DC.

After his morose attitude about the Mika concert and once the concert date had passed, Jaret snapped out of his pure misery. He mentioned he'd made a breakthrough with Jodie and even went dancing a couple of times with Brady. Then he announced he was giving himself one year to find himself, whatever that ambiguous phrase meant. Xavier tried not to push.

Finally, Jaret asked if they could set up their household in Washington, DC, for the rest of the summer. They had.

After settling here, Jaret demanded to meet Catherine. She arrived in all her glory and hit it off instantly with Jaret. Xavier had fretted about his sister reminding Jaret too much of Jenn, but he seemed to cope well and loved Catherine's enthusiasm for life. She pulled him out of his shell unlike anyone else despite all their attempts to do so.

"But you'll take some time to look at the graduate school material?" Xavier asked for the hundredth time.

Jaret laughed. "I have the literature in my room. Applications aren't due until January, anyway."

"You can't wait until the last minute to pull all the materials together."

"I know." Jaret nodded. "We'll get to them. You're going to be back in a couple of weeks. I think we have enough time. Just let me hang out with Catherine. She promised we're going to tour like vampires instead of normal tourists."

This time Xavier laughed. "I don't think I want to know what she means." He paused, still concerned. He always worried Jaret might relapse each time he took a step forward. Though they'd had some ups and downs, so far he'd held steady without any major setbacks. What if he panicked while Xavier was gone?

Xavier recalled Catherine's scolding of him earlier. "What am I? Chopped liver? He's safe. I won't let any harm come to him. I can contact you in a second, and you can run back here in a matter of hours if not minutes, should anything happen. Trust me and trust him. Go do your séance or whatever and leave us alone. We're bored of being with you every minute of the night."

Looking across the table, Xavier almost teared up again, this time at how much more at peace Jaret appeared. He had lost the ever-present hunching over in despair of the last several months. "Okay." Xavier stood up and pulled Jaret into a hug. "We'll talk about your future when I get back."

Jaret let his arms fall to his side and leaned his head against Xavier's chest. "You wear me out. I promised a million times we'll decide my future. It's not like I'm eighty and only have a few more years to figure everything out. We'll talk."

They both started at Catherine's voice behind them. "Are you still harassing him about the future? You're the worst kind of helicopter parent ever imagined."

"Why do I feel like I'm leaving a three-year-old with a child molester?" Xavier said as the three of them moved toward the living room.

Jaret laughed.

Catherine screeched to a halt as she grabbed Xavier's arm and spun him around. She pulled his hand to hers and bit him.

"Ouch!"

"Serves you right. A child molester? Are you serious? It's not even funny to joke about such a thing. And coming from a priest—"

Xavier watched as his hand healed. "I probably have rabies. And, if you'll remember, I'm not a priest anymore."

"But you act like one all the time. Like a sequestered old monk." Thomas looked up from some financial documents as the three entered the living room. Each took a seat.

"Why is everyone picking on me tonight?" Xavier asked. "First I'm too protective. Then I'm a priest again, which I'm not. And now I'm a monk."

"A pouting monk," Catherine said and jumped across the room to peck him on the forehead.

"Are you ready to go?" Thomas asked Xavier. "We need to meet Anthony before the sun comes up." He put away all his papers.

Xavier shot a look at Thomas. Thomas froze in consternation, unsure of how to extricate himself from the situation. An awkward silence descended upon the room.

"Um, guys." Jaret arched his eyebrows and broke into the uncomfortable quiet. "I know his name. I know he's going to be with you. Sure, it'd be easier if you just ignored him, too, and refused to talk about him. But this tiptoeing around his name drives me nuts. Like Voldemort lurks in the shadows. You make me feel crazy. Bonkers."

Catherine burst into laughter. "I've been dealing with this kind of behavior with the two of them for centuries. Can you imagine? They're impossible, especially when they start their silent, lovers' communication. They make me vomit."

"I know!" Jaret grinned. "Like you're not sitting in the room seeing their nonsense happen. Instead, you know something happened but not the details. Like you're the moron. No—I know. It's like you're a dog sitting in the corner waiting for them to be done with each other so you can get attention."

"All right, enough!" Xavier stood and pulled Thomas to his feet. "I think we need to get out of here. Though I'm still questioning whether or not it's a good idea to leave these two together."

Thomas grinned. "Especially since the plans include breaking into national monuments."

Xavier spun around and stared at Catherine, who just looked innocently back at him. "He'll be fine."

"Not if he's in prison!"

Thomas pulled Xavier toward the door. "Ignore Mama Bear. He's going with me."

Xavier glanced back at the house once the two of them got to the sidewalk. Jaret and Catherine stared out the window, waving goodbye and laughing at something Catherine said.

"Seriously, is it a good idea to leave her with him? I think she goes crazier and crazier with each passing decade."

"I agree." Thomas yanked Xavier down the street. "But this way he'll know there are more insane people than him or us. Come on. We have more important business. You didn't tell him, did you?"

"Of course not. He thinks it's a routine matter." No way Xavier would dare mention to Jaret the need to get rid of Henrik had intensified and became mortally dangerous, even for a vampire.

Forty-Four: Empowered Ghost

8 SEPTEMBER 2012
Fremont, Nebraska

Xavier stared at the logs burning in the fireplace while he and Thomas waited for Anthony to return from his reconnaissance mission. He replayed the last few days in his mind, still searching for a weakness to exploit, even though the three of them had come up with nothing to counteract Henrik.

Thankfully, they still had the house they'd purchased after saving Jaret, because none of them knew how long to expect to stay in Fremont, though all hoped for something quick regarding this mission against a crazed ghost. Sometimes the Council's business took minutes, sometimes days.

Here they sat on the sixth night of combat against the ghost, no more prepared to face him or his minions than before. The magic confounded them, which frustrated the vampires who were accustomed to a life of almost absolute power.

*

Anthony had come ahead to begin surveillance and discovered two alarming bits of information that he explained to Thomas and Xavier when they arrived a few nights later. "First, as the Council's magic informed us, three rogue vampires have taken up residence in the Bachmann Home. Worse, I have no power against them when I set foot on the property. Not even the force invested in me by the Vampire Council's magic does anything. I scanned the area with our magic and saw Henrik somehow protects them and probably found a way to call them to him in the first place. I shouted at them about violating the vampire ethic, to which they laughed and taunted me. I had to flee the property when Henrik flew at me."

The next night, because Thomas refused to believe Anthony's story of being powerless against Henrik, the three did another reconnaissance mission. Thomas stormed up and pounded on the front door. Xavier flinched when Thomas went flying through the air and landed in a bush across the street.

Every night since, Anthony, Thomas, and Xavier visited the Bachmann house to find the same thing: Henrik had full control of the block, including the supernatural elements, despite his continued imprisonment inside its walls. Their magic still contained him there. But he commanded these three defiant vampires, none of whom even Anthony could identify other than being run-of-the-mill vampires he met once at their creation.

The biggest threat became the people who lived around the house. They started to hear the rumblings from within and came around to check out the latest happenings at the huge Victorian mansion in their neighborhood—a house long rumored to be haunted. Henrik seemed intent on bringing attention to himself, and thus to the vampires living with him, and by default, also the ones combatting him.

*

As Xavier contemplated what brought them to the current moment, Anthony rushed into the room, his forehead creased in anger. "Still the same. I can approach the house but not step onto the property. They can't come off the grounds. Those three vampires somehow acquired some extraordinary power through Henrik. They feed off his energy." Anthony slumped into a chair. "There's no use for us to storm over there until we can figure out how to counteract him."

The three listened to nothing but the crackling of the fire. What were they doing wrong? Xavier and Anthony had read and reread every part of the vampire ethic, they had asked other spirits for advice, yet nothing they did gave a better answer.

Xavier almost spilled his wine with fright when Thomas, stretched out on the couch, shot to a sitting position and slapped both hands on his knees. "Maybe we're not approaching the problem the right way. We're not angry enough to think straight."

Xavier stared at him in disbelief.

But Anthony smiled. "I thought we got your temper under control. Why on earth would you propose your irrational rage as a viable option in any situation? Your anger makes you insane."

"And none of us know how to think straight." Xavier figured out what had made Anthony laugh. "Never have, even before we knew what being gay meant."

"That's not what I said about anger." Thomas stood in front of the fire and looked at both of them.

"For lack of any better ideas, explain yourself." Anthony poured himself another glass of wine.

Thomas's voice grew more excited as he talked. "On the frontier, when we came up with strategies for defending our home, or in the past against defiant vampires and our enemies, our anger sharpened our minds and forced us to figure out the best way to attack an enemy. Remember, Anthony, when I almost killed you—"

"You mean when *I* almost killed *you*. I'm not the one who fell into the fire pit."

Thomas rolled his eyes. "Whatever. Such trivial details are beside the point. The rage sharpened our analytical skills. Anger put us in the best frame of mind for combat. We went on cunning and instinct and moved fast or we had no chance."

"How does this help us against Henrik?" Xavier asked. "You sound like you want a new excuse to unleash your out-of-control rage. Are you going to hit me again?"

Thomas flashed genuine anger. "Not funny. Still too soon."

"I referenced a moment during the French Revolution."

"Too soon," Thomas reiterated.

"I went low I admit. Go ahead. Explain."

Thomas's face relaxed and the red drained out. "First, we're too sure of ourselves. We have to admit we may never defeat him. Then, we need to concentrate on what he did to Jaret and the awful being he is. The rogue vampires flaunt our laws and threaten our existence. No more passive vampires hanging out and willy-nilly trying to figure out a solution. We need to attack."

Xavier and Anthony sat immobile, oblivious to whatever point Thomas had made. Xavier felt no closer to a solution than he had when the sun went down to awake them.

Thomas reached over and pulled first Xavier and then Anthony to their feet. "Come on. I'll show you."

Forty-Five: Inferno

8 SEPTEMBER 2012
Fremont, Nebraska

"I need both of you to do as I say." Thomas stood a block away from the Bachmann home, giving Anthony and Xavier their last instructions. "We're going to walk right up the driveway. Don't flinch when they come out. When I say attack, we attack as if they have no special power over us. Then follow my lead."

They started down the street when Xavier called them to a halt. "I'm willing to go along with you, even though this makes no sense. But I'm worried about something. Something significant."

"What?" Anthony asked.

"The danger. Whenever we step onto the property, they throw us around like rag dolls. Even the vampire magic has no effect on them. It's one thing to get thrown into a bush. What if they have something more powerful? What if they can kill us? What makes tonight's plan different from every other night except Thomas wanting to be pissed off?"

"Trust me," Thomas said. "The answers will come."

Thinking both he and Anthony had lost their minds, Xavier followed Thomas as he strode toward the house with no plan of attack, no indication of what he intended, except he thought he had figured out how to make Henrik and his posse enrage them. Xavier's head spun in bewilderment.

A few steps from the front porch, the three vampires appeared before them, each yielding a magical torch of fire.

Xavier heard Thomas whisper "Perfect" as he moved with vampiric speed toward them. Each grinned and then cast their torches at Thomas, who blew up into an inferno right before Xavier's eyes.

Thomas on fire. Dying? Xavier froze with dread and complete panic. Thomas appeared beyond saving, and Xavier wanted nothing more than to jump into the fire with him. As he fought against suicide, he glanced over to see Anthony had enchanted some spell to send the three flying through the air. They landed in separate parts of the street and hurried to their feet.

Henrik's enchanted spell cracked around Xavier, almost visibly, with tiny charges of electricity shooting through the air. Did Anthony break apart the energy?

Without waiting to see the next move from the vampires, Xavier hurried to where he had last seen Thomas and found nothing but charred ground at his feet. With blood tears streaming down his cheeks, the hate he so loathed to admit resided in his heart boiled to the surface. He would avenge Thomas's death.

Xavier remembered the magic Jaret had told him about—the gems helping to imprison Henrik in the iron box years before when Jaret first discovered his witchery.

Xavier stormed into the house and shouted Jaret's spell, despite knowing the gems were safely with Jaret in Washington, DC. Instead, Xavier asked the magic of the vampire ethic to appear before him. Purple streaks of energy blasted through the air and formed in front of him. To his shock, he saw the spirit of Henrik trapped inside, screaming in rage and pounding at an invisible wall.

Jaret had left the iron box here when they left Fremont and had given Xavier the golden key when he finally approved of attacking Henrik.

The purple streaks shot one at a time into the iron box, each one seeming to pull a part of Henrik with it, until Xavier saw the last one crashing in with Henrik's eyes staring widely at Xavier in terror. Xavier slammed the lid shut and turned the key. Leaving Henrik in his prison on the floor, Xavier pulled out the key and started toward the front door when he almost slammed into Anthony rushing inside.

"Where are the vampires?" Xavier asked.

"They fled. I tried a different spell with the Council's magic to shoot them into the street and away from Henrik's power. I still had trouble combating them at first. But the protection from Henrik seemed to wear off, maybe because I forced them off the property. I came back to help you when they ran away."

"He's in there." Xavier pointed to the box at his feet. But he could hardly concentrate, wanting to know if Thomas had died.

When Xavier heard the familiar laugh behind him, a combination relief and intense ire coursed through his body. He spun around to see Thomas standing at the foot of the landing, laughing at both of them. Thomas appeared as he had moments ago, except he was bare-chested.

"You two look like you've seen a ghost."

Xavier walked across the entryway and slapped Thomas on the face. "Not funny. You're an asshole." Then he reached over and clutched Thomas into a tight hug.

Thomas kissed the top of his head. "My plan worked, didn't it?"

"I don't see how watching you burn to a crisp helped anything." Anthony's measured cadence told Xavier he was as mad as Xavier.

Still holding Xavier, Thomas picked up the iron box and moved them out of the house.

"Hear me out."

"You've already said those words tonight and look where they got us. This episode wasn't funny." Xavier wanted to slap Thomas again, who still giggled. "I don't want to hear you out anymore."

"I agree. You're a shithead. I don't know what I see in you that keeps me around. And Xavier's a fool for partnering with you for all these decades."

"Not fair." Thomas still grinned from ear to ear. "I'm a genius!"

"Where are your clothes?" Xavier asked.

"I lost my shirt. Part of the plan."

"We'll let you talk, but only once we get home and I have a divine glass of wine in my hands." Anthony launched ahead of them. "I need something magnificent to wash out your bitter taste."

Xavier locked up the Bachmann house and then followed Anthony and Thomas to their own home. Back in its comfortable confines, Xavier took in the fact they had somehow defeated Henrik.

"Can I tell my story?" Thomas asked as he snuggled next to Xavier on the couch.

"I'm giddy with anticipation." Xavier still fought mixed emotions of relief and anger.

Thomas laughed, though Xavier and Anthony still found little humor in having watched him die less than an hour earlier.

"Here's what I couldn't figure out." Thomas played with Xavier's ear as he talked. "I'm with the two smartest beings on the entire planet. I've seen you figure out much more difficult problems and take on much more dangerous foes. But here you sat, incapacitated by a dead guy from the 1800s. Why? Made no sense. Then I figured out the problem—anger. You weren't in the least bit pissed off. You needed something to provoke your genius, so I pissed you off."

"Do you mean to tell me you planned in advance to fake your death?" Anthony asked.

"Yep."

"How did you know they'd use fire?" Xavier looked into Thomas's eyes.

"Some of my success was luck. I needed to die somehow, and they provided the perfect ruse. When they aimed the torches at me, I whipped my shirt off and allowed the fabric to catch fire. I leapt away before a flame could get to me. But see, that moment of despair triggered Anthony to control the vampires and got Xavier to capture Henrik in the box." Thomas pointed to the iron jail nearby.

Anthony got up and walked over to the couch. He kissed Xavier on the cheek then flicked Thomas on the nose. "I repeat, you're a complete and utter shithead. Nobody likes you, least of all me."

"You're lying. You know you love my brilliance."

"You're a daredevil and a fool." Anthony's words only made Thomas laugh again.

Anthony picked up the iron box but tossed the golden key to Xavier. "I'm going to take Henrik to the vampire prison in the Rocky Mountains and make sure no one can ever get to him. I'll see you two later."

Xavier thought of offering to accompany Anthony but then decided against it. Despite wanting Henrik locked away there, he still held bitter memories at his own past incarceration for a week and the thought of so many others who had suffered in those iron boxes hovering over the fire. Instead, Thomas and he hugged Anthony goodbye and then went upstairs to a bedroom to enjoy a night alone.

"Are you still mad at me?" Thomas asked once they had undressed and crawled into bed.

"Of course."

"But I killed myself for all of us. So we could defeat Henrik before he endangered us anymore or risked exposure."

"You had no idea if your plot would work. It was dangerous and foolhardy. The only dumber thing was Anthony and I willingly going along with you, knowing what an imbecile you can be with your safety sometimes."

Thomas licked Xavier's ear. "You love me. You know you do."

Xavier closed his eyes and sexual excitement started to take over. "Maybe I don't anymore."

Thomas's tongue trailed down Xavier's neck.

Xavier moaned with pleasure and licked at Thomas's ear. Then he reached down and grabbed Thomas's rock-hard penis and squeezed hard with his nails pressing into the skin.

"Ow. Stop!"

"Don't ever do that to me again. Ever. Do you remember how you felt when you thought the Vampire Council may have killed me after I freed slaves? There's nothing funny about death."

"You're hurting me," Thomas whispered, his eyes tearing with blood.

"Promise."

"I promise. I swear!"

Xavier let up on his grip. "Don't joke about dying either. Don't ever, ever do that again."

"I understand." Thomas reached over and kissed Xavier on the lips. "I won't murder myself again."

"Good." Xavier slipped under the covers and trailed down Thomas's chest and toward his cock. "Here, let me make your penis feel better." Xavier closed his eyes and lost himself in the taste of Thomas's organ as the shaft slid in and out of his mouth.

Forty-Six: Infidels

11 SEPTEMBER 2012
Creston, Nebraska

"This isn't nearly as interesting as conquering Henrik." Thomas sighed and leaned against the large tombstone inside the Creston cemetery. "Henrik gave us a good challenge. These idiots"—Thomas pointed into the darkness as if the vampires sat watching them—"are nothing but an annoyance."

Xavier grinned. "Don't try to liven things up with a fake death."

"Still isn't funny." Anthony turned around and lifted his eyebrow at Xavier. "And I can't believe you're encouraging him."

"It's actually funnier the farther removed we are. You two have chilled out." Thomas paced in front of them. "Catherine thought it was hilarious."

"Catherine isn't a good gauge of decorum," Xavier said. "Or humor."

"Back to the task at hand." As usual, Anthony kept them focused. "They have some remnant of the power they got from Henrik. We've been hunting them for two days. They can't combat us anymore but seem to have some ability to hide and run despite our Council magic."

"Speaking of Henrik," Thomas said, "how is the old boy?"

Anthony laughed. "I took no chances. He's locked safely in his iron box, which is further locked inside one of the iron coffins and hovering over the pit of fire. I enchanted an extra spell to add a force field around the tomb. Nothing can get in or out of the vault without someone from the Vampire Council." Anthony stopped talking and cast his glance to the ground. "Will one of you please tell Jaret? He'd want to know we're safe, and that Henrik can never get away."

"I already did." Xavier walked over and placed his hand on Anthony's back. "We still haven't talked about what's going on with your attitude toward Jaret. You promised you would."

"His promises when it comes to opening up about emotions take centuries to come about. He can't even email the poor lad, let alone cope with everything troubling him."

Anthony flipped Thomas off. "I'm not reneging on my promise. We've been rather preoccupied of late."

"Speaking of which, back to my original announcement." Thomas huddled near the other two. Xavier still swooned when Thomas took control of a situation. His long black hair fell over his shoulder, his brown eyes glistened in the moonlight, and his strong arm felt powerful around Xavier's waist. "Gentlemen, though I grew up on the frontier, I've come to prefer the urban settings of this modern world. Creston, quaint as it is, gives me hives. I don't think they have a gay bar here yet. I understand these vampires don't threaten us anymore, nor are they capable of doing much to expose vampires so long as we track them. You promised we had a way to get to them soon. Could we speed it up?"

"If my senses are correct, you won't have to wait long." Anthony spun around and looked into a nearby field.

Xavier sensed the presence, too, and then heard them. Thomas tensed and placed himself between the approaching threat and Xavier as vampires headed in their direction. Xavier, Thomas, and Anthony took combat positions, but as their adversaries appeared, they walked in plain view across the field, one holding a white flag.

Thomas eased his stance. "We've been sucked into a time warp. We're back in the middle of the Civil War. Or are they renegade pirates seeking asylum? Who even uses a white flag anymore?"

Anthony laughed but remained vigilant. When the infidels got within several hundred yards, Anthony ordered them to halt.

"We surrender." They spoke in unison.

The female of the three stepped forward. "You have to believe us. We never wanted this conflict. We never wanted to defy the Vampire Council. We came to Fremont to request a favor of the Council. The ghost trapped us against our will. We had no control over ourselves."

Xavier became dizzy. They had set out to assassinate the defiant vampires and thereby protect vampires everywhere. Her plea confused the situation.

Xavier wondered how to determine if they told the truth because, if so, the Council needed to consider the truth. On the other hand, he, Thomas, and Anthony had to guard against a ruse designed to get them off the hook so they could go elsewhere and wreak havoc.

Anthony said something that Xavier missed as Thomas and he moved closer to the three suspects. While they engaged the vampires, Xavier took a step back to consult his magic for answers. He noted Thomas and Anthony had enchanted a freezing spell on the vampires, who couldn't move or do anything except talk.

A glowing orange orb appeared before Xavier. He put his back to the others to conceal his viewing and chuckled, feeling like the Wicked Witch of the West glancing into her crystal ball. Well, thanks to Gregory Maguire, his comparison made him Elphaba and not some nasty hateful person.

There before his eyes appeared the past. The three vampires imprisoned across the way walked into Fremont, laughing and chatting with one another, happy and without any type of a negative vibe. They had a small white sphere glowing in front of them. The only magic allowed for vampires other than those on the Council was this communication system to help them find a member of the Council when needed. Xavier and Harriet had created the system to help alleviate the feeling of an aloof and distant Council, a means these three had followed to Fremont.

The magic also allowed Xavier to hear their thoughts; they could communicate with him even though frozen a few yards away as the orb read their minds. They had traveled from Salt Lake City because they met a human friend there and spent a few years with the person. They sought permission to reveal themselves to her with the hope of converting her. One of the males hailed from the 16th century, the other male and female from the twentieth. They had no prior record.

According to everything Xavier could determine, they told the truth. Still, he wondered why these three had fled the house after Anthony, Thomas, and he incapacitated Henrik, and why they had stayed away since.

Xavier walked over and joined the others so everyone could hear the same information. "Why did you run? If you came to Fremont to tell us about your friend in Utah, why flee once the spell wore off?"

One of the men stammered something but the woman cut him off. "We're afraid. You have to believe us. We went to the mansion because the orb led us there. I can't explain what happened. I felt like another entity took control of my body. I could hear everything and think. Yet I had no power over my actions or even the words coming out of my mouth."

"Everything indicates she's telling the truth," Xavier said.

Anthony nodded agreement.

"They came to us for a favor. There was nothing sinister about their intentions when they got to Fremont," Xavier confirmed.

"If you'll excuse us," Thomas said to the vampires and pulled Xavier and Anthony a safe distance away.

Anthony cast a concealing spell so they could talk aloud without the others hearing, even with their vampiric senses.

Xavier told them what he'd learned from the orb. "I don't think they deserve severe punishment. Certainly not death. Henrik gained power over them, perhaps because they lacked the same protective magic we gain from the Council's sorcery. They wandered to the house looking for us. Maybe they came during one of our failed attacks, which explains why the orb led them to the Bachmann home and not our place."

Thomas scrunched his brow. "It feels risky. And I so wanted to kill them. I was humiliated when they threw me into the bushes."

"And the law states they need punishment." Anthony had called forth the vampire ethic. "They attacked members of the Council and risked exposure. We can't maintain order without some sort of sanction."

"Do we agree Henrik forced them against their will?" Xavier asked.

Anthony and Thomas nodded.

"Then we need to reconsider a harsh punishment."

"But the ethic," Anthony said.

"Oh, I sense the old Anthony talking." Thomas placed his hand on Anthony's shoulder because he could better reach Anthony in these situations than anyone else. "The gray areas, Anthony. Remember the gray. And you don't have to determine all of this on your own anymore. We can decide together how to proceed. This isn't a black-and-white situation."

"Should we consult Catherine and Harriet?"

Xavier thought for a moment before answering. "I don't think the situation demands a full vote. I suppose we could call them."

"What should we do?" Anthony seemed lost. At least he had not demanded they enforce the letter of the law. But without a rule-bound way of thinking, he had no idea how to act.

"I say we strip them naked and make them parade around Nebraska in the nude. Especially the hot little number who's so quiet." Thomas motioned toward the twink on the edge, his perfect type.

Xavier punched him in the arm. "You're not helpful. But I have an idea." Xavier pulled the two closer together. "Let's put them on probation. We'll place a monitoring spell on them to give us a regular report as to their whereabouts and activities. We can order them not to tell this other friend about their nature. If they behave for a year, then they can reapproach us with their request. Probation will end after a decade, provided nothing has gone wrong."

"Is a decade enough?" Anthony asked.

A decade seemed a long time for punishing a deed done against their will. Still, Xavier reminded himself ten years hardly mattered in vampire years. But a short discussion determined the time sufficient.

Soon enough, the present members of the Council agreed on Xavier's proposal. They called both Harriet and Catherine at Anthony's urging, who each declared they trusted the other three to handle the situation. They communicated the punishment to the victims, all of whom expressed their gratitude. As they watched them race away toward Utah, Xavier smiled.

"I admire how you handled this," Xavier said to Anthony.

"I can learn. I'm trying."

Thomas hooked a hand through Xavier's arm and then his other one through Anthony's. He turned them toward Omaha. "Come, I want to see a skyline. Omaha is better than the cow staring at me over there. I have a special case of wine waiting for us. We're going to test whether or not Anthony has become a reformed vampire."

Forty-Seven: Anthony's Pain

11 SEPTEMBER 2012
Omaha, Nebraska

Thomas reserved the best suite at the finest hotel in downtown Omaha. After a drink at one of the most fun gay bars outside of someplace like Chicago or Paris, they returned to the hotel for the last three or four hours of darkness. Thomas opened the first of the bottles of red wine, a case from Ferrari Carano. Speaking of reformed, Xavier had moved beyond a restriction to drink nothing but French wine as he opened his horizons to other vintages. Still inferior, of course, but very nice nonetheless.

After a while, Xavier excused himself to check in with Catherine. He had talked to Jaret a couple times since they left but liked to speak with his sister every night.

"How is he?" Xavier asked.

Catherine sighed and then giggled. "The same as every night when you ask. He's doing fine. He's opening up more and more, still fighting through the pain. He told me to say hello."

When Xavier got back to Anthony and Thomas sitting in a quaint living room of the suite, a comfortable silence had fallen over the room. He sat near Thomas but not right next to him. He wanted the focus on Anthony and not he and Thomas or anything their relationship may represent.

Anthony held his glass up and swirled the wine before sipping and closing his eyes. "Who knew Americans would ever figure out how to make good wine?"

Xavier smiled. "I thought the same thing a minute ago. I can actually swallow American wine."

"European snobs." Thomas stuck his tongue out at both of them and then pointed at Xavier. "I know of other American substances you like to swallow."

"Stop!" Xavier shouted while Anthony bellowed a laugh.

After a pause while they enjoyed the wine, Anthony sat back and spoke. "I'm ready." Xavier detected a slight nervousness but nothing extraordinary. Anthony almost always had control of himself, regardless of the situation. "Agree to one thing. Especially you." Anthony pointed at Thomas. "Hear me out. Let me say everything before you scold me."

Thomas grinned, and both he and Xavier agreed.

"I doubt anything I say will surprise either one of you. There's no smoking gun. No grand revelation to knock your socks off. It's just I've never really articulated my true self before. I've held emotion close to me."

"We know." Thomas laughed. "You're not exactly an open book."

Anthony grinned. "You promised to keep your mouth shut."

"Oops." Thomas wiggled his eyebrows and took a drink of wine.

"Let's get the past out of the way. Julius meant everything to me. I know I sound preposterous, given the centuries since he died, but I think about him every day. When I see the two of you together, I wonder if we would've had the same comfort level still. The same connection. Don't get me wrong. I've moved on enough to embrace life. I enjoy myself. But deep within, I still miss him. I decided to play the field forever because his memory haunts me. I could enjoy sex and have companionship, could surround myself with hot, young male servants, and the circumstances seemed safe. Fun. Exotic, and often thrilling. Yet always safe. I had the vampire ethic as a companion. Duty became my mistress.

"Then in the 1700s I met this hot, brash young American and decided to take a chance again. I'm not rehashing old wounds between us." Anthony held up his hand to Thomas and smiled. "We're fine. It's just important to my story. Your charisma enchanted me. I think I took too long since I tried to grapple with my inner emotion. I'd repressed my feelings so well I seemed to have no idea they even existed anymore. No pain. No worry. I had my obligation and sex drive. I lost myself in courting you. Too easily you fooled me. I had converted you, and we figured out two power tops would kill each other. We became friends and went our separate ways."

Anthony paused and sipped his wine. He glanced at Xavier and then looked at Thomas. "I don't want to make you feel guilty. I swear. But something broke inside me again. I played the breakup as cool as possible and returned to my cavalier ways with sex. But in my mind, our failure proved again why I had to avoid a relationship. Coupling for other vampires made sense, but not for me. I had too much work to do. Too many obligations. And I told myself over and over when I fall in love, I become too careless and lose sight of my responsibility. So I returned to the old me. Until—" Anthony choked on the words. He stopped and stared hard into his wine glass.

After a few minutes of quiet, Thomas got up and poured everyone more wine. "It's okay." He rubbed Anthony's back before returning to his seat. "I don't feel guilty. That's not a strong emotion for me. And we're here. You're safe. Everything you say is in confidence. We both love you."

Anthony nodded and smiled. He took a deep breath. "Repression worked until he came along. I was minding my own business when I detected an innocent in trouble. Wanting to save him, I rushed to the scene. Mind you, there was nothing terribly original about what I encountered. Jock assholes attacking a gay guy. Happens all too often in this shithole of a world. I saved him, punished the assholes, and then fell for him in a matter of minutes afterward. He's funny. Sexy as hell. I mean, not in a Hollywood-model kind of way. He's slim, sweet, laughs easily, and the curls in his hair drive me nuts. His smile could charm anyone.

"Before I knew what hit me, I started a relationship. But this time I remembered myself. I remembered how you had tricked me. I remembered the pain of two lost lovers. I recalled my obligations. After diving in like a fool, I slowed myself and did some investigating. None of what I said about the ethic was a lie. He's so powerful with his magic, more powerful than he even knows. With knowledge about vampire magic, or even the addition of vampire senses and abilities, he could become indestructible. The ethic warns against turning him. I had to pull back. To protect all of us. And, truth be told, myself. Because I couldn't admit I had never coupled again because of how much previous losses hurt. I couldn't admit I had messed around with a different partner all the time to hide from myself. I couldn't face how losing him would kill me all over again. Maybe literally this time. Even typing his name into an address line on email would cut into my soul."

Anthony drank half his wine and refilled his glass. "I'm so glad vampires can still get drunk."

Everyone laughed, but Xavier, and even Thomas, waited again for Anthony to continue.

"I've determined again what I always told myself. It's far easier and simpler to live alone. Adopt some boys along the way, protect them, find a tryst here and there, and do my job. He's too much for me. See? He's the problem." Anthony seemed to swallow an emotion and fought to maintain control. "I desperately love him. You've no idea. I can't even have sex since we broke up, because I just want him back. But I can't become careless again. I don't ever want to lose another lover."

"It seems like you already have," Thomas spoke after letting Anthony's words sink in.

Xavier had thought the same thing but wanted a softer way to convey the sentiment.

"What do you mean?" Anthony asked.

"Don't play coy. You're avoiding the truth." Thomas smiled. "I'm not a psychologist, and I don't play one on TV." They all laughed. "But you're trying to protect yourself, except it's not working. You already lost him as a lover. You're too late to pull back. Sometimes you have to take risks. I know you like everything in order. I know how you loath the gray areas of life, and especially when murky reality threatens any kind of emotion in you. But you don't have all of those duties and obligations anymore. We relieved you of sole responsibility when we reformulated the Vampire Council. The five of us govern the vampire world. Not you alone. We all take turns leading, and we all slip away from time to time to enjoy life. You're the only one unwilling to take the step. Except when you did—with Jaret. Now you're trying to turn back the clock. Even with all of your vampire powers, you can't undo time."

Anthony listened and nodded his head.

Xavier spoke with a soft tone. "Besides, he needs you." This territory belonged to Xavier. "Henrik destroyed his world. He's a strong kid. Regardless of what he thinks, not many people could live through what he's experienced and even try to make a go of living. He's doing a remarkable job. But he needs you. He thinks about you all the time. He still loves you too."

They sat for what felt like hours before Anthony continued. "I'm not shutting down. We'll still talk. But I need you both to respect me as much as I'm respecting you. I understand what you're saying. I'm listening. But

I'm also not ready. I may never be ready." Anthony sighed. "And I know we all have different interpretations of the vampire ethic. Our different ways of thinking is a strength of the Council. I think we need to take the warning seriously about Jaret's magic. I've never encountered such a powerful witch. Who knows what his power could do if he became a vampire?"

"Nothing says you have to convert him." Thomas shrugged. "Who knows? But you don't have to start out by taking him to forever and ever. You need to start by reconnecting with him."

"I operate on all or nothing. I would never string him along a second time and disconnect. And can you imagine loving with such intensity all while watching him age and die?" Anthony grimaced. "If I start, I won't be able to let him go. And the ethic is telling me it's too dangerous, for me, for him, for all of us."

Silence crept over the room before Anthony stood up. He hugged Xavier and Thomas before he went off to his hidden coffin within a trunk. Xavier and Thomas soon cuddled next to each other in their own crate-cum-coffin.

"I feel so badly for him." Xavier held to Thomas, forever grateful for his lover.

"Me too." Thomas kissed Xavier on the head. "But I think we got somewhere tonight."

"I hope so."

Forty-Eight: Séance

29 SEPTEMBER 2012
Washington, DC

"You're sure this is a good idea?" Xavier asked Jaret. He'd been planning the moment since returning from Nebraska a couple weeks ago but had second thoughts. They removed themselves to the basement of the house in DC, closed the door, and locked themselves in for privacy. Darth snuggled into her own little bed in the corner. She had slowed down in the last few months, showing signs of her age. Jaret seemed to ignore her aging.

"You planned for this."

"I know. Which is why I'm unsure."

Jaret sat on a love seat next to Xavier. "Doing a similar thing helped you so much. Whenever you see Michel, you know he went to a magnificent place. What if seeing them helps me too?"

"And what if seeing them is too much?" Xavier reached over and grabbed Jaret's hand. "What if you can't handle the interaction and relapse? I'll never forgive myself."

Jaret studied Xavier for a moment. "Not your fault. Any of what has happened or will happen. You take things too personally."

Xavier laughed. How many times had he heard similar words from Thomas? He also kept to himself another doubt. What if they tried and failed? What if Xavier had gotten Jaret's hopes up for nothing? Not seeing them might be worse than success.

"Besides," Jaret lowered his voice. "You promised. You promised if I got better you'd try with me. Like you have with Michel. You said a connection could help me take the next step."

Xavier nodded. He had no way of going back. He pulled Jaret into a hug and then had them sit next to each other, still holding hands. "Relax. Breathe easily. The space around us will evaporate. We'll be in some white space, bright and undefined."

Xavier and Jaret sat for several minutes with nothing changing. Xavier heard Jaret's heartbeat next to him, quickening with anticipation. Jaret's grip on Xavier's hand tightened and his palm sweated.

When Xavier almost despaired that he had failed Jaret, a mist swooped in around him. Their surroundings disappeared, and Xavier and Jaret stood side by side in the white space. Though Xavier felt a tether back to his vampiric form sitting on earth, he walked about in this heaven-like realm. He smiled as he heard the heavy footfall and then saw the French military uniform materialize before him.

Michel smiled too and held his arms out to beckon his brother into a hug. "You know we're not supposed to meet all the time. Too much interference between the realms." Michel scolded him but smiled and kissed both of his cheeks.

"But you keep coming back," Xavier said.

"I've never been able to resist my little brother. And who is this?"

Xavier introduced Jaret, knowing full well Michel already knew the entire story, everything about Jaret, and why they had come.

Michel walked over and held Jaret by both shoulders. "Speaking of forbidden acts. Our meeting is a risk. You have to promise you can handle this. I can't tell you what it'd do if you gave up and decided to join us instead of staying there. You offer too much to the world."

Michel's frank words and attitude worried Xavier. Jaret, on the other hand, seemed surprisingly comfortable with the entire situation. He acted no different despite the transformation into another realm and interacted with the spirit of Xavier's brother with surprising ease, as if they had met as humans in a bar.

"I haven't offed myself so far. Even when I really wanted to. I promise. Please?"

Michel nodded and smiled. He stepped back and put his arm around Xavier's shoulder, pulling him a short distance away behind Jaret.

One by one, Jaret's family materialized before him. His cousins, then his aunt and uncle. His father, grinning, then his mom raced over and hugged him and stood by his side. Lincoln waved, and last, Jenn appeared. Jaret burst into tears. Jenn hurried to his side and engulfed him in a hug as the rest of his family surrounded and clutched at him. They spoke to him, too soft for Xavier to hear. Yet even at the distance, Xavier felt like an intruder on this most intimate of moments.

Without any way to know how long they had remained away, Xavier found himself once again in the basement of their Washington, DC, home next to Jaret. The only sign time had passed or anything had occurred was how Darth sat licking Jaret's face with exuberance in a seeming panic until he put his arm around her and buried his face in her fur.

Xavier reached over and held Jaret as he cried.

"Well?" Xavier broke their silence, his heart pounding with fear at what he had done.

Jaret pulled away and wiped at the tears. He still cried but not as passionately. "I'm good."

Xavier arched an eyebrow.

"Well, you know what I mean."

Xavier shook his head. "No, I don't."

Jaret picked Darth up onto his lap and petted her head as he talked. "I never thought I'd enjoy emotional pain." He laughed, and so did Xavier. "I mean, I was miserable. Seeing them there—definitely dead—was awful. Then, I really wanted them to, like, go apeshit on me. Yell at me for being careless with Henrik. Get mad because I failed them. I expected anger or disappointment. My parents loved the disappointment card when I was growing up. Instead, they loved me and sent me back. Told me not to give up. Live for them."

"I know what you mean." And unlike people saying those words to comfort someone without really knowing, Xavier spoke the truth. He had a similar visit the first time he went to Michel after his murder. He wanted Michel to lash out for having failed to protect him, for having witnessed his death but being so drunk he had fallen and could do nothing. Instead, Michel had commanded him back to earth with forgiveness. Painful and emotional, Xavier remembered. Cathartic and distressing all at once.

At least Jaret's reaction put Xavier at peace for having taken Jaret on the journey. Jaret would pull through the experience, in no small part because he had seen his family, as Xavier had done two centuries ago.

"Weird. The best and worst part was seeing Jenn. She talked to me alone for a little." Jaret cried hard. "Said she was so proud of me. I didn't believe her, so she kept saying everything was okay. Then she promised to watch over me if I promised to do my best to go on."

Jaret stopped talking when the tears stifled his words. Xavier held him in his arms and let him cry. Darth did the same, laying patiently on Jaret's lap, seeming to understand her job.

Eventually they went back upstairs where Xavier tucked Jaret into bed.

Jaret smiled. "I'm not three, you know."

"The problem is everyone thinks they grow up and don't need to be tucked in anymore."

Xavier walked to the door and turned off the lights. He stepped outside but turned around to look at Jaret one more time, with Darth snuggled between his legs.

"Good night."

"Good night. Xavier?"

"Yes?"

"Thank you. I love you."

"Love you, too, kiddo. See you tomorrow."

Part Nine:

Peacemaker

Forty-Nine: Healing

1 APRIL 2013
Cleveland, Ohio

Xavier braced himself for Jaret's anger and determined to have this conversation regardless of how he reacted. He started down the hall, contemplating the last few months of Jaret's progress and how he so wanted to force him to take the next step.

Xavier observed Jaret had healed well from the tragic losses in his life. Xavier cried and hugged Jaret the day a week ago when he announced a major breakthrough. "I've accepted I somehow survived. I'm doing my best to move forward in their honor. I still have survivor's guilt—Jodie gave me the label—but I'm not feeling as guilty as before. Plus, visiting my family helped so much. Thank you so much. They gave me courage. Anyway, I wanted to tell you. Oh, and I got letters of acceptance from three of the grad programs I applied to! Three out of five isn't bad, and I haven't heard from one yet. I don't know if I'll go. I have to decide. But I'm in a better place to make the decision."

Xavier also noticed Jaret engaging more once again with his friends, especially Brady. While he had stayed in contact with Brady throughout the year, now he went out with him to movies and clubs and had funded a couple trips for the two of them. He often paid to have Brady come visit in whatever city they were visiting or went back to Chicago to see Brady.

Brady had a special energy about him that worked to pull Jaret out of his shell. Too, Xavier thought their bond amazing—as intense as what he felt with Catherine.

"I'll never be able to repay you," Jaret said to Brady in front of everyone after their last gathering.

Brady bounced over to Jaret and hugged him. "Dude, you do every day. By being my friend. You give me a lot; you don't recognize how much you do for me."

Jaret and Brady would leave tomorrow on their latest vacation to Salem, Massachusetts, the two young historians wanting to explore the actual location of the Salem witch trials of 1692.

Jaret had also visited his family a couple more times, always returning sad and yet better at the same time. He took the longest to recover from the visit he'd had alone with Jenn. "I just can't help wishing I had the same thing with her you have with Catherine," he told Xavier. "Instead, I have a guardian angel. Jenn promised I did. I can even feel her presence sometimes if I'm depressed."

As Xavier got to the living room where Jaret sat, his phone rang. Shit. He had to take this call so stepped aside and hurried back to the kitchen.

"Anthony?"

"I got your message. You know I can't see him. Why do you two keep asking me?"

Xavier took a deep breath. His rage almost erupted, making him feel like Thomas, who had ranted and raved just that morning about Anthony's obstinacy in not coming to see Jaret. "He needs you. Give him a chance."

"I won't because I love him too much. I can't bear the pain of another breakup with him, or all the arguments about turning him into a vampire. Stop badgering me. The vampire ethic will not allow his conversion. How hard is this reality to understand?"

"You admitted a while ago you use excuses more as a security blanket because the situation is not as absolute as you pretend. Isn't there anything you can do for him? For me?"

Anthony sighed on the other end. "I've sent him a couple of messages, so he knows I'm thinking about him. He doesn't respond. I'm scared to death every time I write to him. And it hurts when he ignores them."

"I think he ignores them because they're so impersonal. I know they're a big step for you and appreciate your effort. But he needs more."

"I have to go. We'll talk later." Anthony hung up.

Xavier wanted to punch a wall but stopped himself by returning his attention to Jaret.

Anthony's problem went a long way to explaining the one area where Jaret refused to move forward or attempt to cope with his life. Jaret wrapped up all his hurt in the Mika concerts he missed or refused to attend. He stopped himself from moving forward or feeling all his emotions by making those events a permanent stumbling block. Xavier was determined to overcome Jaret's stubbornness. Xavier found out Mika had a huge concert at an outdoor stadium in the summer in Paris. Xavier had not returned to his home city in some time, and the thought of sharing Paris with Jaret while also getting him to a Mika concert invigorated Xavier.

Jaret had shut down when Xavier tried to talk about the trip, though he had agreed to go to Paris. He listed a host of places he wanted to visit, asked about Xavier's and Thomas's flat there, inquired about Catherine's home—the Saint-Laurent mansion—and wanted every detail of history Xavier could remember.

Then Xavier asked about the concert again because Jaret had ignored the Mika part of the plans. Jaret stared straight ahead as if Xavier had said nothing. Try as he might, Xavier could not change Jaret's mind about the concert.

Asking for an explanation got either a three-year-old's tantrum about not wanting to talk about it or a teenager's icy silence. Live Mika hurt too much, though he still cranked the albums throughout their house whenever he got a chance.

Xavier had even caught Jaret using his magic to make a 3-D image of Mika for he and Brady to dance with to their favorite songs.

Xavier walked down the hall and found Jaret sitting by himself in the living room, reading a history of Cleveland. For some reason even Xavier had a hard time articulating, this Midwestern city often called to Xavier. He felt comfortable here. So they had always maintained a home in Cleveland Heights, even though Thomas found the city somewhat dreary and provincial. He much preferred Chicago for his Midwestern haunt.

They had all come to Cleveland because Jaret wanted Xavier to take him around the city. Now, Xavier prepared to send Jaret on his way to Salem while he and Thomas were headed to California to visit Anthony.

"Hey," Xavier said and sat next to Jaret.

Jaret grinned. "Hey. You ready for shitty American wine?"

"Stop. Don't let Thomas hear you, or he'll think I'm being obstinate again. I like the wine there, especially in Sonoma. Are you ready for Salem?"

"Yep." Jaret shut his book and his smile widened. "Brady and I found a secret map online of places not for tourists but related to the trials. Like Gallows Hill. A park now. They don't want people knowing it's where they offed the witches."

"Charming." Xavier reached over and scratched Darth behind the ears. "And we'll hook up in Paris?"

Jaret nodded. "I can't believe you got us a private plane."

"Don't worry. We can afford a plane. Besides, how else would we get Darth over there? This way we can sneak her in without the quarantine."

"Won't we still have to go through customs?"

"Vampire money gets around a lot of obstacles. We'll get her in, no problem."

They chatted about Paris for a couple minutes before they arrived at the moment both knew was coming.

"Please reconsider," Xavier said. He had failed to think of a more subtle way to approach the subject. "I have the tickets. It's been your dream. Brady wants to go. Why not give the concert a try? I'll go. Or Thomas and I can stay home and send the two of you. I don't understand why you're punishing yourself over this. Your refusal doesn't hurt anyone but you. Not going certainly doesn't prove anything."

The stubborn German set into Jaret's countenance. He pressed his lips together and shook his head. "How many times do we have to talk about this?"

Xavier grinned. "Until I get my way."

Even Jaret had to laugh. But he shook his head and grabbed for Darth, a sure sign he'd entered a difficult emotional place. "I made a commitment to myself."

"Will you do me one favor? A small one, I promise."

"Okay." Jaret did not sound convincing.

"First, listen to Brady. Hear him out."

"I never said he can't go."

"I know. But you never listen to him either. Hear him out. Then, once we're settled in Paris, let's reconsider. Please?"

Jaret set his chin on top of Darth's head. "I'll agree for you. But I'm not promising anything."

Fifty: Orchid Inn

12 APRIL 2013
Guerneville, California

Xavier had a hard time believing Anthony's newfound boldness but thought his action refreshing because Anthony always held so rigidly to the ethic. Anthony had discovered the Orchid Inn during a visit to California and fell in love with the setting. He especially liked the two owners, who sat with him and chatted for long periods of time.

Anthony never revealed his vampirism, yet he confided to them he had a disease that only allowed him out at night, away from the sun. They gave him a basement room, kept the staff out of his quarters during the day, and even changed their routine to make him a gourmet breakfast every evening when he woke. Anthony had protested but they insisted. He told Thomas and Xavier he had never had such an exquisite breakfast in all his life. Despite not needing the food, he never missed a chance to enjoy the innkeeper's cooking.

Anthony had been coming here for a few years and invited Xavier and Thomas to join him. They agreed,

Xavier in part so he had a distraction from Jaret's going on a trip with Brady to Salem. Xavier had moved beyond constant worry about Jaret but still had a hard time leaving him alone without checking he was safe. He needed some time away so they would stop bickering about the Mika concert in Paris.

They arrived to greetings from Anthony and a very pleasant introduction to the bed and breakfast's owners. They had just finished arranging some evening wine tastings for Anthony, well after most of the wineries closed for the day. As always, a vampire's wealth could get a lot of nighttime favors, not to mention the ability to sleep all day uninterrupted in the establishment without having to invent awkward excuses.

One of them showed Thomas and Xavier to their room, and then left them with Anthony.

"This is rather open of you," Thomas said.

"Yes," Xavier added. "Rather exposed. The Council may need to assess whether or not you've violated the ethic. Perhaps you need a stint in an iron coffin. I dare say, this comes close to enjoying life too."

Anthony laughed. "Not you too. Normally I only have to hate him." He pointed to Thomas. "These two are wonderful. I love this place. And Sonoma has the best American wine. The boutique wineries are tremendous. Tonight, we're all going to Arista, right around the corner."

They settled into a small sitting room for a while to catch up.

Anthony told them about a few of the places he'd visited, while Thomas told Anthony about a gang of drug lords he and Xavier had attacked in Los Angeles before they came up the coast. As always, Thomas found the entire story quite hilarious, despite the seriousness of the crimes. "I won't be able to feed on other humans for months after all the blood."

"Prince Charming as always." Anthony winked at Xavier. "I see what you found in him. The subtle charm. The compassion."

Xavier laughed while Thomas gave Anthony the bird. "I only fed on what I needed. You know how Thomas overindulges."

Thomas raised his hands in the air. "What did you want me to do? I had no idea when we started so many of those young guys would also be exquisitely hot. I can't fuck them, so I just drink their sweet blood, which gives me visions of their past, where I can linger on the scenes of them jacking off."

"You're disgusting." Xavier rolled his eyes.

Anthony, however, laughed. "I'm surprised at how well you obey the ethic. Who would've ever guessed— Thomas the Vampire Council Enforcer."

"Fuck off." Thomas twisted a strand of hair in his hand. "I only obey to protect you and because Xavier makes me. Besides, killing all those druggies was fun."

"Indeed. You're always the martyr." Xavier reached over and held Thomas's hand. "You never can admit when you're doing something good to protect humans or to help someone."

"Because I don't like people. Except to feed me."

"That's not true," Anthony said. "You protect them more than you ever admit."

"Yeah. Look how you treat Jaret. You're as protective as me." Xavier realized the mistake too late. Jaret's name hung in the air.

"Well, after all," Thomas interjected, "we had to talk about him sometime. I mean, you're superb at repression. But he's part of our lives now whether you want to admit he's alive or not."

"I never criticized you for saving him." Anthony sat up in his chair. "Never. I respect what you've done for him. I'm asking you to respect where I'm at in life in return. I struggle as much as the three of you do."

Thomas blew out an exasperated breath. "You tire me. Seriously, you need counseling more than Jaret. All the drama. Get over your issues and give him a chance. I thought we'd been through all this already last fall. Why are we still at this awkward place? Your silly little notes to him don't help; they only make you think about him and manage to royally piss him off."

"Thomas." Xavier patted Thomas's forearm, trying to calm him.

"We've done the nice approach, Xavier. Look." Thomas motioned toward the stoic Anthony sitting across from them. "He's not even there. Floated right out of the room, like a spirit, leaving his undead body as a prop. Jaret still won't go to Mika. He's come so far, but he needs either closure or something from him. He's still too afraid."

Xavier opened his eyes wide to try to communicate for Thomas to stop.

"I'm still here," Anthony said in a terse tone. "I'd appreciate if you two would stop the monologues. And I did give him closure. I broke up with him in no uncertain terms. I never indicated we had any chance of getting back together. We're over."

Xavier motioned for Thomas to shut up as he started to say something. Xavier leaned forward in his chair. "Telling him the rules forbid your relationship does not constitute a finality to someone's love. Haven't you read *Romeo and Juliet*? If your idea of closure is what you did, you're being unfair to Jaret. And you know as well as I you've hardly moved on. I'm not mad at you like he is"— Xavier said pointing his thumb toward Thomas—"but let's not delude ourselves, either."

Anthony nodded. "I don't know."

"Well, you're going to know soon. The entire Council convenes tomorrow night, right here in California!" Thomas stood up and clapped his hands.

"I never agreed to this meeting." Anthony, too, stood.

"No need to even register a vote." Thomas announced they had to leave for the winery and pushed them all out the door. "The Vampire Council voted, without your participation, to hold a meeting. And according to the letter of the law you so fondly adhere to, no member can be absent from such a called gathering."

"I hate all of you."

Xavier had a hard time telling if Anthony had used his classic sarcasm again or meant the curse as they meandered down the road toward what Xavier hoped would be a more pleasant evening of tasting wine.

Fifty-One: Vampire Council Convened

13 APRIL 2013
Guerneville, California

Xavier woke with dread.

A week before they came to California, Catherine and Harriet had surprised Jaret, Thomas, and Xavier with a visit to Cleveland. One night after Jaret had gone to bed, they sat around discussing the situation between Jaret and Anthony. They all agreed something had to be done, only with Anthony's permission.

Thomas suggested an alternative issue, though he more easily separated the concerns than had the others. To Thomas, the matter of Jaret's relationship with Anthony was entirely separate from the possibility of Jaret ever becoming a vampire.

"Why are we insisting only Anthony can turn Jaret?" Thomas asked. "The Vampire Council as a whole has the authority to bring someone over, not Anthony alone."

Xavier at first thought the whole idea absurd, a mere product of Thomas's anger toward Anthony's handling of his feelings for Jaret. Yet as Thomas continued to make his argument, the more sense the concept made to Xavier.

"Jaret has become a part of our family, not a random human tagging along for the ride." Xavier loved hearing Thomas express the sentiment he himself had come to believe. "We all care deeply about him. If anyone ever made a possible addition to the vampire world, Jaret does. We've got to isolate the matter of Jaret as a vampire from Jaret and Anthony's relationship."

Xavier nodded in agreement. "If we had met Jaret apart from Anthony, I'd push for the Council to allow Jaret's transformation. He's like my child. Or at least as close as I'll ever come to having one."

The four agreed on this newest point and called up the vampire ethic to study the passages Anthony used to deny Jaret's turning. The ethic did warn against making too powerful a vampire. The ancient text described powerful human witches turned vampires and the evil deeds they wrought against humanity and thereby the dangerous exposure to vampires. What struck Xavier more than anything, however, was how the ethic detailed human witches who had already engaged in evil before becoming vampires. Nothing in Jaret's life indicated a bad person who would become evil for no reason because of his eternal life. Xavier came to agree with Thomas— Anthony used this passage as a crutch more than an actual reason to prohibit changing Jaret. Not to mention how everyone agreed Anthony almost always took the ethic too literally, under any circumstances.

Yet even with their consensus, only Thomas could separate Jaret's presence from the looming shadow of Anthony. They had an obligation to their friend, too, and taking care of Anthony contradicted what they wanted for Jaret. Xavier felt pulled in two separate directions.

But in the end, the four had determined to convene the Council, and without saying why, everyone understood their intentions. In part, they convened for Jaret. And in part, they came together to help Anthony, despite anticipating his anger. Thomas convinced them they had to push Anthony to address his angst and emotional issues. At least three of them felt 100 percent convinced about the course of action. Regardless of what Xavier decided, they had a three-vote majority. Xavier still found himself in turmoil over the decision between what he wanted for Jaret and how to handle him in the midst of Anthony's involvement.

Xavier dressed himself in quiet, glad Thomas always woke earlier and, on this night, gave him some time to gather his thoughts before having to communicate with anyone.

They had reserved the basement of Ferrari Carano and the beautiful tasting room down there for themselves. The proprietor had even agreed to leave the bottles of wine out for them without leaving staff behind.

Xavier took his time getting there, moving about the vineyards and enjoying the cool spring air.

He arrived to find Thomas, Catherine, and Harriet already well into a few bottles, laughing and enjoying themselves. He hugged everyone, holding Catherine close. She always centered him at charged times.

They fell into an awkward silence when they heard the footsteps treading down the stairs and then saw Anthony turn the corner. He had dressed in tight black jeans, a light-blue muscle T-shirt, and his long blond hair fell around his face and down his shoulder. To Xavier's surprise, he smiled when he saw them gathered and stepped into their presence.

"I feel like Satan having walked in to crash a communion service."

They all laughed, Xavier relieved Anthony had cut through the tension hanging in the air.

They shared more wine and admired the architecture of the basement. They loved the black iron chandeliers and the beautiful wood bar lining one whole wall with a temperature-controlled wine room behind, agreeing the atmosphere smacked of a vampire designing a moody winery for them alone.

After a time, they gathered into one of the smaller side rooms and sat around a table. The wine flowed and they grew quiet, waiting for the business part of their gathering to commence but no one taking the reins.

"You're all dancing on eggshells because of me." Anthony, as always, took charge, even when the others had conspired against him. "We don't have to operate this way anymore. Whether I agree or not, I accept the judgments of this Council. Each of you need to know something. My happiest day as a vampire came with my first relationship. The second happiest was on the day when we convened the new Council of five."

Thomas nodded, and Xavier wiped at a blood tear trickling down his face. Catherine reached under the table and grabbed his hand.

Harriet smiled. "Then I call this meeting to order."

"Oh God," Thomas said. "We haven't started using Robert's Rules of Order, have we? I can't."

"Of course not," Harriet said.

Xavier noticed of late she had taken to wearing low-cut shirts to accent her ample bosom. Her warm brown eyes glowed in the darkness. "But if I didn't say something, we'd sit here staring at each other all night. Let's get to business. Besides, you were the one who got all uppity about getting started when we met in Washington."

Thomas laughed and then grew solemn. He rubbed his hands over his cheeks before he started. "This doesn't have to be antagonistic or disagreeable." He looked right at Anthony.

"I agree." Anthony smiled and then laughed when Thomas arched an eyebrow. "I do."

"Good. Then let me cut to the chase. This whole thing is getting on my nerves. We're paying too much for this space to waste time on business all night."

"Then speak," Xavier said.

"We're here to address the conversion of another human into the vampire realm." Thomas glanced around the room, looking each one in the eye.

"As you know," Catherine continued, "a majority vote on this Council can allow the creation of a new vampire. The ethic has no exact guidelines for admission and leaves the choice to the discretion of the Council members. Jaret's become an intimate part of our inner circle. He knows about vampirism. He's kept our secret, even from his very best friend. The regrettable death of his family further paved the way for this decision. He makes an ideal candidate. I can't bear the thought of losing him."

At those words, Xavier glanced at Anthony. He sat in silence without the irritation Xavier had expected but looking miserable at the same time.

Fifty-Two: Decision

14 APRIL 2013
Sonoma County, California

The gathering fell silent after Catherine's words of support for transforming Jaret. All eyes fell on Anthony for a moment but next turned to Xavier. He hadn't realized the sigh he emitted to catch their attention. He self-consciously reached for his wine glass and took a sip, more than anything to avoid speaking or looking around at everyone watching him.

A hidden clock chimed midnight, at which Thomas cackled like an insane person. "A fitting omen? The vampires gather at the bewitching hour to discuss their evil designs."

"Vampires-cum-witches, what with our magic. Particularly dangerous to the devout out there." Catherine held up her hands in mock horror.

When they'd satisfied their amusement, attention again came back to Xavier. "You know how I feel," he whispered. "I adore him. He's like a son to me. He's warm and caring but has suffered more than anyone could ever comprehend. Of course, I want to give him eternity."

"Have we decided to dismiss the ethic's guidelines? He's too powerful." Anthony's words sounded bitter.

"Actually," Xavier said, "the law doesn't really say to avoid converting him. If you look, the ethic warns against converting a powerful human witch who's demonstrated hate. The words say nothing about someone of Jaret's nature." Xavier called forth the orange orb containing his copy of the vampire ethic and sat a book on the table in front of everyone. The needed passage appeared before each vampire, at different angles so all viewed the same thing. "See? There's nothing explicit here pertaining to Jaret. Like so much this tome contains, the guideline leaves plenty of gray regarding this decision. Once again, it's up to us to decide what to do. There isn't a strong prohibition."

Harriet and Thomas nodded after they finished reading.

"That's wonderful news," Catherine said. "Anthony?"

Anthony had gone pale, or at least as pale as his fair skin-cum-vampire tone allowed. Xavier guessed he grappled with how they had dismissed his primary argument against them. His shield cracked, and he either had to go along with them or admit his own emotional turmoil.

Anthony nodded. "I don't want to prolong this. You'll outvote me, anyway. I'm not even saying I disagree with you. But I do have one more issue. Does Jaret want this? Have any of you discussed the possibility with him?"

Xavier thought for a minute. He had never had a direct conversation with him. He doubted any of the others had, either, based on their blank expressions.

"Of course, he'll make the final decision." Xavier looked at Anthony. "We'd never take anyone against their will. They always get to decide the matter regardless of our desires."

Anthony nodded. After a long moment of silence, he spoke. Xavier wondered if anyone else saw the blood tears welling in his eyes. "Then it's decided. We'll give him the option, and also allow him to choose the time."

"Does he get to choose the maker?" Thomas asked. Xavier wished Thomas had waited to bring up another difficult topic. He was seldom adept at the subtle moments in life.

Anthony answered with a frown. "So long as the maker agrees too. Both parties must volunteer to enter the agreement."

"I'll let him know," Xavier said to distract both of them.

They began leaving the room and returned to the larger main area. Xavier breathed a sigh of relief everyone had decided to stay and continue to enjoy the wine, with even Anthony slipping out of his melancholy and enjoying himself. Xavier shared a text he received from Jaret, who was sitting on Gallows Hill with Brady in the middle of the night. He stated the location heightened his witch's powers.

At one point, Xavier found himself sitting off to the side, alone with Anthony.

"I'm not trying to push you. I don't want you to shut down on me like you do to Thomas. Still, you're going to have to reconsider everything. This changes everything. Everything. It's about you, now."

A blood tear trickled down Anthony's cheek. He took a napkin and wiped at the stain. "Perhaps. Or perhaps not. I get to decide how much the decision changes for me."

Xavier nodded and stared into his wine. He spoke in a soft tone, hoping none of the others eavesdropped on the private moment. "Even if you can't be in a relationship, I want you to consider something for me. He's heard from me about how I overcame pain. And he's heard from Harriet. Each time he hears a different story the information seems to help him evaluate his feelings about his family and all his life's tragedy. He responds to people who experienced a never-ending pain, because the shared emotion somehow allows him to continue hurting. Your pain could mean so much to him. Perhaps sometime—" Xavier stopped, unsure how to finish. He could have rambled about his request for another hour but decided to leave alone the question.

Anthony stood up. Xavier's heart dropped, thinking Anthony would leave without saying anything. Instead, he walked around the table and pulled Xavier into a hug. He kissed Xavier on the cheek and whispered in his ear. "Thank you." Anthony walked away and grabbed another bottle of Xavier's favorite Ferrari Carano wine, the Tresor.

Fifty-Three:

Remembering Jérémie

15 APRIL 2013
Salem, Massachusetts

The following evening, after the Vampire Council meeting in California, Xavier, Thomas, and Catherine traveled to Salem, Massachusetts, to hook up with Brady and Jaret. Xavier had stopped worrying about leaving Jaret, but Catherine insisted she had to go see him.

When pressed, she explained her reason. "I've never opened up to him about Jérémie. I need to share the details with him about my loss when he died. But I want you to come along for moral support. Remember when you helped me see through Marcel, the awful witchdoctor who killed our brother and who I thought I wanted to marry because of the spell he put on me?"

"How could I forget the lovely scenario?"

"Well, you make my point. I'd never have found out about Jérémie's love without your help. I want you there when I talk to Jaret. You asked me to share my story with him, and I'm ready."

Thomas came along for the ride, though tonight he and Brady had gone into Boston to dance at one of the clubs.

Jaret took Catherine and Xavier to Gallows Hill, where he claimed to feel the hurt and sorrow of the wrongly accused witches but also fed on the supernatural elements they had left behind. Indeed, Xavier's senses tingled from the spot, no doubt meaning Jaret's were even more heightened. The three sat on a swing set, enjoying the night's solitude and quiet companionship.

"Don't you think it's strange modern-day witches are so taken with Salem?" Catherine asked after two twentysomething women romped through the park, doing some ritual to the moon.

"What do you mean?" Jaret asked.

"The Salem witches of 1692 weren't really witches. By most accounts, they were Christians and definitely all innocent of the crimes for which they were executed. The witches today come here as some kind of holy spot, when the events they commemorate had nothing to do with Wicca or witchcraft being practiced."

"You'd make a good historian." Jaret jumped off the swing and motioned for them to follow. He led them to a break in the trees. "Do you feel the energy here? I have no idea why. They weren't witches. Still they left something behind. Maybe an imprint. Maybe the sorrow, hurt, or anger. But something powerful marks this spot."

Xavier nodded. A tingling sensation swept over his arms, a feeling he hadn't had since becoming a vampire, as if his arm had fallen asleep. "What happened?"

"The energy from the departed." Jaret closed his eyes as he spoke. "They died here and left a part of themselves behind. Even if they went to heaven or wherever, what happened left a window into another realm. They created a unique energy. So, witches or not, in 1692, they left something modern witches sense."

Catherine smiled. "Amazing. I've only felt this one other time in my life." She held her hands out and placed them in the center of the power. She spun around in a circle and plopped to the ground.

Catherine slapped the side of her jeans with both hands. "We came to a perfect segue."

"Segue to what?" Jaret asked.

"Come." Catherine patted the ground on either side of herself, beckoning Jaret and Xavier to sit next to her. They obeyed.

She placed a hand on each of their knees and smiled at Jaret. "I'm not one to dwell on these things. It's not my style, not something I'm comfortable with. There's enough people in our group who feel the weight of the world at every minute. Some of us have to let the past go. Harriet, Anthony, and you—" Catherine tapped Xavier on the nose "—honor the memories of anyone and everyone you've ever met." Catherine turned her attention back to Jaret. "Thomas and I have the duty of keeping them moving toward the future. Xavier has times where he sits and reflects on people who meant a lot to him but aren't here anymore. Not me. I don't have time for groveling in the past. Well, I'm exaggerating. You know what I mean."

Xavier reached over and placed his hand over Catherine's mouth. "You started by saying you didn't want to dwell on the issue. But here we're well into your monologue and you haven't even told Jaret what you're talking about. Can you come up for air long enough to focus?"

Catherine's eyes twinkled as she nodded. When Xavier started to pull his hand away, she reached out and bit him.

"Ouch!" Xavier shook his hand as Jaret and Catherine laughed. "You're an ass."

"I'd respond, but you commanded me to get to the point. So I will." Catherine turned so her full attention rested on Jaret. "Xavier thinks you need to see the pain we all live with. I know the notion sounds morbid and perhaps too protective. You know he can't let you go. He frets over you. He's better. Really, he is. But he's always worrying about you—"

Again, Xavier placed his hand over Catherine's mouth. "Focus." He pulled his hand away too fast this time for her to bite.

"Right. Focus." Catherine grinned. "Let's cut to the chase. What you experienced is a tragedy. An awful, painful one. But we all carry shit with us. Everyone. Imagine lugging that baggage around for centuries. Xavier is having us tell you our stories so you'll know you're not alone. And if you let yourself, you can be happy. Even content. You'll always miss them. However, the pain changes, and you'll come to accept the realities of this world, cruelty and all. It's not always wrapped in a neat bow.

"Which brings us to my story. Well, I'm not telling a whole story." Catherine paused for a second as she thought about what to say.

Jaret looked at Xavier. "You're right. It's like she doesn't breathe when she's in the middle of a story."

"I'll bite you too." Catherine snapped her teeth at Jaret and showed her fangs. He laughed. "All right. So here's the thing. When I was young, I had a best friend. He was kind, funny, and supported my feminism. Doesn't sound like much, but to back me in the late 1700s was risky for him. I had no idea he loved me. After some horrid melodrama, the likes of which you can't imagine, we got together. I had many good years with him. Some of the best."

"Is this Jérémie?" Jaret asked.

Catherine nodded. "Yes. And the point, as you've heard from everyone else, is I still miss him. I think about him. Not every day. In some way, though, he's a part of me. He'll always be a part of me. I honor his memory and cherish what I became because of him. And sometimes his memory still makes me a little sad, wondering what it'd be like if I could've shared eternity with him. My story is another way to let you know you're not alone and to keep fighting. I think you've got the idea by now. But doting Xavier wants to make sure you have a connection with as many people as possible regarding your pain. So here I am. And now you know."

Jaret reached over and grabbed Catherine's hand. "And now I know. Thank you." He grew silent, so Xavier and Catherine waited to see if he had something else he wanted to say. "Your sharing means a lot to me. Every time you convey these stories they help. I'm getting the truth behind the lessons. It's hard. And I'm still sad. But I'm learning. I'm healing."

They sat and felt the energy all around them for several more minutes before getting up to meet Brady and Thomas, who would be returning from Boston soon. They walked back to their hotel, content with one another and the strength they felt from each other's presence.

Fifty-Four: Invitation

19 APRIL 2013
Washington, DC

After returning from Salem, Xavier decided to wait a couple of days for everyone to settle in before approaching Jaret about the Vampire Council's offer. He finally got the nerve up and asked Jaret to meet him. He planned to tell him about the decision to allow his conversion, but Xavier hardly anticipated what came before he even introduced the subject. They sat near each other on the living room couch with Darth planted between them.

They chatted for but a minute when Jaret sighed. "I want to say something. You know, before we talk about *the issue*. I really appreciate how much you worry about me. I know I sound annoyed sometimes, but I'm not. Your protection means a lot to me. You're my family. You all are. So, when I don't react or say things or I seem irritated, don't take me wrong. And I love the way you know what to worry about with me. Seriously." Jaret nodded his head with vigor. "But this time I feel awkward you want to talk. Because I'm not ready to even consider the plan. Not at all. Not that your idea hasn't crossed my mind. It has. Not now, okay?"

Xavier stifled a grin. Jaret was adorable. But he had no idea what the poor young man was talking about. "What do you think I want to discuss?"

"I guessed from your approach. Obvious. Plus, I did a little spell to tell your topic was personal and deep. But I am overwhelmed by everything. Maybe the combination of losing everyone and all the depression I'm working through got to me. Probably. Sounds reasonable. Well, okay, and then there's the fact I'm still totally in love with him. There, I said the words. True. I love him a lot. But I'm not ready to even think about going on a date, let alone anything else."

Jaret cocked his head to one side and squinted at Xavier.

Xavier laughed aloud. "Well"—he slapped Jaret on the knee—"I'm glad you released *that* demon. But I needed to talk to you about something else."

"Something else?" Jaret looked shocked.

"Listen, I won't push you on the dating front. Unless you want my advice, I think you can handle the matter for yourself. I know how much you still hurt from Anthony. So no." Xavier shook his head. "I had nothing whatsoever to say to you about dating. But I'm glad you said something. You need to talk about your feelings there if they weigh on you."

Jaret scratched Darth behind the ears. "Yeah. The idea does kinda bother me. But what did you want to talk about? Now I'm way curious. Forget my shitty love life for a while."

"Are you sure? We can talk about dating if you want."

Jaret shook his head. "Nah. Enough. Maybe later. Reminding me about Anthony depresses me. I'm in a good mood so I'd rather not spoil the moment."

Xavier smiled. "Fair enough."

"So tell me." Jaret leaned toward Xavier as he often did when intrigued.

Xavier felt uncertain, which surprised him. He'd wanted to tell Jaret right away, was excited even, but delayed until they had time alone. Now he worried. What if the offer made him angry? What if it spiraled him back into depression?

Xavier drew in a deep breath to calm himself. He knew Jaret better. He knew Jaret could handle the concept, even if he decided against a transformation.

Xavier's delay made Jaret squirm. He patted Darth on the head, grabbed a pillow and held it, and sighed. "What? You're killing me!"

"Okay!" Xavier laughed. "I was trying to make sure this comes out the right way. It's not a light matter."

"Well, I'm pretty good at dealing with deep shit these days."

"True. Perhaps too true."

"Yeah, well, too late to turn back. Spill the beans."

Xavier reached over and pinched Jaret's cheek. "You're right. I'm torturing you. The Vampire Council convened and made a decision affecting you. I wanted to tell you in person. Ask any questions you want. Please don't shut down if the offer shocks you or you don't know how to react."

Jaret laughed. "Stop! Tell me already."

"They, or rather we, approved of converting you into a vampire." Xavier held up his hand to stop Jaret when he started to say something. "Hear me out first. You're part of our family now. You mean the world to me. And all of us. Frankly, if I decided alone, I would've offered a long time ago because I can't bear the thought of ever living life without you. You'll make a wonderful vampire if you want."

"I thought the ethic forbids my transformation?" Jaret's voice had almost no inflection, so Xavier had a hard time reading his emotion. He assumed Jaret first thought of Anthony with their relationship lurking in the background.

"We dispelled the concern. I studied the ethic, which does not forbid converting you. The guidelines caution we need to be certain before converting a powerful witch, because the combination of vampiric power with your witchcraft will be extremely potent. We're all confident when it comes to you."

"It's not true that I'm too dangerous to be a vampire?"

"Anthony wasn't lying to you if you're implying so. He sometimes sees things as black and white, and we have to help him see the grayer areas."

Jaret casually petted Darth and tugged her head into his lap. He leaned over and kissed her on the head. "I thought this required a unanimous vote of the Council?"

Xavier shook his head. "No. Nothing to my knowledge requires such a thing. Merely a majority vote."

"Huh." Jaret stared into the distance. "Was Anthony there?"

"Ah, I see." Xavier nodded. "He was. And the Council voted unanimously for me to approach you."

Jaret spun toward Xavier and stared at him with his eyes wide open. "Really?"

"Yes. He understands what you mean to all of us. He'd never block your transformation."

"But he didn't decide because I meant the same to him, right?"

Xavier paused. Jaret wanted a definitive answer to a complicated question. Or some macabre confirmation Anthony had totally rejected him.

"Our conversation came full circle." Xavier reached over and grabbed Jaret's hand. "Whether you become a vampire or not, you're going to have to deal with this. I know the two are linked. But don't confuse the offer with your feelings for Anthony. As to your question." Xavier got up and opened a bottle of wine, pouring a glass for each of them. He used the activity to give himself time to choose his words, and the alcohol often softened Jaret's harsh responses. He handed a glass to Jaret and then took a sip for himself. "Australian. Not bad, though."

Jaret laughed. "You amaze me with your snobbery about French wine."

"I try to be open-minded. This is one prejudice I've never overcome." Xavier held up his wine glass and swirled the crimson liquid. He smiled at Jaret. "I'm trying to answer your question with complete honesty, but you asked a complicated one. Though in some ways I could give you a short and honest answer. You're wrong. You do mean the same to him as to the rest of us. If you're being honest with yourself, you know in truth you mean

406 - | Damian Serbu

infinitely more to him. So why did he abandon you? Why hasn't he come back? You can guess some of those reasons too. He's terrified. Anthony presents a certain image to the world. He's confident. In control. He likes to lead and makes quick decisions. And he is all of those things. Except after you get to know him—the real him—you come to see a deeper reality. He hurts underneath and is afraid to make himself vulnerable. He lost a lover, and then got tricked by Thomas. He's never talked about his human life, but he obviously has trust issues imbedded in his personality. Listen"—Xavier sat next to Jaret and put his arm around him—"none of this excuses how he treated you. I think his treatment was deplorable. I mean to explain him without excusing him. I don't know what's going to happen. And, even if he won't admit the truth, I think he wants this as much as the rest of us."

Jaret leaned over and put his head on Xavier's shoulder. He seemed ready to burst with emotion. "Do I have to decide right away?" A tear trickled down his cheek.

"The offer isn't an expiring coupon."

Jaret smiled. He wiped at the tear, though both eyes watered. "Good. I'm going to need some time. Like, maybe a long time. I don't know. I need to decide if I really want to live forever while missing my family, you know?"

Xavier nodded. "Of course."

"And seeing Anthony for eternity. That may hurt even more."

Xavier kissed Jaret on the top of his head and pulled him close. He had no answer to the issue of Anthony.

Fifty-Five: Confronting Anthony

12 MAY 2013
London, England

Xavier and Thomas sauntered by Big Ben as the clock chimed 2:00 a.m. Xavier held Thomas's hand and leaned into him. The secluded streets seemed so peaceful at this time of night. Xavier loved his nocturnal walks with Thomas as they toured a city, often saying nothing as they enjoyed the mere presence of one another in a vibrant urban environment.

Thomas lurched to a stop, yanked Xavier into his arms, and drew him into a deep and passionate kiss. Xavier reached around and clutched at Thomas's powerful shoulders. The kiss stopped when both laughed as a passerby honked and shouted out the window, "Go for it!"

"I don't ever want to forget how lucky I am." Thomas took Xavier's hand and continued them on their way to Anthony's London flat. "I'd be in one of those iron boxes for eternity, or dead, if you hadn't come along and saved me. Eternity would mean nothing without you."

Xavier squeezed Thomas's hand. "We're lucky. Not just you. You saved me too."

"We do make a stunning couple, don't we?"

Xavier smiled. "If only we could get Anthony to see the error of his thinking."

"We will."

As they continued in silence, Xavier contemplated their appointment with Anthony. Thomas insisted he would take charge because the soft approach had failed thus far. To a degree Xavier understood the method to Thomas's madness, but his instinct to protect and nurture people spoke against a heavy push. He trusted Thomas, however, and agreed to let him take the lead. Still, he had said he might step in and soften the conversation if he thought the abuse became too much for Anthony.

Anthony greeted them at the door and hugged them both. After they took seats around a very modern living room overlooking the Thames, the room grew quiet.

"I know why you're here." Anthony smiled and swept a lock of hair out of his face.

"Good." Thomas spoke curtly but smiled. "Then we don't have to deal with hours of bullshit before we get to the point. Let's be done soon. We can finish fast if you'll not bury your emotion under twenty feet of earth before we can get to the root problem."

Anthony laughed, though Xavier twitched his leg nervously, unsure about Thomas's approach. "All the mystery as to what you're really thinking."

This time Xavier laughed.

Thomas grinned. "See, you're already trying to deflect."

Anthony tossed his head back and roared with laughter. "Your being pushy won't get you what you want. At this rate, I could piss you off and instead we'll deal with your temper and never get to what brought you here."

"That's why he's here." Thomas jerked his head toward Xavier. "He'll whip off his clothes and seduce me if I get out of hand."

Now they all laughed but fell silent soon enough. Thomas allowed a moment of quiet before pushing ahead.

"Xavier wanted to approach this delicately. I said soft doesn't work with you. You're too adept at hiding, dodging, and avoiding your emotion. Too many centuries of living alone and being the heroic martyr. Blah, blah, blah. But's it's the twenty-first century, so we're doing therapy instead of just bucking up like we had to in the past. We all know you have Post Traumatic Stress Disorder. And I caused some of your hurt. It's all on the table, whether we talk about the pain or not. Good. Now— time to get over your issues. You adore him like nothing I've ever seen. I've seen you bang hundreds and hundreds of twinks over the years. I've seen your lust, and I know your passion. I also know when you're in love. I don't mean temporary infatuation." Thomas got up and went over to Anthony and sat on his lap. "You didn't even react to me as you do him, when we were in passionate love."

Anthony pushed him off and swatted his butt. "You're an asshole."

Thomas jumped up and then sat on the floor at Anthony's feet. "Speaking of assholes, I expected more of a shithead response from you. What gives?"

"With all due respect to Xavier," Anthony nodded his way, "you were right. You're blunt and crass. I assumed as much when you set up this meeting. I'm not daft. I prepared myself for you to bust down my walls like Genghis Kahn. Or a bull in a china shop. Long before you got here, I had our argument about a million times in my mind."

Thomas arched an eyebrow at Anthony while Xavier leaned forward, intrigued as to where this conversation had gone.

"Sounds like you need more counseling than I anticipated." Thomas tilted his head. "For multiple personalities? Who won this argument in your head? You or me?"

"Sybil. Right after we suppressed the superhero figure who emerged and wanted to kick your ass."

Despite himself, Xavier laughed again.

Thomas leaped to his feet and put a hand on each arm of Anthony's chair. He hovered over him, his long hair falling between them and concealing his face from Xavier. "What's going on?"

Anthony pushed Thomas away. "Okay, okay. I'll tell you." Anthony ran a hand through his hair and flung a leg over the arm of his chair. "You can't expect me to change overnight. It's been centuries." Anthony held up a hand to stop Thomas when Thomas grunted and started to say something. To Xavier's surprise, Thomas obeyed though he still stood over Anthony. "Though I must admit the last few years have been a struggle for me, in a good way. I haven't been with another man since I broke up with Jaret."

"No wonder you're an ass. You've got blue balls."

Anthony swept a hand at Thomas, who dodged his punch. "I can still beat off."

"Show me." Thomas wiggled his eyebrows.

"Thomas, stop. Will you let him speak?" Xavier went across the room and grabbed Thomas to drag him to the couch. He sat down and pulled Thomas onto his lap.

"Now I'm going to get blue balls." Xavier pinched Thomas's ass to shut him up.

"I don't know where this will go. But here's what I'm prepared to do. I'm considering the option. The whole thing. And I can promise both of you I won't take forever. I'll decide soon. I need to figure out if I can risk the move. Either way, I'll go to him and explain everything. You won't have to do the deed for me. Some days I want to get over my past and move on. And other days the thought terrifies me more than I could ever articulate. That's the best I can do."

Xavier thought Anthony gave an honest answer. "I appreciate how difficult working through these feelings must have been and then to tell us."

"Thank you."

Thomas, on the other hand, rolled his eyes. "We already knew everything he said. I want more."

"It's all I have, Thomas."

"You mean it's all you're willing to give to the poor boy."

"Not fair."

"And what you did to him was?" Thomas frowned. "You don't have much time. I expect to see you in Paris when he's there. Don't be an ass, Anthony. He's in as much pain as you. Think of someone else for a change."

Anthony slumped in his chair. Xavier had braced himself for another argument between the two but instead Anthony nodded.

"You're right. I promise. He'll see me before the end of June. I'm taking this very seriously. I won't do anything else until I know whether or not I can."

After several minutes of silence, Xavier pushed Thomas up and they both prepared to leave. They hugged Anthony goodbye and went into the hall. Before they got to the stairs, however, Xavier turned around. Anthony still stood in his doorway, watching them go.

Xavier strode back but motioned for Thomas to stay at the stairs. He hugged Anthony one more time and whispered in his ear. "You can. I know you can. Because he's worth more than anything you've had before."

Part Ten: The Mika Concert

Fifty-Six: Paris

8 JUNE 2013
Paris, France

Jaret held tight to Darth's leash as they jogged along the Seine, heading back toward the flat Thomas and Xavier owned. He loved Paris, and this late afternoon jog only confirmed why. The city screamed of history at the same time it offered a modern urban environment. He could explore the ancient past while living as an out gay man. Xavier's pride in his hometown shown through in his enthusiasm as they toured the city. Jaret marveled at the fact you could pass centuries-old buildings here and then on the next block encounter a newly built piece of modern architecture.

Back at the flat, Jaret took his time showering because he still had a couple of hours before the sun set.

He spent several minutes lying next to Darth. He'd noticed of late she had slowed down on their run, and he often brought her home early and had to finish on his own. Her gray muzzle gave away her age, and she slept a lot more than she stayed awake. He stamped down on the panic welling within himself at the thought of losing her even as he knew the inevitability of her death. He kissed her head and then stripped off his clothes to take a shower.

Then he remembered he had to check his email because Brady was scheduling a visit later in the month and needed to know if the dates worked. He also needed for Jaret to transfer the money to pay for his plane ticket.

Jaret logged onto the internet and read Brady's message.

> *Here are my dates. Do they work? Don't go shit crazy sending me lots of money for it. I'm not a call boy and the money will make me feel like a prostitute. Can't wait to see you. I feel like you flew to Mars or something. You okay?*

The dates worked perfectly. Instead of having Brady book his own tickets, Jaret simply made his plane reservation and sent him the information because Brady would never book himself in first class no matter how much Jaret insisted.

> *Dear whore, the details for our next appointment are attached, along with the ticket as payment for your less-than-stellar services.*

Jaret was already growing excited to see his friend. The warmth and companionship always renewed him. Xavier and the others did, too, but something about Brady made the emotion different. Perhaps because of their proximity in age. Or Brady's free spirit and insistence on having fun. He made Jaret laugh and feel loved even at the most depressing moments. Too, Brady had known him for a long time through a lot of ups and downs. They stuck together no matter what.

Next Jaret deleted a bunch of spam, and then his hand shook too much to move the mouse when he saw a message from SexyVamp. At the same time, he involuntarily got excited and reached down to touch himself.

He got control enough to open the message but had to fight against the urge to delete it.

> *Dear Jaret,*
>
> *If you can find the space in your heart to forgive my insensitivity, I would very much like to have a meeting with you. I'll be in Paris June 22. Can we make an appointment? I frankly wouldn't blame you for deleting this message as you did with my previous attempts to write to you. But I hope you won't.*
>
> *Yours faithfully,*
>
> *Anthony*

What in the hell did his message mean? In all of the time he dated Anthony, he'd never seen something so awkward and formal. The email read more like something from his lawyer than from a former lover. Or something out of a Jane Austen novel. Yours faithfully? Was he a dog?

He stared at his computer screen for several minutes trying to figure out the meaning. He knew Anthony had buried emotional scars he desperately worked to hide. Maybe they had something to do with the odd communication. Or did Anthony want to meet to reject Jaret one more time, so he wrote the message to keep Jaret from getting his hopes up?

Jaret almost took him up on the offer to delete the message. Figuratively rip up the letter like he had the notes Anthony had sent. Much safer for his emotion. Instead, he let his dreams get the better of him and decided to reply. But he kept it short and simple.

Sure. Tell me the time and place. J.

There. Two could play at the game.

Still, in the shower he found himself aroused. He closed his eyes as he lathered with soap and recalled the feeling of Anthony's muscled chest pressed against his back, his strong hands rubbing the soap down Jaret's chest, past his belly button, and then the soap dropping to the floor as he wrapped his fingers around Jaret's cock. Jaret manipulated himself as he leaned against the shower wall and imagined Anthony's stiff manhood inside him, gently making love as Jaret blasted a load all over himself.

As he shaved and dressed, he tried to calm his desires, reminding himself over and over Anthony's message hardly indicated a renewal of their relationship.

He got to the living room to find Xavier alone, reading a new novel by Rick R. Reed. "I love gay horror." Xavier closed the book and smiled. "It's nice to have gay characters in my favorite genre now."

"Is Catherine here yet?" Jaret asked.

"We're meeting her on Montmartre. She's hunting for straight American jocks. It's her latest fad. She's only feeding on hot jocks who beat their girlfriends or beat up gay men. She thinks a tourist area will be ripe for the hunting."

Jaret laughed. He hadn't seen Catherine in a while and looked forward to her vibrant personality. He went over and grabbed a Coke from the bar fridge, knowing he'd have another late night out. They had so much fun in Paris, Jaret almost decided to become a vampire so he could stay up all night with them.

"You seem happy." Xavier poured himself a glass of Vouvray. Then he grabbed a bottle of rum and came over, pouring some into Jaret's can.

Jaret nodded. "I am. This has been a good trip."

"I'm glad. It's nice to see you enjoying yourself. Or should I say, allowing yourself to enjoy life?"

Jaret smiled. "Yeah. True. Now I have to work on not feeling guilty about living. Sometimes after a particularly fun night I come home and feel bad I'm having fun at all. Then I miss them all over again."

"Sounds normal. Maybe you're coming to a new understanding of everything."

Jaret played with a tassel on a pillow and gulped back a huge drink of rum and Coke. "I think so. Like, what everyone told me is happening a little. The places where I miss them and the loss can really depress me. But I can also let myself survive. I'm doing well at letting my new family love me. My new Dad especially." Jaret choked on the last sentence.

Xavier, too, appeared to struggle with his emotion as he pressed his lips together in a half grimace, half smile. He twirled the wine in his glass and watched the golden colors shimmer before him. "Your words mean the world to me. I feel the same way. Have you thought any more about the other issue on the table?"

"Why? Is the coupon expiring?" Jaret grinned.

"Never for you. Well, until, you know."

"Yeah. If I get hit by a bus tonight, not much you can do."

This time Xavier smiled. "Right. So, where are we at?"

"Funny you should mention it. You know what I said the other night?"

Xavier nodded. "You didn't think you could convert without something from Anthony. He's a big roadblock for you."

"He emailed today. Or last night, whatever. He wants to meet when he's in town."

"Did he say why?"

Jaret shook his head. "He sent a bizarre message. More like an email to his broker than me."

"That doesn't surprise me. He's as afraid as you are."

"Good enough." Jaret got up and made himself another drink. The slight buzz helped him talk so openly to Xavier about Anthony. "So, no real change in the answer to your question. I can't reconsider the vampire thing until I know what he's thinking."

"Fair enough. But remember, you promised to consider the transformation no matter what happened with him."

Jaret almost blurted out his initial rude thought, about spending eternity staring at the man he loved while he pretended Jaret didn't exist. Instead, he nodded and took a drink. Before he had to come up with a response, Thomas burst into the room.

"Hurry! I just paid a hot little artist up on Montmartre to paint you." Thomas hurried over and picked Jaret out of his chair like a rag doll before putting him down.

With his feet on the ground, Jaret scrunched his brow. "Why me? Shouldn't you want a portrait of him?" He pointed at Xavier.

"Yeah, whatever. I have a million of him. But you promised you'd pose so we could put one over the fireplace of you."

Jaret had agreed to sit for a portrait a few nights ago while drunk and mostly to shut the two of them up. He hardly thought they intended to follow through with the ancient ritual of the rich and famous. Who in the twenty-first century had paintings done?

"Hurry." Thomas pulled Xavier to his feet. "I paid him well, but if someone else comes along, that'll be it. And this is definitely someone you want to watch paint."

Xavier hit Thomas on the arm. "Is this about finding a good artist, or getting your cheap jollies in the process?"

Thomas grinned. "Both?"

Moments later, they had raced through Paris and Jaret found himself sitting on the cobblestone street as a cute twentysomething guy with short brown hair and green eyes tried to focus on painting though he kept glancing at Thomas and Xavier with lust.

Thankfully, Catherine arrived and after a quick greeting took them away because she found a posse of hooligans to feed off. She whispered her plan to Jaret and ran away.

As he sat awkwardly watching this cutie paint, he wished he knew enough French to converse. Instead, he just blushed when the guy winked at him.

Fifty-Seven: Notre Dame at Night

13 JUNE 2013
Paris, France

Jaret had cranked his Mika CDs and was almost done listening to them. He had slept until early afternoon, having converted to vampire hours so he could spend more time exploring the city with Xavier, Thomas, and Catherine. He only had a little time before they emerged and then he'd have to put all his Mika music away because he had to decide whether or not to attend the live concert later in the month. If they heard him playing Mika, they'd force another discussion about the topic.

As he had healed over the last year, and especially since coming to Paris, he grudgingly admitted his reticence to attend the concert had more to do with his inner three-year-old than any real tangible reason for denying himself the experience. Yet he clung to the punishment, as if letting go of this last vestige of the painful past would sever the link to all he had loved and lost.

He'd showered and put on his socks when Catherine stormed into his room without knocking. She grabbed him and then his pile of clothes before lifting him in the air and running outside.

"Catherine! I'm naked!"

"You're not naked. You have cute little red socks on. And we're moving too fast for anyone to see you. We had to escape from Xavier before he got up." She came to a halt and set him on the ground in a deserted alley. "There, get dressed."

"What's this about?" Jaret blushed and grabbed his shirt to cover himself. He started dressing. "You forgot my underwear!"

"Free ball! Come on, before they find us."

Jaret laughed when Catherine waved her hand in a circle to get him to hurry.

"Are we in trouble or something?"

"Not yet." Once again Catherine picked him up and carried him through Paris. Usually, they let him walk and move about like a human, but every now and then Catherine took charge. Jaret always let her because they had so much fun together, ever since Washington, DC.

Before he knew it, Catherine set him on an iron railing high atop the Eifel Tower. As in, above the highest observation deck, above where no human could possibly go. Jaret's senses pulsated and he resisted the urge to scream. When he looked down, the height and fear caused tingling in his crotch and panic as his heart raced. He swayed a little.

"Don't worry. I've got you." He felt Catherine's arm wrapped around his waist in a tight embrace. "Beautiful, yes?"

Despite his fear, Jaret looked out over Paris and was in awe at the view. Breathtaking.

"You can imagine this is risky and illegal for us to be up here. But I come here all the time. No one can really see us. I wanted to share my secret place with you. Xavier freaked when I mentioned coming here last night."

Jaret's phone rang in his shorts pocket. No way he could move to answer without throwing up. Seconds later, Catherine's phone rang. She held to Jaret in one arm and grabbed the phone in her other hand, hitting speaker with her thumb.

"I can see you. Get down here. You're both fools."

Catherine laughed so loud Jaret worried the people below could hear her. She clicked the phone off, and Jaret screamed when she pushed them off the bar and dove toward the ground. They landed but had no time to get their bearings because she ran forward and had them hidden in a nearby park next to Xavier in no time.

Catherine and Jaret laughed so hard they had Xavier chuckling, too, despite his obvious anger.

"You're lunatics."

"I was kidnapped!" Jaret protested. "I'm not even wearing underwear."

"I don't want to know how you failed to dress tonight." Xavier seemed to inspect every inch of Jaret to see if Catherine had injured him. "You need to be more careful."

Catherine dismissed him with a wave. "He deserved a private tour of Paris like no one else."

"What would the Vampire Council say?" Xavier put his hands on his hips.

"You're a stick-in-the-mud."

Xavier rolled his eyes. "Come on. We have to hurry. They're doing a concert in the gardens of Versailles tonight with the fountains going. We can't miss it."

Once again, Jaret was unable to respond before Catherine picked him up and hurried at vampire speed through Paris, out of the city limits, to Versailles. The vampires allowed Jaret to straighten himself up before they started walking around the breathtaking grounds and viewing the amazing fountains of celebrated Greek and Roman gods.

They found Thomas waiting at Jaret's favorite fountain, dedicated to Apollo. Thomas tilted his head and grinned at Jaret. "You don't wear underwear?"

Jaret blushed.

Catherine laughed hard. "It's a long story. Don't torture the poor boy. Free balling was my fault."

When the concert ended, Catherine asked if they wanted to go hunt in the red-light district for more straight young assholes. Jaret announced he'd rather go home to bed since he had no need for human blood.

"Sometimes I forget you're not a vampire. Yet." Catherine pinched Jaret's cheek.

"I'll take him home," Xavier said. "My turn to show him something illegal."

As they walked away, Jaret looked at Xavier. "What do you want to show me?"

"Are you up for another adventure? Or are you too tired?"

Jaret shook his head. "No! Take me."

"Do you want some underwear first?"

"Will you people stop reminding me!" Jaret blushed again. "Is it so obvious? How did Thomas know?"

"You're fine." Xavier smiled. "I don't think anyone can tell. Thomas is a pervert."

They sat at the front of Notre Dame Cathedral and glanced at the majestic church in the moonlight.

"When I was a priest, I hated this building. I had a small parish in a very poor part of the city. The bishops and cardinals stayed here. The majesty signified everything wrong with the church—wealth, corruption. Not everyone could go inside. There are still so many problems in the world. But in many ways, much of the world has improved."

"Does being here still bother you?"

Xavier stood and motioned for Jaret to follow as they walked around the grounds. A young solider walked by holding a machine gun, even at this late hour. "Not any more. The building is stunning. Now the cathedral reminds me of the past. And I admire the beauty and architecture. I love the gargoyles."

"Me, too."

"Good. We're here to go see them. Don't tell Catherine because I'll never hear the end of my own trespassing."

At an inhuman speed, Jaret again discovered himself moving fast and high atop a Paris landmark, Notre Dame Cathedral this time. Yet another amazing view of the city and a private tour of the best gargoyles.

"It's too crowded to come up here when open to the public. If I grab you again, it's because someone saw us on the security cameras, and we have to get out of here."

Jaret studied the gargoyles, thinking the panther-like one was his favorite. He caught up with Xavier, who stood leaning against the wall and looking over Paris, toward the Eifel Tower.

"I've waited to tell you this." Xavier spoke after Jaret leaned on the wall next to him. "Not because I was keeping secrets. I wasn't. I never knew how to tell you, or whether I should. Now as you feel better, I thought the idea might help."

"What?" Xavier had piqued Jaret's curiosity.

"About the crash where I staged your family's death."

"You told me." Jaret furrowed his brow, worried Xavier's news might depress him more than he expected.

Xavier turned to him, then reached over and put his arm around Jaret as they continued to peer toward Paris, more to avoid the intense emotion than anything.

"I knelt and prayed after. I felt so guilty for defiling them further than Henrik had already done. Lost in my emotion, I almost missed the moment. Before my brother, Michel, appeared to comfort me, I caught a message flying through the air. I don't know how else to describe what happened. As if she spoke to me or sent a note right into my head."

"Who?"

Xavier paused. "Your mother."

At the mere thought of his mom, Jaret's eyes teared. "My mom?"

Xavier nodded.

"Why?"

"She sent a plea. To me. To save you. She didn't want you joining them. She was desperate for me to protect you. She said you'd suffered so much and deserved more than to feel guilty over their deaths. She wanted you to live."

Jaret absorbed the words as the city sparkled in front of him. He cried a little, but not the passionate anguish of before. He and his mom had a special connection, even more so after the torture of his coming out and her initial reluctance to accept his sexuality. He was glad Xavier waited to tell him. Otherwise, he would have survived to obey his mother's command instead of by his own will.

But the latest news somehow helped. His visit to his family in heaven had given him the same sense: they all wanted him to continue with life. Somehow knowing she'd pled for such a thing long before seeing Jaret gave him comfort.

"Thank you for sharing with me."

"I thought it'd be okay now."

When they heard someone climbing the narrow circular stairs, Xavier clutched Jaret close to him, ran to the back of the cathedral and across the roof and right by the statue of St. Michel, then jumped to the ground. Xavier whispered into Jaret's ear as they raced along, "The St. Michel statue and I had a moment once. A long story for another time. He came to life. Or an angel possessed it."

Xavier stayed at home the rest of the night with Jaret, saying he would remain even after Jaret retired to bed. Jaret snuggled next to Darth and buried his head in her side. Again, he dismissed the sound of her labored breathing as they drifted to sleep.

Fifty-Eight: Blood Hound

17 JUNE 2013
Paris, France

Xavier rushed into the bedroom he shared with Thomas, then hid his secret in his large closet. His heart beat fast from adrenaline and fear. He started sweating. Since when did vampires sweat? He returned to the closet to peer in but saw nothing to worry him. Well, not much. He whipped around and slammed closed all of the shutters on the windows and double-checked he'd locked the door.

Then he stood in front of the bed, breathing heavily and looking down at Thomas. Thomas lay in his bathrobe with a bemused expression, propped up on one elbow, and watching Xavier as if in the midst of a sitcom.

"Are the authorities after you? Did you steal some bread like Jean Valjean? Don't worry. I'm not afraid of Javert."

Panic set in at what Xavier had done so much he couldn't even laugh at Thomas.

"I did something wrong."

Thomas arched his brow. "Do tell."

"You don't understand. I mean really, really wrong. As in, I should be locked back in the iron box and right over the fire in the Rocky Mountains in the old vampire prison. I've shit on the vampire ethic. Maybe more than when I tried to free all the slaves."

Thomas sat up and leaned forward. "Come here." He motioned for Xavier to sit next to him on the bed. "The Council won't have the votes to imprison you. Catherine and I would never allow a conviction. Unless you vote against yourself."

"I might have to."

Thomas laughed. "Why don't you tell me what this is about. Anything to do with the scratching I hear in your closet?"

"Yes." Xavier nodded and wiped at the sweat on his brow.

Thomas reached over and ran his hand through Xavier's short hair. His own long black hair fell gently against Xavier's cheek when he kissed him.

"Tell me, *abbé*. What's going on?"

Xavier reached into his shirt and pulled out his crucifix. He rubbed the cross, then leaned his entire body into Thomas.

"I panicked. As in, total overreaction, holy-fuck-what-have-I-done, insane panic."

"You're being intense. Tell me already."

"Promise not to judge me?"

Thomas grabbed Xavier by both shoulders and turned him so they faced each other. When Xavier cast his glance to the bed, Thomas clutched his chin and forced eye contact. "Trust me. Relax. We're in everything together. Always. What has you so worked up? You're right. I haven't seen you like this since you went after Duncan in the 1820s. Did St. Michel visit you again? I detest the saint."

"No. Not him." Xavier fell into Thomas's arms and found comfort there. "You remember when I told you I thought Darth was getting sick?"

"Yes."

"Well, she couldn't move her back legs this morning. The paralysis started right before I had to go to sleep, so I helped Jaret look up the very best vet, and he promised to take her right away. I wrote a note, since I didn't know if he'd be able to communicate in French. When I got up, Jaret had left me a note. Darth has cancer."

Blood tears streamed down Xavier's cheeks. He had come to care about Darth and, even more, dreaded what her loss might do to Jaret.

Thomas petted Xavier. "And?"

"Well, I stole her from Jaret. I took her outside and held her in my lap. This would kill him, Thomas. He's come so far. He's done so well. But I know he can't survive without her. I was crying, but she's so out of it she had no idea what was going on. I think the doctor gave her something for the pain."

A dog barked in Xavier's closet, startling them both.

"Did you get him another dog?" Thomas asked.

Xavier shook his head. "No. I put Darth in there."

Thomas opened his eyes wider. He kissed Xavier on the forehead and got off the bed. He opened the closet door, and Darth bounded into the room, wagging her stub of a tail. She jumped from the closet door to Xavier's side in one leap and gave him a big lick on the cheek. Thomas stood with a complete look of shock on his face. After a long pause, he burst into laughter.

"Not funny." Xavier commanded Darth to lie down, and she obeyed.

"I didn't know such a thing was possible. Did you do it like we do to humans?"

"No. It's in the vampire ethic. There's a whole section on converting animals. Of course, you're not supposed to. And they can't convert each other."

"If you're not supposed to, why does the ethic explain how to?" Thomas returned to sit next to Xavier.

"In the section on war. If there's a bad vampire war, the rules say to convert creatures to your side. You can enchant them to link with certain vampires, whom they'll obey."

Thomas played with Xavier's hand and then laughed again. "This is the only vampire dog?"

Xavier slapped Thomas on the leg. "It's not funny."

"It's kind of funny."

"Shouldn't I be punished? What are we going to do?"

"Too late to worry now. What does Jaret think?"

"He doesn't know yet. When he woke, I told him I had Darth and was taking care of her."

Thomas got up and dressed as he spoke. "Let's worry about the others on the Council and the implications later. Let's take her to Jaret first, and see how he reacts. Will she obey him?"

Xavier nodded. "Yes. Him most of all. I made sure. She was attracted to him, anyway. It took everything I could do to get her to follow me and not run to him."

"What does she eat?"

"Apparently the blood of other animals. And only when we allow the feeding."

"Fascinating."

"Will you stop? This isn't good."

"Or she may be perfect." Thomas pulled Xavier back into his arms. "You may have done exactly what he needed. I think the others will be okay."

They started down the hallway with Darth following. "But think of what we'd do to another vampire if they pulled this stunt," Xavier added.

"Impossible. You'd have to be on the Council to know the magic."

"Will you quit justifying my malfeasance? Take this seriously."

Thomas smiled. "I am. You know I'm not a big one for the rules. You made an exception. A one-time exception. I vote okay. Relax."

Outside the door to Jaret's bedroom, Xavier stopped Thomas. "You stay out here with Darth. I'll call you both in."

Thomas nodded, so Xavier turned and went inside. Jaret sat in his pajamas, hugging his knees to his chest and crying.

"She died, didn't she?"

"That's why I'm here." Xavier sat next to Jaret and rubbed his leg. "I have to explain something. I hope you won't be angry."

Jaret sniffled and wiped at his eyes. "What? I didn't get to say goodbye."

"I'm not sure how to tell you this. Maybe I should show you. Thomas?"

Jaret's door flung open and a very excited Darth pounced onto the bed. She controlled her newfound power but nudged herself under Jaret's arms and started kissing maniacally at his face. Jaret's magical jewelry spun to life and hovered around him, seeming to glow with excitement. Jaret told Darth to stop, so she lurched to a halt and sat beside him, her tail wagging.

Jaret's eyes lit with recognition. He opened his mouth and then closed it. The gems floated through the air and returned to the jewelry box.

Thomas came over and joined them on the bed as the vampires waited for Jaret to respond.

Jaret looked at Xavier, then turned his attention to Darth, then to Thomas, and back to his dog. He reached over and tugged her into a hug, then buried his face in her neck. Before Xavier had time to wonder at Jaret's reaction, he heard Jaret chuckling.

Jaret pulled away from the dog and looked at Xavier. "She's a vampire, isn't she?"

"I'm so sorry. I should have let you decide. I was so worried about you. And her. When I found your note tonight, I didn't know what else to do."

Then Jaret frowned for the first time. "This wasn't some attempt to manipulate me into becoming a vampire?"

Xavier shook his head. "Never. Never crossed my mind. I didn't know how you'd cope with losing her. I wanted you to have her. I wish I had come up with a devious plot to deceive you, but instead I can only plead panic."

Jaret smiled again and leaned across the bed to pull Xavier into a hug. The tears came fast and furious. "Thank you so much," Jaret stammered. "Thank you so much."

Xavier retired to bed the next morning resolved he'd done the right thing. With Thomas's help, he felt certain he could persuade the Council to accept this one exception to the rules. He thought even Anthony might come around to understanding.

They trained Jaret in how to handle Darth and made a dark and safe place for her to sleep during the daylight. Jaret said he could not wait until she woke up the next night so he could go on a jog with a vampire dog.

Xavier even learned how to convert the ethic's section explaining how to control a vampire animal into a pamphlet for Jaret.

Something told Xavier Jaret had needed this more than anything in order to survive. A vampire dog had saved Jaret and Xavier decided not to apologize for his actions.

Fifty-Nine: Healing

19 JUNE 2013
Paris, France

Catherine sat next to Thomas on a love seat, both laughing hysterically the entire time. They had gathered in the suite Anthony had rented in Paris. While those two carried on, Anthony frowned, and Harriet sat stoic and unreadable. Observing this whole climate made Xavier nervous.

"What about a vampire parrot?" Thomas snorted. "Can you imagine? I think we should start these experiments on every animal as Catherine suggested."

Catherine laughed so hard she doubled over in her seat. "Vampire mice would be funny. They'd scare the shit out of rats. Imagine when a cat thinks she found her prey and then the mouse attacks her instead!"

"Unless she came upon a vampire cat!" Thomas roared.

"Can you two stop?" Anthony's curt words brought silence to the gathering. Xavier did see a slight smile at the corner of Harriet's lips, however.

Though he'd stopped laughing, Thomas still had a goofy grin plastered on his face. "Do we really need a vote or formal proclamation? We talked about the matter long enough. We reprimanded Xavier, forced him to promise not to turn any other animals, and agreed to allow this exception to the rule. I promised to further punish him in my own secret way."

Xavier found Thomas's rendition of the meeting rather inaccurate. They had discussed Xavier's action at length and determined to permit Darth's transformation, but no one had scolded him or needed to exact such a promise because from the beginning Xavier had made it on his own.

Harriet moved forward in her chair, speaking for the first time. "The ethic demands a vote, regardless of how we all see the issue."

"Very well." Catherine sat up straighter. "I'll cast the first vote to accept Xavier's apology and promise not to repeat the deed. No further action required."

"Here, here!" Thomas cast his vote and sat back without another word.

"Harriet?" Catherine asked.

"I'm in more of a quandary. I agree with all of you. Still, allowing an exception without further reprimand risks making light of our rules. However, I trust Xavier. I agree, but hope he understands the gravity of the situation despite the two clowns over there."

This made Thomas and Catherine giggle all over again.

"Anthony?" Thomas spoke this time.

"We don't need further voting. The decision is made."

"Still, we should all make our feelings known." Harriet walked over and stood next to Anthony, as if anticipating he might need her support.

"I'll go." Xavier interrupted. "I appreciate your faith in me. Your trust means a lot. But I think some sanction is in order. I vote to imprison me in my rooms for a month."

The room grew silent, and all eyes fell upon Anthony. "This disregard for the letter of the law still makes me uncomfortable. I don't know if I'll ever get used to our mode of operation. Nonetheless, I happen to agree with everyone else. Xavier," Anthony turned to him, "you're outvoted on this matter, four to one."

Xavier sat stunned. He had anticipated an exoneration from everyone but Anthony.

When Xavier stared at him in disbelief, Anthony smiled.

"I'm trying to learn. I'm grasping the meaning of following the ethic without the rules becoming mandated laws from above we can't alter. I remind myself often how vampires made the rules originally, not some gods. I'm understanding the need for exceptions." Anthony paused, running a hand through his hair and breathing out. "I'm learning how to deal with my feelings. Losing Darth would destroy Jaret. If for no other reason, I grant the exception to save him." Anthony started to say something else but stopped, leaving Xavier to wonder why. Had he come too close to engaging his true feelings for Jaret?

The Vampire Council considered a couple of other minor issues before going their separate ways. Harriet and Catherine had an art exhibit they wanted to see,

Anthony slipped away without saying anything else, which left Xavier and Thomas to return to their flat.

Once inside, Thomas pulled Xavier into his arms. "Are you going to tell him?"

Xavier nodded. "I'll go. Then you and I can go do something once he goes to bed."

"Or we could go to our room and do something." Thomas wiggled his eyebrows and grinned. Then he kissed Xavier on the forehead and headed toward their private quarters, explaining he had gotten behind on their finances.

Xavier knocked on Jaret's door and laughed when he heard a more passionate Darth than her old age had previously permitted barking on the other side. "Darth, sit!"

The door opened with a grinning Jaret on the other side and Darth sitting as commanded in the middle of the room but wiggling her butt in anticipation of greeting Xavier. Jaret released her and she bounded over and jumped high enough to lick Xavier on the lips.

He laughed.

"What did they say?" Jaret asked before they even sat down.

Xavier lowered himself into a comfortable lounge chair while Jaret sat on the very edge of his bed and fidgeted.

"We're fine. They're allowing the exception."

Jaret jumped into the air and clapped his hands. He spun around and then hurried across the room and fell into Xavier's arms as he embraced him. Xavier returned the hug and smiled.

"I have one other thing to talk about." Xavier lifted Jaret back onto the floor.

"What?" Jaret plopped down in front of Xavier, sitting on the floor with his legs crossed. Darth scurried to his side.

Xavier noticed for a while now Jaret's body language had softened. He'd returned more to the gentle, carefree soul whom Xavier had first met. He didn't lose the hint of sorrow and maturity that had become his constant companions. But he had learned to accept life and even found enjoyment in living.

"Please don't shut down this time." Xavier folded his hands in his lap. "I'll let you make your own decision and respect your feelings. But I hate when you refuse to even listen."

Jaret tilted his head and smiled as he petted Darth. "Me? Refuse to listen? Can't imagine."

"Right. Never you. Will you agree, for me?"

"Sure. What?"

"I want to talk about the Mika concert." Xavier paused, waiting for the eruption. Jaret sat there with a funny grin on his face. "Brady arrives tomorrow. I know you two have a lot of plans. Remember he's excited about the concert. I think you should go with him, not me. Or all of us. I don't really understand why you're denying yourself on this one. Makes no sense. Mika is your favorite singer. You're obsessed with him. Steve didn't like him. And Anthony only did because of you. I can't see what point you're making in—"

"Stop!" Jaret held up his hands and laughed. "Enough with the monologue. My turn."

"You said you'd listen."

"I did. But I can save us a lot of time. I mean, I know time doesn't mean anything to a vampire. Which is what I was afraid you wanted to talk about—the whole vampire thing. Because I'm not ready to make the undead decision yet. Anyway, time is still fleeting for me, so I don't want to sit here and listen to you going on and on about something we agree about."

Xavier paused, gauging Jaret. He still sat smiling and petting his dog. Had Xavier understood correctly? "You're going?"

"Yeah." Jaret sighed. "I suppose you want to know the whole story."

Xavier nodded. "You need to explain a rather sudden change of direction."

"Well, I mean, yeah, I changed my mind. But I took a long time. I talked to Brady a lot. Of course, he wanted me to go. We've always wanted to go to a Mika concert together. Like you always said, and he did, too, my refusal didn't really affect anyone but me. I knew. Even when I was being stubborn. I'm not a complete moron. I hurt so much thinking about all the shit around the concert, you know? First the memories brought back all the shit with Steve, which now includes some guilt I killed him because I failed to see Henrik puppeteering him. How did I miss the magic? I don't even know where Steve ended, and Henrik started."

Jaret held his hands in the air. "I know, I know. I didn't kill him. Henrik did. And Henrik acted on his own. I can't shoulder the weight of the world at every turn. So not my fault. Still, life is a little more complicated, right? Mika reminded me of all the shit. Then, when I got beyond

Steve and my family and Henrik, along comes Anthony. He'd promised to take me, even saying we could go anywhere in the world. Then one day, poof." Jaret waved his hands through the air and a puff of smoke literally appeared before him. Sometimes Xavier forgot he was a witch. "No more Anthony. No more going anywhere I wanted to see Mika.

"Mika's concert became a bad omen. As if my love for Mika became my divine punishment for all the shit I've done wrong in the world. I know this explanation doesn't make sense either. I could've made a really good medieval monk. Whipping myself on the back all the time. But every time I got excited about Mika, something bad happened. I avoided the concerts to avoid my emotion. Whether coincidence or not, my being Mika's biggest fan created problems. Or at least, I associated the two."

Jaret finished and sat with Darth. His monologue had purged a great deal of emotion, and Xavier wasn't sure where to begin. He decided to seek more information. "What changed?"

"Oh, yeah." Jaret smiled. "Jenn told me to grow up." He laughed. "I'm not nuts. Quit looking at me funny. You didn't think she'd be coming to me? Please. We were too close for her to float away. I need a guardian angel. And I'm more high maintenance than you, with Michel coming every few decades or whatever. We talk a lot. How do you think I moved on from losing all of them? Or at least, how I cope? Jenn, of course. She's my Catherine, only dead." He laughed hard this time. "I mean dead in a dead dead kind of way. Fuck. This is morbid."

Xavier still needed to hear more to convince him Jaret had not gone mad or into denial. "Jenn told you to go to the concert?"

Jaret nodded. "She heard us talking and after you left told me I was full of shit. She said, 'Xavier's right. This doesn't make any sense.' She told me to go to the fucking concert and enjoy myself. Sometimes she talks sense to me. Blunt. With anyone else, the words would hurt my feelings or I'd get pissed. Not with Jenn. She helped me decide I was the one punishing myself, and my punishment wasn't doing any good. Going means a lot to Brady and me. We'll have a blast. But we want you and Thomas to go too. Catherine already promised she would."

Xavier got up and sat on the floor next to Jaret. He put his arm around him and squeezed. "You're mature for your age. Are you okay? You let out a lot."

Jaret leaned into Xavier. "I'm cool. I've figured out the truth for a while. I hadn't told you yet because I've been so worried about Darth."

"Darth is safe. She's hoping she has a master for eternity."

Jaret punched Xavier in the arm. "Manipulative. I'll decide when I'm ready."

"I know." Xavier smiled. "I like to let you know where I stand."

"Like I didn't already."

Sixty: Telling Brady

20 JUNE 2013
Paris, France

"Catherine, please. Hurry." Jaret pulled her along, counting on the fact she loved defying the vampire ethic. She had to understand. When they got far enough away from the house, he sat on a bench and motioned for her to join him.

"What naughtiness are you up to? Are you wearing underwear? Red socks?"

Jaret laughed. "Stop. We don't have much time. We need to do this before Thomas and Xavier get back. They won't take long to feed, and this is important."

"And against the rules, or you wouldn't be hiding from Xavier."

"Right." Jaret nodded. "Here's the thing. I can't keep making dumbass excuses to Brady about all the nocturnal wanderings around here. Plus, if I'm contemplating a change, he's going to find out. I know, I know. Technically I'd be required to leave him behind. But you know I won't. Let's not debate the matter."

"Okay. No problem for me," Catherine said. "And I'll be on your side, whatever happens there. This ethic gets stupid with its rigid rules. Anyway, what does this have to do with tonight and me?"

"I want you to tell Brady about the vampires."

"Why me?"

"Because I think I'll get in less trouble if we tell him together. Less risk to me."

Catherine laughed. "You'll throw me under the bus?"

"Kind of."

Catherine tilted her head. "Well, I see your point. I don't know. Does this have to happen now?"

"Come on. Don't start getting all rule bound on me. He can handle the truth. When I told him I was a witch, he hardly reacted. Embraced all of me because he trusted and loved me. He'll do the same with this."

"I do love fucking with the ethic. Maybe even more than Thomas. He talks a good game, but he also hates defying Anthony. Or making Xavier nervous." She rolled her eyes. "He's always nervous so I learned when we were kids to ignore his moods."

"Then come on!"

Jaret got up and pulled Catherine back toward the house. She grabbed him around the waist and carried him the rest of the way. He thought he might plummet right through the porch when she slammed him down.

"Ouch!"

"Get over it! Open the door so we can tell him. I'll keep my senses alert, in case they return."

"Brady!" Jaret shouted as the door swung open.

"Whoa, chief. You'll make me go prematurely deaf." Brady sat smiling at them from the parlor.

Jaret hurried in and sat next to Brady, hugging him and kissing his cheek.

Brady giggled and pushed him off. "Awkward! What is up with you two?"

"We have something to explain to you. Catherine?"

"Yes, and we haven't much time. You two are sworn to secrecy. No telling anyone what you know. Got it?"

Jaret nodded but Brady threw his hands into the air. "What's this about?"

"Promise first," Catherine demanded.

"Okay, I promise."

In one of her classic monologues without seeming to take a breath, Catherine explained the whole thing to Brady, who sat with a funny grin but otherwise nonplussed. She blurted out the story—an explanation of vampires and vampirism, why they had hidden their nature from him, and another promise of secrecy from Brady, or she would kill him. They both thought the killing part only half a joke, even though she laughed.

"All right. I better skedaddle so they don't suspect anything." Without another word, she hurried out of the house.

"Whew. I'm exhausted just listening to her." Jaret tried to gauge Brady's reaction. "You okay?"

"Yeah. The truth is odd. Then again, I kinda suspected something was up. Witches and vampires, and I'm the lame human in the middle. Can I ask you more about them?"

"Of course."

"So, you know, do you think I could ever become one?"

The question did not surprise Jaret. Brady had played too cool with Catherine, interested but not overly interested, too content when she explained she couldn't convert him or Jaret. Jaret knew her explanation did not end the idea for him.

"I don't even know if I want to convert." Jaret grabbed them both a drink and sat back down.

"They've offered to make you one, despite what she said?"

"Yes. It's a whole thing with Anthony I'm trying to figure out."

"What about me?"

"Complicated."

Brady laughed and poked Jaret in the stomach. "Nice dodge. You're being rather vague. You can tell me to fuck off."

"Fuck off."

Their laughter gave Jaret more time to formulate the answer he really wanted to give. "Dude, eternity without you would suck. Listen, there's a lot more to the subject than sucking your blood out and making you a vampire. You have to leave everything behind. You have to leave your whole life, probably fake your death or something. You'd need to decide if you could abandon everything, or even want to. Anyway, here's the thing. I could never tell them this in advance because they'd put the kibosh on wanting me to become one. But if I decide to become a vampire, I'll bring you over if you want. I'll convince them. Somehow, I'll bring you. Catherine indicated she'd help me. She told you what she was supposed to say."

Brady jumped at Jaret and bit at his neck until Jaret pushed him off. "You're a fool."

Then the front door opened, and Thomas and Xavier walked in, ending their conversation.

Sixty-One: The Savior Returns

22 JUNE 2013
Paris, France

Jaret's nose burned as the Jack Daniels moved through his nasal passage and out his nostril. He choked back a cough, which would have spewed what remained in his mouth all over the table or onto Brady sitting next to him. Brady had just joked about wanting to run onto the stage to give Mika a kiss right in front of everyone. They'd been laughing and carrying on for a long time.

Catherine kept making Brady and him giggle inappropriately because they'd told Brady about the vampires but no one else knew.

Brady's joke about kissing Mika had been funny, but the liquid out his nostrils came from Catherine's crack Brady better be careful because Mika might be a vampire and infect him. Then she added something like, "Of course, only if vampires exist."

Across the table, Xavier and Thomas laughed, too, which propelled Jaret's giggling because they didn't even know the best part of the joke.

"Men are disgusting." Catherine smiled. "Even gay men. Always with the penis first, everything else second."

"You're as bad as we are," Xavier retorted. "Remember, I've seen what you're capable of."

Catherine tossed her head back and laughed. "You've no idea. Do you know how many orgasms I can have in one night? You four would be so jealous."

Everyone at the table roared. The alcohol in Jaret's nose still stung because he had hardly recovered from a moment ago.

"I can't believe the concert is tomorrow night!" Brady did some odd dance in his chair with his arms in the air. "I thought the night would never get here. Jaret and Brady, finally going to see Mika!"

"Yes!" Jaret danced around too. Then Brady and Jaret launched into their favorite Mika song.

Jaret heard the doorbell and saw the servant come to inform Xavier he had a guest. He and Brady kept singing away. Jaret thought nothing of a visitor until Xavier returned to the dining room alone but with a solemn face. "I'm sorry to break up the impromptu concert. I think Thomas, Catherine, and I should take Brady on the promised nocturnal visit to the Palace of Versailles." Jaret started to protest his exclusion, but Xavier's stare silenced him. "You have a visitor."

Jaret got up with slow motions, resisting the urge to go fill his glass with straight liquor. He suspected who it was, especially since the visitor worried the shit out of Xavier.

"Go ahead. Nothing dangerous." Xavier grinned, while everyone else froze and fell silent.

"Then why do you look like the Grim Reaper came for me?"

"Because I care about you." Xavier reached over and ran his hand along Jaret's cheek. He took a strand of Jaret's hair and tucked it behind his ear. "Go on."

Jaret decided he did need a drink. He refilled his glass and then left the room. Everyone had remained quiet the entire time. Once Jaret turned the corner into the hall, he paused and heard Xavier mumble something to them. The sounds of their moving around the room and preparing to leave left Jaret feeling alone, wishing he could go with them. At least he had a good buzz going to lighten his mood and make even this tension a little amusing.

Of course, despite his earlier denial, he could predict who waited at the other end of the hallway. There was no one else left, especially who could arrive in Paris on a whim. Besides, Jaret had gotten up this morning and seen the appointment on his calendar—the day he'd promised to meet with Anthony.

He took as long as possible to shuffle down the hall and had downed his drink before he went into the living room. As he inched forward, Anthony turned from looking out the front window and smiled.

Jaret swooned. Those piercing blue eyes, the stunning, long blond hair, and those biceps. A tear trickled down his cheek. Then his left hand started to shake so badly he had to set his glass down before he dropped it on the floor. He stood frozen.

Anthony started across the room and held out his arms, but checked himself and stopped halfway to Jaret. "I've missed you."

Jaret snorted a slight laugh and wiped at his tears. He moved past Anthony, brushing against his arm, and walked to the window. Darth trotted into the room, either because everyone else left or, more likely, because she had a heightened sense for Jaret's needs in her vampiric state. She sat at his feet while he looked into the Paris night.

"I suppose you're waiting for me to say something." Jaret almost continued but had no idea whether to curse Anthony or express his persistent love for him. Jaret felt Anthony's presence closer behind him but didn't turn around.

"No. I can start, if you want."

Jaret turned around. Anthony stood a few feet from him. Jaret resisted the urge to fall into his arms and walked around to the couch and sat. He patted the cushion so Darth jumped up next to him. "No. I'll start. Maybe the historian in me needs to begin. But I've been thinking a lot. Odd to me, you see, how vampires are so shitty at relationships. You'd think with all the extra time to figure things out, they'd master relationships. Instead, sometimes I think they're even worse than humans. Because all I see is a bunch of fucked-up feelings when I look at vampire couplings."

Anthony sat on the couch but a slight distance from Jaret. He scrunched his brow with confusion.

"Seriously," Jaret continued. "Hear me out. Thomas and Xavier have the most beautiful relationship I could ever imagine. But Xavier told me about their beginning.

How fucked up was their start? I mean, all the angst and avoidance and years before they got together. Fuck me."

"It was a different time." Anthony tilted his head, still puzzled. "People didn't live 'out' lives." He made quotation marks in the air with his fingers. "They didn't even know what being 'out' meant." Again with using his fingers for visible demonstration quotation marks. "Twenty times worse than today; being gay could get you killed. It was dangerous. And Xavier was a priest."

"Even with those explanations, Thomas bitch-slapped Xavier across the room. They ran from each other. All the drama before they got together. Then later, after they worked out their issues, Xavier said he ran away from Thomas to go free slaves. They finally figured out being together after so much crap and angst and drama."

"Why the interest in them? As you said, they worked out their relationship. They are a beautiful couple."

"I was just commenting on the fact the best relationship I know comes from two vampires who almost fucked up the whole thing. I only know vampires suck at relationships. Because Catherine won't get in one. Cool. Fits her. Except whatever she and Harriet have, which is another mystery to me. And then there's you. And you fucking suck at relationships."

Jaret could tell the verbal slap stung Anthony as his face drooped and the twinkle in his eyes disappeared. Had Jaret meant to sound so harsh? Maybe. Maybe not. But he had a lot of hurt to get out.

"I deserve your words." Anthony leaned back, creating more distance between them.

"I don't know if anyone deserves anything so mean. I needed to say how I feel. Because I'm not going to sit here and wait for you to smash my face in before we move on. I'm not as swooning as Xavier. He and I are a lot alike, true. But I'm more independent than him. Always have been. I learned early in life to handle things alone. I didn't have anyone to understand I'm a witch." As if to prove his point, Jaret dimmed the lights in the room by using the ruby in his pocket. "I coped with a lot, alone. My parents kept shipping me off to the shrink and everyone stared like I'd gone bonkers when I told them about seeing ghosts. I lived alone with my power and my sexuality. No one accepted me until I had to save their asses from an apeshit, out-of-control, angry ancestor ghost. Then the fag-witch Jaret was okay. Xavier had a lot of support. I had love. Not so much with the support. I want a relationship. But I'm not a punching bag. That's all I'm saying."

"If you're trying to piss me off, you won't."

Jaret scratched Darth behind the ears. He wondered what the hell had unleashed all of his shit. Maybe the alcohol. And the constant F-bombs? Definitely the alcohol. *Fuck it. What did he want?* He had no idea. He supposed it was to let Anthony know where he stood before they even began the discussion.

"Well, sorry." Jaret smiled. "I mean, I was pretty shitty. I meant all of what I said. I guess, you needed to know. Well, and one other thing. Though I don't even want to say this one because then you'll forget about all the other stuff I said and because I'm going to kinda contradict myself. Anyway, what I said was all true. And it's also true I still love you. But I won't wait around for years and years or get abused again. Emotional abuse, I mean. Bad enough how long you took to send one of those vague and distant little notes. Or the businesslike email to set this meeting up. Like, my whole family gets offed and not a fucking thing from you." Jaret jabbed his finger in Anthony's direction. "When what I wanted most—" He choked on the words. "See, I can't stop—"

Anthony leaned forward and placed his hand over Jaret's mouth. Darth tensed, so Jaret reached over and held her by the collar to comfort her.

"Stop. My turn." Anthony removed his hand. He prolonged the touch by running his hand along Jaret's cheek, across his ear, and then through his long curls. He twirled a strand of hair around his finger before letting go. He withdrew his hand, yet leaned forward, a couple of feet from Jaret's face. Jaret could smell the mint on Anthony's breath.

Jaret answered by nodding.

"There's a lot I have to tell you. A lot. Let me begin by admitting I've been a total asshole. I know. I deserved to hear everything you said. Believe me, I know who you are. I know you're different from Xavier. And fiercely independent. To a fault sometimes. I never assumed you were a damsel in distress, waiting in some tower for me to return on a white horse. To use your parlance, I've been shitty toward you. I fucked up. I wanted to reach out to you, but I was always too afraid. If you could understand how much courage I had to muster to write those notes, inadequate as they were. I know I'm giving you an awful excuse. I'm trying to be honest. I was afraid my contacting you after your family died would make things worse. I'll ask forgiveness, but only after I explain myself."

Jaret laughed. "Parlance. Who says that? So nineteenth century."

"Very old people say parlance." Anthony smiled. "May I continue?"

Jaret nodded. He felt his muscles relax, some of the tension slipping out of him. He was glad Anthony did nothing to change their close proximity. He checked himself to make sure he protected his emotion and resisted the urge to forget the hurt too fast.

"I know you have a hard time understanding, anyone would, because my pain happened over centuries. A time frame impossible for humans to comprehend. I lost two lovers. One ripped from me when I thought we'd be together for eternity. He was sensitive, funny, and so caring. I would've done anything for him. I still hurt. I'm not trying to make an excuse, but reality can sound like I want one. I avoided relationships afterward because I never wanted to experience loss again. Ever. Then, when I decided to move on, Thomas tricked me. We joke about his subterfuge now."

Jaret giggled again. "Subterfuge."

Anthony smiled. "This is serious! Stop!" He shook his head before continuing. "And I understand what happened. But what never comes out is how much he hurt me. He set me back centuries. Centuries. Back into protecting myself. Back into the fear of loss and humiliation. Some of this is because we lived in a different time. The world moved more slowly. I try to change with the passing of eras and live in the moment. No matter how much I try, I can't stop the angst and slow movement when I deal with my emotions."

When Anthony paused, Jaret spoke. "I know. I get it. I understand. I always did."

"I'm just explaining what I did. Or didn't do."

"Did what, when?" Jaret had relaxed but remained on high alert, because without consciously calling them forth, several of his jewels had floated into the room and hovered near the ceiling above them.

Anthony glanced up. "I'd never hurt you."

Jaret laughed again. "I don't know why the hell they're up there. Maybe because my emotions are all fucked up right now. So, explain what?"

"Why I abandoned you like a total dick. One of the ways I hid from my pain was with the vampire ethic. I hid on the Vampire Council. You know the story. Xavier told me he told you. Forever, I was the only one on the Council, enforcing all the vampire laws. I used my sense of duty to avoid dealing with my own pain and fear. If I got close to someone, I could dismiss them and forget about them because I had too much responsibility and could never tell them about the truth. When Thomas exposed himself as a dominant top, I tried to convince myself his trick didn't matter to me. I didn't have time for a relationship, anyway. I had too many obligations."

Anthony took a deep breath and leaned closer to Jaret. "I don't want this to take forever. Forgive me." He reached around and cupped his hand around Jaret's head and pulled their mouths to one another. He kissed Jaret on the lips then pulled away, but pressed their foreheads together.

"I manipulated what I knew about the ethic to pull away from you. I used my service on the Vampire Council to find the excuse to end our relationship. Why? Because I'm an asshole. Whether I distanced us consciously or not doesn't matter. Here's the bottom line." Anthony inched closer so their knees touched. He kept one hand clutched around Jaret's head and with the other held one of Jaret's hands.

"What are you trying to tell me?" Jaret's voice quivered. He fought the urge to raise his hopes. He almost laughed aloud again because he had grown rock-hard.

"All of this stuff defies all logic. I know I don't make any sense. I took a long time to admit this to myself. Do you understand? The hardest part—making myself admit the truth to myself. Reality was obvious to you. Thomas and Xavier both said they knew. But I didn't know about myself. I'm trying to tell you I hid like a coward from myself."

"I still don't understand." Jaret's lips brushed against Anthony's as he spoke. They kissed again.

"I did all those shitty things and ran away from you because I was afraid. Of myself, not you." Anthony's tongue brushed across Jaret's lips. "I was terrified because I love you much too intensely. Staying with you meant being vulnerable. Our relationship meant opening up to you. And I wasn't strong enough to risk the hurt."

Jaret reached over with his free hand and ran a finger along Anthony's muscular thigh. He stopped inches before going too far. "So where does this truth leave us?"

"Do you understand what I'm saying?"

"Maybe. I think so." Jaret leaned forward. Darth got scrunched between them and jumped off the couch. Jaret listened as she spun around in circles before landing with a thump on the floor beneath them. She let out an irritated dog harrumph.

"I'm asking for forgiveness. I'm telling you I learned a lot about myself. I hide behind duty and rules to protect myself. I did for centuries, which kept me distant from friends and unavailable for a relationship. I got over the friendship part and accepted the protection and love of those around me when we formed the new Council. But I still couldn't go the last step. I was still hiding. Still too afraid."

Anthony leaned over and kissed Jaret's ear. Jaret closed his eyes, bursting with excitement.

"Where are you now? I mean, did your feelings change? Or what?" Jaret brushed a finger along Anthony's hard cock.

"I took the final step. I've come to terms with what I did, and why. I'm ready to try again. I desperately need to. But I can only move on with your permission and forgiveness."

"But I'm afraid." Jaret scooted over, entwining their legs together.

"Of what? Talk to me."

"Afraid you'll leave me again. Abandon me. I guess I don't understand what changed you or brought you to this. Are you holding something back?"

Anthony wrapped his arms around Jaret and pulled their bodies together. He kissed Jaret on the head, ran his lips down to his ear, and licked across his neck. Then he moved up and stuck his tongue in Jaret's ear. Shivers ran down Jaret's spine as Anthony whispered into his ear.

"Not holding something back, no. Saving something for last."

"Tell me."

"I love you. I don't mean in some flippant Hollywood kind of way. Jaret, I'm only scared now because I love you so much. A thousand times more than I ever loved Thomas." Anthony pulled away and grasped Jaret's face in both his hands. He kissed him hard on the lips again. "I love you more than anyone, ever. Anyone. Anyone. Do you understand?"

"I think so. More than him? Even him?"

"God forgive me, yes. More than anyone. I want you. I yearn for you." Anthony kissed him again. His hand slid down Jaret's back and into his waistband, under his underwear, and down the crack of his ass until his finger pushed at Jaret's anus.

Jaret breathed heavily. "I love you too."

"Do you forgive me?"

"Only if you promise never to fuck me over again."

Anthony chuckled. "You have a way with words." He pulled out his hand and ripped Jaret's shirt off. He flung the pieces to the floor. Jaret fumbled with the buttons on Anthony's shirt. He licked at his hard nipples. Anthony lifted him effortlessly into the air and had his pants off in moments. Anthony's lips locked around Jaret's penis, making him almost come immediately.

Jaret pulled away and leaned down to release Anthony from his pants. They kissed and touched and panted together on the couch.

When Anthony moved on top of Jaret, Jaret grabbed his hand and stopped him before having sex. "You didn't promise. I don't want you to toy with me."

Anthony kissed Jaret again. "I promise, love. Never again. Never. I'm here. Here with my little witch, whom I love."

Jaret licked his hand and grabbed Anthony's penis, guiding Anthony to his ass and stuffing his cock in. He begged Anthony to fuck him and grabbed for his own dick, shooting come all over his stomach before Anthony had even pumped in and out of him a few times.

He clung to Anthony's back as he fucked him. The rhythm of his cock sliding in and out, his muscles flexing in Jaret's hands, his lips finding Jaret's mouth, his ears, his eyes, sent Jaret into a wave of pleasure despite the fact he had already spent himself.

"You're mine." Anthony grunted as he climaxed inside of Jaret.

"Forever." Jaret stared hard into Anthony's eyes to communicate his meaning.

Anthony brushed Jaret's hair out of the way and bit hard into Jaret's neck. Jaret grew excited again. Without touching himself he shot another load. Next he sucked at the blood with intense passion when Anthony got up on his knees before Jaret, cutting with his finger nail at his penis so Jaret could drink the blood. As Jaret sucked in his new life, Anthony came again, all over Jaret's face. Jaret licked at the blood and the cum and held Anthony's ass firm in his hands to push his organ back down his throat.

"You're mine, love. All mine. Forever." Anthony licked at Jaret to clean him up. Both maintained their proximity and refused to lose the connection, afraid not to touch one another.

After they stopped breathing heavily, Jaret realized he'd become a vampire. Jaret loved how he allowed the conversion without a drawn-out contemplation or days of angst and questioning. For a long time, he had wondered if Anthony should prove himself before Jaret fell again but tonight the answer came, crystal clear: he loved and trusted Anthony with all his heart. In all the fantasies about getting back together with Anthony, never had he lost himself like a star-crossed lover and yet tonight that felt like the most natural outcome imaginable.

"You know I'm only yours because I let you own me. I can undo your possession, you know?" Jaret lay naked on the couch in Anthony's arms.

"I know."

"But I do like a man who takes charge."

"I know that too."

"Do you know what I want now?"

"Oh yeah."

Jaret felt Anthony's strong grip around his ankles as he raised Jaret's legs in the air, this time spitting on his anus, and moving to plunge back inside.

Sixty-Two: Mika in Paris

23 JUNE 2013
Paris, France

Xavier woke the next evening, wondering what to make of the note Jaret had left the previous night.

Can't go with Brady tomorrow. Please give him lots of cash and tell him to do something rocking in Paris. Tell him I told him not to be a pauper shithead and to spend money on himself because you're wickedly rich and need to use up money to help the economy. Then please make arrangements for all of us to meet for the concert. I guess you can deduce things went well with Anthony. I'll fill you in. Promise. J

Xavier left the note for Brady with more than enough money and a list of possible things to do for a day on your own in his home city. He penned notes for everyone else, deciding to leave everyone's ticket on the counter and arrange a rendezvous point inside the stadium. Brady had indicated he planned to get there early. Who knew when Catherine would grace them with her presence, and Thomas and Xavier were inclined to get there just before the actual concert began.

He and Thomas spent the first part of the evening making love, getting dressed, and then deciding to walk like humans to the concert.

"Do you think Anthony gets reality now?"

Thomas chuckled. "Are you asking if I think Anthony will become a shithead again?"

"I didn't mean anything so harsh."

Thomas laughed again. "Here's what I know. Anthony won't toy with him again. Whatever he said, he meant. I trust him. Moreover, I trust Jaret to take care of himself."

"I'm worried."

Thomas opened his mouth and slapped both cheeks with his hands as if shocked. "No! You? Worried? I'm sure there's a good dose of guilt in there, too, if we dig deep enough. Want me to check?" Thomas grabbed Xavier's ass.

Xavier spun away but laughed at Thomas. "Why do I love you? You're the shithead, not Anthony."

"But I'm your shithead, which makes my shittiness more special for you." Thomas reached over and took Xavier's hand. "Seriously. No guilt. No worry. They're fine. You're fine. Let's enjoy this concert."

"You've grown to like Mika, haven't you?"

Thomas nodded. "I totally dig his music. Jaret converted me. Though I'm still more drawn to Katy Perry's sassiness."

Outside the stadium, Xavier marveled at the huge crowd. They had a few minutes before Mika appeared on stage. They'd skipped the opening act and now saw the stage curtain drawn and heard with their vampiric senses the scurry of activity behind it.

Their tickets were for the very front of the audience where they stood in a mob near the stage. Xavier first spotted Catherine's glowing blonde hair off to the side and noticed she held Brady up a couple of feet off the ground. She apparently had decided to let him know about their being vampires, since she was using her strength to give him a better view. She was near one side but only a few people from the front of the crowd. He shook his head at the thought of Anthony scolding her for defying the ethic once again because of her fondness for someone, not to mention using her vampire strength so obviously in public.

Then Xavier glanced next to her and saw Anthony standing at the very edge. How had he missed him? Sitting on Anthony's shoulders with his legs wrapped around Anthony's neck, Jaret held Anthony's hair for balance and was screaming for Mika.

They looked so comfortable together, surprising Xavier. But as he and Thomas pushed closer, his heart raced at what else he detected. The more defined but still slight musculature. The ease with which he balanced on Anthony's shoulders. The tingling of Xavier's senses to warn of other vampires, telling him of four other vampires in the vicinity. Not three others, as in Catherine, Anthony, and Thomas. But four.

Xavier and Thomas hugged Catherine and greeted Brady. Xavier whispered something to Catherine about exposing the young man to the vampirism before they talked. She waved him away and warned he was lucky she hadn't converted Brady.

Xavier grinned and then turned to Anthony. If not for their vampiric hearing, he could not have heard anything but the roaring of the crowd as people chanted for Mika.

"Anthony." They embraced. "You're looking—" Xavier paused, searching for the right words. "—happy."

"I am."

Thomas had turned his attention to the stage, joining the calls for Mika, probably more because he liked yelling than from any real desire to shout for the singer.

Xavier looked up into Jaret's eyes. He reached over and grabbed Jaret's foot and shook his shoe.

Jaret held their stare and grinned more widely than Xavier had seen him smile since they first met, his sharp incisors visible to Xavier's vampire sight. Jaret winked at Xavier but then cast his eyes to the stage and screamed in happiness.

Xavier turned around as guitar sounds filled the air, drumbeats rumbled through the stadium, and the crowd noise became deafening. Mika ran onto the stage singing and smiling at the adulation.

About Damian Serbu

Damian Serbu lives in the Chicago area with his husband and two dogs, Akasha and Chewbacca. The dogs control his life, tell him what to write, and threaten to eat him in the middle of the night if he disobeys. He has published *The Vampire's Angel*, *The Vampire's Quest*, *The Bachmann Family Secret,* and *The Vampire's Protégé*, as well as *Santa's Kinky Elf, Simon* and *Santa Is a Vampire* with NineStar Press. Keep up to date with him on Facebook, Twitter, or at www.DamianSerbu.com.

Facebook
www.facebook.com/Damian-Serbu

Twitter
@damianserbu

Website
www.damianserbu.com

Other NineStar books by this author

The Realm of the Vampire Council
The Vampire's Angel
The Vampire's Quest

Also from NineStar Press

The Vampire's Angel by Damian Serbu

As Paris devolves into chaos amidst the French Revolution, three lives intertwine.

Xavier, a devout priest, struggles to hold on to his trust in humanity only to find his own faith threatened with the longing he finds for a mysterious American visitor. Thomas fights against the Catholic Church to win Xavier's heart, but hiding his undead nature will threaten the love he longs to find with this abbé. Xavier's sister, Catherine, works with Thomas to bring them together while protecting the family fortune but falls prey herself to evil forces.

The death, peril, and catastrophes of a revolution collide with a world of magic, vampires, and personal demons as Xavier, Thomas, and Catherine fight to find peace and love amidst the destruction.

The Bachmann Family Secrets by Damian Serbu

Jaret Bachmann travels with his family to his beloved grandfather's funeral with a heavy heart and, more troubling, premonitions of something evil lurking at the Bachmann ancestral home. But no one believes that he sees ghosts.

Grappling with his sexuality, a ghost that wants him out of the way, and the loss of his grandfather, Jaret must protect his family and come to terms with powers hidden deep within himself.

The Vampire's Protégé by Damian Serbu

A sinister vampire offers Charon a choice he can't refuse: play a deadly game of winner takes all, losers die.

Charon relishes the competition and molds himself into a sexy vampire who defies vampire law, savoring his power and embracing the role of villain. He also loves surrounding himself with hot young men. But when an alluring vampire stalks him and threatens to turn him into the Vampire Council unless he helps with a seemingly impossible task, will Charon risk his perfectly narcissistic life on the challenge? Does he have any other choice?

Connect with NineStar Press

www.ninestarpress.com

www.facebook.com/ninestarpress

www.facebook.com/groups/NineStarNiche

www.twitter.com/ninestarpress

www.instagram.com/ninestarpress